D1026610

Stargorod

STARGOROD

{ a novel in many voices }

PETER ALESHKOVSKY

Translated by Nina Shevchuk-Murray

Russian Life

BOOKS

Cover: Torzhok, the Cathedral of the Transfigured Saviour
and the Church of the Entry into Jerusalem, 1910.
From the expeditionary photography files of Prokudin-Gorsky,
collected in the US Library of Congress

This book is an original translation of
Институт Сновидений/Старгород, copyright © 2009, Peter Aleshkovsky.
English translation copyright © 2013, Russian Information Services, Inc.

Copyright to all work in this volume is governed by U.S. and international
copyright laws. All rights reserved. Work may not be reproduced in any
manner without the expressed, written permission of the copyright holder.
For permission to reproduce selections from this book, contact the publisher
at the address below.

ISBN 978-1-880100-80-6

Library of Congress Control Number: 2013935581

Russian Information Services, Inc.
PO Box 567
Montpelier, VT 05601-0567
www.russianlife.com
orders@russianlife.com
phone 802-234-1956

CONTENTS

2010

AUTHOR'S PREFACE

Stargorod and *The Institute of Dreams* (two books published separately in Russia, but joined together in this English volume) are two parts of one whole. For me, they are not collections of short stories, but a single world; a single expansive story, woven by a great multitude of voices. This is why the book is subtitled as "A Novel in Many Voices." The world around us always speaks in voices, in many tongues, but it is always talking about the same things. A writer's task, then, is to create his own world, one in which all of those he loves and hates could live and suffer. Without a world of his own, a writer becomes a journalist – and that's a completely different, although in its own way also wonderful, profession.

I was not the first to use the name Stargorod. I stole it from one of the best Russian writers, Nikolai Leskov, who lived in the nineteenth century. Leskov, in turn, was also borrowing, in part, from Nikolai Gogol. Gogol, a truly titanic figure in Russian fiction, wrote a collection of short stories he titled "Mirgorod," after a real town. Gogol's Mirgorod, however, is vastly more than an aging smattering of buildings under the hot Ukrainian sun. The first part of the name, Mir, means "community," "all of us" – it is a force that holds people together as a part of a larger world, that makes them a sliver of the universe that reflects, like a shard of the broken mirror, all the small but telling features of humanity.

Nikolai Gogol is the giant on whose shoulders most of our literature stands. All of us who write in Russian continue to draw from him, and this continuity is important as long as everyone contributes something to the map he had laid out. Sometimes, the new is what takes one far and wide from one's point of departure. But the road is vastly more important than the mile markers or the signposts along its sides, and only a walking man draws breath deeply and freely. After Leskov, the brothers Ilya Ilf and Evgeny Petrov, writing in the 1920s, populated Stargorod with their own extravagant characters. So, as you can see, all I did was follow my predecessors' good advice. Stargorod – which in Russian means "an old town" – a place that is by definition on the margins, on the far edges of the known world, is a sort of a Russian Yoknapatawpha County, a place where the nation's metaphysical essence is held longest, if not in perpetuity. Stargorod is Russia's test pit, to borrow a term of my earlier profession – archeology – which concerns itself with digging up all kinds of old towns and burial places.

Twenty years separate the two parts of my book – enough time for an empire to collapse and for things to take what seemed like a most radical turn. "Twenty years after" is also the title Alexandre Dumas, *père*, chose for one of his D'Artagnan romances – books we read compulsively back in the days when Russia was called USSR and lived behind a concrete wall that effectively separated our country from the rest of the world. A particularly inquisitive reader will find this and many more allusions in my book, along with inside jokes, shameless quotations and stolen plots. To steal, for a writer, means to take a thing and think about it anew, to homestead on land someone else discovered and to argue with the discoverer all along. But hasn't this been a human preoccupation since times immemorial? From the day a Stone Age hunter committed breath-taking images of horses and bison, birds and skiers, and spear-wielding hunters to a cave wall coloring their bodies with sacred ocher or etching them into the face of the rock with his stone chisel? I challenge anyone to step up and tell me that this older predecessor of mine (and no less of a giant) merely recorded his everyday life – that's laughable! No, sir, I say – that's no everyday life. It is a life seen anew.

This, I believe, is the task of any art. What about telling a story, you say? A story is a must – without it, the reader falls asleep along the way, and will never travel the full length of the road. The road must be shared with a good company of like-minded people – and that is precisely the kind of journey I invite you to take in these pages. Happy travels!

Peter Aleshkovsky
Moscow, Fall 2012

1990

Stargorod is emphatically not big. It is located at
The Lake. There is a chemical plant, the State Bearings
Factory No. 4, a brick factory, an agricultural machinery
plant, a furniture factory, a kremlin and a great number
of old churches and monasteries. Renovation efforts are
ongoing.

A Guide to Stargorod

Sad! I feel sad beforehand! But let us return to the story.
Nikolai Gogol, "Old World Landowners"

ABOVE THE FRAY

The sun is high. Tourists cruise by, like fish, in schools. In couples. Half-naked metropolitan tourists and foreign tourists, with hairy legs, in foreign shorts, in streaky, bleached denim, in bright, sexy T-shirts.

Pishchutin ignores the species known as "tourist." Today is his day off. He has come to the riverfront promenade. To rest. To think. He thinks a lot, and then spends his evenings writing into the small hours. Pishchutin is a writer.

He is dressed in a navy blue, velvet suit: Pishchutin abhors modern populism. He may have just one suit in his wardrobe, but this suit is fashioned from serious fabric – Finnish velvet, real Finnish velvet from the discarded curtain of the local theater.

Out of the corner of his eye Pishchutin notices people noticing him. He knows that the extraordinary figure he cuts draws attention. He understands the people, and he pities them – they are wasting their lives, with no thought for the eternal. He forgives them. He tries to love them. But he doesn't always succeed. Because still, they are the unwashed masses. Small souls. Sometimes at night he cries at his desk, unable to write – his pen is merciless, but he is not.

He has a gold-tipped pen from China – these are the most comfortable, easy on the hand. After all, what is Russian literature? It is love, plus pity for the oppressed and the aggrieved, plus the fierce chastisement of the plebeians and the burgers. The real literature is all in the past, and it is aristocratic. The task today is to bring it back. One could spend a life at such a task. This is why a writer must be above the fray, above the crowd.

Pishchutin takes a seat in a terrace café. Today he will have some champagne. But the waiter does not come – he is a local, that eyesore; he knows Pishchutin, and one must be patient and wait with a disinterested attitude. Patience is the most important thing in life. A real writer is always lonely and poor in the beginning. Sometimes, his entire life.

Now, when his fame comes, then he'll donate to the church and orphanages. And, of course, he must donate something to the City Parks department; it's intolerable how dirty the city is. The riverfront is the only place they care to maintain; they make a Disneyland out of it for the foreign tourists. For shame. He'll have to give them a hundred thousand or so.

The calculations consume Pishchutin. In half an hour he orders a bottle of champagne, casually, and a bar of chocolate. He drinks slowly. He enjoys the drink. He nibbles on the chocolate delicately and rolls it around inside his mouth, submerged in champagne. But he maintains a disinterested attitude.

He sits, one hand with an intentionally cultivated long pinkie nail draped at his side. He tries not to look at the tourists.

Not to yield to the moment, not to relax – to think, think through the myriad plots and stories he has in his head. It is amazing what imagination can do. What his imagination can do. It's too bad he won't live long enough to write everything down, everything that daily presents itself to his gaze. He must work, work!

Today is off, comp time for tomorrow's working Saturday, followed by Sunday. Today he is looking for the plot, he finds it and polishes it. Tomorrow, after a trip to the market (he needs potatoes; life is prosaic), he will sit down to write the story he will conceive today.

But plots, too many plots swirl and flit about him, like tourists.

Champagne disappears irretrievably, like time (that's a great simile – he must remember it!), but he mustn't drain the bottle. He'll leave some at the bottom. And he won't finish his chocolate.

No, life is beautiful, like his trusty Finnish velvet. It sparkles, full of stories, and his soul catches its breath, and pities, pities them all…

"Are you crying, pops?" asks an overly-friendly tourist, but Pishchutin wipes his tears and proudly turns away.

"Leave him alone – he's our local nut, a planner from the museum. He always comes here, once a month, like clockwork: drinks, cries a little and leaves," the waiter explains as if Pishchutin weren't sitting right there.

And that's when Pishchutin rises, puts money on the napkin – with a 70-kopek tip – and leaves.

He walks along the waterfront; he does not see the crowd. He mutters: waiter… tourists… knife… policeman, no, better a retired colonel… and he sees it all so clearly, it is all so alive to him that he cannot stand it anymore and again begins to cry.

"Again, again," whispers Pishchutin, stunned. "I wanted to take revenge, to satirize, but I instead I pitied them… again tragedy comes instead of laughter."

Where does this come from? Where? It is a mystery. He does not know. He walks home, not seeing the tourists, or the crowds that hurry home from the bus stop, past the empty stores. He walks, almost to the other end of the city, to his five-story cinder-block apartment building.

He has a small, one-room flat. A closet stuffed with manuscripts, and a large ledger where he records the stories, novellas, and novels that he has sent out to various magazines. He likes order. He cannot take the humiliation of sending someone the same thing twice – that's why he needs records. He keeps them accurately and he does not despair.

He is not married. He is only 52 and there are so many unwritten stories ahead of him. And the Fame, too, somewhere out there, in the distance, where he cannot yet hear the call of its trumpet.

TWENTY YEARS

"Would you believe it, it was only at his funeral that I learned he used to be the school's star, 20 years ago. He danced! Can you believe that? He was an officer, you know, he'd seen fire. I can't even picture it – him, dancing, with his military posture. The school was famous then, not like now, the students from those old classes went places! Sashenka Stroyev sails a merchant vessel on international routes, he's a Captain; Lenochka Korneva married a Moscow diplomat, last year she sent me Teacher's Day greetings from Prague; Lyoshenka Stepanov is the party organization secretary at the Kirov plant. Pavlik Boldin – he's in outer space somewhere, all I know is he prepares our Soyuz rockets for launch. Those old classes don't forget – they come to their reunions every 10 years; it's the newer crop that don't care for the school that much... I only knew him after he'd already started drinking. Sometimes he even showed up tipsy to teach, and the kids didn't pay him any mind, did whatever they wanted. He buried his first wife 10 years earlier – his son now teaches, also geography, in School No. 2. It was at the funeral that the thought really struck me, for the first time perhaps: here was a man, and now he's gone – and nothing is different. Of course, in those last years he only kept his job because of the School District Head, Kirill Georgiyevich – he used to be our principal. They started together. They retired from the army together and took the entry exams for the Leningrad Pedagogical Institute at the same time; when they graduated, they got their assignments together. Only Kirill Georgiyevich had the party streak in him, and the other one wasn't a real fighter. Whenever I chaired the party meetings, he'd always sit in the corner, quietly, but if there was any task to be done, he'd wrinkle his face like so, and sigh – but would complete it conscientiously, with military precision. Eventually, I only charged him with political information sessions for the teachers, but soon he wiggled his way out of that, too. He'd started drinking by then, but I don't think it was a regular thing yet. But I'll tell you a secret – Kirill Georgiyevich himself goes on binges as well. The ladies and I worried that he'd lose it after the funeral. And he'd just come out of the hospital, his heart is worthless. They were friends, he and the old geography teacher, you know, real, wartime friends. And another student of his, Sashenka – he cried. His widow stood there like a rock. If you think about it – what's she got left? They couldn't have children. Just lived, you know. And the school – it was the school, of course, that did him in. He always carried a big load; he had to work. His second wife is a restoration technician – you know what they make, something between 105 and 120. But to imagine him – an officer! I wouldn't have believed it. Women couldn't keep their hands off him, apparently, he was their pet. I never knew him to be like that in all my ten years at the school…"

All this suddenly surfaced in Yegorshin's memory after Taisiya Petrovna's own funeral, 20 years after that of the geography teacher she'd been talking about. The former officer. In the late sixties, Taisiya Petrovna was at the peak of her glory: children would follow her anywhere, and the teachers adored her, too, although she taught high school history and was, at the time, the secretary of the school's party organization. Of course, she had a lot more energy then: she regularly led field trips to historic battlefields, or excursions around the city – and always gave it her all. And her trivia contests! Her *Do You Know Your Native Land?* was even broadcast on national radio. When they had that prize of a trip to Bulgaria, to the Golden Sands, she was the first choice, of course. But she was strict. She could beat parents into submission like no one else, and vetted the candidates for the parent advisory group herself – all for the betterment of the school, of course. And her husband hadn't left her yet, then. And her mother was alive – she babysat the kids. Now her son serves up North on a submarine, based next to Murmansk; her daughter's got two of her own and lives with her husband close to the chemical plant – he is the senior nitrates engineer. They all came to the funeral together. There were people from the School District and the District Party Committee too, but the teachers all felt like strangers. Yegorshin was the only one from the school who had been her student. There was something so absurd about her death: she died of pneumonia. Who dies of that anymore? It was a grim funeral, too solemn, morose. And all because there wasn't anyone left who knew her when she was young.

Yegorshin sat in the empty teachers' lounge – he had a break between classes. Next door, the leader of the pioneers and a young history teacher were putting together a poster for the "Memorial" society. Yegorshin could understand why they didn't like Taisiya Petrovna.

Then the bell rang and children filled the room:

"Alexander Alexandrovich, what time is our rehearsal today?"

Yegorshin directed the school's musical theater.

Turyansky himself, when he came to Stargorod on tour, watched one of their shows. And liked it. Afterwards, they spent the night in the Yegorshins' kitchen, drinking vodka and singing.

SOUR CREAM

Natalia Petrovna Kivokurtseva came from the same Kivokurtsevs that were bodyguards to Tsar Alexei Mikhailovich.[1] But, you know, only now we can mention this; before – not a peep. She told no one, and no one knew, so somehow she managed to keep it secret and not get into trouble. And come to think of it, why would anyone bother with her? She never married – times were such that she couldn't possibly find a proper match. You could count the decent bachelors in Stargorod on the fingers of one hand. Her father died in 1920, mother in '24. What did she know? Embroidery, piano, French. She asked around at the music school and worked there until she retired, and since she didn't have a university education, her pension was just a notch above that of a *kolkhoz* milkmaid. Later, they increased it, twice, and she was grateful for that. And then what? Before the war there were the Gryaznins, the Korobovs, the Ebermanns and the Shirinskys, but they were all gone; the last one, Nikolai Nikolayevich Monteifel was in the museum's employ, with the paintings department – she buried him in the sixties. His children were all in the capitals – they had degrees. She had colleagues, of course, but some had died, and the others had forgotten about her. She was alone.

She got used to it. To the ladies on the bench she never said much – they had little to talk about. They got used to that, too: they'd greet each other, and that was it. Once, people from the museum came. They wanted to buy her painting, but she refused; instead, she bequeathed it to the museum in her will – the painting was all she had left, her mother used to say it was Italian. Recently, however, it hasn't

---

1. Father of Peter the Great; ruled 1645-1676.

mattered to Natalia Petrovna where the painting came from: she'd look at the little painted cows and their young cowherd, and the tiny castles and towers up on the hill, and remember things. Her eyesight has gotten poorer, but she can still see the picture in her mind.

The museum people mentioned that the Assembly of Nobles[2] had started up again in Moscow, and that women were now being admitted as well. But this, pardon me my dears, is nonsense. It's all in the past, and if someone's got the taste for playing dress-up – well, it's not dangerous anymore, apparently. But she doesn't. And not with those people. Her eyes don't see, her feet barely walk – she's ashamed of herself, but she gets around.

It was her eyes that let her down in the end. One morning she went out, first to buy some canned mackerel. She spent three hours in line and they ran out right before it was her turn. Then sour cream. Another line. She got some. She was on her way home, when, near the home for deaf children, a drunk stumbled out from behind a fence, knocked her into the mud, broke her jar of sour cream and, for good measure, cursed at her: "Damn blind hag, high time you kicked the bucket, you bitch."

High time indeed. She headed home, having more or less scraped off the dirt; tears swelled to a lump in her throat, but she held strong. The Kivokurtsevs don't cry, that's what her Mama had said when they took Uncle Kolya away.

She remembered it. She remembered her whole life. She didn't go to college – not with her background. And as to whitewashing her pedigree by working in a factory, no, thank you. She taught children music, quietly. And just as quietly, like a mouse, she slipped into retirement.

And now she couldn't even bring her sour cream home. It was very upsetting.

Chin up, knees straight, past the old ladies on the bench, with a "Good evening!"

---

2. An institution of self-governance in Russia from 1766-1917.

"Hello, hello, Natalia Petrovna, what happened?"

She didn't even attempt an answer. Went upstairs, took her clothes off. Coat into the bathtub to soak it before the dirt caked. Afterward, a cup of tea. She had no strength left. She boiled the water for tea, to have with a *bublik* and a piece of hard candy, instead of sugar.

The museum girls – good, nice girls all – sometimes asked her, "Natalia Petrovna, what do you remember?"

And she'd always answer, "Nothing, girls, absolutely nothing..."

She took the cup to the sink, put it down with a clang – her hands shook, her head was spinning. High time, bitch.

For the first time in her life she didn't wash her dishes.

She went to her room and fell into the armchair. She looked at the painting on the wall. The Kivokurtsevs' home was long gone and the one that had been Ms. Goncharnaya's was gone too, but the Shirinskys' still stands. How strange...

They think they've got themselves an Assembly of Nobles...

"I-di-ots!" she said, hitting each syllable hard, staccato.

But she didn't cry. No, she did not. She felt better, after a while.

THE LIVING WELL OF THE DESERT

Tatyana Zlatkova stood in line for cottage cheese at the grocery store. She felt a painful poke in her side and snarled back, but, thank goodness, the spat didn't turn into a scene. The other woman, wearing a blue tweed coat, apologized. Tatyana sighed and apologized, too. She had no choice but to be in this line – it was imperative that she buy cottage cheese.

Tatyana Zlatkova had fled to Stargorod from an ill-fated, cruel love affair in Leningrad. She purposely chose the job of tour-guide. If there was one thing her time at the Hermitage had taught her, it was that the research department was a life-sucking swamp. She'd spent ten years in one of those and she wanted to be free, to walk around, stare, and talk about the things she loved most in the world. She also believed in educating people.

At first things went smoothly. She and the indigenous expert Osokin – short, with a small voice, his eyes completely faded at 43 – were the museum's two best tour guides. Osokin never changed. Between his groups he sat on the bench in the nook behind the tour-organizers' kiosk, read *Knowledge is Power* and delighted in engaging whomever approached him in long discussions about the latest scientific discoveries. Osokin was very good at his job, but at heart he was a rapturous fool, and Tatyana could not stand men like that, not to mention the rest of his ever-humble countenance… No, she could not possibly understand why the girls in the department felt so sorry for him and made plans – smiling but nonetheless earnest – to get him married. Tatyana was stern with Osokin, but, naturally, chatted with the girls, though she tried to avoid their endless tea-breaks as much as possible. She was well respected and a bit intimidating.

Sometimes, Tatyana spent all her time dashing around the city, with one group after another. Other times, when her mood changed, she kept to the museum collection. She was readily forgiven for these sudden swings, since there were never any complaints about her, only thank you's from her rapt audiences.

Her little Nadyushka, who was just a baby when they moved from Leningrad, grew up in day-care, and later pre-school, but strangely enough, rarely got sick. After work, Tatyana would pick up Nadyushka from extended hours and they'd walk home, where they read books and built a cardboard city. They were happy together.

But then school started, and with it came school infections: measles, mumps, and scarlet fever all in one year. And all that came with bills. Money became short. Tatyana took on more groups, worked harder, and pulled through. In the summer, when the girl got stronger, they went on vacation to Sudak, to the Black Sea, and in the second grade things went back to normal.

Only somehow, after that summer, everything at work changed instantly, as if a veil fell from Tatyana's eyes; she suddenly felt an all-consuming hatred for the public. She hated people for their pettiness, bad manners, and rudeness. Especially the kids – they were undisciplined, inattentive, and loud. She must have just ignored them before, speaking to those who were listening, but now she was possessed – she could snap, she could even yell at someone. She was also tired. A single vacation was not enough for the year she'd had.

Something was missing. She felt suddenly and completely bored. She was tired of getting up at the same time every day to go to work. Now she looked at Osokin, that meek Stargorod lamb, with a new incomprehension that bordered on envy: how could he do it? He noticed nothing around him, as always. No, she felt no pity for him, only disgust.

It was known that Osokin rose early and before going to work made his rounds in the neighborhood, where he shared a small house with his elderly parents. He scattered crumbs for the sparrows and dropped morsels for every stray cat (who sat waiting for him) – a bone, a piece of fish, a slice of bacon or even some sausage. As if nothing had changed in the stores.

Tatyana once made a caustic joke about him at the office, and then couldn't forgive herself for it. She should have kept her mouth shut, but no – it was coming after her, the familiar life-sucking swamp. Inexorably. Inescapably. It had been pursuing her for nine years, ever since she left Petersburg, and it was about to catch up.

And that's when she realized that it was going to be like this forever. Until she died. Because she hated standing in lines; she lost all her dignity there. Because she'd taken on more groups and still couldn't afford to buy meat. Because she hated her job. She'd even considered asking for a transfer into the Country Painting Department: it was nice and quiet, a cushy gig.

Someone prodded her from behind, "It's your turn, miss, come on!"

She bought her cottage cheese and felt slightly better: she could fry up a batch of cheese pancakes and not worry about dinner for two whole days.

She picked up Nadyushka at school and, on the way home, now cursing absolutely every bit of her existence, took a spot in a line for frozen pollock. It didn't look like it would take more than half an hour, but she was still appalled. She wanted to go home, where it was warm, to her kitchen, to her green-shaded lamp. Nadyushka perched on the radiator trying to read *The Adventures of Huckleberry Finn*, clearly with little success.

The child had an idea. A secret. She said so when Tatyana picked her up: "Mom, I've got a surprise for you." And now she kept fidgeting – she couldn't wait to go home.

At home, when they finally got there, they had no time for surprises at first: they had to change, wash their hands, and make dinner. A school notebook lay on top of Tatyana's plate. She noticed that her daughter shut her eyes when she opened it.

The title was written in colored marker: "Essay: Why I love My Mom." A simple piece. Naïve. Written and read a thousand times before.

Everything became clear. They hugged, and the cheese pancakes got burned on the stove. Tatyana made a new batch. She opened a can of condensed milk, and declared a feast. They sat together, drank tea with cheese pancakes dipped in condensed milk, and watched Good Night, Kids!

Then Tatyana gave Nadyushka a bath and put her to bed. She read *Huckleberry Finn* to her, breaking her own rule: Nadyushka was old enough to read on her own. But they made it an event – and once was okay.

She put her hair in a braid before going to bed, and the braid came out thin as a rat's tail. She lay in bed, looked at the sleeping Nadyushka and thought about the essay. It was funny, it said: "My mom's the most loved mom in the world because I love her very much!" But it was still nice.

It was really not that different from one of her tours: "Here's a depiction of the Savior on his throne, look how detached and lonely he is, but still all-powerful..." She always used the same words to describe the image, the facts were not important – only the intonation was. Such a small thing.

She yawned, but she wasn't ready to fall asleep yet.

"Yes, the intonation..."

She picked up the day's *Izvestia* from the nightstand, skimmed over it, then read:

Facts and Commentary: The Living Well of the Desert. Of course, the desert means sand, first and foremost. Dunes can be as tall as multi-storied buildings. But even here some vegetation persists – camel-thorn and various grasses thrive in the dunes. Could there be a way of obtaining moisture from these living symbols of the desert?

Turns out there is: half a dozen plastic bags, pulled over different plants, could collect from two to two and a half liters of water in a day, as condensation. Of course, the liquid doesn't taste like tap-water – it's more like strong green tea.

Salsola Early and Salsola Southern are the best plants for this.

Funny. Tatyana tried to picture these "salsolas" and the dunes… the symbols of the desert. And the life-giving water hidden inside them. Dunes rose in front of her eyes and she fell asleep.

The next day Tatyana found herself on the bench next to Osokin. The spring sun was warm, and the nook between the buildings where the bench stood protected them from the wind. There was decidedly nothing to do. She told him what she had read in Izvestia. Osokin listened attentively, even though he had heard of this phenomenon before. In return, he told her about a new science, synergistics. Tatyana never understood anything related to physics or mathematics, but Osokin made it sound so interesting that, listening to him, she lost all track of time.

IRON LOGIC

A tiny sun-bunny – hop! – flips from the window, from the crack in the lace curtains – hop! – onto the mirror, and crackles, and pops, and skitters all over the room: onto the ceiling, the floor, the Yatran typewriter, the desk and into Shishmaryov's eyes. The chairman squints, pushes budget sheets away, leans back in his chair. On a day like this one should be out in the field, waiting for dusk. When things go still, the sun sets, and only pink streaks, then scarlet, then purple – then dusk. That's when they come: wizz! – jet-quick teals, whoosh! – golden-eyes, swoop! – fat mallards. And after – wild onion, fish stew over the fire, and Pal-Petrovich, serene, happy, Pal-Petrovich finally at peace, and Andrei Yevgeniyevich – with all his troubles sent to hell, and a story, a joke! And in the morning – out in the mist, whistle to the grouse: a hard full trill like a cock, one cut-off quick, half-garbled – like a hen's.

"Yes, siree..."

But there is the Plan. Norms to fulfill. The harvesting of things. Of bark, for instance. And there are huntsmen. The Forester. The hunting season's around the corner... And where are the huntsmen? The huntsmen are ready – but he's got no money for staff. And where can he get it? From Pal-Petrovich, of course. Pal-Petrovich: we take him hunting, he gives us a staff position. Although, truth be told, Pal-Petrovich doesn't need anyone's permission to hunt; if he wants something, he gets it. But no, he won't just go over the chairman's head like that – they're friends, aren't they? So, what then – to beg? Calling, cow-towing, pleading? And Pal-Petrovich is stern at work, oh, very stern. It wouldn't look good. Not good at all, quite disgusting in fact. And if he refuses – then what? Flattery, ingratiation, so on?

Right? Quite logical indeed. And wasn't there a Lefaucheux rifle procured for Pal-Petrovich? Such a piece of work that rifle – pretty as a picture! A perfect toy. I'd love to shoot one myself: for bird there's nothing better. But it wouldn't be right. You wouldn't look right with it, Mister Chairman of the Stargorod Sporting Society, you would not indeed. You have to wait. Be patient. When Colonel Yegorov croaks, someone'll have to find a new home for his Sauer – the old soldier promised to bequeath it to you, didn't he? A three-ring Sauer, the real deal! A trophy. That's even better than a Lefaucheux. Certainly not worse. And Yegorov's got cancer. The hospital won't admit him again – Vdovin refused to operate, said it's pointless. So there you have it. Ready, set, march – the grouse will still be there. Trilling.

And that's when the phone on the desk, a Hungarian model, with buttons, trills just like a grouse: "Bee-bee-bee-beep!"

Perk up, like a spaniel, grab the thing – gently, like a shot bird – carry it to your ear:

"Shishmaryov speaking."

Sound stern, sharp. Take pride in the sharpness – you can't keep things in order without being sharp and stern.

On the other end of the line – the regional administration chairman, clearly irked.

"Shishmaryov? Shestokrylov here. Is there a reason you're not cleaning out your toilet?"

"Which toilet, Savvatei Ivanovich?"

"What do you mean, which toilet, damn it? You know perfectly well! I have to apologize to my Italian tourists for your toilet, and you want to fool around? Who's in charge of the portable toilets on Solikha dig, me or you?"

"I am, Savvatei Ivanovich, I am indeed, but you know, those archaeologists..."

"Shishmaryov, do you understand the words that are coming out of my mouth? You have three days, and I don't care if you have to scoop it out by hand, do you hear me? I don't give a flying hoot about your damn archaeologists, and you better think long and hard about why the chairman of the regional administration should have to clean up your shit! All right, that's it, Shishmaryov. If you don't get it done – I'll see you in my office."

Shishmaryov placed the receiver carefully back on the phone and only then cursed. Without any special anger, however – a snap, as if at a passing fly. That's life right there, isn't it? Like he's got nothing better to do. And, of course, it has to be the scientists! He's just about had it with their kind – you give them an inch, they take a mile, never fails. But not this time, no sir – they'll clean it up themselves!

He rubbed his hands together, let himself chuckle even, put on his suit jacket, looked himself over in the mirror, straightened his tie, sighed and grabbed a leather portfolio for added solemnity. Then he went out onto the porch.

All this is happening why? He knew it – he didn't want to move into Syrtsov's lush offices, he did everything to get out of it. But no, they just had to move him there – twisted his arm, basically. Said it was temporary. It's been ten years. And it's a *his-to-ri-cal* landmark (like they'd ever let him forget about it)! It's good historical wood heating – that's one thing. Then he had to give up one of his precious huntsman lines for a stoker – that's another. Then he had to build them an outhouse – with six holes, a beauty of a thing, that was the third. Except now, every batch of snot-nosed kids that comes through on a school trip just has to stop by his, Shishmaryov's, place. And use the toilet.

"Who's in charge of that toilet?" he repeated, mocking the chairman's tone. Rather than yelling at him, why couldn't he build a regular public one? But what are you gonna do, eh? You live in Russia.

But – it's your own damn fault. You let them in. And how could you refuse? Who hasn't heard Professor Koldin speak on Stargorod radio, who hasn't seen him, damn his cotton socks, on national TV – he is a public figure, that's for sure. And he came to Shishmaryov himself, asked for an appointment, said, "We're beginning an archaeological project right outside your door…"

An archaeological project, right. The hole'll be here when we are all gone, that's for sure. They have a conveyor belt for the dirt in there. A whole swarm of school-kids – there was a special order to send them all to the dig, for "practice." Barns, laboratories, a lean-to for when it rains. And a chicken-wire fence around the whole thing – can't have just anyone walking in and out, it's a site!

But – you do what you have to do. How could you not? It's history! Shishmaryov has great respect for history.

He pushed the gate, walked into their territory, sniffed the air. Yep, it stinks alright. You bet. Could've at least closed the door in this heat. Oh, they'll clean it up – he'll see to that! Look how many kids they have tooling around in that hole, and every last one of them's getting paid. Of all things, money here is not a problem. Anyone can see that.

He introduced himself to a student – the nice girl who sat at the desk, reading a nice red book. He asked to see the professor. She gave him a displeased kind of look – for interrupting her nice work, how else – but stood up and went to get the professor.

"Please, wait here a minute," she said when she came back. "Pyotr Grigoriyevich is climbing up."

And indeed, Pyotr Grigoriyevich is climbing already. Tiny steps, short, exact, one foot in front of the other on the plank – planted firmly, solid on the good pine boards (they made the footpaths from one-by-fours). Professor's rubbing his hands, professor can't wait to see him. Professor is smiling, but Shishmaryov can't see his eyes behind the sunglasses. It's hot out here, of course.

Looks like it might just work. It will! Professor's in the right mood.

"Andrei Yevgeniyevich, my dear, to what do we owe the pleasure of your company?"

A bit old-fashioned, but Shishmaryov actually likes being addressed like this.

"Are you here on business, or did you just decide to stop by, to be a good neighbor?"

"Business, I have to admit, just business... I just can't seem to make it here otherwise – work, you know, is keeping me busy..."

"Oh, don't I understand? You must be running off your feet getting ready for the hunting season. I'll tell you, in the old days, I used to love tracking around with a gun myself... But if it's business, I won't bore you with my chit-chat. Please, come in, here, to the laboratory – we won't be disturbed in there. Nadenka," professor says to the student, "please make sure the log house foundations are reflected on the drawings accurately, I'll check it myself. And yes, I am not available for anyone – Andrei Yevgeniyevich and I have some extremely important affairs to discuss, I see. Affairs of the state – you know what I mean, Nadenka?"

He's sharp, Shishmaryov observes, but with a sense of humor too. It might just work, it just might.

The Professor leads Shishmaryov into a walled-off laboratory. Nadenka follows them with her gaze, then goes back to being absorbed by her book.

In the laboratory – an old threadbare couch, a table on trestles, a plank-board bench, shelves along the walls. The professor carefully deposits his soft plump body on the couch; Andrei Yevgeniyevich perches on the bench, his portfolio on the table before him.

"So, I am at your disposal."

He doesn't take his glasses off, the bastard. Shishmaryov – grab the bull by the horns! – goes straight to the heart:

"I had a call from Shestokrylov today..."

"Yes, well, Savvatei Ivanovich and I go back a long time."

"Basically, we have one toilet between the two of us, right?"

"Yes, of course, Andrei Yevgeniyevich, but don't get so worked up about it, please. I'm here to help."

"So, like I was saying, we have one toilet, and you have many people. So, the toilet's overflowing, and foreigners see it. It doesn't look nice, Pyotr Grigoriyevich, it should be cleaned up."

"I understand you completely and agree wholeheartedly. I want you to know, I'm all for it. I myself don't actually use that restroom – it doesn't seem proper, in my position, but it's highly unhygienic, it's only a matter of time before the health inspection gets a whiff of it, pardon my pun. I agree with you wholeheartedly. So what is the problem?"

"What do you mean?" Shishmaryov thought he explained everything plainly. "You, then, have all these people, an army, and what do I have? And a truck, you know, is liable to cost eighty rubles, no less, we'd have to hire it privately, our fleet's all tied up."

"You see, Andrei Yevgeniyevich, I am a man of science, and I've gotten used to putting my faith in numbers. You must forgive me, your sentiments have little effect on me, although I can see you are very upset. I can also see you are a man of action. Splendid, then. Say, what if someone told you there's little grouse to be had this year, but I heard with my own ears three females trill just this last Sunday. What then? Which do you believe? Neither, of course! You show me a figure, or at least some calculations, and compare the numbers with the last year's count, and then, yes – then you can make a logical conclusion. Am I right?"

Damn it, he's a hunter, too... But Shishmaryov nods obediently.

"So, let us do some math here."

The professor sits up on the couch so he can reach the table, grabs a sheet of paper from a shelf, produces a pencil and inquires, apparently with no intention whatsoever to mock him:

"Could you by chance recall when the toilet was last cleaned out?"

"Geez, before you guys came, it was doing fine – it's been here for five years, and never bothered anyone."

"Splendid! We'll say five years. In what units would you like to measure its contents?"

"What do the contents have to do with anything?"

"How do you mean, Andrei Yevgeniyevich? It's our facility, isn't it, shared that is – so we're the ones responsible for measuring its capacity, aren't we? Ancient Greeks in our position would have suggested the amphora as a unit of volume, and you and I, if we put our minds to it, could probably manage with barrels, remember, like the ones horses used to pull around when we were children? But buckets would do just as nicely, or mugs, even, it doesn't matter."

"But I don't understand... what are you trying to do?" The joke, it seemed, was no longer funny.

"Bear with me, dear Andrei Yevgeniyevich, I beg you. I assure you, I'm not trying to avoid the problem, I just want us to agree on the method of our approach, as a first step. It's all perfectly natural, a common outcome of a human function – so there's nothing to be ashamed of, is there? Let's count in liters, to stick to the metric system. By the way, you have five accountants on your staff, plus the huntsmen, the senior forester, a typist, drivers, and, finally, yourself – about 25 people in all?"

"Twenty-two," Shishmaryov confirms, curtly and with the grim determination of a man who'll fight to his last drop of blood.

"Splendid, plus two, three, four, sometimes six visitors every day, and sometimes more. You have fifteen districts under your jurisdiction, with huntsmen, foresters, and a manager in each, so for the sake of simplicity, we'll just round it up to 25 people a day."

"All right, but you – your expedition..," without really wanting to, Shishmaryov is drawn into the process. To be completely honest, he's rather appalled, really disgusted, but it appears this is the only way to get anything out of the Professor.

"Just another minute of your patience, Andrei Yevgeniyevich. So, on this side we have 25 healthy adult individuals consuming a high-calorie, high-protein diet. Because I will not be convinced that elk or boar, not even to mention bear, are any less nutritious than the pollock and catfish one buys at the grocery store. Your 25 against my 75 schoolchildren and four students. Let's take the volume at..," the Professor trails off, writing a column of numbers.

"There you go with your volumes again, Pyotr Grigoriyevich! Can't you see – it's plain: there's a toilet, and it must be cleaned!"

"Here... I think it should be about four cubic meters, multiplied by six days a week – 24 total. I have 75 six- and seven-graders on paper, but I don't ever get more than 55-56 of them to show up. Then, if we compare a six-grader against a grown-up hunter, based on average weight, we'll get a ratio of about one to four, right? You're a hunter, Andrei Yevgeniyevich, you know what I mean: a piglet is not a boar, right?"

"Yes, of course, but..."

Goddamn it!

"No 'buts'. Logic is a merciless thing. You can't argue with it, my dear. So, 60 divided by four (meaning, four kids equal one hunter) comes out to fifteen. I am getting one point six cubic meters of, pardon me, the substance in question per six-grader. Doesn't add up to much over the two months we've been here, does it, Andrei Yevgeniyevich? And by the way, the kids only work until lunch, while you and I are compelled by law to carry out a full eight-hour work day."

The Professor dabs his forehead with a hanky – it's hot even here, inside the little building.

"So, my dear, do you see the logic? It's rather compelling, isn't it? Twenty-five versus 15 – it's like two times two. And, beyond that, do you know how much our beloved government allocates for archaeological research per year? A million! For the entire country! That's the price of a single mid-range bomber, and it's supposed to cover all, mind you, all expeditions across our boundless country, plus the salaries of laborers, guards, cleaning crews and myself. I dare say you make more from harvesting birch bark. And the kids who work for me? I can't pay them more than two rubles a day. How much pollock or catfish can you buy for two rubles?" The Professor rises and maneuvers Shishmaryov towards the door, out. "That's where the matters stand, Andrei Yevgeniyevich, and now I must excuse myself – I am late for a meeting."

"Yes, of course. I see now. I am sorry for having disturbed you..."

Shishmaryov is defeated. He is smitten, in fact – what a penny-pincher, and a Professor! He runs, cursing the science of archaeology and all its professors in general, and Professor Koldin in particular, and then cursing himself. In the office, an idea occurs to him: he will call the plant, and he will ask not for three, but for five new huntsmen positions! Pal-Petrovich, as he's wont to do, will not give him all five – he'll back off two and get his three. Of those, two will employ actual people and the budget for the third will pay for a sanitation crew to vacuum out the damn toilet, and whatever's left he'll use to pay the night-guard who's been watching his bark warehouse for free (in exchange for a boar license), but still... Damn it all to hell! Shishmaryov picks up the yellow, Hungarian-made receiver he hates so much.

Pyotr Grigoriyevich watches the Chairman disappear inside his office, shakes his head, and rubs his hands together – it's a habit. He takes off his glasses, stuffs them into his breast-pocket. He looks at his watch.

"Smoke break!" he calls out.

The students raise their heads from the trench like war-horses at the sound of the trumpet, and echo: "Smoke break!"

The mechanic transporter line stops; kids run to the shade, splash at the sinks.

"Nadenka," the Professor turns to the girl still sitting behind her desk reading her book. "Nadenka, I am going to the museum for a meeting of the renovation committee. I won't be back for dinner. If I don't get a hundred and fifty rubles to fix that transporter line, we'll have to carry the dirt out by hand next year."

He touches the pocket containing his glasses, but does not pull them out; instead, he walks away towards the kremlin. The committee is waiting for him. The museum's director has spent the morning staring at her budget, trying to find 1,264 rubles in cash somewhere between its lines. Last night, the roof above the Likhonin Chambers leaked, there's been water damage to the icons kept there. She needs to find cash – no one will fix her roof in exchange for a piddly IOU.

High in the shade above the dig, Nadenka sits behind her desk, reading. The transporter line starts up again, rattles. The sun beats down on the dirt. Nadenka is reading a samizdat translation, a thick book in a red cloth cover. She reads: "The real difference between a mortal man and an angel does not lie in the fact that a man possesses a body and an angel is fleshless; the true distinction can only be revealed in the comparison between a mortal and an angelic soul. A mortal man's soul is endlessly complex. It is an entire world constituted by different essences, while an angel is a singular essence and, in this sense, one-dimensional. Moreover, because of its multiplicity, its ability to contain mutually exclusive instincts, and because of its central gift – a share of the Divine which constitutes a mortal soul's true strength and resilience, and makes a man human – because of these capacities of his mortal soul, a man has the ability to differentiate things, to tell the good from the evil. A man can ascend to great heights, but he can also fall from what seems like a secure, well-established path. None of this is possible for an angel. In his internal essence, an angel is forever unchanged."

"Nadezhda! Are you ever coming out to work, or what?"

Nadenka stops reading, but does not look down, into the dig, to see who's calling her; instead, she gazes upward, at the clear, distant August sky and mutters lines from a poem:

"*Fear the open road in the middle of the day*
Noontime is the hour when angels go to pray..."[3]

The noontime Stargorodian sun is hot, very hot. The barely noticeable breeze brings a distinct waft of the toilet. One of the kids forgot to close the door again.

Nadenka reads.

---

3. Lines from a poem by Mirra Lokhvitskaya, 1869-1905.

BLESSED ARE...

"...let us commend ourselves, and one another, and all our life unto Christ our God."

"To Thee, Our Lord," the congregation responds. A moment later, a confirming, albeit discordant "Amen!" resounds through the church.

The deacon steps down from the ambo. From the choir, the reader, in a clear, measured voice, recounts the beatitudes from the Holy Scripture. The congregation – and it is sparse today – repeats The Savior's words after the reader, whispering meekly, obediently:

"Blessed are the poor in spirit, for theirs is the kingdom of heaven..."

"Blessed are those who mourn, for they will be comforted..."

"Blessed are the meek, for they will inherit the earth."

A man in a long gray raincoat slips into the refectory sideways, glancing about him, and takes a spot behind a column. His eyes search the congregation; he is looking for someone specific, but he is not seeing him or her. He crosses himself in time with the old ladies next to him.

The reader continues:

"Blessed are those who hunger and thirst for righteousness, for they will be filled."

"Blessed are the pure in heart, for they will see God."

The man in the gray raincoat makes an inconspicuous motion to adjust the stub-barreled, small machine gun, so tiny it is almost toy-like, hanging on his chest beneath the coat. The man glances around him, but people are preoccupied with their own thoughts and no one pays him any attention. His eyes keep scanning the front row of old ladies, but the one he is looking for doesn't seem to be there. This is bad news. Very bad news. The man is tense: what if she is late? What if she comes in now – it would be easy to spot him, she'll recognize him. He presses his whole body into the column, becomes one with stone.

The reader's cadences roll forth, peaceful and heart-felt:

"Blessed are the peacemakers, for they will be called children of God."

"Blessed are those who are persecuted because of righteousness, for theirs is the kingdom of heaven."

"Blessed are you when people insult you, persecute you and falsely say all kinds of evil against you because of me. Rejoice and be glad, because great is your reward in heaven, for in the same way they persecuted the prophets who were before you."

Solemnly, slowly, the Royal Doors swing open, as if the Pearly Gates themselves allowed mortal souls to glimpse the Kingdom of Heaven, and the congregation beholds the magnificent altar, the seat of the divine glory and the supreme fountain of knowledge whence the Truth issues forth and the news of eternal life is brought.

The priest and the deacon approach the altar, lift the Holy Scripture from it, and carry it through a side door to the people.

Peacefully, with measured steps, they proceed to the center of the church. Both bow their heads. The priest looks at the floor; he is silent, focused. The deacon lifts his orarion, like a wing, at the gilded Royal Doors, and inquires loudly:

"Do you Bless, Master, the holy entrance?"

"Blessed is the entrance of Thy holy ones, always, now and ever, and unto the ages of ages," the priest responds.

And that's when the man in the raincoat sees it – the familiar headscarf in the crowd, a glimpse of the woman's face: his mother is gazing steadily at the Gospel, crossing herself. Yes, he is certain – it is she!

"Thank God," he whispers.

She is here, and this means nothing stands between him and the pantry in his mother's apartment. He adjusts the gun again – a motion that looks as if he's shrugging his shoulders – and begins a slow retreat to the exit.

"Wisdom!" the deacon's bass thunders, the last thing the man in the raincoat hears.

He has made certain: his mother is here, in church, and she will be praying for a long time. She will pray for him, too, among other things. Usually, he doesn't care one way or the other, but today he wouldn't turn down a bit of protection from the higher powers, even if he doesn't believe they exist.

The man checks his watch. Everything is going exactly as he has planned, perfect. He's got plenty of time. He looks at the street, the side alley. The alley is empty. Behind? There's no one behind him either. Excellent.

Through backyards he knows so well, through nooks and alleys, avoiding the brightly lit boulevard, the man makes his way to a large barrack-like apartment building that belongs to the railroad. He grew up here; here he knows every in and out. The man pauses for a moment behind a woodshed, checks his approaches: there's no one around. He runs up the stairs, leaping over the fifth and the seventh step – they've been creaking for years now. He slips into his mother's little room, and closes the door behind him. Just in case, he locks it.

He is home now.

The man takes off his raincoat, pulls his machine gun off over his head and places it neatly on a bedside table. He opens the pantry, pushes a sack of potatoes aside. Here's the floorboard he had cut out, and below it: his secret cache. There, wrapped in a rag, is a revolver and a half-dozen wonderful little bullets. The man unfolds the rag carefully, checks his weapon, strokes it affectionately. He opens the cylinder and slips in the bullets, pressing each hard with his finger: six gleaming capsules, six exactly – he counts them with a gravity that befits the occasion. The revolver is also short-barreled, foreign – it took him forever to hunt it down. The boys from Petersburg helped. Those guys are gold – they never let him down.

The man slips the revolver into a holster, and adjusts it under his arm, next to his heart. He can't deny himself a moment of joy: he whips out the gun, pretends to aim it – Bang! – spins it on his index finger and throws it smartly back into its nest. Everything will go just fine! He'll pay them back for everything. He checks his watch again: plenty of time until show time.

Now, the machine gun. It's a splendid piece, just splendid, but it'll have to wait its turn, it won't speak today. From looking at it, you'd never know it was homemade: it's small, compact, and it cost, let's be honest, a fortune, but money means so little when you remember what the goal is. And Petrovich is an ace! An expert! He just studied the drawings (that was a separate story, how he got those), named his price, and voila! – two months later, he had it made! Excellent.

The man stroked the steel of the barrel, pulled out the cartridge, and laid them both out on the rag. Then he wrapped it up, tied it with a rubber band he brought with him specifically for this purpose, and rested the bundle at the bottom of his cache. He put the board in place, swept some potato dust over it, and finally dragged the sack back into place. No one would ever think to look here. And even if someone did – the board looks no different from all the other floorboards around it, he made sure of that.

Suddenly, the man thinks about his mother. Let her pray, what else has she got left to do in her old age? What was it they said in church? Rejoice and be glad! That's right – watch out now, you sons of bitches, he's about to go do some rejoicing! He's spent a long time planning it, and he's got every second laid out.

The man puts on his raincoat – a wonderful piece: so large, it hides the revolver even better than it conceals the machine gun. Not machine gun – his "little toy." That's how he likes to think of it.

Retreat, through the yard. And he's lucky again – there is not a soul anywhere. And it's beginning to drizzle. And dusk is seeping into the air.

He is lucky! Lucky!

The man is now walking down the main street. He is walking calmly, confidently. He doesn't care that the street lamps are bright – it's even better that way, it'll be easier to take aim.

The man checks his watch – everything is going according to the plan. Excellent!

And here's the Park of Culture and Leisure, which people simply call "the spot." Some are already beginning to gather at the spot – the open-air dance floor on Merry Hill. The man crouches, ostensibly to tie his shoelace – and dashes into the bushes. The bushes are wet – it is drizzling – but the man can't think about that: it's now or never!

Holding his breath, he sneaks up closer to where the police patrol usually stands. There they are: two policemen in raincoats next to a traffic-police Moskvich sedan. They stand with their backs to him, smoking, talking about something.

It's quiet in the park, only once in a while does someone walk by – the bigger crowd flows down the main street: back and forth, fat on its free feed, dumb as cattle. Trucks thunder by.

The man pulls out his gun, raises it, aims with both hands, knees slightly bent, back leaned back just a bit.

Pss! Pss! Pss!

Damn it! God damn it! All six – misfire!

Were the bullets wet? Did Vityunya let him down? Oh, you just wait, you bastard!

Disappear – right now! Everything's been planned!

Through the park, past the kremlin. Stay calm. Those two didn't even hear anything – the street noise swallowed the sound. Double-up, come back. Just like that. Now, go past the post, take a look.

Everything is fine: the pigs are standing where he left them, suspecting nothing. And only five minutes ago... All right, let it go.

His nerves are strung so tight they seem to hum.

Now go, mix with the crowd, vanish. Get on a bus. Go home!

At the door – hug her, so warm, cozy, and also tense, worried, she's been waiting. Kiss her on the lips, pull her close, hold her tight.

"Did it... did it work?"

"No. Vityunya, son of a bitch, slipped me bad bullets – either they were wet, or the caps didn't fit the firing pin. But they seemed fine when I tried them at his place!"

The man, defeated, shrugs off his raincoat, drops the holster with the toy Italian revolver, but doesn't let it hit the floor – he catches it and puts it carefully on an armchair. It's a nice piece, really. Four-hundred and fifty rubles kind of nice. His wife comforts him:

"That's alright, Valya, don't worry about it now. Everything went as you wanted, didn't it? So you just think of it as done. Go wash up, quick, I've made pancakes with cheese and honey, the way you like."

He goes to the bathroom, and splashes ferociously in the sink. He looks at himself in the mirror, and makes a face, like a fearsome gangster. Screw it!

"You know," he shouts to the kitchen, "Petrovich did make me a machine gun. Wait till you see it! I'll go to Petersburg on the weekend and show the guys, they'll flip! Even Semyonov's Parabellum is not as good, and he had it made at the Kirov factory."

"You'll have a great time, Valya!" his wife has come into the bathroom, put her hands on his shoulders. "You're such a boy, really. Thirty-seven, and you're still playing at guns."

Valya turns and grabs her – the whole smooth, warm, delicious bundle of her – but the wife struggles free:

"Oh no, not right now. Off to the kitchen, Mr. Secret Agent!"

"*Oui, mon général!*"

The two scarf down the pancakes; each thinking about his or her own. The wife is happy that the not-entirely-safe game has ended well, that no one got into any trouble. Let him go to Petersburg for the weekend, hang out with his guys at the dacha, and shoot to his heart's content. They call themselves "Scouts." When they were little, they played Indians, and now they spend hours chasing each other in the woods and shooting paint at each other. She doesn't mind, though – he needs to let off some steam, anyone would after sitting at a desk all week, drawing boxes at the architecture office.

And the main thing, of course: it's long been clear they won't have a little one of their own to play with, but it doesn't mean you can't play at all, does it?

"Hey! I've got an idea," Valya perks up suddenly. "You know what?"

"What?"

"What if I buy Semyonov's bow, like he offered, and you and I go duck-hunting at the lake? He's had new arrows made too, from bamboo, just like Thompson Seton wrote, exactly. They are awesome. And he only wants 500 for the lot."

"That'll be fun!" the wife agrees in advance.

"You know, we could go, make a fire, maybe we'll even catch a fish to cook. Spend the night there! Nights are still warm. What do you say?"

"I'd love it, Leatherstocking!"

"Katya, come on, I mean it."

"I mean it, too. We should go to the Senga, to the channel, there's never anybody there."

"And you don't have to worry about the money – there's a bonus coming at work."

"I never do – what's money, if you can't buy anything anyway?"

Valya gives her a peck on the cheek, goes back to the room and turns on *Vremya* on TV. While he watches the news, Katya clears the table and washes the dishes. Then she joins him, sits in the armchair and picks up her knitting.

"Come here, Katya," Valya says, patting his knee. His wife slips out of her armchair and nestles in his lap, and he presses his face into her hot chest.

"You are such a miracle! I just don't know what I might have done to be so blessed."

"So am I, sweetie, so am I," she says, stroking his hair. Eventually, she says, "Why don't we turn in now."

"Yes, I'm tired... You know, it was quite a rollercoaster today, nerve-wise. It's just a game, of course, but still... it takes its toll. You'd think it was for real."

Katya turns off the TV.

MASHENKA

This story dates back to the fondly remembered bygone days of old when one could still buy something at stores like Balaton or Yatran without special sale coupons and when some of our Stargorodian girls still went to Moscow in search of husbands. It wasn't like they all enjoyed unmitigated success there, but some got lucky, and a few got really lucky: Marinka Kuzmina, for example, now lives in Detroit and sends her old friends from Stargorod's telegraph office sentimental letters about her little boy Christopher and her little girl Natasha.

Mashenka G., unlike her proactive girlfriends, resisted the idea of going to Moscow for a long time. Trapping some poor slob in a shotgun marriage, to be completely frank, rather disgusted Mashenka, and, being an honest and pure-hearted girl, she naturally dreamed of a mate who would be both an intellectual and young and handsome, and if he absolutely had to happen also to be rich, then only a little, because everyone knows money can't buy happiness. So it was that all her friends from the bookstore where she worked had already made their pilgrimages, but Mashenka kept holding back, waiting for something. Of course, she was tempted by the stories of Moscow theaters and beautiful stores. Some girls even managed to meet apparently good guys, and the way they told it, things sounded perfectly simple and not at all shameful as some impotent prudes would have it, but... Mashenka was a dreamer; Mashenka wore her hair in a long braid and was a bit old-fashioned.

Lyudka was another story – Lyudka the whirlwind, Lyudka the lucky one. She ruled over the bookstore's glamorous fiction section, while Mashenka was supposed to guide potential readers to "political literacy." Lyudka seemed to know every other person in Stargorod, and still, somehow, she had cast Mashenka G. as her best friend, and it was Mashenka who was the first to hear about Lyudka's adventures and suitors, it was with Mashenka that Lyudka shared all her plans and aspirations, and it was Mashenka from whom Lyudka came to ask permission to have an abortion (it's not like she could ask her parents). Better than anyone else, Lyudka knew how to have fun in Moscow: she had some family connections (kept active with regular doses of hard-to-find titles that gathered dust on Stargorod's provincial shelves) at the Soviet Hotel (no less!), so she always had a place to stay, albeit not a cheap one. But who counts money on a trip to Moscow? The whole point is to save up and then blow it all, so you have stories to tell!

It was Lyudka, of course, who finally convinced Mashenka to go. The girls secured a pair of advance return tickets for Sunday (two French novels for the railway ticket office), met at the station on Friday night, and early on Saturday morning were inspecting their "luxury" singles at the Soviet Hotel (which used to be "The Pit," where, as Gilyarovsky[4] assures us, the rich Russian merchants so loved to burn their money in the old days).

The girls spent the day shopping. They didn't find the biggest items on their respective lists (Mashenka was after a winter coat and had 300 rubles set aside for this purpose in her make-up case, and Lyudka wanted a pair of crème-colored Austrian boots), but there were other bits and pieces – Moscow always makes a dent in one's budget. They wrapped up their shopping excursion with a meal at the "Crystal Room" restaurant on Kalinin Prospect, where two rather persistent hucksters attempted to insinuate themselves into the girls' company but were told, in no uncertain terms, to get lost by the fearless Lyudka. Happy and well-fed, the girls rolled out into the frosty Moscow air, where the swirling flakes of the first snow only added to their celebratory mood, and, despite the fact that 150 rubles

---

4. Vladimir Gilyarovsky, a journalist, best known for his reminiscences about life in the pre-revolutionary Moscow, *Moscow and Muscovites*, published in 1926 (in English from Russian Life books, 2013).

had already been spent, it was decided to go hunt for tickets to the Bolshoi.

Neither the great heaving mass of people nor the buses filled with foreign tourists intimidated Lyudka. She parked Mashenka at one of the columns in front of the theater, and instantly vanished, gone to look for scalpers.

Mashenka was standing at the doors of the Bolshoi theater! Natasha Rostova's debutante ball was nothing compared to this. Of course, Mashenka dreamed of being inside, where everything swirled and gleamed, and she couldn't take her eyes off the doors, which was why she did not hear it when someone addressed a question to her.

He stood there with a bouquet of pale yellow roses, dressed in a double-breasted coat with a white scarf, and wore a large Seiko watch with a built-in calculator on his delicate wrist. His happy blue eyes openly sized up Mashenka, and were now inviting her to the theater.

"You see, my girlfriend stood me up – would you mind taking her place?"

Mashenka agreed on the spot, and he gave her the flowers. When Lyudka emerged from the crowd a second later, she instantly grasped the situation, nodded approvingly, winked, and cooed by way of blessing: "You go ahead, kids, I'll head home – it's not my night."

Lyudka was a real friend.

The ballet was magnificent! The theater – everything there was magnificent! They had second-tier seats, not very far from the stage at all, and in the intermission Andrei (that was the young man's name) bought her champagne. He was a person of style and manners, polite and solicitous, but Mashenka could also sense he could be passionate. He said he studied Philosophy at Moscow State University, but he wasn't one of those nerdy softies – his Dutch suit (one of those with a tiny rooster on the pocket) fit snugly around his manly shoulders, and his handshake was firm, which is rare these days, and his blue eyes could go from piercing to bottomless in an instant, but never dangerous. It was easy to be with him.

After the show they had some more champagne, then Andrei bought another bottle, "just in case" and they got a cab back to the hotel. And in the cab – they kissed!

Andrei was duly impressed with their rooms at The Soviet, behaved graciously, and Mashenka made him come along to Lyudka's room. There, they had a bite to eat – Lyudka prudently made a batch of sandwiches when she came home and bought some éclairs and mineral water from the buffet downstairs (she also had a bottle of cognac she had brought from Stargorod) – and spent the rest of the night talking and laughing. Andrei asked the girls to tell him about Stargorod, swore he'd pay them a visit the very next weekend, wrote down the address, and entertained them with tricks he could do with his electronic watch: it had a whole set of memory functions, and a phone book... and, heavens, the champagne went straight to Mashenka's head, and everything was just so easy and fun. When Andrei guided Mashenka into her room, God knows, she did not resist.

Everything was easy and fun, and she didn't even see her friend wink at her conspiratorially when they parted.

In the morning, Andrei rose early, took a shower, dressed, then came and sat down at the edge of the bed, kissed Mashenka, and asked kindly:

"Did you have a good time?"

"Of course!" Mashenka reached to touch him, but Andrei politely guided her hand aside.

"And you know all good things come at a price, don't you?"

"Of course. And what's the price?" Mashenka asked readily, going along with this new game.

"300 rubles."

"All right, go ahead and grab my make-up case. There's three hundred in there exactly, I was saving it to buy a coat."

She watched him as he opened her purse, dug in her make-up case, pulled out and counted the money and put it in his pocket.

"Well, then – *Ciao, principessa!*"

And he left.

Lyudka found Mashenka at the edge of her wits. Who could blame her – a part of her still waited, hoped the joke would play itself out in some surprising, beautiful way, that he would come back... but another part knew what happened.

Lyudka assessed the situation on the spot. She hugged the wailing Mashenka and shoved her, almost by force, into the shower. Then she packed them both quickly, and led her fooled friend out of the hotel. Lyudka hailed a cab, and they rode somewhere for a while, until they were in a *shashlyk* cafe in a small park somewhere. Only there did Lyudka allow herself to laugh.

"So, Prince Charming cleaned you out, didn't he!"

"Stop it!" Mashenka wanted to jump up and leave, but her friend held her down.

"You silly thing!" Lyudka just couldn't stop laughing. "Look at this!"

Next she produced out of her purse the super-computer watch Andrei had showed off the night before.

"I got up early in the morning – I wanted to give it back to him, but now – oh, Mashka! this is just too funny! – it's like he sold it to us. Don't you worry about a thing, we'll sell the watch – I know the people – and get a coat like you've never had before! Furs! I bet we'll get at least six hundred for it!" Afterward, they went on a long walk around Moscow and Lyudka comforted Mashenka as best she could, and by the time they boarded their train it seemed she had succeeded.

On the train (Lyudka traveled only first-class, sleeping car), the girls had tea with biscuits and then turned off the lights. In the dark, they sat together on one birth, hugging each other, Mashenka whispering breathlessly, in a happy voice, and Lyudka giggling, and then they fell asleep.

CLEVER ELSA

Really, it's enough to make us laugh. Picture this: just the other day, these two girls show up at our doorstep, fresh-faced students from the Moscow State University Slavic Department, in Stargorod for the first time; they stayed with us for the night. A friend of mine had arranged this, and sent us a package, much appreciated. They brought the usual things: some sausage without too much fat, three packs of Indian tea, and a whole kilogram of buckwheat. That's nothing to sneeze at, especially the buckwheat – we'll do it up with some onions, and a bit of garlic, and some bacon fat, and a tiny drop of oil so it doesn't burn, and "It's a treat, for those who know!" as our mother-in-law puts it. The metropolitan maidens enlightened us that, beside familiarizing themselves with Stargorod's many historical sites, they wished to collect folklore, because... well, suffice it to say that upon hearing their nonsense, my wife and I saw the urgent need to talk them out of this project, because what kind of folklore could the poor things possibly find in our city? They'd just perish, vanish off the face off the earth, and no high-placed friends would help you find them. Long story short, we rerouted them to Kargopol. We hear people there are nicer, and an old lady storyteller lives there – for ten rubles she'll sing to you about Eruslan Lazarevich until the cows come home. You've never heard such folklore.

The girls got excited, bought new tickets, and, basically, we haven't seen them since. And thank God for that. We know plenty well what Stargorod is like, and they'd never end well here. And this way, they probably wrote long papers, and nice ones too. The girls were smart and cute, not the kind you could let roam Stargorod on their own. Well, "any serious pursuit requires a habit of intellect" as our boiler-room stoker Mikhail Nikanorovich used to say, God rest his soul, you don't find people like that these days.

There's hardly any folklore to speak of: our *gusli* ensemble Russian Skomorokhs and the Birch spoon-players from the Red Proletariat factory spend all their time touring places like Finland and Sweden these days, you hardly even get a chance to hear them at home. So we have to admit that whatever folklore we had is all gone to seed, so to speak. But we do have stories every once in a while.

People around here are for the most part not especially rich; the co-op guys – they've made a pretty penny,[5] and did the Intourist-type moonlighters, but you know their kind – they spend more in one night at the Riflemen Izba than they make in a month. When your money's quick, it's work holding on to it. We have our misers, too, of course, who doesn't? Now, a friend of ours – a lieutenant at the detox that's housed in the White Monastery on the hill, Anatoly Kretov is his name – told us that he is personally aware (this is through his old connections at the Criminal Unit) of at least two old ladies in town who have 300,000 and 500,000 rubles in their savings accounts respectively. You'd think they'd live a little – and you'd be wrong. Instead, both beg about, look for bottles to turn in for small change, spend their entire days combing through the Victory Park, and haunt the bathhouse. They live in two tiny holes under the merry-go-round on Jolly Hill and pay nobody no mind. Anatoly said they are under secret surveillance – they've no family, so it'll all go back to the government when they croak, but they seem to have plenty of life in them yet...

Or take Stolbyshev, Matvei Semyonovich. You've probably heard of him already, only you didn't know his name and where he came from – we ourselves heard his story in Moscow and Leningrad presented as a genuinely local tale. I wouldn't be surprised if people in Tver, or, say, Arzamas, soon followed suit and laid their claim on Matvei Semyonovich, but do not let them fool you. We know

---

5. A 1987 law allowed limited private enterprise in the form of cooperatives.

this for a fact: Stolbyshev is ours, born and raised in Stargorod, and a widely known nut, who's been to the clinic many times, but was always ultimately let out to return to his usual pursuit – going to the dump to collect various pieces of trash, such as old galoshes, smashed pots, dead birds' wings, ratchets, padded blankets, and soiled railroad workers' vests. He wasn't above picking up a handful of nice dry dirt or some moldy bread crusts either. He dragged all this loot into his tiny room, where he stomped it nice and tight until he packed the entire space up to the ceiling, even blocked out his only window and only left himself a narrow path and a bit of space to set up his cot for the night. The neighbors, finally, caught a whiff of it – you can imagine the smell. Terrible! They sued. They won, of course, and brought in a marshal. This made Matvei Semyonovich very happy: "I've been waiting for this for so long," he said, "I want to make sure the assets are transferred to the government in a proper and legal manner." By then he'd chained himself to the radiator, so they couldn't drag him out of his room. "The assets in this room," he declared, "are worth more than a million! I wish to turn them all over to the government, and in return I would like very little: a room in a first-category retirement home and a military funeral." And how are you supposed to fight with him, if he'd hidden the key somewhere and you've got a court order to clean the place out anyway?

To begin with, they sent for some carriers like they use in field hospitals, and piled stuff on those to take it out. It stank to high heaven – the neighbors rued the day they went to court. But alright, you gotta do what you gotta do. Somewhere in the middle of this cultural layer, so to speak, they came across a giant-sized *valenok*[6] with a hole burnt through it, and inside it – 400,000 rubles in hundred- and fifty-ruble bills. They called the Colonel, and began addressing the old man politely as "Grandfather."

They kept cleaning, and eventually made their way to a couch – they uncovered one in the corner. By this time, obviously, the police

---

6. A felt boot.

sent the neighbors back to their rooms. And in the couch, sewn into the seat were these hefty little sausages: stacks of Imperial ten-ruble coins, a thousand of them altogether. I'll let you do the math. At the very end, when they cleared the floor, the old man himself showed them a spot under a floorboard where he had hid a small jewelry box, which was filled with pearls and precious stones. We, personally, saw neither the inventory nor the protocol, only know that there was a lot, so much that our Colonel was soon handpicked for a promotion to Moscow. What do you imagine the going rate these days is for a General's star if the regular 15-kopek-a-glass apple juice sells for twice that much in the co-op? This is what I'm saying.

And the other thing – grandfather's family did turn up after all, direct heirs, but all they came to say was, "We know nothing, and have no claims." It might be there was blood on that treasure, or maybe they really just got it all from the old man's father. Matvei Semyonovich's father, you now, owned a hardware store back in the NEP[7] days, and Matvei Semyonovich himself spent most of his life in the kerosene stand in the Old Market – a nice spot to be sure, but not the pearls-and-gems kind of nice! I'll let you do the math: how long did NEP last? And how long have the new co-ops been around? There, you see the difference? That's what I'm talking about. There's more to it, of course: people didn't start from scratch back then, and they didn't, old-timers say, use to drink as hard and as deep as they do now, at the Riflemen's Izba, and the caviar didn't cost what it does today...

Where do we get all this? From the same Anatoly Kretov, of course – back when this all happened, he had just come back from the army and enlisted as a private in the Criminal Unit, which is how he was able to be personally present at that famous search and property transfer. He only moved to the detox job later: "The criminal life," he used to say, "is not for me – too nerve-racking." Well, one can certainly see it that way: he has a family, small children, and they

---

7. The New Economic Policy, put forward by Lenin in March 1921. The policy was tolerant of small enterprise and engendered a short-lived economic revival in post-revolutionary Russia.

promised him an apartment. Only his nerves are no good anyway; any little thing can start him screaming, and his breath smells of alcohol, like that character in Gogol, you know (and he probably gives the same excuse for it too – that he was born that way).

"You could have snatched a rock for yourself in a blink," Anatoly once told us. "They all went into a stupor when I pulled out that box."

But he didn't take anything. His conscience wouldn't let him. He turned out to be an honest man, young Criminal Unit officer Anatoly Kretov, and that's why they made him a sergeant. And honest people don't make good stories – everyone knows everything about them anyway. One day, maybe, we'll mention him again – he is an interesting soul, after all, as is any soul, so unique and individual from the moment it comes to this world. But now we'd rather tell you a different story: the one about a dishonest policeman and the clever Elsa.

Listen then:

Elsa Pavlovna Goff came to Stargorod after the war. One way or another, she came to possess a small house on the Right Bank near Kopanka, where our sectarians live. One way or another, she also acquired a son. She went to work as proofreader at the city's paper, worked there until she retired, and sent her son to the army.

People knew she was German; people also knew she came from somewhere in the Urals or Siberia, or maybe even from Kazakhstan – somewhere far, anyway – but they didn't pry, and Elsa was German in every way: quiet, neat, her house, albeit decrepit, always painted some happy color, and the gooseberries and raspberries in her orchard, people said, were big as a fist. And her flowers – no one else has such glorious flowerbeds: there were asters – the plain reed kind, and the fancy tubular kind, in yellow, and purple, and red, and some others, terry ones; and chrysanthemums – Betsy, and Golden Star, and Measure, and Slogan, and Sunset (purple with pale white), and Elegy, and Stakhanovite, and Svetlana, and Mariana, and I'm not even going to talk about her sweet peas, and tobaccos, mums, nasturtiums, pansies and lilacs – the plain ones and the Persian ones. You couldn't possibly count them all. And the apple trees – she had about a dozen of those: late Chinese, early Antonov, Cinnamon, Pippin, Baltic Gold and White Gold – plus a smattering of currants along the fence: black ones to eat, red ones for the jelly – but that's about it.

Elsa fed herself from her garden, of course, but she never sold much – just a bit here and there, enough to buy tea and sugar, and some potatoes; no one ever held a particular grudge against her, which must mean she was never rich. She didn't have much time to go to the market anyway: she worked all day, and after work she had her son and her garden to tend. She was just... German, you know? No one envied her, and it was too much trouble competing with her at flowers and stuff. Everyone knew, for example, that she would happily share her seeds or cuttings with her neighbors, and would even come over and show them how to tend her plants, and her little tricks, so that the neighbors came to take a sort of family pride in her and would boast to the downtowners and the folks from the other side of the lake: "Our Elsa – she's really clever!" But as far as chatting or gossiping went, she never had the time for that; as we say around here, different strokes for different folks.

And so everyone was just getting along fine until one summer a gentleman paid a visit to Kosmodemyanskaya Street. You couldn't call him anything else – this was an honest-to-goodness capitalist: you would have said so too if you'd seen his trousers, and his jacket, his gold-rimmed glasses, his boots – atop real white India-rubber soles! – and his mustache, oh, his mustache was absolutely not how we do things around here. He went here and there, asked a few questions, and sort of filtered himself through Elsa's gate. This, then, was her cousin, come all the way from West Germany.

I won't even waste my breath telling you Elsa was terrified. Put yourself in her shoes: not a peep, not a trace, everything's forgotten, water under the bridge, and here he is, and it all comes back like in her nightmares: the barge sailing down the Volga, and Kazakhstan...

No! And yet – there he is: a living, breathing, flesh-and-blood (and quite well fed) gentleman, and presents his passport issued to one Erik Hoff, and brings out old family photos. Even their family name got passed on, and imagine this – he tracked her down through the Red Cross, bought himself a proper ticket, obtained a tourist visa, and there you have it: "Uncle Peter died in Bonn three years ago. He was ill at the end, didn't feel well, you know, his mind was... he began to remember Russia a lot, his brother Paul, and you... he made us promise we would find either you or Paul, and..." Basically, she, Frau Elsa-Katarina Hoff was entitled to 10,000 American dollars, her Uncle's diamond ring, the family silver, and, most importantly, a villa with a lake view and a Mercedes-230 automobile. There was, however, one condition: should she and her family be unwilling to move to Germany, all of the above, except the money and the diamond ring, would be inherited by her German relatives. And before Frau Hoff could even open her mouth, her cousin added that there were quite a few relatives indeed, and it was unlikely that she could ever win a lawsuit over the villa and the lake with the family silver, given that her Uncle was not quite altogether well in his last years.

The clever Elsa happily signed the release, wrapped the cash in piece of cloth and put it in a drawer in another room, and then hid the ring in a different safe place – and hid it well, you won't ever find it. She poured her newfound relative a cup of coffee with a piece of her famous coffee cake for the road, saw him off to the gate, and rushed back inside.

She locked the door and started thinking.

To the neighbors, of course, she revealed nothing, only said that the German tourist stopped by her place by accident, and kept thinking. And the more she thought, the more she grew scared. It's a big, terrifying thing, you know – having foreign currency in your own home, and having gotten it from a foreign German person on top of that. But – what are you going to do? – she tormented herself for a week, and then decided to act. She couldn't stand it anymore. So she went to the bank, showed them a copy of the gift document, certified by a notary, told them everything, and asked to have a foreign currency account opened in her name.

You can imagine the response. They dug around in all their books, called somewhere higher up, leafed through their manuals, never, of course, found anything, and finally said:

"You're not allowed to have one, in accordance with such-and-such order, issued on such-and-such date, end of story."

Elsa went home in low spirits. Visions of prison and freight-trains rolling somewhere very far away haunted her. She was scared to be alone in the house, and too afraid to write to her son and, God forbid, get him mixed up in this trouble as well – he had nothing to do with anything, his name and last name were both Russian, and he didn't even speak a word of German... Which, of course, never stopped anyone before.

She was scared.

And rightly so. They came. Meaning, at first, just like the last time, a single officer came: a field-operations KGB Lieutenant Sidorov. He started off mildly, but later, when she wouldn't tell him anything, raised his voice and threatened to dig up her old file: "We've got everything about you all written down!"

That's when Elsa confessed, and told him how things were: that her uncle had died, and she had not seen this uncle since she was little, and no one knew where he went and where he lived, so she was shocked to get this inheritance, but she's a smart woman, she was born here, and she'll die here, she's not about to move anywhere from her Motherland, and that's why she only got ten thousand dollars for giving up her portion of the estate – mind you, she didn't say anything about the ring – which ten thousand dollars she, as an honest citizen, hurried to put in the bank, but they turned her away.

"You should have called us right away, citizen Hoff. It wasn't proper to hide this, but alright, no harm done – we were informed anyway. Let's go ahead and take care of this right away; I'll come back tomorrow, say, after four, with an accountant. We will accept your dollars with all the proper documentation, of course, and will exchange them for five thousand rubles you're due according to the current official exchange rate: fifty Central Bank kopeks for one dollar. You did well to refuse the other things: it doesn't really behoove a Soviet citizen to have property abroad."

That's where he slipped – that was too much. Elsa was smart – she smelled a rat, she knew their kind: last time they confiscated even brass tea-glass holders, and now they were turning down a car and a villa just like that? She didn't let anything show, of course, but she got this sinking feeling inside. She saw her guest off to the gates, saw that he had come in the police car with the flashing light, and began to have some serious doubts.

But – the good Lord was looking out for her: her neighbor, Grishka Panyukhin, her son's classmate, stopped by to borrow a tenner for a bottle and to ask, among other things, what "that cop from the double" wanted from her.

"What cop, Grishka? From what double?"

"Aunt Elsa, would I lie to you? I just got out of there – spent two years staring at that mug at the gates, I'd know him anywhere."

"What's a double, Grisha?"

"The slammer, Aunt Elsa – the city jail."

"All right, Grisha, I'll give you a ten, but when are you going to quit drinking?"

She hesitated, digging in her wallet unnecessarily long – trying to decide: to tell or not to tell? Grishka had a good heart, her Andryusha liked him, only Grishka fell in with thieves, and got burned. She couldn't see another way out – she wouldn't find anyone else to stand up for her. So she told him.

"Aunt Elsa, are you kidding me? Dollar's now worth two and a half rubles, and he's giving you fifty kopeks! Well, that's a neat trick, you son of a bitch, and where did he get the uniform, Aunt Elsa, he's just a stinking sergeant, who does he think he is?! Oh, this is good. This is a stroke of luck, this is awesome – so, he's gotten greedy, he's too good for what the brothers pay him to sneak things into the slammer, he wants more. All right, let's play..."

And they made a plan.

The next day, just as they had agreed, a GAZ pulled up to Elsa's house right after four o'clock, but the "lieutenant" got out of it alone, without the promised accountant.

He came in, apologized dryly that the accountant could not accompany him, put his briefcase on the dining table, pulled some papers out of it and a "Paid" stamp, and arranged it all neatly on the table. Neither did he neglect to produce a stack of banknotes in a white bank wrap – five thousand rubles.

"All right, citizen Hoff, let's get it done."

"You're right about that, let's get it done. Come on, Katso!" Grishka yelled, jumping out of the wardrobe. From the other room, like a hawk, Katso swooped in – Grishka's friend, about the size of Aunt Elsa's wardrobe. The boys knocked the poor "GB officer" down, shook him a bit, and fished his police badge out of his pocket.

"See, Aunt Elsa, and you were scared! Out with him, let's take it to the street."

Outside there was a ruckus. Grishka paid a bunch of Gypsy kids to gather a crowd. The boys dragged the fake inspector out of the house, bared his behind, and tethered him face down to a bench. Then they gave him a hundred good lashes, to the crowd's great amusement – Grishka and Katso did a nice job there. Afterward, they explained the lay of the land to him – to keep mum, or else, they had plenty of witnesses, and they would pack him off to jail at the slightest provocation. Then they kicked him into his car and let him go, only Grishka took his briefcase as "material evidence." With the five thousand in it.

Later, Katso quietly exchanged Aunt Elsa's dollars for twenty-five thousand rubles (she gave Grishka the "GB" five on the spot, as they had agreed) and disappeared. No one ever saw him again.

The next morning, Grishka, naturally, woke up famous. People said he even got a laudatory letter from the double. The fake GB-man quit his job in great hurry, and left town – folks wouldn't let him be. They ragged the girl from the bank who'd dated him for a while for months. Clever Elsa wasted no time either – she put the money to work: put a new foundation under her house, got hot water, raised a heated greenhouse and a garage, bought her son a Dnieper motorcycle and a Sony tape player. Andryusha, however, when he came back from the army, yelled at his mother at first: the dollar, by then, was running between one-to-five and one-to-seven, but cooled off fast – Grishka threw him a couple of welcome parties and they had themselves a grand old time riding the bike around town. They played hard for about six months, and then Andryusha straightened up – his German blood must've made itself known – he passed the exams into the Polytechnic and got into books. Grishka also settled down – he now cuts meat at the market.

And what about Elsa herself? That's why people say she's smart: she made sure to spend the money as quickly as she could, only put away a thousand – for the funeral, and three more – in an interest account, for a headstone, and then went on living as she always had, nice and quiet.

"They can take four thousand if they want it – I don't care," is what she says to the neighbors.

And the ring? How do we know about the ring? Well, no one around here knows for sure, but it's not for nothing they say "the land fills with rumor," do they?

STARGOROD VENDETTA

Things are not what they used to be. Things have lost their gravitas. Their weight. Gone from the Lake are the famous roach, each of which weighed a man's arm down to his knee; gone from the Monastery Hill is the grove of great pagan oaks, uprooted one day by a sudden hurricane. A single stump remains as a memory, and it is mangled by fire – every summer, weekend lovers of *shashlyk* and loud music set it alight but can't burn it down. Gone is the mighty ancient tribe of *bogatyr* heroes from our land: where is the cunning Alyosha, the iron-armed Dobrynya, the spear-wielding Peresvyet? Who are the new Taras Bulba and his son Ostap? You couldn't even find a man to match our own Opanas Perebey-Gora,[8] who found his way to Stargorod from the provincial Gradizhsk, where in Gogol's times any kozak could easily trace his lineage to the glorious *atamans* and colonels of the Sich.[9] The Ukrainian famine of '33 and the times that followed scattered the last descendants of the free steppes far and wide. Opanas' family was one of the first to retrace the historic route from the Vikings to the Greeks in the opposite direction, and settled in our lands for good. The father plied his trade as a smith, and the son, thanks to his granite fists, native Ukrainian musicality, and long linen-blond curls, instantly became the ringleader of his Kopanka neighborhood. Even the downtown high-rollers considered it a great honor to be counted among Opanas' friends. But of his entire retinue, Opanas was most attached to the quiet Vassily Panyushkin. It

8. His last name literally means "break a mountain."
9. *Kozak* is Ukrainian for Cossack. The Sich refers to the independent military republic that existed on the Dnieper in the sixteenth and seventeenth centuries.

was their unbreakable bond that led, in the end, to Opanas' untimely demise.

To be fair, his death was in a way predicted by a roaming Gypsy woman back in the blessed pre-war times. After the fortune teller saw our golden-haired hero, appraised him, and bestowed on him whatever gifts she had to give, she prophesied him a death not of bullet or bayonet, but of common wood, and hearing this, Opanas lost what little fear he ever had in his mighty heart and, armed with his uncommon strength and significant wits, won himself on the fields of the last war the glory of a merciless and elusive partisan. Opanas became the right hand of Vanka Grozny, the Terror of the Krauts, later fought all the way to Berlin with the regular army, and came home unscathed: medals all across his chest and a sack full of lighters, silver spoons and famous Solingen knives, each with a pair of twins emblazoned on the blade, dancing their German *gopak*.

Opanas died as he had lived his short life: wildly and heroically. One quiet Sunday noon, an NKVD truck arrived in Kopanka to pick up the falsely maligned citizen Panyushkin, Vassily. Opanas, who by that hour, as was his custom, had already imbibed a significant amount of home-brewed mead, reclined in repose under an apple tree next to his smithy. When he heard Maria Panyushkina's wailing, Opanas Perebey-Gora rose and without bothering to sort things out any further, or perhaps taking the apparitions in blue cockards for the devil's own minions, picked up his heavy sledge-hammer and went to fight the noontime demons. The NKVD guys were at first taken aback by the sight of the fierce kozak, and even let go of the unresisting Vassily. They shouted a warning, trying to reason with the ferocious descendant of the glorious steppe warriors. But what was their yelp, their serpents' hiss, their crows' caws to a partisan full of honey-mead? Opanas struck once, and then again, and the NKVD bastards were dispatched straight into the gaping maws of hell. Their heads burst like ripe pumpkins; their impure blood squirted and poured onto our long-suffering land and stained their well-shined chrome-leather boots. For the third time the sledgehammer rose –

and fell into the side of the truck, splinters flying in every direction. The rookie at the wheel, white with fright, hit the gas, and the lopsided truck lurched and got stuck in the Panyushkins' fence. The lieutenant in charge of the arrest finally recovered his wits, tore at his holster, and whipped out his TT gun so glorified in movies and songs, and fired the entire clip into Opanas. But so great was Opanas' strength that even shot-through with bullets and blind with pain, he raised his hammer one more time and crashed it again into the wooden side of the trapped truck.

Why did Opanas choose to fight the inanimate truck, the one object on the scene that was truly, when you think about it, innocent? Why did he not lunge, with his last breath, to finish the evil lieutenant? Somehow, he must have seen doom itself in the spasms of the growling, foul-smelling machine; he must have sensed somehow that it wasn't the scoundrel that shot at him he had to fear – but this, the iron beast that trembled and shook in its rage. Opanas' last strike threw the driver off his hard seat, and when he fell back, he hit the reverse, the truck jerked again – and its half-shattered wooden back crushed Opanas against the willow tree behind him.

So perished the son of *kozaks*, Opanas Perebey-Gora – not taken by a bullet, not pierced by the honest bayonet, but buried in a pile of wood that crashed upon him and took out the light. His soul was received by the angels of heaven, but his body was left to the mercy of his enemies and vanished forever in the dungeons of their building as material evidence of his attack. Along with his body disappeared Opanas' mighty sledgehammer and the primary cause of the battle, the harmless beekeeper Vassily Panyushkin. Thus did the Gypsy woman's prophecy come true. This transpired in the year one thousand nine hundred and fifty one.

Our province, we must admit, has always lagged behind metropolitan trends. The arrival of postal service and telegraphic communication, which ended both the style and the desirability of epistolary correspondence as a soul-restoring pastime of the eradicated classes, which now delivers Moscow's orders with lightning speed to the most distant cities and towns of our far-flung empire, stretched the long hand of the law and, in the early fifties, tightened its grip on the throats of all the not-deported-far-enough. Their sympathizers and collaborators could do little in our province to extinguish the old, well-nurtured hatred for the mysterious and ever-scheming Trotskyists.

Grigory Panyushkin, a humble Petrograd priest, was arrested by the Cheka the morning after the attempted assassination of Lenin during the night of September 1, 1918, did his time on the Solovki,[10] and upon his return felt no desire to reside in our northern capital. Instead, he settled in Stargorod, where, since he had no chance of ever fulfilling the grain quotas required of independent farmers, he signed up for the Kopanka *kolkhoz*. In 1941 he went to the front, and vanished there without a trace. The only thing he left behind was his son – the above mentioned Vassily, who plied his partisan trade on the Lake's Black Shore with his mighty friend, Opanas the smith.

In his own time, Vassily, before he, too, vanished without a trace in the dungeons of the Stargorod NKVD, also begat a son who was subsequently raised by his mother in complete ignorance of his father, an enemy of the people. Maria Panyushkina lived in an instantly acquired and never abating anxiety vis-a-vis Stargorod's special organs, so decisive in their actions and so doggedly persistent in tracking down anyone they might have missed. Here it is important to note that the report that drew said organs' attention to Vassily Panyushkin was written by none other than Stepan Kandyba, a disabled veteran who, in his youth, had served in the Petrograd Cheka and arrested Father Grigory. Kandyba once stopped by the priest's son's bee farm, got a good deal on some stolen *kolkhoz* honey, and became curious about the origins of the beekeeper's last name. Over a glass of excellent mead, the innocent Vassily happily shared his family's hard-scrabble story with this total stranger, which

---

10. The attempted assassination of Lenin in 1918 accelerated the Red Terror. Solovki is Sol-vetsky Islands, the White Sea monastery that was transformed into one of Soviet Russia's first political prisons.

prompted Kandyba to look up a few dates, connect the dots, and report his suspicion to his own son, Pyotr Kandyba, a lieutenant of the Stargorod NKVD. Pyotr ordered his father to submit a full, anonymous report in the required format; in due course, it brought about the bloody and heroic battle described above.

Many years passed. The veterans all got their medals; even an Order of the Red Star found its addressee after years of zig-zagging through various offices. The Young Historians Society produced a display titled "Partisan Heroes of Stargorod" and placed it in the large window of the Stargorod Telegraph. Time erases old grudges, heals old wounds, and restores heroes to their rightful place, no matter how long they've been forgotten or how much they've been despised. Portraits of both Opanas Perebey-Gora and Vassily Panyushkin graced the Young Historians' display.

As one might expect, they ran out of room before they could post the picture of the Grozny Ivan. But by this time the grave of the old partisan – who had died after being stabbed in the neck with a thief's fillet after losing his legs in the post-war GULAG, as a result of which misfortune he came to occupy the throne of the local holy fool – was considered by the female population of Stargorod to be a miracle-working and sacred site. Women made pilgrimages to the cemetery because rumor had it that the old man could cure many maladies from beyond the grave. The authorities at the time were only just beginning to shake off their uniformly atheistic proclivities; the pictures of Opanas and Vassily were placed at the very top of the display, where they appeared to claim the status of the partisan movement leaders. The Memorial society awarded Grandma Masha regular food assistance, but the old woman, terrified once and for all by her husband's arrest and sudden disappearance, refused to accept it, hiding her deeply-seated fear beneath false pride.

Without Memorial's sausages and other fats, Maria Panyushkina's life took a turn deeper into poverty, aggravated by the fact that her son Grigory had fallen in with the wrong crowd and managed to land in the local prison with a two-year sentence. One can't judge the lad too harshly, however: he returned from the army to an old mother sitting on a threadbare couch before an ancient Temp TV, a flee-ridden dog, and the oppressive poverty of living on a single pension. Visiting Grigory in prison, Maria finally told him the story of the bloodbath in her black yard, of Uncle Opanas' heroic intervention, and of Grigory's own, unlawfully persecuted father. Somehow, the tale inspired a hope for a new life in her wayward son. The Kandyba family was also mentioned, and firmly fixed in Grigory's memory. Having found, albeit belatedly, a real father, the boy decided to avenge him, and even applied for parole, which he did not get. Nonetheless, he was a changed man when he came out.

Never having seen anything good from people in uniform, Grigory now had an ancestral bone to pick with them. So, soon after he came out, he won himself new fame in the story with Elsa's inheritance: Grigory defended the foreign fortune that had befallen Elsa, his neighbor, out of the blue, by fighting off a crooked prison guard who aimed to confiscate the money by pretending to be a KGB officer. The thirst for vengeance dimmed a bit in Grigory's heart after this incident, since he had the opportunity to whip the crook publicly – in the streets – for his misdeeds, before a large crowd of guffawing locals. But it did not die completely. His success, however, made him popular and some good people got him a job as a meat cutter in at the Stargorod market – a position passionately desired by many but available to almost no one.

Old Maria Panyushkina lived her last days in luxury: Grigory bought her new furniture, acquired a color TV and a VHS player, and married well. Before she died, his mother had a chance to play with her grandson, who was named, naturally, Vasilko. Maria died in dignity and comfort, yet still fearing for her high-flying son and praising the Good Lord daily for not abandoning her and letting her sleep on clean linen sheets in her last days. She died, and her son buried her in the Stargorod cemetery, affixing to her grave a large cross welded of stainless steel.

In the course of all this, he almost forgot his desire for vengeance – he had too much going on: a butcher's work is hard and stressful, and not only gives, but also claims much in both spiritual energy and nerve cells, which, as we all know, do not regenerate.

In the meantime, a certain lieutenant Stepan Kandyba arrived in Stargorod after graduating from the MVD[11] training institute. By sheer accident, he had attended school at the other end of Stargorod and up till this moment, fate had kept his and Grigory Panyushkin's paths far from crossing. Fate was saving him; fate waited for the proper occasion; fate raised and educated him, fed him and brought him up in the safe harbor of a retired major's home. Fate then ensured his political literacy in the halls of the MVD institute, and finally returned him to his native city, where it placed him right at the exit from the bridge where you turn to go into the suburbs.

Stepan Kandyba was honest, principled, and did not, unlike many of his fellow officers, accept bribes, for which he was disliked by his superiors and cursed at not only by motorists violating traffic rules but, of late, also by his wife, who was trying to feed and clothe a family of four on the combined income of an honest traffic cop and a typist.

The momentous encounter occurred on a Sunday afternoon. Grigory Panyushkin was in a hurry to get home: he had picked his wife up at the hairdresser's, and they were worried about their boy being left at home alone for so long. Grigory drove, as always, fast but carefully. At the exit from the bridge, he obeyed the stop sign, but the front wheels of his car edged just beyond the white line.

The violation was duly observed, and a traffic policeman's wand appeared, ordering Grigory to pull over; a very young lieutenant saluted the shocked Grigory and introduced himself as Stepan Kandyba. A short exchange followed:

"You have got to be kidding me. I drive here twice a day and know all you guys by name."

---

11. Ministry of Internal Affairs.

"You have violated the rules!"

"Really, pal, are you sure you want to mess with me? It'll come back to bite you."

"License and registration, please."

"You can have those, of course, but you look new to me. What did you say your name was?"

"Inspector Kandyba."

So transpired the first round of the Stargorod vendetta: the inspector won an easy victory and Grigory got a traffic violation on his record. Grigory threw the license onto his wife's lap, and said to the lieutenant, quietly but very clearly:

"Tell your guys the butcher Grishka said hello, and told you to tell them that the only meat they'll get from me is a dead ass's ears."

He pulled away, but just couldn't get over how bold and rude his blood enemy was. At home he let off some steam by yelling at his family.

Stepan Kandyba, when he returned to the station, reported the incident, and was immediately dragged over the coals, with much cursing. It was not among his duties to quarrel with the only butcher shop in town. At home, his wife also had some very unpleasant things to say to him. They fought, and as a result, the young Ms. Kandyba put her foot down on the subject of conjugal relations, and banished her spouse to the couch for a week. Ragged and unloved, poor Stepan began to contemplate taking his radar gun out to the highway, but inside him there was a feeling, something like pride, that kept him from breaking his oath for the time being.

On Friday, his boss Terebikhin ordered Stepan to ready a car.

"We need to buy some meat, bro. Let's go see Grishka at the market."

Kandyba was in urgent need of meat. A good roast would be just the thing to appease his wife, but the memory of Sunday's encounter made him deeply uncomfortable. He determined not to go into the store with his boss, but Terebikhin ordered him to follow, and the order, together with the irresistible pull of flesh, both the pieces of it hanging on the butcher's hook and his own, starved for a woman's touch, won.

"Aha! Here you are, my friend. You came yourself," Grigory greeted them from the manager's office.

"Greetings, Grigory Vasiliyevich!" Terebikhin either forgot all about his officer's misstep or was pretending that he knew nothing of it.

"I've no meat for you."

"Grisha, my dear, whatever is the matter with you?"

"Ask your lieutenant there why he put a thing on my record."

Given such an occasion, Grigory told the heart-rending tale of how he was hurrying home, with his wife fresh from the hairdresser's, and how he was suddenly and rudely stopped, and fined, his pure record violated for nothing.

"Oh, Grisha, he's new here. What's the problem? Give me your license. Stepan, fix it!"

While the meat was being carved and weighed and packed for his boss, while soothing, respectful conversation was being had in the butcher shop, Stepan Kandyba sped in the station car to the DMV, clear at the opposite end of the city, to get the hated butcher's record corrected. He fixed it, and he returned, and he gave the license back to the butcher, and... unable to stand it any longer and blushing like a boy, he asked, with a stutter:

"It's done, Grigory. Are we... good, then? Could I, by any chance, have some meat?"

Grigory roared with laughter, and his mighty voice bounced off the arched ceiling of the old butcher shop, much like the legendary roar of the heroic Opanas Perebey-Gora, the kind of roar you don't hear these days.

"Come, come, my friend, I'll cut you some. But mind you, Terebikhin pays three rubles, but for you it's five-fifty, so you'd know your place."

Grigory prodded Stepan to a door, and he went down the stairs into the basement, with a shamed little smile on his face. Behind him, Grigory Panyushkin whistled a prison tune as he walked and played with his heavy dummy – a short-handled butcher's hatchet, razor-sharp.

A lump of pork was hacked off in a blink. Weighed. Wrapped. An excellent cut from the back side, from the leg's very pink, tender center. The bill came to 52 rubles. The poor Kandyba had no such money on him, and was forced to request a loan from Terebikhin's fat wallet.

The entire uncomplicated procedure was accompanied by such nasty snickering (performed by Terebikhin himself, the store's manager, and Grigory, who snickered while he wiped his glistening blade on his apron) that poor Kandyba cracked: he took his boss home, stopped by the station where he stuffed the meat into the fridge, grabbed the radar gun and went out on the highway.

That night, slightly tipsy from the vodka his wife poured him at dinner, and with his flesh appeased (to his wife's own satisfaction as well; she, too, was tired of fasting), Stepan Kandyba cried quietly into his pillow next to his wife's blissful, soft snoring.

On the other end of the city, Grigory Panyushkin tossed and turned in his own hot bed. He should have been happy, he should have been enjoying his victory, but for some reason all he could do was turn from one side to the other and whisper a curse at someone. He finally realized he would not be able to fall asleep, and so he got up, went to his son's bedroom and stood there for a while, looking down at the sleeping boy. Then he ran his heavy hand gently over the boy's fuzzy hair and went to the window: the moon hung, large and orange. The sight of it so captivated Grigory that he stayed at the window, not moving, unable to take his eyes off of it.

"Just look at that," he whispered, utterly mesmerized by the moon's alien, frightening beauty.

He had never before seen such a moon, even in prison, where such things can claim a man's attention to a degree that is truly extraordinary.

TWO-HATS

Take Vanka Grozny – who was he, really? Little old ladies had him for a holy fool, priests all were afraid of him, cops let him be. To be sure, there was something to him, a colorful character, but nothing more. Back during the war, when he was a partisan, people scared kids with his name. "With a name like mine," he used to say, "what else could I do?" In '46 he was still a bit of a hot-blood, straight from the woods, and he whacked one cop who was thieving – just walked straight into the station one day and shot him point-blank with his Luger. "That's the only way to deal with you," he said, "bitch." Given his service record, they only gave him 10 years, but he wasn't about to become a changed man just because he was sent to a camp in Komi – he started a war with the old cons, and you know how it goes with the real convicts, they've got simple ways. They dropped a fir tree on Vanya. He lived, but they had to saw his legs off at the hip.

He rolled back into Stargorod on a cart: beard wider than a shovel, shirt forever unbuttoned, another beard's worth of hair sticking out on his chest, and in that nest – a copper icon that shined from a mile away (while bumming around the tundra, he managed to learn the Bible almost by heart – he'd rattle off whole chunks of it if the spirit moved him), and a padded *vatnik* in all weather, a backpack on his back, and two iron-shod pedals in his hands, to push himself around. An invalid of war, and his leg don't hurt, coz' it's chopped off at the root – pay up if you look, that was his gig.

First he set himself up by the telegraph office, and that's where they started calling him "Two-Hats": he wore a cap on his head, you see, and had a flop-eared hat for coins on the ground before him – that's how it was in summer, and the other way around in winter.

Then they chased him away from there – you're not supposed to beg in our country – so he moved over to our Electropower plant. He'd sit there at the gate (and he never begged – people gave him money anyway), speak kindly to some, bicker with others, especially if it were a woman – he was big on trash-talk. And little ol' ladies – that's a separate story with him, he took a shine to them. He'd see one going to church past the factory, roll up next to her, and bark – loud, so the whole street could hear: "Rejoice, daughter copulative, the cup shalt reach you too, and drain ye thou shalt and bare yourself drunken!" Or something like that. We'd be standing in the bushes with our cheap port and laughing our heads off, and the old ladies always took it very seriously, bowed to him, and gave him a dime or two. And the thing of it was – we never saw him set foot in church, but if he were going by one, he'd always cross himself. But for priests he had no love whatsoever.

"Vanya, hey Vanya," we'd bug him, just for fun. "Sell your icon."

"No way – it's a gift, from a good man."

"Then why is it, Vanya, that you wear your icon, and read your Bible, but never go to church?"

"No way, I can't: if I see a priest, I'll kill him, and I've sinned plenty already."

"What's a priest ever done to you, Vanya?" and the guys are already giggling.

"They've all turned greedy, only think of money."

"You must be jealous, Vanya, you only got a million in that hat of yours!"

And, of course, he'd fly off the handle, and start cursing at you – he was a pro at that, better than an old Gypsy woman – and we had fun. He kept calling us "bus-tards," but we knew he loved us – always came with a clean glass, and shared if he had any food, and never said no if we invited him. It's only lying he never stood for.

This one time he spotted two of our guys at the railway station: tipsy, naturally – and when they're tipsy, they'd do anything – and the cops' van pulling up. He grabbed them both by hand:

"Quick, take me to a cab!"

"Uncle Vanya, you don't have any money."

"None of your business, do it!"

They roll him up to the curb – and there's only one car there, everyone knows the guy, he's always there.

"Put me in the back, boys!"

So they start loading him into the back seat.

The driver, of course, recognizes who it is – he's an old rounder, too.

"I'm not driving that stinking bastard anywhere," he says.

But Uncle Vanya tells him:

"Don't worry, son, we're not going far, just over this way, to Lomonosov Street."

"I said, I'm not taking you."

"I'll pay you well."

And everyone knew – Grozny had a coin-purse on his belt. So at this point, he pulls it out, reaches into it, and pulls out a whole wad of cash.

"See this?"

"Thirty!" the driver declares.

"No problem, man, just take us."

They get there. The guys get out, pull out Uncle Vanya. He rolls up to the driver's window – to pay. Then starts looking around, digging at his belt, and says:

"Son, d'you have a light? Looks like I forgot me purse on the back seat..."

The cabbie puts two and two together, steps on the gas, and is gone – figured he can find the purse later. Only, of course, it was right there, hanging off Uncle Vanya's belt, where it never left. The whole town made fun of that cabbie after that: "Found Grozny's purse yet?"

He was fearless too. Our Boss, he never rode to work, always came on foot – that was his way of promoting democracy back then. That's how they ran into each other on the bridge one day: Vanya Grozny rolled one way, and Himself was walking the other. The Boss saw an invalid and decided to show how he cared.

"What's your name, grandpa? Do you need..," and stopped mid-word when he saw the icon on Vanya's chest.

And the next second Vanya howls:

"Lord Almighty, take pity on us! See what befell us: our wealth has gone to others, and aliens took our homes!" and so on. That was his favorite act. Whenever he drank a bit, he would rattle the whole spiel off to us, like a poem.

The Boss's eyes went all glassy on the spot; he turned and marched off at his best commanding gait, but Grozny wouldn't let him get away – rolled behind him and hollered:

"They whip us like cattle, we work and see no rest!"

The Boss' security team freezes: people are staring at the scene from everywhere, and the old man's a cripple, it's kinda' awkward to go chasing him off, so they decide to ignore him. The Boss – he tries to walk faster – but Vanka keeps right up. The security's hissing at him, but he pays them no mind, and just keeps piling it on thick: "Slaves have come to rule over us, and no one will deliver us from their hand!" – he's having a ball. He heckled the Boss all the way to the government building. And got away with it. And the Boss, they say, rode in his car for two days after that, but then started walking again.

He gave our priest the same treatment. They sent us one from the capital – he must've messed up somewhere, a fat guy, round as a barrel, and greasy as a tar-pit. When one of those gets sent to Stargorod, it's the end of the line for them – can't jump any higher or fly any further from here. So, you know, he got bored in a hurry and started ripping off old ladies and drinking vodka with the government types on their boats. You can't keep anything a secret very long around here. Word got to Vanya Grozny – and it wasn't long before he decided to set things right. Vanya – he never could stand things being messed up for long. So, he ambushed the priest right at the church, went up right into his face and took off: "You, bloody sell-out, stinking money-bag..." The priest was so shocked he couldn't move from where he stood. Vanka just kept going: "Repent, my son, for ye do not have much longer to live – know that the snake shall gnaw ye liver!" And it was like he was reading it from a chart, you know? Six months later, the priest kicked the bucket from cirrhosis, right in Dr. Vdovin's unit. Now that got the old ladies whispering for real. Come to think of it, it could be he had a feel for those things – it wasn't just that priest whose death Vanya predicted, and now they're talking about biofields and auras on every corner.

Healing – yes, Vanya would try to heal, too, but he couldn't fix everyone. One time Kostya Terentyev came to him with a finger – Vanya packed him off straight to the hospital, said: "Chop it off right now, or else you've got a month to live!" Kostya freaked out – and for a good reason, Grozny only missed it by three days. He'd seen enough gangrene for ten men in his Siberian days – he told us stories. And another time, these guys brought an old lady to see him, she was their mother-in-law, and a snake had bitten her. I saw it with my own eyes – her leg was swollen up as big as a coffee table and so blue it was going black. Vanya rubbed and massaged it for a good long time – must've been pushing the lymph around – and after a week, the swelling all went away and the old lady pranced like a new nanny-goat. So, if I see something, I ain't gonna deny it. Like Grozny himself used to say: "Yes – then yes, no – then no," he was full of sayings like that. But he never healed anyone just by looking, although he had an eye – oh, man – could go heavy as a pick-axe in a blink. Once, I remember, we were drinking beer at Veterok, and this hot-shot from out of town started talking big, like, "I been places, seen things" – and Grozny just rolled up, glanced at this guy once, and he was gone with all his talk, like he's never been. Vanya's eyes could gleam like he was mad, sometimes, and other times, he'd just be sitting there staring into space, and wouldn't even see you – it's true, he could be weird like that, but no weirder than you or I. One thing I can tell you for sure – he'd never whine about his hard life, as guys like to do when they've had a bit, and you should've seen the hole he lived in – one old hag let him stay with her. But he went on living!

So there he was, rolling around on his cart, and we got used to him.

One day (his old lady later remembered that he had said that morning, "I've lived beyond my time, old girl, time for me to rest") these two guys from the chemical plant happened by. They spotted his hat, and there was just enough in it for a bottle: the first shift had just come to the factory and dropped change in there. So they took it from him. Vanya Grozny shouted after them: "You bloody goats, what've you done to my legs!" So they came back and asked: "Who's a goat here, you stump?" and he said: "Well, it's not me for sure!" So they shoved a fillet knife through his throat, and that's that.

At least Lyudka Selivanova, from the electrolysis department, saw it and came running to our workshop: "Guys, they killed Uncle Vanya!" Whatever we had in our hands, we all ran out carrying it. We caught them boys, alright: one kicked it right there, the other made it to the hospital. Vanya'd be proud of us.

Then we buried our Uncle Vanya. Old ladies came out in droves, paid Pashka Smolin to set the little icon Grozny wore on his chest in a stainless steel frame and make a cross around it. He did a heck of a job – no one'll ever pry it out – and only asked a hundred for it from the old ladies. And actually it wasn't the old ladies who paid – turned out Grozny had about three thousand put away, and the girls used it to pay for everything, a proper fence and a headstone. We were the ones who did it all too, and we worked hard for Uncle Vanya – he even thought to buy us a round from beyond the grave. And the old ladies – there ain't nothing you can do about them, they're all nuts. They hung a little lamp like in church on his cross, and ever since then, line up to get to the place – they do their repenting or whatever it is there, bowing, kissing the icon, and spreading rumors like you won't believe – like this Stargorod's holy fool heals everyone.

It could be that some actually get relief: first, the copper itself from which the icon is made can be good for people – it's got negative ions that slow down our fields' vibrations, and second, don't forget the element of self-delusion – focusing hard on one thing can relieve stress. I've read all about it; it's interesting, but whatever's going on there, one thing's for sure – Uncle Vanya was a whiz at healing us from boredom. He'd roll up to our bushes, greet everyone, and holler like it's the Judgment Day: "All right, pour me a drink, you pagan seed!" and things would all of a sudden look up, just by virtue of him being there. We'd snicker and chuckle, but then his stories would make you think – man, he'd really seen things in life that few men had seen.]

Even now, when we get together, someone always brings up Uncle Vanya and raises a glass, and someone else always says: "Rejoice, daughter copulative, the cup shalt reach you too, and drain ye thou shalt and bare yourself drunken!" Not a single one of us knows what a daughter copulative is, but it's funny anyway. So we laugh first, and only then do we drink.

A MIRACLE AND A VISION

Dear Editors!

I must confess I do not read your magazine much for the reason that it's all but impossible to get here in Stargorod. I mean, it must sometimes come here, when they send an issue or two to our Soyuzpechat,[12] but I've never come across one. Except that the other day, in our foreman's office, I found an issue, the one in which you describe all the miraculous things that happen to the Shroud of Turin, and what scientists have been doing with it, and it made me feel like I should write to you about our own, local, so to speak, miracle.

Why am I writing about it? Well, it's not just because I'm the sort of person who likes to waste paper with whatever fancy strikes them – I think it's important that you record this. Maybe someone will make use of all this material. Nowadays, when everyone writes so much about religion, people have started to take a second look at their attitudes towards this subject, but many have stuck to their old views. Personally, I don't think science can add much to the debate, but neither could I possibly not share with you how I myself witnessed an unusual miracle. In the philosophical dictionary, what does it say? A miracle is something that cannot be explained, and a phenomenon is an event that is scientifically explainable. So it is the inexplicable I want to tell you about.

We have a lot of new people now living in Stargorod, but, as a true old-timer, I can vouch that Raika Portnova is a true, born and raised Stargorodian. How do I know? Well, I used to live right next door to

---

12. Soyuzpechat – the centralized Soviet network of bookstores and kiosks through which printed media were distributed.

her – she was on Rosa Luxemburg street, in the railroad dormitories, and I was on Liebknecht's, where the DOSAAF shooting range[13] used to be. I used to go to her store at the market, too, how else – it's the only one that's close to our neighborhood.

Raika Portnova was short of stature and a fright to look at. Even if you didn't know anything about her, you'd think she'd done time, and a lot of it. She never denied it, either. She'd bark sometimes, loud as a thunder: "Sure I did time, but I'm not hiding it – deal with it!" She had a hoarse, smoker's voice, really raspy, and a gray beard grew on her chin; whenever she'd go on a drinking binge, she'd forget to cut it. If she had any goods to receive that day, she'd just lie down under the counter in her store – on the floor, on her vest or something – and zonk out – she wasn't afraid of no one, not the director, not OBHSS.[14] But she always looked out for her friends – she'd open the doors for you even during the lunch break, if she had anything in the store.

When things got tight around here, I did, I confess, go knocking on Grishka the butcher's back door (I do not provide his last name here, for obvious reasons). And Raika, even if it wasn't her shift, would always be there, just hanging out – it was packed at the dorms, where she lived. So she'd just be sitting there, at the butcher's, on a crate, drinking beer and shooting the breeze. For example, we'd start talking about Vysotsky. And Raika just had to put in her two cents: "I don't like him. He's stolen all his songs from us. It wasn't him – it's us that came up with all the words. We'd be sitting around at night, bored, and one of us would say something, like such-and-such, and that'd be the first line, and another girl would add to it, and by the end of the night – we'd have a whole song. Like, for example, 'Forgive me, mama, for what I've done...'" I'm sorry I don't remember how it goes – Raika was the one who knew all the songs by heart. She'd sing,

---

13. DOSAAF stands for Volunteer Association for the Support of Army and the Fleet, and was a youth-oriented program teaching paramilitary skills like shooting, flying a plane, riding a motorcycle, etc.
14. OBHSS stands for Department against Misappropriation of Socialist Property; it was the Soviet financial police.

too, often, in what she called "the fourth voice." But she was good at sales – it didn't bother her if she'd never seen a person before, she'd make a crack, and the next thing you know, the whole line's laughing. Raika was a fun-loving soul.

The other day, I picked up the brochure entitled "What's in a Name?" produced by a Zhitomir co-op Olesya, sold for one ruble a copy, and it says there that "Raya" means "Easy-going" in Greek. And our Father Yevtikhy also says that a name doesn't come to a person just by accident. He must be right about this – Raya did live her life easily.

"I," she used to brag, "have six kids, 14 grandkids, and five great-grandkids. And the more the merrier."

Her life, of course, was not in any way special. A common life. She just always tried to make sure to work someplace not too far from meat: at the slaughterhouse or in a cafeteria – she had mouths to feed, you know. How do I know about this? She said so herself.

We'd be standing in Grishka's basement, where he cut cooled carcasses. The ones that don't come frozen, you have to cut – can't chop them with a hatchet – and the meat's so fresh, it's still bleeding a little. Raika would pop up out of nowhere. "I," she'd proclaim in her graveyard basso, "just love drinking blood. Always loved it. Whenever they'd fell a cow, I'd slice it across the throat, and it'd just pour out. We all lined up with our coffee mugs."

She was a real fright to look at, worse than the devil's own mother, short, bristly, topped with a man's hat, but she'd crack something like that and you'd just be laughing your head off. And that's just what she was after.

But where am I going with all this? What I want to say is, it's not like her life was especially Christian in any way. She didn't go to church, except to baptize her kids, or get them married or something. She herself, everyone knew, had her six kids with six different husbands, and not one of them stayed for very long. Yes, she worked hard, and she fed her own, but who doesn't, and she'd sometimes help people out with something from the store through the back door – I think that was more out of habit than any sort of malfeasance. And who would say no to a friend? She was really fun to be around, that's true. She lived, in a word, like a butterfly – not a care in the world, never took things to heart, had a great time, and sometimes drank hard if she came into some good money.

But I should say this one thing, lest I be accused of lying. Even before people started writing about church the way they do today, Raika would announce, like thunder, for the whole store to hear: "I know for sure God exists. And I wear a cross – my mother's cross." And then she'd show it to you: a plain little cross. Like they make of copper, you know.

This finally brings me to the main thing – Raika's death. Because what happened? Here's what happened and, mind you, it wasn't on a special church day, or anything, just a regular day. Old ladies, as they always do, came to church early, way before Mass, and Aunt Zoya was right there waiting for them, sobbing: "Ladies, ladies, if only you'd know!" Out of her mind, almost. She was the one who told them.

Aunt Zoya trudged to church early, as always, when it was still dark, and sat on the bench under the cottonwood tree to wait, and it's quiet there, the spot's sort of hidden in the bushes. She was just sitting there, to the whole world invisible. Suddenly, she saw Raika walking down the street, and she was walking in this strange way, hands pressed against her heart. Raika went through the gate, and looked like she wanted to go into the church, but her legs folded under her, she fell onto her side and remained lying there, still as a rock.

"I was just getting up to go to her," Aunt Zoya said, "when all of a sudden I saw this great paw, black and hairy, come from under the ground – it grabbed her leg, and dragged Raika into the ground. It got her down half way already when a light burst all round, and then wings, beating wings, and white doves came down from the bell tower. The doves hit the ground and became angels. Such a light came from them – you couldn't look at it with your mortal eyes. And the hairy one crawled up out of the ground – all black, soiled, and coughing like he's got no air to breathe.

"Who," he says, "do you think you'll be taking here? It's mine and I'll have it."

"Not yours – she's ours," the angels answered.

"How so? She's served me how many years, and now I'm supposed to give her up, just like that?"

"She has repented," the angels said.

"What do you mean, repented? She never made it into the church – how'd she repent?" the devil was all by shaking with laughter.

But the angels said, "As soon as the Good Lord saw her repentance, he accepted it. There was one thing that was in her power – and that's to repent, and the Good Lord of all things was the lord of her life."

At this the devil sneezed hard, in anger, and yelled: "Let me then eat of her flesh at least!"

He grabbed her, smashed her against the ground, and vanished back into Hell. And the Angels received Raika's pure soul and it shone forth with the same light as came from their wings. Together, they rose up, to the bell tower, and flew away as white doves, and vanished in the clear sky.

So the devil was thwarted.

And that day there was a great thunderstorm, and down came hail as big as pigeon eggs. The old ladies, naturally, connected the weather with Raika's disappearance, but they can be forgiven, they don't read books and don't know that it's long been shown that hail that big is a rather common meteorological phenomenon, and the fact that it occurred on the same day – well, there've been more stunning coincidences recorded by scientists.

You'll say all this is just old wives' tales about the devil and the angels. If I hadn't happened past that church myself, I probably wouldn't have believed it either. But I remember it like it was yesterday: here's our church, and the old ladies are standing in a little circle, and in the middle of it is Raika's green coat on the ground, and her man's hat she always wore, her boots, and some sort of underthings, and on top of it all – her little copper cross, and it smells of incense all around, but they hadn't even started the mass yet.]

Since that day, no one has seen Raika anywhere around here, and it's been five years. Father Yevtikhy later served a mass for the repose of her soul, because her daughter confirmed that on that morning her mother had complained about a pain in her chest, and said she needed to go to church. And before that, you couldn't drag her there on a rope.

I struggled to solve this puzzle for a long time, and, having come up with nothing, went to my old history teacher Semyon Petrovich Ogurechnikov. He heard me out, then squinted at me just so and said, "People need miracles to believe in, because life is hard. And what you just told me here is all myth, pure and simple."

Meaning, he didn't believe me.

I probably wouldn't have believed it either, but then what happened to the body, and who burned incense?

I went to see Father Yevtikhy next. He is our monk. He's still young, but he's very good, and you just know the first time you meet him – he won't lie to you, and neither, by the way, would Aunt Zoya. She's one straight-living holy soul, always has been, ask anyone here.

Father Yevtikhy listened to my doubts (he actually wasn't here yet, when Raika disappeared), didn't say anything, but leaned forward a bit, bowed his head with his eyes closed and just made this quiet, regular motion with his right palm around his heart. And such a change came over his face then, it was like a light had come on inside it and burst forth, and he opened his eyes, and there was nothing but joy in them, and joy was on his lips, and in his entire countenance. Suddenly, I too, felt a great elation – there's no other word for it – and my heart sang, and there was nothing I needed to hear or say any more. And he just looked at me and didn't say anything – we understood each other without words. I kissed his hand, quick, and ran out.

But what it was that became clear to me in that moment – I cannot explain it to you, I have no words for it. Things are not as simple as they seem, is all I can say. I still have my doubts about the hairy demon and the white doves, but the coat was right there on the ground, and that's the thing.

I'll tell you one thing: I climbed into my excavator cabin that day, and such strength was awakened in me that I dug a whole ditch in one shift, although I was supposed to be poking at it for three days straight according to the plan. My boss, naturally, didn't give me a prize for that, and the other guys, when I told them after work, only shrugged their shoulders at me. On one hand, who here didn't know Raika, but on the other I could see they too had raked their brains about it – it's not every year that miracles like this happen, right?

This is why I am writing about this to you – to inform you. I know you must have materials like this sent to you from all over the world. Please, record this accident in your catalogue, maybe someone can make use of it. Even though I can think of no scientific hypothesis that would explain this, I testify to the appearance of the coat – it was there. I not only saw it with my own eyes, but also touched it.

After it became clear they couldn't find Raika, her youngest daughter Lyuska put on her little copper cross. Lyuska has two kids, and also two different husbands who have each gone astray. I wonder if there's any sort of a connection there?

It would be very nice to have your opinion on this matter as well. If you know of any relevant statistics, I hope it wouldn't be too much trouble to send them to Stargorod.

Sincerely,
Yakov Smirnov
Excavator Operator,
Stargorod City Landscape and Maintenance Department

THE MAGIC LETTER

Viktor Ivanovich Ropin is a born outdoorsman, camper and hiker, and in summer, when he has a chance to get out of town, pitch his tent, arrange his campsite just so, sit down before a fire and grab his guitar... well, then he is truly happy.

Viktor Ivanovich is a music teacher, but the most important thing in his life is summer. In summers he works as a camping instructor at the Stargorod Tourist Camp and he also takes groups on boating trips. A hundred miles of rowing's just the thing to separate the men from the boys. Sometimes he gets real whiners in his group – and woe to them; Viktor Ivanovich doesn't cut anybody any slack. Eventually, though, they always find the rhythm, get used to the work, and thank him in the end, of course they do – he takes them to see places they'd never find anywhere else, the lake, the little tributaries – and they get there rowing, by the work of their muscle alone.

Oh yes... His last trip went really well – everyone left happy. People became friends. Working together – it brings people closer. It was only he, the guide, who got into a bit of trouble: the woman who seemed to favor him during the entire trip, as soon as they got back to the camp, went out with a man from Moscow. And the most upsetting thing was – it was his 50th birthday yesterday, not just any birthday – his 50th! They had talked about how they would celebrate it together, made plans; Viktor Ivanovich had put away some money – and then she dumped him! Still, he tried not to get too upset about it – all women are the same.

She said she was sorry for him!.. Oh no, he wouldn't have any of that – no tear-jerking sentiments, that's what he told her, up front. He's gotten used to being straight with women. She can take her pity and stick it – he knows how their pity works, he's seen his good share of it. He's been burned twice; he's had to trade his apartment that he'd worked so hard to get for two smaller, separate ones – but now he's got his own place, and no one can reach him there. And why should anyone pity him? It's all games... The woman left in a huff. Good riddance! There's a new tourist group coming – there'll be others. The thing's to stay calm, not to get worked up about it. Stress is unhealthy.

And still – it hurt. It was his 50th birthday, and even his son didn't come – the boy's also pissed at him. He'd come to ask for 40 rubles – wanted to buy some special sneakers at the market. He'll be fine without – it's not the end of the world. Viktor Ivanovich at that age didn't have a pair of sturdy boots, never mind some shitty sneakers for 40 rubles. It was his big birthday, and he'd only put aside 50 to spend on it – and here was the kid wanting 40 for a piece of junk.

It's too bad it didn't work out, though. He really wanted it.

He went to bed angry and sober, and didn't even watch the TV.

Come to think about it, this summer hasn't been good at all. He'd spent the whole winter looking forward to it, rearranging and fixing his equipment, and suffering through the classes he taught at the school – he hated those more than anything else, it was torture. He let the kids play punk rock on the school's rattling tape deck and dreamed of summer.

Viktor Ivanovich hated his students. He taught choir, and even his fifth-graders couldn't hold a note together – they were all rickety, weasely children of alcoholics, juvenile delinquents. He left them alone. He understood it was pointless to teach them choir. He'd come into the classroom and sit behind his desk. The kids turned on the tape, and he spaced out for 45 minutes. And then another 45. And another. He dreamed of summer.

If a fight started in the back of the class, he'd get in and twist a couple ears, but more often he'd just grab the broom and give the instigators a few jabs on their behinds. That's all right, it'd only do them good: the kids saw much worse things at home and didn't hold a grudge against their teacher. Viktor Ivanovich remembered his own strict upbringing well – in a home for the Leningrad blockade orphans.

The kids today – you don't even want to think about them... Everything's just going to hell in a handbasket. Old ladies say the End is near, with a capital E. Who knows, maybe they're right: everywhere you look is sloth and ignorance, no one wants to work. And the women? He doesn't count them as really human. At first, he tried – he wanted to make a home, have a family. But no – all she wanted was him to give her money. Women are all the same – they use you, they rob you, and then they move on to greener pastures. And sometimes they sue you. They'd put you in jail if they could.

He was raising his son right – as a real outdoorsman. The kid'll thank him when he gets drafted. But his mother... She just couldn't leave well enough alone, and she ruined everything. She keeps spoiling the boy – and what happens? All he thinks about is going out to discotheques and his damn sneakers. He runs in for a minute, asks for a tenner, and disappears. God forbid you say anything to him: he gets upset and cries. The boy cries! He's got no manhood in him. And when his son cries, Viktor Ivanovich can't help but feel sorry for him, and gives the boy what he wants. What kind of a future generation is this?

This is precisely why Viktor Ivanovich has decided to ignore the young people, and to keep his emotions strictly under control. You can't feel sorry for everyone; plus, being felt sorry for has never done anybody any good. And one's nervous cells do not regenerate! So it's like he's ordered himself to stay healthy. He'll live a long time yet: he bikes almost everywhere, and lifts weights, and takes cold showers. He doesn't smoke or drink, reads *Arguments and Facts* and *Ogonyok*. For a while, he joined the Stargorod Green Movement Society, but got disappointed and left. He realized no one wanted to hear what he had to say – so he left. He doesn't need any favors from anyone. They all thought they were smarter than him. Fine. All they did was talk, and he doesn't need more talkers in his life. He doesn't need anyone. He went home alone, boiled some potatoes, and ate them with sardines and sauerkraut. Great stuff! Who needs women?..

He can have his pick of them in summer; he's not one to go to the city's Over Thirty Club – that's just plain embarrassing. No, he's done everything alone, all his life, and that's the only way to make yourself happy – you have to do it, no one else can help you. Nature, nature alone can heal. The quiet. The fire. The fish soup boiling in the pot. The moon. Do you know the kind of moons we have over Stargorod? You don't see moons like that anywhere else in the world.

He takes hiking groups because they need him. He can whip up a tent in a blink, and start a fire from a single match – and these big-city folks from Moscow and Leningrad... Well, let's just say they have a lot to learn. Book smarts is one thing, but he's graduated from the Culture Institute too (correspondence course), yet he doesn't shout about it on every corner.

And after every trip, they thank him. They always thank him. "Thank you, Viktor Ivanovich," they say, "It was a trip of a lifetime!" And they do remember these trips – of course they do, look at how beautiful it is all around here, it's the real Russia! She, she alone heals a troubled heart.

Because of his large bald spot, some call him Pleshner.[15] He knows they do. He knows who these people are, too. His colleagues from the school, all those gossips and ne'er-do-wells, and the women from the tourist camp – he tries to avoid them all. Not one of them said as much as a Happy Birthday when he turned 50. Could have sent a card, at least. One from the whole staff, it wouldn't have killed them. But no, instead he gets nasty notes stuffed into his mailbox. To heck with it – he's managed just fine without them, and he'll be fine just the same. And the woman can take her pity and stuff it.

Soon, soon enough the new group of tourists will come, and with them – new women. He'll have his trips. And his peace. And his islands. The still expanse of the river. The fish-soup in a pot over the

---

15. *Plesh* is Russian for "bald spot."

open fire. And his guitar. When asked, Viktor Ivanovich plays Russian romances and sings. And people enjoy listening to him. They do.

✳ ✳ ✳

Viktor Ivanovich went down the stairs carrying his bicycle – it was time to go check in at the camp. He had no particular reason to be there, but he went every day anyway, as if to work. Sometimes there were things to be fixed or painted. And all they paid him – it's a shame to say it! – was 40 rubles a month, part-time. But he wasn't doing it for the money – money can't buy inspiration, as they say.

He checked his mailbox purely out of habit – he wasn't expecting anything good there. There was a single sheet of paper in there, a page torn out of a school notebook. Viktor Ivanovich pulled it out – he already knew what it was. Another note from the kids.

They'd been tormenting him all winter: there were notes with a skull and bones, or unprintable obscenities, or threats to set his door on fire. Little sons of bitches – what had he done to them? But he bore it patiently for a long time. Once or twice he tried to ambush whoever did it. Finally he couldn't stand it anymore, went and complained to the precinct duty policeman. The cop just laughed at him: "What do you want, boys will be boys!" he said. Boys! These are underage criminals! His son is turning into one of them, never mind how much his father might beat him. These are the boys who changed the points on the siding at the train yard – it was just luck the trackman saw it before anything happened. That made quite a stir. And it was this same precinct captain who saved their little asses then, the bastard – he had to cover for his own kid. Law and order, my ass! Look at all the muck in the stairwells, and the words carved out in the elevators, and all these young punks hanging together at night – it's a miracle they haven't raped anyone yet.

After that conversation at the precinct Viktor Ivanovich commanded himself to ignore the captain, too – and he used to say hello to the man whenever he saw him.

But the note turned out to be something out of the ordinary. Viktor Ivanovich read:

This is a good-luck letter.

This letter brings good fortune. The original of this letter is kept in Holland. Now the Letter has come to you. With this letter you will receive good fortune and happiness, but on one condition: you must send the letter onward. This is not a joke. You will receive happiness. Money can't buy happiness. Send this letter to someone you know who is in need of happiness. Do not delay. You must send 20 copies of this letter in the next 106 hours (4 days). Even if you don't believe in magic. This Letter began its life in 1842. Arthur Conan Doyle received this letter and told his secretary to make twenty copies. Four days later, he won a million. One office worker got this letter and threw it out – and was in an accident the next day. Someone placed a copy of this Letter at Khrushchev's dacha in 1964, and Khrushchev tore it up. Two days later, his colleagues from the Politburo toppled him. Under no circumstances can you tear or shred this letter; treat it kindly. You will see the results four days after you send all 20 copies.

Do NOT alter the text of the letter.

That's what it said. On a piece of ruled paper. A handwritten carbon copy.

For whatever reason, the letter struck Viktor Ivanovich as funny. It's too bad none of his neighbors were around – he'd have shown it to them. They're all old ladies, though – stupid old hens, they'd probably make a fuss over it.

He's gotten some "holy" letters before, but this was the first one that promised happiness. Good fortune. On a silver platter, so to speak.

So, what's going on here? Little old ladies with nothing to do are now after good fortune and untold riches? They'd want it free, of course. Just copy the thing 20 times, and here you go, here's your million. Like Conan Doyle. An elevator ride to heaven, wouldn't you like that... But there are no elevators – this ain't the place with miracles we live in, he knows that for a fact. A man has to make things happen. With his own two hands. You reap what you sow, that's right.

But he didn't toss the letter – he thought he'd show it to the folks at the camp, they'd have a laugh. Or maybe he'll give it to the old Leshcheva – let her copy it and get some happy times come her way. She does nothing but complain about her life and her son. Her son drinks, and his wife drinks too, and Grandma Leshcheva feels sorry for them all – usually for a week or two, then she goes right back to cursing them. Than back to pitying, and back to cursing again. That's how they get along; she mostly sits on the bench by the apartment building, waiting for someone to come by and talk to her – when she's had a chance to complain to someone, mourn her lot, shed a tear, she feels better, and another day's gone. But what else do you expect: she'd raised that boy without a father, he'd basically grown up in the juvenile system. You won't get a decent grandkid out of a son like that either: the little one just takes after the father.

That's it – he'll give it to her. She'll copy it and send it around. All her country friends – they believe this nonsense. They believe everything you tell them. Dreams – they believe in those. The Evil Eye. Jinxes. That, if the priest's wife were to take a swing with the incense burner, all the drowned would come up from the bottom of the river. UFOs.

UFOs are a special topic, Viktor Ivanovich's favorite. He enjoys telling stories about aliens at campfires, knock those arrogant Moscow types down a rung. They try to argue with him – bring up the so-called facts from newspapers, but he beats them at physics. There is no natural law anywhere in the universe that would allow an object to travel faster than a speed of light, is there? He shoots holes in their theories with natural laws – they don't know their physics from their botany. And as far as the newspapers are concerned, there's a reason journalism is called the second oldest profession on earth, the first being whoring, of course. Whores is what they are, those journalists.

Journalists... He had one in a group once; the son-of-a-bitch was only good at drinking and eating, you couldn't make him work with a stick. He'd probably believe a letter like this, too. Never mind there's no logic in it whatsoever – that never bothered them before. Viktor Ivanovich, they said, doesn't understand the supernatural. Supernatural or not, but when he made them row across the lake – in the rain, he did it on purpose – they changed their tune, didn't they? They barely made it. He'd put the fear of God in them that day, better than any UFOs! They thanked him later, of course – until the day they left, they talked about how he saved them. He didn't know whether to laugh or to cry.

The thought of that poor journalist (the wimp!) instantly improved Viktor Ivanovich's mood, and he effortlessly sped off on his bicycle. Only at the camp's gates, near the village, did he again remember the letter: he spotted the old woman Leshcheva at her post on the bench, she was watching her grandkids, as always. The kids, also as always, were dirty, snot smeared under their noses, and covered, at the moment, in clay – they were making tanks out of mud. Of course, when your parents sell your toys to buy vodka, you make do with mud. How else? And if you're in third grade already and can't read, that's not a big deal. How could anyone raise a decent kid in a pigsty like this?

Viktor Ivanovich stopped and gave the old woman the letter; it'll keep her busy all night – she's barely literate, too, reads syllable-by-syllable and writes horribly. The silly woman was happy, though, and kept thanking him and bowing after him. He laughed at her a little after he pulled away.

And then it started – as soon as he got to the camp. First, the director dragged him over the coals for leaving the little window in the warehouse ajar last night: someone had stolen four sleeping bags and a tent. He had to think on his feet to appease her – he was lucky he thought to remind her how he covered for her during the last audit, when the linen counts didn't add up. She said she wouldn't take it out of his salary, this time. But everyone's stealing – he's the only one who hadn't taken even a single nail! Pleshner's always guilty. How else?

He went to check the window: turned out the glass was cracked, so whoever got in, just pulled out the broken-off part from the frame, reached in, unlocked the window, and then put the piece of glass back where it was. Viktor Ivanovich took the window of its hinges and started replacing the glass – and then sliced his finger. Blood spurted everywhere; it took him forever to stop the bleeding by sucking on his finger, and the taste of blood lingered in his mouth.

And then his son showed up.

"Hey, Dad, thanks for the cover-up," he said. "I hoped you wouldn't be mad – we just went camping last night."

The boy dropped a backpack at his feet. Inside: everything that was missing. Apparently, he and his friends decided to celebrate the end of the school year, and Mom let them spend the night outdoors.

Is that so? Of course, the bastard knew where to go. He didn't go for the used or worn stuff, oh no – he picked the best sleeping bags and the brand new tent! Why didn't he just come and ask for it?

Viktor Ivanovich wanted to control himself, but couldn't. He grabbed his belt and... the worst thing was, the boy didn't even understand why he was being punished. He just clenched his teeth ("That's my boy!" Viktor Ivanovich thought) and then, after he broke free, snarled over his shoulder, like a stab:

"You bloody tight-ass!"

He said it and ran.

He – a tight-ass! That was too much. Viktor Ivanovich got on his bike, caught up with the kid in the village, and stopped him – to talk.

They talked for a long time, walking up and down the road. Viktor Ivanovich did most of the talking – he tried to make the boy understand that what he did was shameful. Finally, it seemed he got through to him. The boy broke down and started crying, and at that point he had to go ahead and give him the 40 rubles for the sneakers.

The kid had been dreaming of those forever, and Viktor Ivanovich never got to use the money he put away for his birthday anyway.

They parted peacefully, more or less. Viktor Ivanovich went back to the camp; he wanted to fix the roof on one of the cabins – the shingles kept coming loose, so he climbed up there to nail them. Below him, music was playing; the group he'd just taken camping had gotten together to grill – and no one even as much as glanced at him, up on the roof, tapping with his hammer. Later, he ate at the cafeteria, the cooking lady gave him lunch; he ate it in the kitchen, didn't go to sit at a table in the dining room – to heck with them all!

In the afternoon, he went to the spit. He wanted to look at the Lake. He sat there for a while, and felt better. He almost got attuned to nature, but it just wasn't his day: that woman, who refused him for a Muscovite, she showed up arm-in-arm with that man, and he wearing only his swimming trunks, she in her swimsuit. They were laughing. At least he saw them first – he darted into the bushes, before they could notice him. Next to him, under the bush he spotted the mutt from the camp, Niurka. The little bitch found the shade to hide from the sun. She panted. He'd just seen her a minute ago mating with a village dog, and now she was here.

When the dog saw Viktor Ivanovich, she crawled towards him, wiggling solicitously, tail tucked between her legs and wagging. He stroked her head once, twice, and then suddenly kicked her, hard – she flew up into the air, and fled howling towards the village. He saw she was limping.

Tears burst from his eyes – he was so angry. He couldn't breathe for a moment – his throat closed in a bitter spasm. No, you can't go on like that – you can't let your nerves do this to you!

Gradually, he felt himself again. For a while, he just stood there and looked at the setting sun – it always made him happy. It was almost dark when he locked the warehouse and his little office, got on his bicycle and rode home.

The sun was almost gone beyond the Lake. Everything around him was settling down, growing still. And everywhere it was green, and the water shimmered, and it was beautiful. This was peace.

In four days (exactly as the letter promised!) new people would come to the camp. Who knows what new good fortune might come his way. Viktor Ivanovich even snorted softly, caught up in the pleasant daydreaming.

He'll handpick his next group, oh he will. He'll put them through hell and high water – he'll get all that big-city ennui (or whatever they call it) knocked out of them. They'll come back revived, tanned, happy – they'll remember him. And they'll thank him.

When he stopped in the village, he heard women talking: Niurka, the little dog, had gone rabid. Grandma Leshcheva raised a switch at her to chase her away from the kids, and the dog turned on her and bit her leg. Vovka Leshchev, the old woman's son, promised to find the bitch and shoot her. And he'll do it for sure – he's big on killing things.

Viktor Ivanovich rode home; he pushed the pedals, not feeling any exertion – the bike rolled on smoothly, at a good pace, as usual. He remembered the magic letter and smiled. Some luck it brought the old lady – three stitches. There's your miracle on a silver platter.

EENY, MEENY, MINEY, MOE

"Eeny, meeny, miney, moe, Catch a spider by the toe..."

"Eeny, meeny, miney, moe, Catch a spider by the toe..."

The boy walks back and forth on the veranda.

He walks slowly and sings to himself, under his breath:

"Eeny, meeny, miney, moe, Catch a spider by the toe..."

He's been doing this for an hour at least. He is wearing nothing but his boxer shorts. It's hot outside, but he can't go swimming – Granny scares him with talk of the undertow. The undertow is cold like a sea-dog.

And where the sea-dog lives there are drowned people. The sea-dog eats them. Granny is in the garden, Mom is at work. The boy is some number of years old. He doesn't know how many exactly. That's why he is walking and singing:

"Eeny, meeny, miney, moe, Catch a spider by the toe..."

Sometimes, when he comes to "toe" the boy stubs his toe into the floor. Other times he doesn't, just goes on singing, but he doesn't stop walking. He walks like this: "eeny" he steps on a floorboard, "meeny" on another, and "miney-moe" he skips over one. Then again: "Catch" is a board, "a spider" is a board, and "by the toe" – skip a board. Sometimes he sings quietly, and sometimes he sings out loud.

Finally, Lyudka can't take it any more and comes to the veranda door with a slipper in her hand. The boy freezes.

"Will you stop your damn singing, you bastard?"

The boy is silent.

"I've had it with you, you hear me? I hear one more peep from you, I'll bite your head off. I want to sleep."

Lyudka goes back into the house and slams the door. The boy chuckles, remembers the name Granny calls Lyudka, "heathen." And – he can't help himself – begins to sing again:

"Eeny, meeny, miney..."

But Lyudka's smarter – she hadn't gone anywhere, she waited behind the door, and now she jumps out and slaps him with his slipper, once, and again!

The boy breaks free, tumbles down the steps into the yard, and yells back at her, angry, through tears:

"You heathen, heathen! You go out God knows where all night, you're a curse!"

Lyudka doesn't come down from the porch, preferring to yell back at him from there. She calls him a rickety bastard.

The boy goes out to the street, scratches his butt – the slipper left a mark. Heathen! But you just wait, when you bring one home in the oven we'll see how you sing! That's what Granny says. What's supposed to be in the oven? The boy doesn't know, but it must be trouble, if Granny keeps talking about it like that.

It's better not to mess with Granny right now – she'd bite his head off too for her tomatoes and cucumbers.

The boy takes up his complicated song again, but just as he figures out his steps and makes a skip down the street, he stops short again. The mailman has come to the Koldayevs. His horse is grazing untethered, which means Uncle Vova the mailman has come drunk. He'll be totally drunk when he comes out – the woman Koldayeva makes her own booze.

The boy crawls ahead close to the fence; there, in between acacia bushes, he's beaten a special path. He is crawling closer to the horse. To Star. First he stares at her, without moving, then finally, slowly, emerges from the bush. Star rolls her eye at the boy, blows air onto his hand, and licks his empty palm. Is anyone listening? The boy looks around to check, then says,

"Star, hare-ware, wonac?"

No, no one's heard him. Star nods her head in agreement. The boy picks up the reins and climbs onto the cart. Star obediently walks off. She is thirsty, and she pulls the cart to the lake. She goes in deep, until the wheels sink in the mud to the axle. She drinks.

The boy is cut off from the shore. Star stands in the water quietly, waiting for someone to pay attention to her; she moves her ears every so often, and swishes at the flies with her uncombed, burr-studded tail. The boy is scared – there's water all around him, the cart is stuck. He begins to sing, in a begging, tender voice, "Star, Star, harrico-warico, wo, wac?"

Star doesn't move, only turns her head now and then to look at the boy with her big, dark eye. She is waiting for help to come.

There's nothing else to do – the boy resigns himself to his fate and, not letting go of the reins, starts under his breath:

"Eeny, meeny, miney, moe, Catch a spider by the toe..."

Uncle Vova the mailman comes running along the shore, cursing as he runs and swinging his arms like a windmill. But there's nowhere to hide – the boy's trapped by the water, and in the water there's the undertow cold as a sea-dog. Uncle Vova has a long switch. He pulls off his boots and his pants, walks gingerly on the slippery bottom, sways, shakes the switch at the boy. Uncle Vova reaches the cart, grabs the reins from the boy, but loses his balance, slips, and falls into the muddy water. Uncle Vova is very angry. He gets up, and, instead of helping Star, begins whipping the boy with his switch. It hurts a lot.

The boy can't think straight, dashes around the cart, but there's nowhere to hide, and he rolls off into the cold water. He runs to the shore, wailing. Undertows or sea-dogs, he'd rather drown!

"You bitch! Bitch!" he yells at the mailman. He picks up a rock but he can't throw it far enough.

Whimpering, the boy crawls deep into the acacia bushes. His shorts, his belly, his legs – everything is covered with gooey mud. He can't go home now. Granny will twist his ears, she sure will.

The boy sits in the bushes and rubs spit into his arm where the switch left a red mark. The boy howls in short, small bursts. Then he lies back on the grass – there's a small patch of green turf in the bushes; here, when the older kids come home from school, they have their headquarters or the trench. Sometimes, they tell scary stories: about the Red Mask, and the dead man, about the White Sheet, and the Black Door, and the Red Boy, and the White Glove, and the Cut-Off Finger, and the Bloody Mary... He is afraid of all of them, but he listens every time, even though he knows the stories by heart. The boy rolls over onto his back, looks at the sky and very soon begins to hum:

"Eeny, meeny, miney, moe, Catch a spider by the toe..."

"Eeny, meeny, miney, moe, Catch a spider by the toe..."

He even begins to drum the beat on his muddy belly. What is this "eeny-meeny-miney-moe" anyway? And where do spiders have toes?

PETTY OFFICER

When he is drunk, he sits on the bench with his head thrown back, mouth open. He stares into the sky. When he is very drunk – his head is in his hands, between his knees. He cries when he is very drunk. He smears his tears across his unshaven cheeks with his dirty, motor-oil stained hand. He cries because he is sorry for the kids. Afterwards, he goes to give Nadka a beating. But she's wised up, too – she jumps at him first and grabs his hair, and aims to get her fingernails into his eyes. That's how they live: he forever scratched, she forever covered in bruises.

In the morning, he goes to the sailing club's boathouse – there, he works on the boats' diesels, welds and rivets things until half past four. Then, if he hasn't had anything to drink yet, he spends a couple hours working on the small side jobs people send his way. Then he takes the cash he's made from these and spends it on liquor, for himself and the other guys. Sometimes he drinks with Nadka. He likes to chase down his booze with kvas, but first he lets his favorite – Svetlanka – have some. The three-year-old Svetlanka is smart: when she rattles off her "motherfuckers," everyone cracks up. Svetlanka is his fifth. The last one. Nadka swore not to have any more. But she's always like this: she swears on her mother's grave to this or that, and he forgives her. He's all right with it – she'll tell everyone if she's knocked up, way before she shows. After four boys, who knew they'd get a girl? Nadka now uses her as a shield, when he comes to beat her. And he backs off. He never beats her when she's got the girl in her arms. He goes to sleep instead. And leaves the next morning without breakfast. His boys – they're always trying to slip away from school and hang out with him in the boathouse instead. He doesn't send them back – no point in forcing it if they don't want to. The three oldest had to repeat each grade anyway. Grandma Katya, his mother, only shakes her head: why torment the poor kids if they just don't have school in them? She, for one, never learned to read and has lived her life just fine; she's had a good, working life – some'd be lucky to live like she did. And books are trouble, that's all they do. There's an example right here in the family: Olen'ka, his sister's daughter, got into reading, and read day and night, you couldn't drag her away from the books. And then she started feeling sorry for everyone; all she did was cry – out of pity. Now she doesn't even recognize anyone; doesn't know her own mother when she comes to visit. No, thank you – it's better without books.

Grandma Katya goes to church. She knows the service by heart better than some literate folks, but she's had to stop singing – her thyroid's got the better of her. She got all ready to die last winter, but her oldest daughter, Valyusha, came and rescued her. She carried grandma out of their place in her arms, warmed her up, and nursed her back to health. Now grandma Katya stays two doors over, with Valyusha. She comes out to sit on her bench, and her son sits on his bench, head rolled back, staring into the sky. Or crying. Because he's sorry for the children.

Grandma Katya also feels sorry for the children. Whenever they run over to her place, she feeds them. The older ones are now embarrassed and don't go so often. They find crusts at home – spread them out on the floor, pick through them to find the good ones, and soak them in tea. And Svetlanka crawls all over, back and forth, until she falls asleep on the crusts and pees herself. Or sometimes she also sleeps standing, like a horse – she puts her head on the couch and sleeps.

Nadka makes 100 rubles a month at the sailing club – she washes the floors there. In summer, she makes another 70 for cleaning the toilets at the tourist camp. There, they also give her leftovers from the kitchen, soup or meat entrees – in summer, the kids eat well. Sometimes she also goes into town and gets her state aid for multiple children – then she buys a bottle of liquor, and spends the rest on the kids. She brings kvas for Svetlanka, and little one says: "Mom, it's beer! It's beer, mom." It makes Nadka laugh: "It's not beer, sweetie, it's kvas." Svetlanka then smiles – like a fox – and washes her hands in the kvas. Or drinks it. Or the other kids drink it. Kvas is tasty.

First thing when he comes home – Svetlanka. She says, "Papa!" And her papa, if he's able, picks her up, and strokes her head sometimes, and sometimes tickles her velvety cheek with his stubble. On Nadka's paydays, he gets drunk and wants to beat Nadka. This is why Nadka now runs away on her paydays – she takes the money and goes to town. Before, she used to run away without the money, too – someone gave her booze in town – and now she only does it when she has cash. Is she now paying for someone else's? She's gone two or three days, then she comes back. Broke, of course. Eyes bulging. She lies on the couch and moans, and the kids tiptoe around, fetching her tea. They love their mommy.

He'd come home, take one look at her there on the couch, and go to his bench outside. When she's lain for a bit, she'll feel better and grope her way out. She'll sit next to him, and they'll eat sunflower seeds together, and she'll complain about her gallbladder. Or tell him she's sorry and would he forgive her. Or not. Sometimes they just sit there.

If they see people walk by, they say hello. People say hello back, and then go on their way to gossip about Nadka. What else can they do? They feel sorry for the kids.

He does, too.

He sits on his bench until late. Nadka, inside, watches a movie. She's big on movies. The kids also watch, until they fall asleep – wherever they were sitting.

He sits. If he cries, that means he is really drunk.

He is 36. But you wouldn't know it by looking at him. He's forgotten already when he came back from the navy. He served on a nuclear submarine. Then he came back and got Nadka – he won her over, she used to go with another guy. She's been on her own since she was 17 – her folks threw her out. And he was a catch – he was handsome then. Then they had kids. Not right away, though, after five years or so. He'd actually gone to the doctor after the submarine, and the doctor said he'd never father his own. But then added the good news: otherwise, everything works just fine!

He'd came back decorated, all stripes and ribbons. Petty Officer First Class. He's got a picture to prove it. Grandma Katya has it on the wall above her bed, with the pictures of all her other kids and grandkids.

"Say what you want, he came back a prince – any girl would go for him. Why'd he have to choose that slut is what I don't know," mutters grandma Katya sitting on her bench.

Two doors down, he is sitting on his bench, crying. He's crying for the kids, and himself, and Nadka – he's sorry for the whole world.

Next door there isn't anyone left to feel sorry about: the neighbor killed his wife with an axe a month after the wedding. He thought he saw something about her he didn't like. Now the family sends him packages somewhere up North.

STAR

Sunday. The morning tea is finished, but the garden can wait. Maxim Maximych kneads a filterless Belomor cigarette with his fingers, lights up, and watches the street through the window: he wonders if his daughter will bring the grandkids from the city today, or if she'll stay there to party again. Everything went out of whack when she got mixed up with that highway criminal of hers. She was sorry for him, you see... So she had the twins. Then got divorced. Said, Papa, I'm not ever getting married again – won't touch that mess with a ten-foot pole. And what's the point of going out then? Soon, though, she'll have to bring the kids for the summer – the school break has already started. And it's only 20 minutes by bus... Half-an-hour tops.

Antonina Pavlovna is finishing her curd pancake.

"Do you figure they'll come?"

"Huh?"

"You're deaf as a post, aren't you? Are you done there yet?"

"Aha."

"Then grab the paper and read what the boys will tell me at the shift tomorrow."

Maxim Maximych used to be a second lieutenant at the meteorological-station in Motovikha, and now guards the furniture factory. He goes in for a 24-hour shift, then is home three days to work in his garden. Antonina Pavlovna is also retired. She worked as an accountant at the city bakery, but quit a long time ago.

"Aha," Antonina Pavlovna says reaching for the newspaper and her glasses. "From the beginning?"

"Of course not! Like you don't know... Start at 1700."

She begins to read:

"Monday, June 9, Channel 1. 17:20. 'Sound your trumpets!' A happy, joyful song opens the performance by the Pioneer propaganda brigade from the capital's Kuybyshev district. The brigade is the winner of the Russian National School Propaganda Brigades contest. Its performances are fondly remembered by the builders of the Tomsk Chemical Plant, the Kalinin Nuclear Power Plant, by the sailors of the Black and Baltic Sea fleets, and by the hardworking *kolkhoz* workers of Udmurtiya. But the propaganda brigade is not the only brainchild of the Kuybyshev district Young Pioneers' Headquarters..."

Maxim Maximych is unmoving. He listens; he no longer watches the street, however. Instead, he's fixed Antonina Pavlovna in his motionless gaze. She takes a sip of her cooled tea and continues:

"Twenty-four years ago the Headquarters initiated an honorary guard and commemoration event 'Remember Everyone by Name.' Since then, every year, on Victory Day, the Young Pioneers stand to attention at the Defenders of Moscow Memorial in the Preobrazhensk Cemetery. This year alone, the boys and girls have raised 1,400 rubles to be distributed to the Peace Fund, Orphanage No. 73, and the Foundation for Battling AIDS. Neither do the Pioneers neglect those who live next door: Operation 'We Care' has become one of the headquarters' biggest projects."

Antonina Pavlovna looks up from the paper.

"It's all pure torment for those poor kids. Boys told me, one of the girls at our school had to be taken to the hospital by ambulance after they stood guard at our Eternal Flame – it leaks gas, you know."

"You know what, you better just stick to reading," Maxim Maximych turns back to the window out of frustration. "That was about Victory Day they wrote – just one day, and our guys stand there all year round!"

Pavlovna nods in agreement and turns the page. She studies it for a while. Suddenly, she is transformed:

"Maxim Maximych! Hamiddulin, the one who stabbed Prokhorov! He's now a star – fancy that!"

"Oh yeah?" Maxim Maximych turns back to face the table, much faster this time. "Come on then, what does it say?"

"It's right here, let me mark it – I'd like to see it too: 'Man and Law: Drinking Causes Crime.' Channel 1. 18:40. Recently the Stargorod City Court sentenced the 28-year-old Hamiddulin to 14 years in prison. Hamiddulin was convicted of a serious crime: an attempt at murder. What began as an act of hooliganism ended in uncommon cruelty. So what really happened at Stargorod's furniture factory, where Hamiddulin worked? One day, the young man entered the boiler room not having cleaned his muddy footwear, in direct violation of the factory's operating procedures. The boiler room operator demanded that he leave the premises immediately and Hamiddulin was forced to comply. Several days later, in a state of drunkenness, Hamiddulin unexpectedly entered the boiler room, attacked the operator, and stabbed him 10 times before attempting to flee. He was detained. The surgeon's skill and the EMTs' quick response saved the victim's life. But would the emotional wounds sustained by the boiler room operator that fateful evening ever heal? Would the shock loosen its grip on the minds of the operator's family, his colleagues' minds?"

"Now that's a load of bull if I ever heard one!" Maxim Maximych waves at the paper dismissively, kneads a new Belomor cigarette, lights up.

"That Beanhill – Kolka, the one they call an 'operator' – he's a dyed-in-the-wool thief and bandit, and the auditor lady was there in the boiler room the first time: she heard him call Hamiddulin a dirty goat. That day, Igoryok – Hamiddulin – he was drunk too, so what? He had a good heart, it's just that Beanhill bullied him, so he was his whipping boy, ran to fetch him booze and such. That Beanhill, he had it coming – he wasn't such a big boss on the inside, mark my word. And now Igoryok's gotta sit 14 years in a special prison... and you say, he's a star! Some star indeed..."

Maximych is so angry he jams his unfinished cigarette into the ashtray, grinds it. He gets up, goes to the door.

"In violation of the factory's operating procedure," he mocks. "You couldn't get into the fucking boiler room on a tightrope, you hear me?" He doesn't know why he is yelling at his old wife, so he adds, softly: "All right, I'll go water now. It's no use waiting for them now – they don't show up 'til dinnertime."

He leaves.

Antonina Pavlovna clears the table, washes the dishes, thinks. She plans how she will share the news with her neighbor. It's not anything special, of course, just a regular bit of news, but the fact that it made the first channel – that's different.

Maxim Maximych waters his potatoes. It's been dry, the earth is hard and caked solid; chinks of it come off like flint. He swears at the dirt, the sun and the potatoes, and in-between, when he stops for a break at the well, he repeats in amazement: "Would the shock loosen its grip on the minds of the operator's family, his colleagues' minds?"

"He ain't got no family – that bitch – never had one and never will!"

He fills his bucket-sized watering can and, bending under its weight, carries it to the next row of potatoes.

DEVIL'S BRIDE

That Alexandra Konstantinovna Zaikina was a witch was not doubted by anyone in her neighborhood. One – she kept her curtains drawn, two – her fence and gates were solid plank, three – she had no TV set, and four – her cat was black and her chickens piebald. And if that weren't enough – she'd go spend two months every winter with her grandkids in Leningrad and lock her place with two locks. No one, mind you, would ever be seen going in or out of there, feeding her animals, but in the spring – voila! – they're all there and in perfect health.

"And she's proud, too! I asked her once to put a blood spell on my Lyoshenka, so he'd finally get rid of his mange, but she just laughed at me," complained Tanka Solodkova, Zaikina's neighbor and, in the old days, her closest friend.

"What else would you expect from that crippled bitch! I wouldn't ask her for a drink of water."

"No, ladies, I know better – she used to do spells for me in the old days, before she got mixed up with those devils."

Everyone knows Zaikina's devil story.

A while back, in '47 or '48, Tanka and Alexandra – people called her Shurka then – were thick as thieves. Tanka was always a go-get-em kind of girl, and Shurka was born sort of lop-sided, grew up awkward, not a match for quick Tanka – so they stuck together. At work, they were side by side, but spent their nights apart. Tanka went out with the *zampolit*;[16] Shurka listened to her stories the following morning, and sighed to herself, but she didn't envy Tanka. Tanka

---

16. The political officer embedded with a military unit; a white-collar job responsible for keeping the troops ideologically sound.

was a beauty, Shurka was a cripple, and she knew it; to each her own, that's how her mother, Lord rest her soul, raised her. Tanka, then, waitressed in the officers' cafeteria, and Shurka washed the dishes there. And the zampolit was a handsome man: shiny boots with steel heels, brown strap across his chest. Single. Quick to laugh. Kind to Shurka, too – Shurka let him and Tanka into her hay-loft, why not, her house was too big for her alone anyway.

And then one day this happened. Shurka went to bed, and forgot to lock the doors. She was just lying there, without lights, and couldn't sleep. Maybe thinking of Tanka's stories – no one could go to sleep doing that. Shurka was dreaming. And suddenly she heard this click-click sound, like someone in the mudroom was stepping lightly on shod hooves. She pulled the blanket over her head. And then the door to her room opened all by itself, and closed just like that. Shurka peeked out – there's no one there. And the next instant – something black, and smelly, and creaky darted to the bed from the corner, and reached his arms under the blanket.

"Sh-h-h," the thing hissed.

"Who are you?" she asked and froze.

"The devil!"

Shurka couldn't make another peep. And he climbed on top of her, pressed down on her, tickling her with his stubble, and whispered, "Don't be scared, I'm not a scary kind of devil, I give gifts to those I love."

And indeed, she felt with him like she got a great present. Then he vanished – and she didn't even see how.

In the morning she was angry with herself: she knew better than to believe in demons, but then she'd remember the way his hooves clicked on the floor... and the feel of goose bumps on her skin, and a sweet, sweet tingling.

She kept mum that day, and didn't say a word to Tanka. The following night, she left the door unlocked on purpose, but thought up a trick: put her bedside lamp under the bed, so she could click it on when he showed up. She wanted to see him.

She waited and wondered: would he come? Or not? He didn't.

He came two days later. Clicked in the mudroom. Shurka lay quiet, as if she were asleep, and held her hand on the switch. He asked: "Are you asleep?" and that's when she pushed it – click! But the light didn't come on – she only knocked the lamp over under the bed – that's how scared she was. And he made a sort of a bubbling sound: "Oh-ho-ho, you can't look at the devil. I make the lights go out just by being there." Then he rolled on top of her again, the beast!

The lamp convinced Shurka. The next morning, she told Tanka everything – her friend laughed her head off:

"You, Shurka, are long overdue for a real guy – you're liable to go nuts if you keep carrying on like this. I'll set you up with one, if you want – he's not much to look at, but serviceable."

"No, Tanka, he's really a devil: he turns lights off just by being near them."

"I've had enough of this – you're making it all up!"

Tanka had no interest in devils: first she had the zampolit, now she found herself a Gypsy with money. Shurka, however, took offense, and said mean things to Tanka. So they fought. And it's lasted forever. "Stupid cripple" and "fat rat" are about the mildest things Shurka's heard ever since.

Shurka kept to herself, but she didn't need Tanka anymore anyway. She could spend her day dreaming, and then at night her devil would come. As soon as she'd hear him clicking in the mudroom, the lights would go off, and he would come in. He was nice and kind to her.

So all right – let's say he's a devil, that don't make it right. Shurka got to thinking. And the more she thought, the scarier it got. She tried to remember what her mother told her about devils – and it was all scary! He, meanwhile, was telling her how he flew in the sky, and flew to visit her.

"You, Shurka, are a witch. You've got some mighty spell on me, I tell you that," he'd say, and she'd feel happy. And then scared again – in the morning. When she couldn't stand it anymore, she went to see the priest one Sunday. The priest, Father Amvrosy, listened to her, but she could tell he wasn't paying attention. Clearly, he didn't believe her. He's heard enough of those stories. Father Amvrosy used to be Metropolitan's sub-deacon. There were great hopes for him. But when the Metropolitan died, they shipped Father Amvrosy off to Stargorod, and that's the end of any career: you just sit here, reading books and listening to old ladies and stupid girls. He absolved her, and told her to do a hundred bows, and read Our Father and Hail Mary before bed. Shurka took offense at him too. This was not what she came for.

She stopped going to church. But waited. Every night – she waited. Then she'd hear the nettles rustle – that's him, walking through the vegetable patch.

"I can't go in the street, Shurka. If someone sees me, they'll go mute."

"Why didn't I go mute?"

"You're special."

And then he'd tell her such things – her head would spin!

About three months went by. Shurka noticed things were not as they were supposed to be with her. She went to see an old lady – she took one look and said, "You, my dear, are pregnant. Who'd you get it from?"

"The devil," Shurka said.

"I'll show you the devil, you little bitch! Don't you sin in my house. Out with it – who was it?"

Shurka told the old lady everything. As she knew it. The old lady didn't believe her, but just in case gave her a little icon of St. Nikita the Exorcist and some holy water.

"When he comes next, sprinkle some on him. If he's a man – he'll marry you, and if not..."

"Then what?"

"Then I really don't know. You go now."

At night, Shurka was afraid to sprinkle him at first, but told him everything. He just laughed: "That won't hurt me!" It's his own fault then: she sprinkled him later on the sly.

The next morning she went out into the mudroom and found one of the breakers flipped in the breaker box. She flipped it back. And got to thinking.

The next night she left the door open – he didn't come. He didn't come the night after that either. Or the one after.

Whether it was the holy water, or the icon, or maybe it really couldn't hurt him – who knows. But he never came again.

Shurka had her baby. The neighborhood filled with rumors – women kept asking, but didn't get a single peep out of her. They shamed her, didn't believe her, but she stuck to the same tune – the devil came to see me. So they didn't believe her and didn't believe her – until they finally did. Shurka, in the meantime, changed radically – kept away from people. Stopped saying hello. Moved from the officers' cafeteria to work at the technical school.

The cafeteria was soon closed anyway: they dismantled the military airfield, handed the buildings over to the city, and transferred all the soldiers to Motovikha.

Things only got worse from there. Shurka Zaikina got herself a black cat and some piebald chickens, and raised her son a little bastard. He kept apart from the other kids ever since he was little; he was always by her side, doing chores at home, or in the garden, and got all A's in school. After school, he passed the exams into the Leningrad Shipbuilding Institute. He's a big boss there now, and comes to visit his mother in a black Volga. Doesn't say hello to anyone either. His wife too – she's either Jewish or French. And our reader at church said that the Antichrist will come from the French – it's from a book that scientists dug up in Palestine, it says so right there.

Alexandra Konstantinovna for the most part stays at home. She limps around her orchard and drinks tea. Tanka says that the cucumbers and tomatoes in Shurka's greenhouse ripen faster than anyone else's in the whole neighborhood.

"And she's too skimpy to share. And I wouldn't take any from a witch anyway, I'd be scared."

"No," Tanka admits, "I've taken plants she'd offered me, but they don't come out right. She must have a spell on them."

"Of course she does – wouldn't you?"

So Zaikina stays in her kitchen and drinks tea with gingerbread, and the neighborhood kids nail all kinds of iron things, horseshoes and such, to her gate. When her son comes to visit, he takes them all off, but she never does. She's a proud old lady – her pension's a pittance, so she sells produce in the market, but other than that, she just keeps drinking her tea and lumbers around in her garden.

"Did you see Zaikin the other day? Had a trunkful of jellies again, he did!"

"And where, pray tell, does she get all that sugar on her pension?"

"Like you don't know. He's a boss – so he must be stealing somewhere. Everyone does."

PETRUSHKA

"Petrushka, is the beer here?"

"Mhhhmmh," he grins and moves his lips trying to say something, but words never come.

"How many thousands do you got there already?"

"Mhhhmmh"

Everyone knows Petrushka counts money. He's been caught at it more than once – writing columns of numbers on a piece of paper, all in thousands, doing sums.

"Petrushka, what are you going to do with all that cash?"

"Mhhhmmh," he makes a scooping motion with his hands. It's all his, all his. He sits in the store's backroom, stares at the picture of the actress Nemolyayeva pinned to the wall, and counts something on his fingers. He mutters sometimes.

"Watch out, Petrushka, you'll get to be a millionaire!"

He shakes his head happily.

Why would Oleg take someone like that to work in the store? Well, no one else would come, would they? Petrushka doesn't know any better – so he went to work for Oleg.

After work, Oleg is building a house. A mansion. Two floors, an underground garage, yellow brick, a fireplace. He's put a welded iron fence around the plot. And the first thing he did was build a greenhouse. Then he parked his boat next to it. And his UAZ.

The construction crew is Oleg himself, his wife, his wife's cousin and Petrushka – he's the runner, the go-there-get-me-that guy. Oleg doesn't have any children. He makes sugar-coated cranberries. Not himself, of course: he drives around making deals and heads out to the villages to buy cranberries when they are in season.

"Oleg? He won't touch anything less than a semi! Everyone knows that. But you can't build all summer from cranberries alone, if you know what I mean."

They are always at the site. Every Saturday. Every Sunday. They got the roof done, and started on the inside jobs, were laying the parquet floors.

"Of course he's got parquet floors! You should see his fireplace – Stepanych charged 500 for the work alone."

"Five hundred? Didn't I hear he borrowed 25,000 at the bank, though?"

"Twenty-five? Well, let's see... The brick for the fireplace – it's the special yellow kind, fire-proof. Then the insert itself, the grate..."

"Mhhhmmh, Mhhhmmh," Petrushka's right there, follows the men around. They sort of – wave him off, let's say, not hard. He stayed down for a bit. But then he got up and walked away like nothing; it's not the first time for him. He wiped the blood that was coming out of his nose and muttered – was he counting something? He had to have been.

At night, on Monday, Oleg's house caught on fire. Oleg got there after the firefighters – to see what was left. He lives in town, at his wife's flat. Out here, on the Lake, this was supposed to be their winter home. The women had to hold him down, or else he would have pulled all his hair out. You would too if your house burned down.

At the other end of the village, in his own house, Petrushka lay on the couch. After his mother died, he moved onto her couch – his other bed is falling apart really. He lay and sniffed at his hands: do they smell of kerosene? He'd sniff, and then snicker, and make small noises, and then cry, sobbing, choking on his tears. He shook his clean-washed finger at someone invisible and kicked the arm-rest.

THE MAN WITH A SENSE OF HUMOR

I'll tell you where you might've seen me: In Riflemen's Izba – I used to man the bar there with Lukeria, back in '79. I moved on to Cooptorg and Zagotskot after that, drank some good cognac there, but got out just in time – boys don't end well if they stick to those gigs: easy money is sure death for our kind. Did you know Seryoga Kostyurin? The guy was 39 and had kidneys like Andropov – they hooked him up to the machine in Leningrad, and all for nothing. Whatever was in the coffin we buried wasn't our Seryoga, I'll tell you that much.

All because why? Because it's free. How much can a man drink really when it pours faster than from a kitchen faucet? And the nerves? Now you'll tell me you know some who get along just fine sniffing glue, and paint stripper ain't stripped anything off them yet, but it's not about what you drink, and not even how much – it's about your margin of safety. Take a man who drinks to numb his pain – people say he's just muffling it, and he'll pay for it, just not right away. But do you know what kind of reserves the human heart has? How many times it's made to beat? I'll tell you – there are enough zeros in that number to put a fence around my place. Twice. And take the liver. Under laboratory conditions, it can handle rat poison, no problem. What does this tell us? It tells us we humans have all kinds of reserves we don't even know about, and you can't live without a sense of humor. If you just go at it dead-serious, just for the money – you won't last.

Trust me, I know, because I did it all. Tatyana, that wife of mine, she's not the sharpest crayon in the box, but she's got a heart of gold: she let me try everything. Why? Because she understood this one thing about me: I have to reach out and touch it. Whatever it is. And not just touch it – I've always got away clean. Back in the old days, I'd burn through three grand in a single night in Petersburg, and that was when you could still buy caviar at the old price. But I've done my share, and at some point that cognac just wouldn't go down any more. I had a heart murmur, and my liver was acting up, but as soon as I realized I had to quit I felt better. And Seryoga, the poor soul, he snapped. I tried so hard to get him to quit Zagotskot back then, you wouldn't believe it – I tried everything. But he wouldn't budge.

"I can't go back to living with a ruble in my pocket," he said to me. "And Svetka would never understand."

Crash and burn, he did. And did he even enjoy drinking all that vodka? Not a bit. He sucked it like a vampire – 'cuz he couldn't do otherwise, but it made his heart groan. But God gave us drink to make us merry, isn't that what they say? You can't force yourself, not forever. All my old pals – they're all living the good life, high the whole time, and when you live like that and get depressed – that's it, man, lights out. There ain't nothing scarier than that. The stuff that gets into your head, you can't get away from it, and you can't drown it either. You know, I've paid a thousand rubles for a case of Coke, can you believe that? We were having a good time once, late into the night, and, what do you know, we ran out of stuff to chase our booze down with. We got up. We went looking. We found the barman. At home. Woke him up. That's what we mean when we say the good life, and who cares if no one took a sip of that Coke after all – that's not the point. But how do you go on like that? Play harder? Go sit at the table for 48 hours straight playing blackjack? You could of course, but then you sleep it off, and you wake up, and the world's so black it makes you want to howl like a wolf! And you don't do it once, or twice, or just for a month. That's your life – and it's the same, day in and day out. And I can't live like that, I'd had it – to hell with the money, I'd rather be free like a bird in the sky, you're only free when you're young, am I right? Maybe I'm not. I don't know.

I just didn't have it in me anymore. And if you don't have it in you, it's time to run. It wasn't fun. I wasn't laughing, at least. And I can't live without laughing; who lives like that – owls and peasants, and let me tell you, if they ever ran into each other, they'd fall over laughing, it'd be like looking into a funhouse mirror, no?

That's what I'm saying: a sense of humor is essential. It's the only thing that's kept me alive. People say I'm easy, travel light – well, that's because life makes me laugh, and if I get depressed, I don't get down, I've got an answer for that too: change everything, go to a new place, and look – here I am again, alive and well! I know no one can live your life for you, and I've always stood up for myself ever since I was a kid, and others... other people also do what's best for them, they just don't like admitting it. Anyway, I ran away. Some will tell you that was a stupid thing to do, left as I was without a penny in my pocket, but I got my warning call, and I heard it good and clear.

For Seryoga it was the kidneys, and for me it was my back. Oh man! First it didn't hurt all that bad – I'd feel better after a hot banya, but you can't live like a walrus, can you? Then it got worse. I went to see Lukeria's mother, she's our resident witch. She rubbed me this way and that, and gave me some herbs to make compresses with, and did her soothsaying thing, and at first it helped, but then the pain came back bad enough to make you howl. This, she said, means it's not your back that's hurting – it's your soul that's gotten twisted by ill-gotten money. You've got to leave it now, easy money's like a jinx – you'll never get better while you're around it. If that's how it is, I said, why don't you get your Lukeria out of that restaurant if cash is so bad for you? The old woman took offense and refused to heal me any more, and it was probably for the best, else she'd have healed me straight into the grave. I'm not saying she doesn't know things – she probably did save Lukeria's life after the drive shaft had gone through her, and all the doctors gave up – but she just wasn't the one to help me. Still, I could feel she was right – I knew somehow money wasn't going to make me happy.

I quit drinking. It still hurt. I left Zagotskot – then I felt a bit better, but then the pain came back again, and wrung me so bad, I couldn't take a piss. It felt like someone took out my spine, and put in an iron rod instead, and it wouldn't bend in any direction, and the rest of it is on fire as if a whole bunch of Chingachgooks were skinning me alive. At the time, I got the cash collector's job at the bank, driving around in an UAZ, and you can just imagine what a back like that can do to a man on our roads. You can sit on a down pillow and wrap a rabbit-hair shawl around your midsection – none of it helps. You're in hell, literally: you're sitting in a pool of molten lead and someone's pouring boiling oil down your spine. I kept mum at home – it didn't feel right to let Tatyana down, but I was starting to think some dark thoughts. There, Oleg Petrovich, I said to myself, looks like it's the end of the party for you. But Tatyana's a good wife: she sized me up, packed me up, and dragged me into the Central Hospital – and you know I did everything to get out of it, I know what these hospitals are like where they have the same pill and the same enema for the whole floor.

But whatever. They put me in bed and tucked me in with a warm blanket. To the right was an asthmatic guy with bronchitis, to the left – one with arthritis, up by the wall – a dude with ulcers, desiccated as a mummy, and up by the other wall a couple of half-paralyzed folks with strokes who had their own stroke talk to pass the time. And there I was – with whatever I had – in the middle. A circus! You, my dear Oleg Petrovich, Doctor Vdovin said, have podagra, the disease of kings. That's what he called it. But I hurt like hell after the exam, so I told him to go kiss an Eskimo's ass, milk a walrus, make some ice-cream and feed it to baby penguins, so he left without saying anything more.

Things are looking rotten: scream – no one will hear you. The paralyzed dudes pee on themselves, the ulcer guy's mute as a log and just keeps checking his tongue in the mirror, and the guy with asthma sounds like he's about ready to go pay St. Peter a visit. The gramps to my right is all I've got: he seems to have a sense of humor – when he heard me send Vdovin to hell, he chuckled and I glimpsed this mischievous glint in his eyes. Aha, I thought, you're my guy; you won't let me rot here – and my back's on fire, Vdovin's made it all worse with his poking and prodding.

I could see gramps was bored, but with me being the new guy, he was hanging back for the time being. Instead, he went to work on the guy to my right.

"Semyonych, you sound like a steam-train pushing uphill – are you fixing to die or something?"

And Semyonych, of course, can only lie there and gasp for air like a fish out of the water – he's got asthma. Mitryunchev (that was the old dude's name) won't let go:

"Semyonych, I tell you what – you oughtta' ask for a different bed. That one you got's cursed – no one lasts longer than two days on it, trust me."

The poor Semyonych went into a bit of contortion then, coughing and wheezing, so I had to throw my slipper at Mitryunchev – it hit the top of his head, and he vanished.

A bit later, he came back, with tea for Semyonych: of course, he wasn't nagging him out of meanness, he was just bored. He helped him drink his tea, like a nurse, fluffed his pillow, and got him talking. Old dudes, they only have one thing to talk about: the war, and who fought where. Turns out, they both stormed Budapest. Well, you should've seen the uproar: they jumped up and waved their arms, and went hugging and kissing each other – obviously, they were going to want a drink. Sure enough, five minutes later, Semyonych turns to me (Mitryunchev got him turned around in a blink):

"Olezhek, help us out here – we've got to celebrate."

Why shouldn't I help – that's about the only joy those geezers got left in their lives, and Semyonych sat there glowing like a marine's belt buckle, all his asthma disappeared. He pulled his wallet out of his bedside table, found a 10-ruble note in there, and handed it to me (Mitryunchev, of course, was broke – his whole life he'd never had much). I called a guy I knew, asked him to run over a bottle for us – my old connections worked like a charm for stuff like that – and handed the bottle over to my veterans. I didn't drink.

They finished it in a flash. Old Mitryunchev only looked fragile, and when it came to business, turned out he was in the penal battalion: he could tie that bottle into knots and squeeze it dry.[17] He threw them back in six seconds each – I saw it with my own eyes, and his pal Semyonych wasn't far behind.

Finally, they called lights out. In the glow of the night-light, I could see Semyonych was feeling good: his eyes glistened, he even got up from his bed.

"Guys! Guys, why did I listen to them, I should've done this a long time ago – I'm breathing now. I'm breathing!" he said, glowing like a first-grader. He held his pillow in his hands and dabbed his face with it: tears were running down his cheeks. It must have really been a long time since he felt so good.

He spent about an hour in this bliss; then the blood-vessels must have contracted again, and he turned for the worse: he couldn't stay lying down, but he couldn't stay sitting up either, his breath went in and out quick and shallow with this small sort of whimper:

"Nadya, Nadya, Nadenka..."

He was trying to call the nurse. As soon as I'd get up – "Semyonych, do you want me to go get her?" – Mitryunchev would hiss from his back: "Just go ahead and croak, you old bastard! Croak but don't give us up!" And Semyonych shook his head, he was hard as a flint, too.

After a while, he got up and walked around a bit, then came and sat at the edge of my bed, leaned against my head rail and whimpered his "Nadya, Nadya, Nadenka..." as if raving. Mitryunchev stuck to his guns:

---

17. Penal battalions in World War II were comprised of convicts who were given the choice of fighting or serving their sentences (including receiving the death penalty). They were thrown into the fray in the worst of conditions, underarmed and with machine guns at their backs, to keep them from retreating.

"Croak already, you bastard! You've got nothing left, but don't you dare give us up."

I looked into Semyonych's eyes – his pupils were wide with fear, huge, but he still wouldn't let me go get the nurse. At some point, he felt ever so slightly better and begged me:

"Oleg, please, can I rest on top of you just for a bit? If I can have something hard under my chest, it helps."

What could I say? He lay down across my chest, and he was heavy as hell, so my back cramped right away, but not too badly, I could live with it. So there we lay. Semyonych started gasping again, but in a different way: he could inhale, but couldn't let the air out – it was like he was choking. The choking made him shake. He lay on me, twitching, for another ten minutes or so, then went to get up, but keeled to his right and went down on the floor. Like a sack.

Mitryunchev jumped up, felt for the pulse, then closed Semyonych's eyes and folded his hands on his chest.

"End of the line," he said. "Go fetch the nurse," he ordered, and ran out, ostensibly to smoke in the bathroom where no one would find him. I believed him on the spot; he'd seen more than his fair share of dead people, I figured, so he knew what he was looking at. And I was right: later he told me some stories that would make your hair stand up; he doesn't see death the way you or I do.

Of course it was I who had to go to the nurse station. Mitryunchev wouldn't show his face: he was afraid someone'd smell the alcohol on him. It was also I who helped Nadezhda carry Semyonych to the morgue on a stretcher – you try finding anyone else in the hospital in the middle of the night.

In the morning, at breakfast, I saw Mitryunchev put his boiled egg in his pocket and then reach for the one that was meant for Semyonych. I thought, whatever, let him eat for two, but the old weasel had something else in mind.

At noon, Vdovin entered our room and headed straight for the two of us. Gramps was ready though: he was already squatting on his mattress, under his blanket draped on him like a tent. He made small clucking noises like a chicken in the roost. Vdovin, of course, has seen enough of the old man's tricks and was not going to be taken in.

"Mitryunchev!" he thundered. "You drank with Semyonych, rest his soul, didn't you? Pack up and get the hell out of here back to your village!"

Gramps looked as if he hadn't heard the doctor; he stared into the middle distance and mumbled:

"Yes, yes, Sergei Sergeyevich, just a second, I will, right away, just as soon as I lay this egg."

Vdovin couldn't help it – he chuckled, and, of course, that's exactly what the old man was waiting for: he flailed his arms, and twitched all over, exactly like a hen, and then pulled the egg from under himself and offered it to Vdovin with an absolutely innocent face.

"Here, Sergei Sergeyevich, send it to the Academy of Sciences to be studied, I swear I don't know what's happening to me. I've been laying eggs for two days now. Here, ask Oleg, he won't let me lie," he said pitifully and made such a grimace that Vdovin burst out laughing in earnest.

Vdovin took the egg and fingered it, and the old man started oohing and aahing again, and gasping and clucking, and in between all that managed to talk, in starts and stops:

"Sergei Sergeyevich, my dear, OOH, do something, I beg you! What is... AAH... happening to me?! This thing – once it starts, ain't nothing can stop it! Argh!" he gasped and pulled another egg from under himself, still warm. And he made it look so natural – with his head moving side to side, cheeks puffed out, eyes rolled – you could charge admission.

Vdovin, however, was not impressed.

"Thank you for the eggs, Mitryunchev," he said. "But do pack your stuff, you've been here long enough. Tell me honestly – why'd you drink that vodka yesterday?"

But Mitryunchev's also an old hand at these games, so he didn't give up so easily either.

"Oh, oh, doctor, please, it's coming again! Another one! Oh, it'll kill me, please – you don't believe me, then feel for yourself!" he grabbed the surgeon's hand and pulled him closer, and all with such desperation in his eyes it'd melt a stone. Vdovin went along with it and stuck his hand under the blanket – he must've wanted to pinch the clown from under there – and that's when Mitryunchev dropped the bombshell: he tensed for an instant, then ripped one – loud enough to rattle the windows.

The room just fell over laughing. The guy with the ulcers slid off his bed, he was laughing so hard, and the paralyzed dudes just made one high-pitched whine – "eee-eee-ee!" with tears coming out of the their eyes. Vdovin froze for a second, then cursed and fled.

The next day he came back as if nothing had happened – meaning, he'd forgiven the old man. Vdovin pulled up a stool, and told us that Semyonych had no more than a few days left to live, and that was a miracle in itself, given that his lungs were worn to threads. So, really, the vodka only cut his suffering short by a bit. Still, the doctor promised to catch Mitryunchev red-handed the next time he tried to pull something, and to throw him out no matter what – even if the eggs he laid were golden.

Gramps perked up after that; strutted around all proud.

"Vdovin," he informed me, "is always like that: he keeps threatening to kick me out of here, but he doesn't really mean it – he knows my situation."

The victory kept the old man in good spirits for the day, then wore off. At night he sulked; his heart ached – he remembered Semyonych. He grabbed me by the shoulder:

"Olezhek, you say we should all fight and live, but what have I ever seen in this life? I only got out of Stargorod during the war," he lamented.

He started telling me about his life, his childhood and stuff, and I'm an orphan myself – I don't need stories to know about hunger. I grabbed my grandpa and carried him to the bathroom, gave him a bath, took his mind off his blues, and brought him back to bed.

Only it was scary to look at his body – it's all holes. It sort of made me gasp, and gramps perked up: he's a hero compared to me! I said, you're full of it, gramps – people only fought in the penal battalion to first blood. And he goes, oh yeah? How about second? Or third? They sent me right back into the meat grinder five times – from the hospitals.

I really don't know what part of what he said was true and what was lies, but there wasn't an inch of him that hadn't been mangled, and that's a fact.

So there we were, the two of us – clean (I took a shower too, while we were at it), warm in our beds and not the least bit sleepy (you do nothing but sit around all day) – and that's when Mitryunchev confessed to me that he only pretends to be sick.

"How should I put it, Olezhek? At nights, sometimes I get so sad – it just comes over me, like goo, this sadness, like it crawls in through the window and under the door. I started dreaming of dead people – there were days I used to sleep on top of them, you'd be so tired in the trenches, you fell where you stood, right onto the dead. This must be their payback for me now: they come and talk to me, but I can't understand what they are saying. Probably, they want to take me with them, but what the heck do they want with me – I saw worse things in the war, they've nothing new to show me. Sometimes, to be honest, I do wonder if I'm losing it, but then again, I don't think so, the wheels seem to keep spinning. That was a long time ago, in the war, when I was wild. I'm quiet now. So, you see, in winters, I run away from them, the dead, here, to the hospital. I've a whole stack of maladies – I just never had time to pay them any mind before, but now they come in handy: I'd dig around in my magical bag of tricks and pull out something shiny for Vdovin. He can't do anything about me: I'm a veteran, and disabled to boot, and I've got heart trouble, and hypertension, and what not. He lets me in. I usually spend about three months here. They can't really fix anything, but I get three meals a day, and that, if you ask me, is a good start. Vdovin's a kind man, not like Pankratov. Vdovin – he, if he doesn't understand why something does what it does will cut you open, dig around in there for appearances' sake, and put everything back the way it was – he'll never do any harm. Pankratov, on the other hand, is a pure Nazi: he likes experimenting on his patients, you know how many he's dispatched to the next world already? All for his dissertation."

He was a funny old geezer, my Mitryunchev. We got to be friends. Whenever he'd sulk, I'd yell at him and find him a chore. Meanwhile, one of our paralyzed dudes kicked the bucket, and so did the guy with the ulcers after Pankratov's surgery. That happened in the ICU, not in our own room, but still. They brought in some new people, but the gramps and I didn't take to them, and mostly kept to ourselves. We had nothing to do all day, so he nagged me to play cards with him. All right. I was bored too, so I started beating him. Little by little, I won all his clothes and all his medals too (he always came to the hospital decked out as if for a parade). This got him perked up again: I could see the old gleam in his eyes – he's gotten into the heat of it, but he had nothing left to gamble. So he was stuck.

I saw him trying to figure something out; he paced the room, and I pretended I was sleeping – in fact, my back hurt and I didn't feel like talking to anyone. Finally, he couldn't stand it any longer, came to my bed and perched on the edge:

"Is it hurting bad today, Olezhek?" he asked, all concerned-like.

"Go away, you mooch, I don't give on Tuesdays."

He saw he wouldn't get far on kindness alone, and decided to be bold:

"Son, give me my suit-coat back, I need to go to town."

"What suit-coat?"

"What do you mean, what? This one right here."

"And did you, Gramps, forget that it's now mine? Here, I was just about to grab me some scissors and cut it up into a nice big pile to put under my back. It hurts, you know."

"You can't do that! What'll you do with all the medals on it?"

"I'll take them to Leningrad, trade them in for booze."

"Oh-hoh-ho!" he sighed, like a horse, and shook his head. "Are you sure you won't give it back to me?"

"Nope. Be strong, Gramps, you got what was coming – you shouldn't have gambled it."

"Oh, come on, Olezhek. You always think of something."

By this point, the whole room is watching this show – they want to know how he'll trick the coat out of me. Except Mitryunchev is really worked up about it: he's already pictured his coat cut into pieces, and he doesn't see or hear the room around him. I'm sorry for him, but I know better: if I just give him the coat back for nothing, he'll have had no fun. He might even get mad at me.

Then it came to me:

"Gramps," I said, "I bet you couldn't stick your naked ass out into the hallway and sing a couplet."

"Would you give me the coat back if I did?"

"I would."

"And the medals with it?"

"You're pushing it, Gramps."

"What do I care – I can strip naked."

"We're not in a banya, Gramps. All right, I'll give you the medals too."

You should've seen him – he was so happy! Quickly, before I could change my mind, he dropped his pants, stuck his ass out the door and bellowed out a couplet so loud the light bulbs above our heads rattled. Naturally, Nadezhda ran up and yelled at him that she'd throw him out, but you could see she was fighting her face not to laugh. And so Gramps got to be the room's hero again.

He took his coat and his pants, too (on the sly – we didn't say anything about the pants), climbed back onto his bed and sat there fingering his medals; he didn't put it on right away – was enjoying the moment. He sat there like that for a bit, and then suddenly – splat! – threw his suit on the floor, dove face-first into this pillow and started sobbing. I rushed to pull him up by the shoulders.

"Gramps, please, don't! I didn't mean to insult you!"

And he looks back at me and – just picture it! – chokes back laughing through tears.

"Man, are you stupid! What are you talking about, insult me. I'll show you now – you'll never even dare set foot in my village!"

I, believe it or not, felt my knees buckle when I realized what he meant.

"You old bare-assed weasel!" I yelled at him, and gave him a noogie, and rolled him around on his bed a bit, and, of course, promised – even swore – to come visit him in his village.

Soon after that, Tanya took me home from the hospital; really, what good's the hospital for, if you can take the same pills at home. Next, she took me to see this guy all the way down in Taganrog – now you'd call him a fancy word, "chiropractor," but I prefer the good old Russian "bone-setter." He was the one who cured me once and for all, and without any drugs, pills or compresses, but I tell you, if I'd known ahead of time what his curing would look like I'd never have gone there – it was a trip to a Gestapo dungeon, not a doctor's office. Once I got in there, I really appreciated my gramps Mitryunchev. He was the one who taught me: it is only those who are tired of living that die, and the ones who want to go on for a bit longer and hold on with their teeth – they always survive. He must have said that five times a day at least.

So picture this enormous dude, close to seven feet tall, with arms to scale and fists like a Clydesdale's hooves. He puts you on your stomach, runs his finger down your spine, and then all of a sudden – whack! – slaps you flat on the back. You hear your bones crush and it hurts like hell! I'm lying there screaming in tears, and the son-of-a-bitch just chuckles.

"Go ahead, scream your heart out. I like it even better – makes it easier to figure what's where."

And again – crack! I blacked out. Came back – I can't get up, and if I'd had any energy I'd have at least bitten his finger off. I couldn't feel my arms or legs though.

But you know – I felt better when I got to the hotel. I took a long warm bath, and you know, I felt better! For the first time in forever, I felt I could bend my back. Two days later I went to see the dude again, willingly. He had me go to a different room, and the set-up there was quite simple. You ever read about the Inquisition? So, picture this: I'm stripped to the boxers, and they tie me to a huge wheel, and this damn gorilla starts slowly pulling my feet towards my head – and all very calm, with a smile. I figured this was it, and bid farewell to my old bones, this world, and my wife; I screamed and blacked out again. When I came round and rested a bit, you know... Words don't do it justice. I was born again. I took him flowers, that bonesetter dude, to thank him, but he only chuckled at me – he knew what he was doing.

We came back home and I got back into my UAZ. I actually enjoy the job now – I can ride on any road without pillows, and I'm not the least bit sorry that I left Zagotskot when I did. Over the year that I was sick, the new power squeezed my old buddies so hard, they're scared of their own shadows. Funny: I was getting meat through my job now without all the old headaches, and when you've got meat, what else do you need? So I figured I was ahead all around.

I went to visit Gramps Mitryunchev too. I flipped the siren on as soon as I got to the village – you know our cars are special, with flashlights and everything – so I made a show of pulling up to his door. Gramps dashed out, made a huge fuss – he was happy as a pup. I brought a bottle with me; we sat together for a while, drank some. And you know, he kept holding my hand and didn't want to let it go. Such a funny old man, I swear: it's not like I could vanish into thin air after I drove all the way over to see him.

He went right back to work, picking mushrooms and berries, and stuff; he loaded me up, and when I offered to pay for it, he naturally took offense. But I turned him around quick – I just reminded him of the couplets he sang in the hospital, and he gleamed like a new penny. Before I left, he asked me to give him a ride to the village store. He said it as if it weren't a big deal or anything, but I could tell – he had a plan, Mitryunchev never does anything just because he needs to.

Well, that's no hair off my back, so I gave him a ride. He climbed out at the store, turned, and winked at me, very importantly – there were people around, of course, folks stopped to stare – and ducked into the store looking purposeful. What a clown.

Nowadays, before he turns himself over to Vdovin for the winter, he always comes to stay with us, and every September Tatyana and I go to visit him – they have more mushrooms and berries there than you could mow with a scythe. Especially cranberries. So I had this idea – and talked it over with my guys – if it all works out, we'll start a co-op, and make the Gramps our main cranberry buyer. He's too good to just slave away at the *kolkhoz*, and he's not that kind of man, anyway, our Mitryunchev!

You'll say, "What is this, Oleg, are you after easy money again?" Nope. This is a whole different ballgame. First, it'd be my own business – I'm getting fed up driving someone else's cash around, to tell you the truth. Second, you do have to think ahead. I'll save up a bit and build myself a house at the Lake, it doesn't have to be big, I'm not greedy. All I want is a place of my own and no one sticking their nose into my business. What's wrong with that? So. Laugh all you want, but it might work – cranberries are all the rage these days.

Gramps' village – that'll make you laugh for real. Whenever I show up, I can tell folks are eyeing the car like it came from the organs, you know. I couldn't care less, of course, but I know the old geezer had to have told them all kinds of stories, so they'd mind him better. Folks in the village don't like him all that much, because he's like me, you know – always been his own boss – so he never misses a chance to pull their leg and laugh about it. And I'd do anything for him – I like to see him go at it; some say you can get a sort of a second wind in your old age, enjoy life all over again, and nothing'll bother you. But he's not much to look at it, that's for sure – just a little wrinkled gnome is what he is, a funny old gnome. I like his sense of humor though – it's what keeps you going, right?

LUKERIA'S HILL

"And his whole body was covered with camouflage film, and underneath it – wrapped with antennae wires."

"Come on now, Katka!"

"No, girls, I'm telling you! And when they went to load him up into the truck, this stuff came out of the bullet-holes – in little clumps, like jelly, and some green hairs came out too. They sealed them up in zinc boxes and sent them off to Moscow."

"Well, I don't know... it could be true. In America they've been keeping a couple of humanoids on ice for years, and that journalist who found out about it disappeared without a trace."

"Of course he did! They just whacked him quietly, so he wouldn't go around sticking his nose where it don't belong."

A door slams – it's Ninka from the grocery store.

"Girls, put in your orders – we got in a shipment of sour-cream, who wants some?"

Everyone does, of course.

"What about that thing you promised me? They haven't brought it yet? Do me a favor, Lukeria Ivanovna, do remember what I asked – when my Andryukha brings some fish, I won't forget you either."

Ninka runs out again; Katya and Svetka renew the argument they suddenly remember having.

"I'm telling you, salmon fights with its head! Ask Lukeria Ivanovna."

"Lukeria Ivanovna, have you heard of this from your Aslan?"

"Leave me alone, girls!"

"Yes, Katya, you leave Lukeria Ivanovna alone now, she is now our Khokhloma painting specialist..."

It goes on like this all day. A habit. No spite. Only their tongues get a bit tired by evening. And their feet. But you can't compare this to working at the restaurant – there you're running around in a lather the whole time, it's mind-numbing, and here you just get a headache sometimes. But you've got troichatka to help the headache – doctor Vdovin sends some from the hospital. Not for free, of course, the first leather jacket that ever came went to him.

The consignment store is not the restaurant, not a buffet even, but if you got brains, you can make a living here too. Again, 45 is not 17, you don't need so much. But still. You need to pay at the garage – for body work and a coat of paint, then you need something for Terebikhin at the Traffic Police – to get the accident off your record... Vitenka, son of a bitch, finally crashed the poor old car. As she goes through her mental to-do list, Lukeria thinks of her Vitenka. The thought makes her smile. It makes her stretch behind her counter. Even though you wouldn't think there's much to smile about – Valya's words are also stuck in her mind. But that's the kind of woman Lukeria is – these things are not mutually exclusive.

"Here's what I'll tell you, girls: no one can replace my Aslan, but when the pickings get slim, Vitenka's pure gold, it's worse without him, isn't it, girls?"

Katya and Sveta smile knowingly: they have husbands and children, too, and it's quite a load to pull, you don't have much time for yourself, so all they've got are their little smiles, their giggles and jokes, and their dreams and memories of how things were when they were young. It's quiet at the store – middle of the day, no customers. Lukeria stretches again, intentionally seductively and makes an obscene gesture with her hand. The girls chuckle into their fists. But again without spite or envy – how could anyone be angry with Lukeria?

The woman at the cash register, Terentieva – an almost-retired grandmother – looks up from the till and sighs.

"Lushenka, sweetie-pie, you'll get into trouble with your appetites. When are you going to settle down, huh?"

The question hangs in the air. The thick sugary silence holds for a bit, and crumbles again – the women move on to the subject of a child's outfit with a picture of Tom and Jerry on it. For this one item they have received three requests: from the laundry and dry-cleaners, the bakery, and Orsov cafeteria. The bakery wins – the feast of the Trinity is around the corner, and everyone is running short on yeast.

Lukeria drops out of the conversation – she has to think some more. Try as she might to get Valya's words out of her mind, she can't stop thinking about what she said about Vitya. Valya, from the campground, stopped by this morning, took her aside, and told her in a whisper that the night before Vitya rented a boat and took a girl from the conservation department at the Museum for a ride to the island. He's quick like that...

Lukeria goes to the pantry to make lunch for everyone. She's alone. She can think. She peels potatoes.

✳ ✳ ✳

She came to Stargorod as a 15-year-old from the Lake Country. Having dropped out of the technical school, she went to work at the Riflemen Izba where she spent five years living with the director and by the age of 23 rose from a waitress to the buffet manager. The director procured himself a new one-room apartment and went to jail.

That's when she found Vassily Antonovich, the head accountant from the conservation department at the museum. Lukeria moved into a three-room apartment, moved her mother in with her from the village, bought her first car and learned to drive – back then, a woman behind a wheel was big news in Stargorod. Vassily Antonovich together with the then Director Syromyatnikov (he was there before Zhorka Pronichev) were building the Bishop's mansion and the dachas for the Oblast Party Committee. Lukeria, still working at Riflemen Izba, moved her sister and husband to the city and made sure her nephew passed exams into the Polytechnic. A bit later, however, Syromyatnikov turned Vassily Antonovich in: 120 cubic feet of imported lemon-tree lumber destined for the museum's parquet floors, Finnish floor tiles, cement, brick, and an excavator given to some friendly moonlighters – enough for him and Lukeria to get close to seven years, plus confiscation of their property. They weren't married, however – and that's what saved her. A year later, Vassily Antonovich died in prison under circumstances that remained unclear. Lukeria was left with the bank assets and her freedom.

In the meantime, she turned 30. Children were not materializing. Somehow, the restaurant smoke congealed into a former boxer named Stas, who drank like a horse but played the guitar with great flair. Just after their one-year anniversary, he disappeared. Lukeria inherited his guitar, his debts, and his constantly muttering old mother, who scared Lukeria a bit. Lukeria loved her anyway. Four more men flew by barely to be remembered. She must have found them somewhere; she picked them up, dusted them off, cleaned them and gave them a new life, and then they vanished just like Stas, only remarkably faster.

Lukeria, to give her her due, when she crossed onto the far side of 30, did not get fat, like most, but preserved her narrow hips, straight back, and impressive breasts, desired by many. You could not find a bigger optimist among women over 30 in the whole of Stargorod. You could always ask her for a loan; she was always willing to go to the basement to fetch a bottle of vodka late at night after the register's been closed out, and the head of the Traffic Police himself, lieutenant colonel Terebikhin who once a year, without fail, put on a blow-out for a hundred of his closest friends behind closed doors at Riflemen Izba, invariably greeted her with a peck on the cheek.

Lukeria's courage would have done a Chechen rebel proud: whenever she interfered to break up a fight, the rabble-rousers in her presence faded and retreated to neutral corners in a blink. On a few very rare occasions, she'd taken a couple punches herself in the heat of the moment, but such perpetrators were forever banished from the Riflemen Izba, and those who owed Lukeria a favor (never few) made it their business to ambush such characters in a dark alley and give them a thorough ass-kicking.

It seemed things would go on like this forever: to her friends, Lukeria announced that she would choose her men herself from now on. The stories with the accountant, whom she had, apparently, loved, and Stas the guitar player whom she loved undeniably, made their impact; the four men that followed were temporary pets, profoundly needy, albeit endowed with the physical stamina Lukeria required. But nothing more.

It was Aslan Dzhioyev, a fiery Ossetian with gold crowns on his teeth and a map of deep scars on his forehead, once his division's weightlifting champion, who threw everything out of balance. He knew how to live large, but he also knew the price of money, and never wasted any – like a gold prospector who's hit it big. He could pay for everyone's food and drink. Or he could let someone else do it. He was persistent and ardent, but gallant. He was like steel. He won Lukeria, as the waitresses whispered, right there in the pantry and she could not resist him.

He was a figure, of course. A king. Aslan didn't care for jeans; instead, he appeared in English suits that made him look like an heir to the throne. The country girls at the Riflemen Izba coat check, its weary cooks and its independent director – they all smiled as soon as they saw him. No one ever observed an expression of contempt on Aslan's face. He owned a gas station at a highway exit and a used car consignment business.

Polite and solicitous, but somewhat distant in public, Aslan, whose mountain upbringing did not permit public displays of affection, was at home as loving as a good child, and his filial respectfulness melted even the heart of Lukeria's bitter old mother, who never called him anything but Aslanchik.

For five years this Ossetian prince became the source of bliss and passion in Lukeria's life. His half-Ossetian, half-Chechen army confidently moved to acquire Stargorod's remaining gas stations, then opened the first video-theaters in the city, and was eyeing the

Cooptorg and the furniture factory when one dark August night Aslan, on his way to the restaurant, was gunned down by a boar-grade rifle wielded by a Gypsy he had crossed in some affair.

The Gypsy managed to disappear from the scene, and Aslan's empire, that had appeared to be so solid, cracked and began to disintegrate. What no one could have guessed, and what became clear in the aftermath of the shooting, was that the whole kingdom had been held together by the will of a single man, a brilliant man, one shot with such matter-of-fact impunity right in the center of Stargorod. At a traffic light. With a hunting rifle.

Lukeria heard the news immediately: the restaurant was only beginning to stir to life, and the gallant Ossetian's life had been cut short not 500 yards from the building. Lukeria took it stoically. She stayed and worked her shift, even after the director offered to personally drive her home. Lukeria refused, and only at the end of the night, after she had closed out, did she jump into her car and leave the restaurant's parking lot for the unfinished winter dacha Aslan had put in her name.

She crashed ten miles down the Stargorod-Leningrad highway, as she was descending a small hill. Somehow, a low concrete post from the roadside barrier speared the car in the front, and it rolled three times before coming to rest in the ditch. The emergency team on duty made it there, miraculously, just in time – had they come even a bit later, Lukeria would have bled to death. The accident, monstrous in its cruelty, remained deeply wedged in Stargorodians' collective memory. For a long time afterward, they passed on the detailed accounts of how the emergency team scraped Lukeria from her smashed car. The drive shaft pierced her peritoneum, but to Doctor Vdovin's amazement (he did the surgery), no vital organs were damaged. Nonetheless, after they had to stitch Lukeria back together like a rag doll, the doctors were convinced she would not live.

Lukeria survived. Her mother nursed her back from the brink of death with herbal remedies known to her alone, thus securing irrevocably her reputation as Stargorod's resident witch, and six months later, Lukeria took up her post behind the counter of the consignment shop, which her own Aslan had founded not long before. She did not return to the restaurant.

On a somewhat different topic, when the local GB[18] followed the route of Lukeria's "panicked flight" (as it appeared in their reports) to the unfinished dacha, they extracted a significant sum of money from a secret cache, but Lukeria said she knew nothing about it. No matter how many times they called her in for questioning, she stuck to her story, and they never charged her with anything.

In obvious concern for her mental well-being, people never brought up Aslan to her, but one day Lukeria herself mentioned him, and from then on spoke of him often and without any prompting. She came back to life and even bought a new car – an act that struck Stargorodians as particularly extraordinary. For some reason, no one ever envied her, even though, when you think about it, between her Japanese TV-VHS combo, her new car, and the unfinished dacha she had inherited, there were plenty of grounds for loads of gossip at least, if not a touch of envy.

A year later, Vitenka entered the stage. A painter who had graduated from the Moscow Architectural Institute, he somehow landed in Stargorod, started drinking shortly afterwards, and gradually debased himself to the task of painting signs for the traffic police. That's where Lukeria Ivanovna picked him up. She dusted him off. She dressed him up. She took him to a mentalist and got him coded against drinking. Then she got him a job at the coop – painting samovars in Khokhloma style.

"Lukeria's got her second wind," her former restaurant friends observed admiringly, before shaking their heads and indulging in reminiscences of Lukeria's wild life, so wide-open to any inquiry and commentary. Usually, this reminiscing ended with the mention of Lukeria's Hill – as the site of her accident had been baptized, to

18. Short for KGB.

everyone's satisfaction. You can be sure that in another hundred years, when spreading Stargorod swallows the tenth mile marker, developers will call the neighborhood they build there Lukeria's Hill. Once something gets a name around here, it doesn't go away.

* * *

Meanwhile, it's lunch time at the consignment shop. Lukeria has fried a pan of potatoes, but hasn't come to any conclusions. She fished a few pickled tomatoes out of a jar, stacked them into an attractive pyramid on a plate and began arranging sliced bologna around it; she was so engrossed in her lunch-time ministrations that she began to hum a tune to herself.

The other girls put the "Closed for Lunch" sign in the door, came to the back room and gushed over the beautifully set table. Terentieva, unable to resist the temptation, snatched a tomato and bit into it with great gusto. She was moved by Lukeria's care, she couldn't help it, and blurted out her secret: "Lush, just don't take this personally or anything – Valka said she saw your Vitya yesterday with one of those drafter girls. Said they rode a boat to the islands."

Lukeria by now has her mouth full, and has to choke on the hot potatoes to answer, with a dismissive wave, "Let him ride his boat wherever he wants – he isn't going anywhere. And if he does – big deal, I won't cry for him. We'll find another one, won't we, girls?"

The overweight 30-year-old "girls" and Terentieva laugh in chorus, jealous as one.

GREED

It's like somebody jinxed the job: no one ever has any luck at Stargorod's Conservation Bureau. So many directors in the last couple of years, and it's the same thing every time – they don't last long. For a while there, we had Pesteryev – everyone had such hopes for him when he came, and then he too went under. Call it what you will, but greed does have a special rotting effect on a Russian soul. Take Pesteryev: you'd think he had everything he could possibly want, why, then, why did he want more? A man is weak, that's why – weak and pliable, and before you know it, he's caught up in the infernal machine of greed – smack! and it pins him down. Savvatei Ivanovich Shestokrylov even called Pesteryev, personally, about this very thing.

"Semyon Ivanovich, are you sure you want to build that deck?"

"Yes, why?"

"Well, it doesn't look good. Why don't you just rent a party room at a restaurant – that's nice, and cultured, and not as conspicuous. No one in the oblast can get any lumber, and you're framing a stage with four-by-sixes – isn't it a bit too much?"

"When my only son's getting married? I don't think so."

"All right then, but don't say I didn't warn you."

"But that's just leftovers, Savvatei Ivanovich – I sent the actual lumber shipment over to your dacha. Or have you perchance forgotten about that?"

"I, Pesteryev, never forget anything."

That's exactly what Shestokrylov said, right before he hung up. It sounded like he was offended. But Pesteryev did not heed the warning, and finished the deck. Not even a deck – a platform. A whole stage.

Yevgenia, Pesteryev's wife, went to talk him out of it – he all but killed her (he was drunk): "It's okay for them, but not for me?!" he yelled. He chased her around the yard for a while, until she left him alone. He didn't listen to a woman's intuition either – means he'd gone hard inside, cocky.

And in the old days, when he used to work in the Construction Trust, first as a foreman, then a head engineer, then as a director – he was just a regular guy. With a temper, yes; demanding, yes, but fair, too – bonuses without fail, and union trips to Moscow (where you could get sausage and cheese) for the guys. He looked out for us. It was when he got transferred to the Conservation (he got caught on the bathhouse project, there was something about marble, or the tiles, or maybe both) that he'd gone sour.

Technically, it was a demotion, but then word came from on high that he was to "renovate" dachas for certain people, and Pesteryev rose again. He arranged for his wife to be transferred from the Game Preserve to the District Executive Committee and things picked up steam: he couldn't get used to living in the city, so he "conserved" a whole mansion for himself out in the suburbs, with gold-leaf everywhere, and had his gates hand-made with lots of curlicues. He had a motorcycle with a sidecar, but rode in the Department's GAZ whenever he went hunting.

So all right, some guys put up this stage for dancing in front of his house about a month before the wedding. He stocked up on vodka (Yevgenia pulled her strings) – at least ten cases, but in the weeks before the wedding, folks made quite a dent in that supply. And here's the thing: he'd sell it to some, but not to others, and in the old days, he'd never have turned anyone away, he knew how things stood: you're a big boss during the day, but at night, if a fellow man's feeling down, be a good neighbor, especially when you grew up on the same street and everyone here has known you since you were in your momma's belly. But – he was flying high now.

At work, too, he'd been working his boys to pieces. He quit paying them, only kept promising: "Everyone here gets what he earns. If you do a thousand rubles worth of work in a month – you get a thousand. Do two – get two." But those were just words. What are you going to do if he's got a seventeenth century window frame priced at two-fifteen and it takes you two days to cut it and put it in right? The prices, of course, are crap, but in other towns people manage somehow! Instead, he had a *stroyotryad* – a bunch of construction students on a "summer apprenticeship," do the entire plan for him, and he paid them proper. They of course, were there from dawn to dusk, just plugging away; a couple of our guys, the younger ones, tried to keep up with them, but dropped it – you'd sooner hurt yourself working like that, without weekends or holidays, but still, that's just not how we do things around here: he paid them thousands and couldn't find two hundred for us. He didn't do it just out of the kindness of his heart, of course – they paid him back, and paid him good. Still, our boys were all feeling down, and how much can a man in a funk do in a day? They kept sighing about our previous boss, Zhorka Pronichev. He used to run things straight out of a restaurant. He'd go get a table in the morning, and just stay there, and that's where you went when you needed him to sign something. He'd sign a paper, and sometimes would pour you a glass, too. In his days, a man could scare up three hundred a month easy. But Zhorka crashed and burned too – they fired him from his job, booted him out of the Party, and struck him from their lists. He's now a free contractor – builds houses around the district, free as a bird. "I drink when I want, and I work when I want," he says.

No, but this Pesteryev with his stage! I bet he just wanted to outdo the Shestokrylovs' wedding, when they took over the entire Riflemen Izba. He hired the band from the Izba, too, got electricity to the stage, hung it about with colorful little lights, made sure the whole street had something to drink, and somehow commandeered a whole bull-calf at the *kolkhoz*.

And it all may have turned out all right, if it weren't for the bride. The girl convinced her newly-wed husband Valerka to take her for a ride in the *stroyotryad's* Zhiguli. So he did. Valerka came back without a scratch, the car was totaled, and the newlywed ended up with a broken leg and completely unconscious. They dropped her off at the surgery like a log, where doctors more or less put the leg back together and sealed it in a cast (Vdovin's handiwork), but the girl wasn't coming around. The X-rays spelled out the bad news: a fracture at the base of the scull and a hemorrhage into the brain.

Good thing Pesteryev's a really stubborn man: he brought in a neurosurgeon from St. Petersburg, didn't spare the expense. The luminary scratched at the X-ray picture with his nail, picked off a bit of mouse shit, and roared so the windows rattled, "You should've treated the girl for shock instead of taking pictures with expired film!"

He yelled and yelled at them, then cursed some more, and then moved the girl to his own clinic – brought her back from the other side, only she was left lame for the rest of her life: her leg rotted – they thought they were working on a dead woman, you know, and didn't try particularly hard.

So the wedding came with a bigger bill than Pesteryev had planned. And then he had to feed the police so they wouldn't pursue the accident. And the doctors! And the car! He was pulling his hair out. They took the stage apart, and sold his motorcycle (Timofei Andreyevich, a fellow hunter, got himself a good deal), but it wasn't enough – so he had to go see Shestokrylov, to find a way to give the *stroyotryad* its Zhiguli back. Savvatei Ivanovich watched him squirm for a bit, raked him over the coals, but did find him a car – took one from the shipment going to the chemical plant.

So all right, the car was taken care of, Valerka was clean and sent off to the army, to serve at the local base, but Pesteryev still had other debts to pay off. And this is where he got caught. And with what! Pennies! He paid the deaf kids' school three thousand to have the kids fish logs out of the river and cut them up into firewood. Everything on the sly, of course, so word wouldn't get out – it was kind of embarrassing. But someone did rat on him – there's always someone. An audit came down from on high, people said Savvatei Ivanovich himself made sure of it. They pulled up the budgets, and they all had Pesteryev's signature on them – he wrote them up himself. And there you go: he was 104 rubles short!

At the court hearing, he kept bringing up some jumpsuits and boots, that the school was supposed to use for work and then give back to Pesteryev, but then didn't, so they figured the cost into the budget. The school's super got a year probation, as he was a veteran, but Pesteryev's case was looking worse and worse. He could have still gotten away, if he'd kept his big mouth shut, but he just broke down one day. When they were taking him to the courtroom (and he knew by then no one would help him there), he pointed his finger at the whole Executive Committee, to their faces, and called them by name: "You took, and you did, and you, and you!" – and said in court who specifically, and how much, and what for. Naturally, he got two years of forced labor at his place of residence. Could have been a lot worse. He got to stay at home, only had to check in every day, and the work they made him do was building shipping crates at the winery.

He started drinking, of course. Yevgenia is a handsome woman, grand, attractive, but he looked like a dung beetle: black brows, black mustache, and mad eyes on fire. It was tough on her. And just before his time was about to end, somehow he got hit on the ribs with a log unloading train cars, and it bruised his lung. It wasn't a serious bruise even, but you can't hide from your fate – sarcoma came and got him. When they laid him out, he looked like an angelic old hermit: all skin and bones, and his white beard. You wouldn't recognize him.

The last month before he died he lay there at home and just kept groaning: "How long? How long? How long?" Yevgenia took care of him in silence: she'd come, clean his bed, turn him this way and that so he wouldn't get bedsores, and he'd keep at it: "How long before I die? Is it soon? I'm sick of it, Yevgenia, sick of it!" And she'd just fix his pillow, turn on the radio for him and go to the office.

Valerka came late to the funeral – couldn't get a ticket. After serving in the highway corps in Voronezh (construction crew, basically), he got packed off to be a lieutenant out in Tajikistan, paving roads for the local goat herders. He came back alone, leaving his wife with the baby. He visited his father's grave, and then spent the next five days in a drunken stupor with the guys. Then he got up, put his uniform back on, and left.

And Yevgenia soon married Timofei Andreyevich, the hunter. He got her transferred from the Executive Committee back to Fish and Game. People say they live quietly and never fight – Pesteryev, he used to beat her up pretty regularly, especially after he started at Conservation. That job's cursed, I'm telling you. Maybe someone really put a jinx on it. People say Lukeria's mother was seen on the night of a full-moon, walking backwards thrice around the Conservation office – right after they gave Lukeria's then husband seven years for selling the museum's parquet on the side. True, that was a long time ago, in the early seventies, but women believe it – the old hag's still alive and is the scariest witch for miles around.

VICTORY

I, for one, have great respect for the Tatars. One – they don't ever touch moonshine or port, because it's death to the liver; two – when they get a mind to do something, they don't let up until they get it done; and three – they're loyal, and always stand up for one another. Kind of like the Chechens almost, only Chechens are more headstrong and as far as being afraid goes – they don't even know what that means: you know their mothers hold babies above mountain gorges by their heels, just hanging there, to teach them bravery. But that's Chechens, and we're talking about Tatars here; they're a proud people, you know, but it's a special kind of pride they have – not showy like the Chechens', but quiet. You, for example – you ever been to a banya with them? Oh that's a whole other story. We used to have this one nut – a total egghead, boys said he used to work for Aleksei Tolstoy in the archives somewhere, until he lost his marbles, and they sent him to pasture to Stargorod. So this loon, his thing was – he was always cold. He'd go into the steam room, climb to the very top birth and just stand there, and sort of weave about, and make these mincing steps in place – like a tiny dog that's wanting to pee – and there was no way anyone could drag him down. He'd dance up there for a while, and then – flop! – and get a ride to Doctor Vdovin in the emergency van. So this one day, a Tatar came in with his son, and our Dancing Pete's been hanging out on his perch since the start of the shift. When the old Tatar went to work on his son, our guys all split from the steam room, but the loon stayed. Then the old man got done with his kid, and sent him out to the *predbannik*, and set the steam room to his own liking – and that's when our egghead couldn't take it anymore: I tell you, he howled

like the factory siren, and shot down from his birth like an eagle –
whoosh! – straight through the showers and into the pool. A good
fright can make you do just about anything: he gulped a lungful of ice
water, went all goggle-eyed, and, as he was, glasses and all, plopped
there at the bottom like a damned flounder – took three of us to
get him out of there. But now, whenever we think he'd had enough
steam for the day, one of the guys just shouts, "Hey, you up there,
I see your Tatar coming!" and he shoots out of the steam-room like
a bullet. 'Cuz, you know, he could croak on us any day, standing up
there, Doctor Vdovin said so himself – he'd have a heart attack and
wouldn't even know what hit him.

So, what I'm saying is, Tatars are special, and I personally can totally
see things their way. But then, on the other hand, life is life, and you
can't do anything about that either. The Tatars, by the way, had their
women in line longer then everyone else, but they've given up now,
too. The old guard – those still hold strong, but with the young ones
– there was trouble. Take Ravil Nigmattulin with his Gulnara. This
all happened right before I retired from taxi-driving, and Ravil – we
called him Igoryok – only just came to the trade. Ravil's not exactly
a tall guy, but sturdy, you know – big bones, shoulders like a pair of
tires. Only a fool doesn't like good food, and then you sit behind the
wheel all day long – Ravil started getting fat, and the guys talked him
into taking up body-building. He was made for it, too – he was such a
softie, a real teddy bear. He got hooked up with Tolya Kazak, the one
with the striped pants, and started lifting in Tolya's gym. It was only
later I figure out that getting fat wasn't the whole story.

As far as drinking went, he never really did any. Very rarely, once
in a great while he'd have a glass with us on payday – he was afraid of
his Gulnara, and I'm here to tell you, that's how you spoil a woman.
And I'm not just saying so – I was there.

This one time, the guys were parked at the railway station, and I
just came to shoot the breeze with them – I was already retired, and
had gone to work at the banya, been sitting here ever since – when all
of a sudden, we heard a fight. We went to take a look: here's this one

massive dude cleaning up private cabbies like puppies – he'd grab one by the scruff with one hand and slam him on the head with the other, like hammering nails, and go for the next. They're beating on him, but he pays them no mind, just works them over like that: grab, slam, toss, grab, slam, toss. Guys, I yelled, they're beating up our Ravil – let's go help him! I knew he wasn't the kind of guy to get himself into a bind over nothing. I knew it: someone crossed him – asked three times the meter rate when Ravil wanted a ride home, and it's not kosher to rip off your own, folks supposed to look out for each other, any one of us'd give a brother two meters if he could, but you don't ask, it's a matter of honor... But these young punks – they're wolves, never mind they park with us; they have their own rules, especially at night, so they just told him to pay up or beat it.

Long story short, we extricated our Igoryok from the pile, and I took him home – we lived on the same street. But here's the thing: the boy was wasted, drunk as a fish, I've never seen him like this.

When I got him to his gate, Ravil pulled on my sleeve – he wanted to sit down on a bench outside, and you couldn't get away from him if you wanted to, he had an arm like a crankshaft. So we both sat down. Being drunk, he started talking. Turns out, Gulnara works at the furniture factory, and they just made her a section head. So he was out of options: try as he might, fight as he might with other drivers to get the fattest cats, he had no chance of catching up with her. No equality in his family. And for a Tatar – that's worse than a knife under the ribs. Plus, the neighbors started talking that Gulnara had fallen in with some bad women. She, of course, told him that she was late all the time closing out and settling accounts, but he was like: "I don't buy that!" I set him straight: my mother-in-law's sister's daughter works at a store, and is forever stuck there till late with the books, they have to – if they get audited, and something's not right, it's her head on the plate. But this was now, and the day before he decided to teach her a lesson: when she came home late again, Ravil locked the door and wouldn't let her on. She must have heard him inside, though, because she cried a little, whined a bit, and then went ahead and yelled: "Help! He's raping me!" That's no joke – Ravil ran out of the house. That's when she, the fox, snuck in, and locked the door on him – let him sit outside or go sleep in the woodshed.

So alright. He went to the garage, borrowed about two hundred from the guys, bought everyone drinks, drank himself, and now was ready to come home. Only he was afraid to go in: "Brother," he said, "I'm afraid I'll kill her."

"Don't you worry about a thing," I told him. "She is afraid of you herself, and loves you a lot, and respects you, too. Want me to prove it?" Man, you should've seen him – he started kissing me, slobbered all over, such a teddy-bear. I told him to wait there on the bench, and he couldn't be happier: he just rolled his head back and zonked out. And thank God, I thought – I needed him out of my way at the moment. Women, you know, they are all the same, but the Tatars are even more so – she bought into it right off the bat.

First, I knocked on her window – nice and polite. She peeked out.

"Gulnara, open up."

"Who is this?"

"Mikhal Mikhalych from the taxi garage."

"Oh, it's you! Has something happened?"

"Did you or did you not lock your man out of the house?"

She's just standing there, looking. Then I see her face turned stony. That's a good sign.

"Do you know where he is right now?" I asked.

"What happened, Mikhal Mikhalych?"

"You heard of Nelka and Lyubasha? (and everyone in town has) So. That's where he went, your Ravil, and borrowed two hundred rubles from them, to party with their whole crowd, I barely pulled him out of there. Mind you, they let me have it on my word alone – if you wait till tomorrow, it'll be two-fifty, not two hundred even. You know those girls – he's not the first one to get on their hook, and generally speaking, I thought it might not look good if people start talking."

"Oy, Mikhal Mikhalych, how could I ever thank you?"

"You," I said, "just run and fetch me the money."

"Oy, one second."

She dashed off. Brought the money.

"Are you sure this is enough?"

"Sure, sure, don't you worry now. Just, next time, think twice about it."

"But he's the one who started it, being jealous and such."

"If he's jealous, he loves you. You be nicer to him, softer. You girls are all the same – takes a man to teach you how to handle one."

"Oy, thank you, Mikhal Mikhalych, I'll never forget it."

The two of us went out to the bench, and lifted Ravil up to lead him home. You should've seen her leading him in – she rubbed him behind the ear, like a bull-calf, and whispered something to him in their own language, and he just shook his head and smiled in his sleep. Finally we got him to bed. Gulnara, bless her heart, gave me another bottle as a present she was so moved. And ever since then, she always says hello to me whenever she sees me – and she's a big boss now, a director, her earrings alone could buy a Zhiguli.

My Ravil, though, soon quit taxi driving (of course, I gave him his two hundred back the next morning, and we had a good laugh about it) and became a butcher. No sooner did he get ahead in the meat business (and he, by the way, always sold me meat at the government price) as Gulnara outran him again: she got promoted to deputy assistant director. Of a furniture store – a man's job, really, which only made it worse. That's when Ravil challenged this one out-of-town guy to arm-wrestle, right here, in my banya. The other guy warned him that he was the Arm-wrestling Champion of Sverdlovsk, but Ravil wouldn't listen – he's a real game cock. He gave it his best, squeezed as hard as he could – and got hurt. He tore a ligament. Vdovin referred him to a surgeon and banned him from weight-lifting, and Ravil switched to isometrics and working only on the muscle definition. That's tricky business, I'll tell you – if you quit suddenly, you just turn into mush. Long story short, it took six months and three surgeries and a whole ton of money. Finally, they patched his arm back together; it wasn't going to atrophy, but his old strength was gone for good.

And the amazing thing was – through all of this, he didn't turn to drinking. A bear of a man! He went to work at the gas station, with the coop guys, and you know what kind of business that is – I don't have to tell you how they run things. I ran into him once, told him, "Ravilka, quit messing with this bullshit, you'll get in trouble." And he says: "Don't I know it, Uncle Misha, but a man's got to do what a man's got to do," and his eyes were so sad – a teddy-bear, a real teddy-bear. "You," I said to him, "can't ever catch up with the furniture factory. Your only chances are to go apprentice yourself with the Isors[19] with their gems and enamel, but they're kind of like you, Tatars – they only teach their own. Or you have to start a construction co-op, and you don't have the education for that, so I'd say you're better off just to make peace with it and enjoy the ride."

He didn't listen. Instead, life gave him a checkmate. Gulnara eventually made the director and he... he became a sort of a hero.

When the Chechens and the Ossetians came to town and went after the gas stations, Ravil put up a good fight: there were three guys with broken spines on his count, one with a cracked skull (Ravil pulled his hammer number on him with his left fist – he's had time to adjust), and one he dispatched all the way to his brave mountain ancestors. They kept their gas station, but Ravil wound up in court.

I went to his hearing. The room was packed. Chechens on one side, locals on the other. Both sent for lawyers from Moscow, and both, of course, bought the judge and the prosecutors well in advance. Still, no matter how you sliced it, Ravil got five years – they called it self-defense, because the Chechen came at him with knives. A lot of other things came up at that hearing, and a lot of them got swept back under the rug – you know, the way it always goes, we have cases like that about every two years. Folks, of course, were all behind Ravil, except the reporters. Those are forever after the same thing:

---

19. Armenian Assyrians.

"Mafia Brought to Justice!" Make you laugh. And the Chechens, by the way, later bought that gas station anyway.

When they took Ravil away, Gulnara started to wail, but he just shushed at her, like: "Quiet, the boys will take care of you." She choked back her tears.

I saw the way she looked at him when they took him away – the same as back then, when she was leading him up the steps to the porch, but he – oh no! – he went out proud, like a big bear. He finally beat her, that he did. You don't worry about guys like that in the camps: they'll make him a barrack boss for his biceps alone, and then there's his legend – how he worked over those Chechens. And then there is Gulnara's money – on the inside, money is everything.

LADY MACBETH

That's it. She's had it. She's started saving up pills.

She's heard women say police never do autopsies on drunkards. And even if there were one, it's no proof: maybe he swallowed the pills himself. People imbibe all kinds of junk these days. A handful – and he's done.

She's made up her mind and started saving up the pills the doctor prescribed for her when she got out of detox last time.

How'd that come about? Well, he'd been drinking and living his high life for a few months, half-a-year maybe. Not a penny of his wages made it home. That day he came in already loaded, naturally, and it was his payday, she knew his schedule. All right. Dang it, she just had to have this bright idea to get him even more addled and then trick whatever was left of the money out of him. Pull it out of his pocket if she had to. She poured him some, and, the idiot, had one herself – for her nerves. He got woozy all right, but she lost it a bit too. So when she asked, "Where's the money?" he just started laughing, and then swung at her. She called the police. Well, by the time they got there the son of a bitch had his teeth brushed, and his head freshly washed under the shower, and as soon as they rang the doorbell, he grabbed a pot of pea-soup from the stove and flipped it onto his head. The police comes in and he's standing there hollering, "Help me guys, she's blinded me!"

Who? What? How? No one believed her.

"Did you drink?" they asked.

She said she did.

"The man brings you money, what else do you want, stupid?"

She looked: there was the money, on top of the fridge – he managed to lay it out for the cops. She screamed. Something possessed her – she shook and almost threw up – and he just went on with his show, groaning and moaning under the pot. She kept screaming, and screamed at the whole lot of them, as it turned out, enough to land her in the slammer for fifteen days.

Her mother took little Seryozha to stay with her, of course. When she got out, the walls were bare: he'd sold everything and drank through the money. There he was, waiting for her on the couch, grinning:

"Shall we start a new life or what?"

Her knees buckled under her... she fell onto her knees and wailed, and such love came over them both as they hadn't had since the days when they were making their little Vasya.

Vasya was how it all started. He ran out into the street and got run over by a car. And he was gone, on a trip for work. Her neighbors, kindly souls, made sure he knew she had a party that day – 'twas her girlfriend's birthday. And that was it. He beat her – he beat her a lot, and cursed her, then started drinking.

And what about her? She was the mother, was she not grieved? She had to live with her guilt. She had to live with the memory of it – but wasn't there supposed to be forgiveness in the world somewhere? She was ready to beg for it, do whatever it took when she came out of the detox.

He's not a man any more – a wild beast from the forest has more heart. And little Seryozha is growing up and watching all this. In the evenings they sit together behind the locked door – she's got two locks, a guy from work put them in for her – and there he is, banging on the door, yelling, "I'll kill you!" He's started stalking her too. And anything she ever does is a crime. And she's ruined his life.

No, this has to stop. She's made up her mind – she's saving up the pills. He's an alcoholic – she is scared. Men like that – how many people have they killed already? And children too. "Let's sell the flat and live apart," she said. Nope, no go. He doesn't come to sleep with her, but wants to know her every step anyway. And how can she sleep if he's at the door every damn night... She's not 20 anymore.

After her detox, he toed the line for a week. He was like before. Then they went to the movies on Sunday and had a bit of champagne after. That was it. He hasn't been dry since.

If she'd turn him in to the LTP – he'd kill her.[20] She's afraid of him. She can't forget what she did. She has to live with that. Girls said, screw it, find someone new, let the new guy beat him up. But, how to put it? It's not about beating him up. The guy who put in the locks for her – he didn't do it for free, but bumming from man to man like that... it's not what she's after. She's got to stop it once and for all. Autopsy, or no autopsy – she's got to do it.

Just yesterday, he barely made it – crawled up to her door and lay there breathing, stinking of burnt rubber – they must be getting high on formaldehyde glue. No, she's got to do it!

In the middle of night she woke up; at first, she couldn't tell what was happening. He was screaming, howling – she thought, it was the usual thing, but then he fell out into the hallway, she took one look at him and – Lord Almighty! She called the ambulance. They pumped his stomach, but it was no good – he'd drunk acetic acid concentrate. He had some in a vodka bottle under his bed. The doctors decided he'd drunk it by mistake, but she knew better – he'd been threatening to do it for a long time. So he made good on his threat – and she didn't have to use the pills.

But at the funeral, when the priest said to say goodbye, the girls couldn't pull her away from the coffin – she was screaming. Steam trains used to scream like that when she was little – it was frightful to hear them up close.

---

20. LTP stands for "Labor therapy preventative clinic," a variety of Soviet penal institution which basically amounted to a forced-labor detox facility.

FORTRESS

Through the thin air of an early morning, through the city drenched in sunlight, down its streets flush with the new greenery of cottonwoods and lindens, among sparse pedestrians, moves a small man. He is not young, but neither is he old enough that one could call him "grandpa." More than any physical signs of age, it is his appearance that ages him – a look he adopted once and has stuck to ever since, having fixed it in his peculiar clothes: a small gray hat, wrinkled but donned carefully and handled lovingly, like an adopted mutt in a lonely home. Then – a pair of glasses with special lenses: barely concave, and with thick glass disks cut into the middle – and his eyes behind them, washed out with work, eyes that sometimes look gullible but more often detached, almost haughty in their refusal to focus on the quotidian. Lower lies the collar of the man's thick, unseasonably warm coat, with a thick belt and a fat black button that locks the mighty gates of this worsted fortress. Lower still are trousers that lack any conclusive personality, and heavy boots of the ugly stitched variety cranked out by the local factory. A brown briefcase in his hand.

Thus he moves, through a spring-time city, as if completely oblivious to the kind of pure beauty that descends on it only once a year, this armored little man – because he does not walk, not at all, he has to move, to heft and roll. He is a fortress, walled off and locked to the outside world not because he does not give a damn about it, but, it seems, because, having once detached himself from this world, he sees himself as having very little to do with it. He advances with a slight forward tilt – not like a man bent down by illness or frailty, but rather like someone fighting against a strong wind: his work sitting daily behind a desk has given him this shape.

The little man bears right from the bridge, past The Young Sailors Club, through the back alley of Public Bathhouse No. 1, through stacks of the brewery's old crates, until he makes his way to the five-domed Church of Jacob and Anna, "on the gorges." He climbs to the gallery, pushes the heavy door of the city archives open, enters and greets the guard.

Pavel Anatolyevich Ogorodnikov always arrives 20 minutes before the start of the workday. He takes off his coat neatly and hangs it on a hanger in the wardrobe. He remains in a checkered jacket, worn over a checked flannel shirt closed at the throat with a solid tie with a pin. Then he puts on his over-sleeves. He pulls out his pencils and pens, his razor and his pen-knife, his sharpener and his erasers – the red one with powdered glass and the gray Coh-i-nor one with the tiny mammoth on it, his black-ink fountain pen, and a second one exactly like the first – a spare, just in case. Then: a light switch clicks; a green-shaded desk lamp comes on, as it always does, even on a bright spring day, even in the middle of the stuffy Stargorod summer: Pavel Anatolyevich's nook is walled off from the archive's shelves with large oak wardrobes moved here from the diocesan offices in March of 1919. He flexes and warms his fingers. He sits down to his desk, pushes his chair in, nice and tight, and takes the first folder from the pile on his right: opens it, leafs through, counts pages, checks the count against the last inventory. Then he studies it closer – he savors it, reads it, moving his lips along the more rhythmic formulas: "And by the order of our lord the Tsar it was decreed to carry out such acts in perpetuity..." or "and the cannoneers' children, should they resist learning and despise letters, to be found and, at first, warned with ferocity," or "by the mercy of God and through your Lordship's blessed governance this was so done. And I, your humblest servant, do now have the honor of laying this petition at your Lordship's feet," or "a Pyramid is a Body, sometimes dense and sometimes vacant inside, with a base that is broad and commonly of four corners, ending on top in a pinnacle." Who can write like that today?

Denunciations, personal letters, complaints, writs, chits, suggestions for the benefit of the Motherland, accounting sheets, traveling papers, indignant epistles by the wrongfully righteous and reports on the progress of long-forgotten construction projects, notations to thunderous speeches delivered at an unknown date to an unknown audience, sometimes put down by the skillful hand of a professional scribe and sometimes in a amateur's scrawl, a myriad of loops, squiggles and apostrophes – for Pavel Anatolyevich there are no secrets here. There is a special kind of bliss in this, a beauty – of the language itself perhaps, or maybe of the scribe's penmanship – it doesn't matter really! The cursives, the capitals, the cinnabar savers. Somewhere outside, a day was on its way, but here he was surrounded by beauty.

"To learn how various countries and kingdoms, into which the universe is divided, had come to be; by what means and steps they had reached the grandeur we behold in our reading of history, and into what kind of union did families and cities have to join in order to form a single body and live collectively under a single authority, obeying common laws, one must return, so to speak, to the days of our world's infancy, to the time when people scattered all over after the separation of tongues and began to fill the Earth."

Reading that, how could you not start thinking about the days of our world's infancy, about the immense base of an Egyptian pyramid that does, on top, "end in a pinnacle"?

He thinks about these things in passing, because his hand never rests, but continues to make entries in the ledger without pause: the hand's hard at work on the archive's inventory; the hand pencils in page numbers on unnumbered pages and binds loose leaves together; it holds up the paper to the light so that the eye can discern the watermark; and it can note, "Lipsia, 1785, Crown and Cross," and he can pull up the main index, which he knows by heart, and yes, there is already a folder for this case! His hand fills the appropriate cell in the record – quartern – his creaking pen draws its own loops, fixes, records once again forever, and only at the very bottom of the record will he add a few squiggles for "entered by P. A. Ogorodnikov." Personally, he would have preferred not to do even that – he long ago conquered the youthful vanity of all neophytes.

He too had once been a neophyte, a student at the local Pedagogical Institute who looked around and could not see a place for himself in the world; he didn't know it then, but he was looking for diocesan wardrobes and the worsted coat he would wear until his penniless archivist's final days. But this is now, and that was then. Back then, he was assigned to the archives for his summer practicum, and the ancient gnome Tsvetonravov, who came from a long line of priest's children, pointed his withered finger at the paper landslides produced by the Red Army in the same 1919 and said: "Here. This – is work!" Pavel Anatolyevich (nobody addressed him that way back then) began to dig; he wanted to make a discovery. A breakthrough! An accomplishment! But Tsvetonravov chastised him: "You must proceed in order; what have they done to you to be tossed around like that?" 'They' were the cases. Pavel Anatolyevich obeyed and, once he sat down at his desk, never really got up again, except, people seem to remember, when he stepped out to get married and the second time – to bring his baby daughter home from the hospital. But home was his second fortress, if not the third, the archive being his first, and his coat the second.

Here, behind the shelves and the wardrobes, a new zeal took over – the zeal of a keeper and a preserver, and with it came a different vanity – not the kind that is common among academic historians who are seriously convinced that they are, in fact, revealing the truth – but the pride of the expert that is nourished by imagination. Life among dead sounds caught on paper became joyful and sweet like the delicacies that he found sometimes in dull inventories: "four *tesha* sturgeons, a side of hausen, assorted salted fish – two large barrels, dried raisins, Gilan millet (meaning, imported rice), ginger, cinnamon bark." This was a monastery kitchen's ration. He remembers the same monastery's inventory, compares it mentally with the order's charter, and he can almost see it: early morning, the novices are building fires under the cauldrons in the kitchen, the sky is just turning pink, it is spring... Pavel Anatolyevich is interrupted: a scholar from Leningrad is asking for help. She is writing a history of Stargorod's fortifications and is trying to find the city inventory conducted after the fire of 1724. Pavel Anatolyevich looks up from his work – his eyes look gullible at the moment, they regard his petitioner kindly. "Just a minute, just a minute..."

He gets up, walks away between the towering shelves, pulls out a drawer, runs his finger over the catalog cards as though over the strings of a giant instrument or a fat stack of banknotes. He pulls one out. He reads. It's simple now: the scholar can take the card to circulation, and they will bring her the case that, Pavel Anatolyevich remember, had to do with the burnt out settlements beyond Kopanka, with the destruction of the city's moat and the newly-paved Pozagorodnaya Street. Of course, of course: the moat then was overrun with weeds and the water in it stood "mainly rotten," and "it wasn't good to take that water even to water the orchards." He turns back before the scholar is finished thanking him. The man in the over-sleeves walks back to his desk – with his thinning hair, his forward bent as if he is struggling against a gale, and his shuffling, heavy soles. The scholar hurries in the other direction, to the circulation desk, where she may strike up a conversation with the girls about the televised debates, or perhaps will just wait until they bring her the records to spread out before her and stare out the window until she is either too tired or too lazy to stay awake.

Pavel Anatolyevich walks between the empty desks in the reading room – how many eccentrics out there, really, spend their time on Stargorod's history? He is lost in his own thoughts, lost to his world, when suddenly he catches a teary gaze and the rest of the apparition before him: fuzzy, helpless. He changes course and approaches the apparition's desk, quickly. A very young student holds out a sheet of paper, "I'm sorry, I can't make out any of it... Could you possibly?.."

"Just a minute, just a minute."

Pavel Anatolyevich holds the document closer to light and immediately begins reading, "By the order of the Great Tsar, the Lord of all Russia, Great, Small and White..."

He reads without pauses, but steadily, as if reading a newspaper for a blind man. The student tries to write it down, can't keep up, fidgets, and finally throws his pencil down on his notebook.

"No, it's just too hard! It's impossible."

"Nothing of the sort, young man, just the common shorthand of seventeenth century scribes."

"But these are hieroglyphs – they don't even look like letters!"

"Of course they are hieroglyphs, and rather beautiful ones. You'll get used to them, don't worry, it's just a matter of practice. Let's go again from the beginning..."

Ogorodnikov reads again, slowly now, making sure the student can write everything down. Finally, it is done.

"Thank you, thank you so much! I have just one more little text here, could you..."

"I'm afraid I can't, young man, I do have other things to do, you know," he says, looking haughty now and walks away from the student's desk, shuffles steadily back to his corner. He thinks, if the boy really wants to know, he'll figure it out – he's got enough written down to compare, to decipher the shorthand and start reading. And if he can't – he shouldn't be here anyway.

A minute later he is back at his own desk, working again.

Pavel Anatolyevich Ogorodnikov – a small fortress of a man – sits behind a big solid desk. Look at him: his over-sleeves, and his boots, and his glasses in their impossible black frame, and his briefcase of the kind no one carries anymore – everything about him is fundamentally permanent. Could this be why the archive's girls, who forever dream of happy, romantic love, dote on him so movingly at lunch? He chews his sandwich, stirs the tea in his glass with an aluminum spoon, and when they ask him, tells them one of his peculiar stories, like the one about coronet Savelyev who was so desperately in love with the merchant's daughter Pilgina that he shot himself in the White Tower when she turned him down. The girls listen, unblinking, hanging on his every word. Who would have thought such things were possible? Pavel Anatolyevich does.

Then they go back to their respective corners. The girls scurry between the stacks and the reading room, pushing carts loaded with case folders, books and microfilm boxes, chat with rare visitors; he works. "Feed inventory for the 4th Royal Guard Uhlan division quartered in Anninskaya Sloboda," another one – from the following year, "The case of Coronet Sergeyev's lost rapier," "Note by widow Vechtomova about her degraded situation due to the non-payment of her dead husband's pension," and more things like that, gray and trifling, a litany of complaints, cowering petitions, the usual fervent Russian begging laced with despair and abandonment. And all of it local, Stargorodian. The city, the town but a tiny dot on a large map, yet there are so many cases, so many files have piled on in the stacks and there is no one but Pavel Anatolyevich to take up the tedious work of sorting through them.

The work day is over. Pavel Anatolyevich neatly collects his pens, pencils, erasers, his penknife and his razors, dusts off his desk and nods his goodbye to the girls as they dash out ahead of him. He pulls on his heavy coat, seals himself behind its massive buttons, and steps out to the gallery of St. Jacob and Anna's little church that's "on the gorges." A long time ago there was a grove of trees here. Later, when the plague came – a cemetery with a tiny temporary wooden chapel, and later still they built the five-domed church. He does not walk past the brewery, oh no – he is walking down the non-existent rows of the Klykov merchant family, past the old fish market, over the three-span oak bridge with heavy breakwaters, and on through Potters' Corner. And if someone should think that this little man in his coat is oblivious to the charms of spring, if someone should judge that "the briefcase guy" does not breathe as fully and joyfully as the judge himself, the judge would be wrong, very wrong indeed. Although sometimes it is true that one's own joy can make one completely blind to the world, and the joy of others seems all but repulsive, and one does not want to share this momentary, private bliss with anyone else, well then, there's nothing wrong with that, is there?

Pavel Anatolyevich has gotten hungry. Against his will, he stumbles into the wonderful prose of life – he begins to daydream about the hot borsch and the potato pancakes with mushroom sauce that his wife makes so well. He enjoys an affectionate home, where the best of dinner is always set aside to wait for him.

His gaze is still distant, aloof, his eyes almost haughty in their refusal to focus on the quotidian.

METAMORPHOSES, OR THE ART OF INSTANT TRANSFORMATION

For A. Arkhangelsky

Let me spin a tale for you, a fable like in the old days, one to delight and amuse. Let me sweet-talk you – only give me kindly of your time and do cast your gaze upon this piece of paper I have filled with ink. I promise that you will marvel at the transformations of fates and of the human forms themselves, and at their return, by same miraculous means, back to their original state. I shall begin.

But who am I, you'll ask. Listen then: our name is the Lyamochkins. I am a Stargorodian, a son of a Stargorodian, and a grandson of a Stargorodian's grandson, and very few of us remain these days. Captured for a while by Moscow, I studied there at the Moscow State University in the Department of History, pursuing the thoroughly forgotten Lucius Apuleius.[21] Here in Stargorod I now labor at the local paper, although back then people expected a great future for me, a great future indeed. But that is all in the past; now I am just making regular progress up the career ladder, and Filimonov even let it slip recently that he might make me his Executive Secretary. That would be logical: I am meek and clever. But I am a Stargorodian, born and raised, flesh and blood, I am Lyamochkin who writes his tales sometimes and puts them in his desk drawer – I have a fancy to compile a chronicle of my generation. Thus, first and foremost I beg you not to take offense should you find in my crude prose some folksy turns-of-phrase and foreign words. A shifting dialect does

---

21. Lucius Apuleius (died December 100 BC) was a Roman popularist and tribune.

befit, when you think about it, the art of instant transformation, and the latter is my single and most compelling subject. Metamorphoses – or perhaps, fate itself. I do begin. Lend me your ears, reader, and let me please you.

* * *

It's not that long ago that they made me head of a department, and Filimonov announces, "Do hustle tomorrow. Tomorrow we are going to pick up comrade Karponos at the railway station. I want you there early. Before. Half-an-hour before the train pulls in."

All right. I run. I take flight. I curse my fate as I rush, but I obey – though it is Thursday, I've got work to do, and instead I must stand here, wait, greet: Karponos is an auditor, come all the way from Moscow to inspect us. Is it good I've been included? I don't know. I really don't – I rather think it's bad. Before, I only heard of these meetings in passing, but now that I've climbed higher – here I am, they bring me along. And thank God for that. I run. I fly. I curse the day I was born – I'm embarrassed.

But. The sleeping car pulls up. First, a Gut emerges. A Pot. A Cauldron. Everyone's on the platform now affecting great liveliness, only I'm bent over under the luggage, silent. They do bring me around to shake hands – I'm the last one. The driver takes up a couple suitcases. The Volga rolls away towards the dacha, our van – with its death rattle – hangs back. We've got someone else to pick up: the city's head architect, naturally, Ilya Semyonovich Razkin, then the unions – Boris Borisovich Draftin, the city administration – Bobchinov, district committee – Dobychin, and so on down the list. Filimonov is in charge of the list; our boss rides in the Volga with comrade Karponos. They must be sitting down to dinner already, and we're still making rounds, still fetching people: Alimzharov – the market, Eaglov – the furniture factory, Patrikeyeva... Wait a second! Who's this Patrikeyeva? Oh, it's Patrikeyev – the gathering is men only. Pardon me – he is tiny, small-boned, and a leather coat obscures his shape. He is the bank. Is that all? All. Off we go then – to the pier.

"Where's the Armenian?"

"Suren Biglyarovich? He's already on the boat – grilling *shashlyk*."

Suren Biglyarovich is our independent retailer.

And here we are at the boat, and it's moored off the main pier, by the Fishing Guard motor-boats. This way, the tourists won't notice us, and they've got better things to do anyway – it's summer, it's Thursday, it's a beautiful day, who wants to poke around with the Fishing Guard?

We climb the boardwalk. The Boss is right there – a one-man receiving line.

"Lyamochkin? Didn't your father work at the printing shop?"

"Yes, sir!"

"Look at you now! The new guard. Why don't you go to the galley, given Suren a hand with the *shashlyk*."

Shashlyk. More *shashlyk*. Onions and tomatoes. Lamb shoulder.

"Sweetie, why vinegar? Marinate in cognac, vinegar ruins it."

The *shashlyk* is divine.

"Let's go, boys!"

We take the food to the deck. It smells! It oozes! Some dill, a salad. Sliced lemon for those who want some.

And the little steamer's pretty as a picture: blinds are down over the portholes, no one can see in.

I sit off to the side, alone, and gorge quietly on my *shashlyk*. I've eaten too much already, but I keep wanting more – it's so good! My face and hands are soiled with fat. I keep my mouth shut – I love a good *shashlyk*.

The toasts wind down – it's time for the banya. A real Finnish sauna right here on the boat! Now, that's a wow!

"Come on, come on down everybody – don't upset your Boss!"

Men shoot the breeze on the benches. Comrade Karponos shares news from the capital; Patrikeyev farts inappropriately. He blushes. Men hoot. I'm embarrassed.

And now we're back to the deck – in our swimming trunks. "The Pot" is pink as a piglet and steaming. Someone squeals with delight. Someone is talking up the pleasures of Stargorod's river. Men egg on the fat Razkin – jump, here, overboard, cannon-ball. It's deep here, the water's clean. Here, on the Senga, on a channel no one will bother you – you can be sure of that. Once in a great while some idiot sails by, but they rarely come here.

And suddenly – it comes, from around the bend – the stench! A pair of muddy, stinking Stargorodian scows covered in clay dirt – smoky, tarred, fishing nets dangling in oily balls, and on the decks piles of fish guts, rot, fry. The stench! Everyone turns away, only I stare. I know what you have to do to get that fish. The fishermen, as if on command, turn away to hide their alcoholics' noses, and only the man at the wheel stares back at me, steady and vicious. Not a gleam, not a spark in his eye. I am embarrassed, scared.

* * *

"Lyamochkin, wake up! Lyamochkin, the day's over. What are you supposed to say to that, Lyamochkin? You're supposed to say, 'And to hell with it!'"

It's Timofeyev from the Letters Department, the eternal drill sergeant. Lyamochkin stretches, wipes off a bit of spit from the corner of his mouth – less than a drop, really, more a perspiration, the sweet drool of a midday nap. Did anyone notice? And if they did, who cares! He waves, at no one in particular, and heads for the street door. Some dreams, man! Sometimes you don't want to know where they come from.

Lyamochkin goes straight to the beer stand – to have a mug or two, shoot the breeze, maybe hear a story. In advance, he prudently takes off his tie. He sips his beer. He listens.

"That Potyekha, son of a bitch, did he fuck up today or what! Captain's on vacation – you ain't getting no fish. Potyekha's in charge. Made us haul ass all the way to Senga, the knuckle-dragger, to this side channel – and there's fish alright, but you ain't getting it, except maybe with a trammel. Thought I'd sprain something for sure, but we got it all pulled up – and what did we get there? A load of thorny coontails! We dragged right over it – twisted our nets nice and tight."

"Coontails? Gramps used to say, they fed it to goats after the war."

"Gramps? You just go on and listen to that old fart – he's the biggest mouth for miles," the story-teller says before turning around and sizing up Lyamochkin. The man's dull eyes are pure beer – not a single spark glows there. The beer pushes him; it pushes him towards Lyamochkin. A fork-like paw shoots out, grabs Lyamochkin's lapel and reels him in, like a boat's propeller spooling weed.

"What are you... staring at? Huh?"

"All right, just take it easy, man," Lyamochkin says. He knows how to deal with these types.

"What are you now? Who'd you think you are? You from around here? I fish, dude, I am a man, you get it? And what are you now?"

Suddenly, Lyamochkin recognizes him – recognizes his eyes, the same eyes he'd seen across the channel – and gets scared. That's bad, that's really bad – he cannot be scared now. That's the worst thing he can do. Lyamochkin makes a step back; he's in trouble.

✳ ✳ ✳

Filimonov comes to visit him in the hospital. He arrives; he congratulates Lyamochkin on having been approved for the promotion to Executive Secretary, and inconspicuously slips a glass flask of cognac under his pillow.

"So you can celebrate."

He then proudly places a pair of lemons on the bedside table – greetings from sunny Greece. ("Konstantidi Georgius" read the tiny, bright stickers, the name lettered carefully in minuscule brown script, sharp and dark, as if inked with the pure oak sap. Now, that's a transformation!)

It's a shame he doesn't have his wings here, but it's all right, he can manage, he'll just have to try harder. Lyamochkin closes his eyes – and his broken jaw does not hurt anymore: he is far away already, in distant and sunny Greece. This is his personal secret. He flies away light and quick, and returns healthy and full of energy.

But being an Executive Secretary is a dog's work – you get heckled from all sides, and there's never a break from it. You're up to your ears in meetings, strategic planning, reporting, budgeting, schedules, complaints, people ratting on each other, people backstabbing – and it's all you. Still, Filimonov knew what he was doing when he picked Lyamochkin to be elevated. Lyamochkin took to the job; he began to shine. Carved out his own niche. Spread his roots. Bought himself a new mug for tea, bigger than the old one, and a cast iron ashtray with the image of a hound dog, a set of fountain pens and an electronic Smena watch. Strange as it may sound, everyone came to love him. That is, everyone to the last man. Only his wife at home knows what it's cost him – how hard it's been. But it's always hard. And not everyone knows how to get things done.

Lyamochkin returns to his pantry-sized bedroom, pulls out his old wings from the wardrobe – washed by his wife countless times in a special tub, white swan wings that he inherited from his grandfather, who picked them up for a dime in a tavern somewhere in Galicia in 1915 – puts them on right over his tshirt and flies out the window.

In a suburb of Rome, maybe perched on a pier facing the deserted sea, or perhaps on the deck of an ancient, creaky galley, seated on a spool of rope on the stern, hidden from prying eyes, Lyamochkin unfolds his scroll. Lyamochkin reads; he recites the lines out loud: "Some things are in a haste to become; others – to cease; even in the becoming, a flame is extinguished; change and the flow of things keep the world young exactly as limitless time is eternally young in its every speeding instance. Thus, how could one admire any of a myriad things flowing past in this river any more than another, if one cannot even stand close enough to touch it? It would be the same as to give one's heart to a fleeting sparrow – a blink, and the bird's gone, never to be found again..." Lyamochkin contemplates. No, he cannot agree with this... yet he also can. But how could you not love a sparrow? A tweet – and it's gone!

Yet it stays. It is here. Lyamochkin writes. Another fable, a tidbit of a story, a morsel of news to be fixed in his thick, clothbound notebook. It has room to spare for sparrows, of course, and it's true: up and down fly the swings of time, but the motion is not the reward, the merit is elsewhere – in the miraculous transformations he re-lives alone.

✻ ✻ ✻

His wife calls him to the table; the family gathers for a late dinner. Ivanov and his wife stop by – they are friends and neighbors. From a fogged-over bottle, Lyamochkin pours thick, lazily flowing vodka infused with the peel of Greek lemons. Then – clink! – and he bites a pickle, crunches it loudly with his teeth. Ivanov tells a joke; the women laugh.

He is at the same paper, the same editorial office still – the unhurried, thoughtful Lyamochkin who can sometimes be as restless as a sparrow in springtime, our Lyamochkin, the irreplaceable one. He is no longer afraid of anything; sometimes he goes to the station to receive important visitors, then rattles all over town in the decrepit editorial van, picking up other banya fans. More often, though, he finds an excuse to stay behind at the office.

And if he doesn't stay late there, drinking countless cups of tea with the guy responsible for closing the issue, and if he manages to get everything on his list done early, Lyamochkin heads out to the beer stand. To get a mug or two, to shoot the breeze, to hear a story perhaps. He goes there with his tie on; he never takes it off now. He sips his beer, smokes his cigarette, and, unembarrassed about his advancing boldness, looks with a quiet joy at each passerby.

VLADIK KUZNETSOV

Stargorodians are a special tribe. While it is unlikely that anyone has ever taken it upon themselves to determine the exact number of emigrants from Stargorod, it is well known that Moscow and Leningrad are constantly receiving large numbers of former Stargorodians, and one can reasonably believe this process to have begun long before the Great October Revolution. Later, the flow of Stargorodians increased quite a bit in the aftermath of the Great Patriotic War, which significantly curtailed our ancient town's native population. But it feels unseemly to talk about it; after all, the whole country knew of Stargorodians' heroism – among the likes of Lyonya Golikov and Marat Kasey, young pioneers everywhere revered Billyakhut Maxuddinova, whose deeds on the Black Shore of the lake won her first a Hero of the Soviet Union star and later an honorable seat at the Professional Unions' Association of the Russian Federation.

Indeed, we should not talk about those whose faces are familiar to every schoolchild; let us rather turn to the unknown and the forgotten. Their name is legion, and restoring their memory is an honorable pursuit, undertaken, in particular, by the Red Scouts of School No. 2 of Stargorod's Left-bank district. Their displays present for public consumption much that is instructive and curious; hence we shall refer any members of the public who find themselves at leisure and with an interest in local history to the modest, cottonwood-shaded building of the school on Vera Zasulich street.

We, however, shall tell a tale of another hero – a hero of our own time.

The old man Kuznetsov was still young when he broke away from the despicable world of Stargorod's pre-revolutionary stockyards into which he'd been born, and signed up for the Red Army. From that distant but romantic period of his life, he retained for the rest of his days a special affection for the color green, discipline and the principle of unitary authority as embodied in the chain of command. Kuznetsov retired into the rank of an infantry Colonel, felt no desire to return to his forgotten hometown of Stargorod, and instead was perfectly happy to settle in the small town of Lyubertsy, where the garrison allotted him an apartment, to be used in perpetuity by Kuznetsov and his descendants. History has not preserved any information as to the whereabouts of the old man's only daughter, Svetlana, lost to the immense expanse of our land; one could well have doubted the very fact of said daughter's existence, were it not for little Vladik, left in his grandparents' care. Grandmother Kuznetsova died a mere three weeks before her grandson's high school graduation, and was buried in the Lyubertsy town cemetery without a church service – something her husband, the old Red Army veteran insisted upon. Vladik, who was considered a wunderkind in the school, was deeply affected by his grandmother's death, but nonetheless graduated with the Gold Medal which, combined with his unimpeachable proletarian pedigree, gave him a free pass to the alma mater – the History Department at Moscow State University named for Mikhail Lomonosov.

Much like the provincial boy who lent his name to the university, Vladik Kuznetsov arrived at the department in humble attire: he wore sturdy green pants that looked like they'd been re-cut from his grandfather's, an army-issue officer's shirt without shoulder straps but with two capacious pockets filled with sharpened pencils, a fountain pen with regulation black ink, a thick plastic comb and a military-discount railway pass for the Moscow-Lyubertsy line. Unlike his more comfortable local classmates, Vladik lived on his 55-ruble stipend (which included a 15-ruble bonus for his perfect grades) and had a crystal clear idea of what he wanted. While the

snobs around him debauched themselves in decadent luxury and
skipped classes, instead laying siege to the One-Armed Man pub,
Vladik methodically studied Latin and prepared to write his thesis on
Cato the Elder and his tract *De Agri Cultura*.

Many readers, of course, will be familiar with this work as well
as the biography of its author, a luminary of Ancient Rome. For
those whom circumstances have prevented, thus far, from reading
Cornelius Nepos' *Excellentium Imperatorum Vitae* or Plutarch's *Lives*,
we offer here the plain but exhaustive entry from the *Great Soviet
Encyclopedia* (2nd edition, v. 20, p. 383):

Cato, Marcus Porcius (not to be confused with Marcus Porcius Cato
Uticensis, commonly known as Cato the Younger) (234-149 BC)
– one of the great Roman politicians and writers. He came from a
wealthy plebeian family, from the city of Tusculum. In 199 BC was
elected Aedile, in 198 BC – Praetor to Spain where he suppressed
an uprising of the local tribes. During the war with the Syrian King
Antioch III, C. secured for his countrymen the victory in the 191 BC
battle at Thermopylae (not to be confused with the one fought by
King Leonid and 300 Spartans). In 184 BC, he was elected Censor.
Once in a Senatorial position, C. defended the aristocracy and its
privileges; he held significant real estate and liquid assets. C. became
the voice of those nobles who had made the transition to new forms of
estate management by organizing large, slave-labor-based latifundia
aimed at producing surplus for the marketplace. All his actions
aimed at promoting an active foreign policy and the expansion of the
Roman conquests. C. advocated for destroying Carthage – Rome's
major trade competitor. Being, at the same time, a representative of
conservative views, he introduced strict anti-luxury laws and fought
the growing influence of the Greek culture.

C. is also a major figure of Ancient Roman prose. He was fluent
in Greek and well acquainted with Greek culture, in particular the
works of Thucydides and Xenophon. C.'s most significant work was
The Origins, which relates the history not only of Rome but also

of other Latin cities. Of his many speeches, only fragments have survived. The tract *De Agri Cultura* is another complete work; it contains fundamental information about contemporary economy and agriculture.

We shall admit that we were not among the lucky few who had an opportunity to leaf through the young historian Kuznetsov's thesis; rather, we watched from the shadows. We cheered from the sidelines. Kuznetsov's work (415 pages long!) drew immediate attention from the department's senior professoriate and, submitted to the contest for student research, rightly won Vladik first place and a special gift: a copy of Edward Gibbon's *Decline and Fall of the Roman Empire*, which was widely available in bookstores at the time. In any case, we are not in a position to judge the merit of Vladik's work, but we do know for certain, from Vladik's close friends, that no work of such length, exhaustiveness, and, most importantly, elegance – nothing written in such a vivid, lively, elegant style so uncommon among our homegrown historians – has been produced by a student ever since the department's founding. People saw a great future for Vladik; the old Latin professor, Dr. Troitsky, recognized Vladik publicly, before the entire class that had so much trouble memorizing *Exegi monumentum* (*The Odes of Horace*, book 3), for his virtuosic command of the toothache-inducing but eminently useful Latin. "*Ab uno disce omnes*" (from one, learn all) Vladik's classmates said in the hallways, expressing their respect. "*Quidquid Latine dictum sit altum videtur*" (anything said in Latin seems more profound) Vladik answered, dazzling the class with his erudition and blushing ferociously.

We don't know whether Vladik's hero, Marcus Porcius Cato, also possessed the gift of turning his countenance a healthy rosy color at the drop of a hat, but he can be presumed, with a great degree of certainty, to have undergone physical training of the same exacting standards as Vladik's. The young Kuznetsov, who has been taught that every man is a master of his fate, and that *mens sana in corpore sano*, followed every prescription of the old Colonel to the letter, and these, rumor had it, included running six miles every day in full combat gear, which in peacetime was replaced by a special set of bricks loaded into a backpack on Vladik's back. It was clear that Vladik intended to live, like his Ancient Roman hero, to be eighty-five – no more, no less.

Gaining a certain degree of fame among his classmates did nothing to check Vladik's passionate pursuit of achievement. Even his appearance – his very image as the fans of Western borrowings would call it – dramatically set Kuznetsov apart from the rest of his jeans-wearing, sloppy-looking cohort. Always trim, although not at all tall; always in perfectly ironed grandfather's trousers and a clean shirt with a narrow officer's tie, with his hair cropped short, and with a pair of plain, wire-rimmed glasses and his unchanging fake-leather briefcase of immense capacity, even in winter Vladik did not wear anything that was not absolutely necessary. Once, during the ferocious frosts of '75, he was seen in a simple gray sport coat with neatly stitched leather elbow patches.

During the annual September trip to the vegetable warehouse, where the students were used as cheap labor to help with the harvest, Vladik always stood post at the packing machine, and while others found countless excuses to go check the fruit room, he spent his shift filling sacks with wet potatoes, the sight of which invariably prompted him to lament the poor storage conditions and, sometimes, express his personal, deeply held belief:

"My grandfather," he might say to a really close friend, "did not fight the war so that some little thief from Armenia could nickel-and-dime the Empire."

The warehouse manager, as chance would have it, was a stunningly handsome Armenian who got his start in the History Department in Yerevan, but later traded his humanitarian bona fides for a Moscow degree in Food Technology.

"All my friends are now PhDs," he would tell the students. "But I've no regrets. I've been here three years – and I'm driving my third car."

We must also mention that, back in those archaic times – the mid-70s – even the most critically-minded students who may have been reading *The Gulag Archipelago* on the sly and occasionally tuned in, for lack of better things to do, to the Voice of America broadcasts, were not nearly as politicized as they are today. Sure, you could easily tell who was opposed to the regime, but things never went beyond a political joke or two. Neither were Moscow's suburbs as stratified and divided as they have become: Lyubertsy, for example, was yet to produce its famous tribe of body-builders. We do believe – and let it be noted that we are the first to formulate this historical hypothesis – that it was Vladik Kuznetsov himself who planted the seed of this Schwarzenegger movement on one particular occasion, especially when one recalls that, in addition to running, Vladik also lifted weights according to a unique method developed, again, by his legendary grandfather.

The occasion was this. Vladik was always gallant. He was gallant to a fault and without any ulterior motives. One night, he and a friend were going home after classes, and came upon the following unattractive scene next to the Dawn movie theater: A gorilla from among the local thugs who even back then were considered dangerous, stood at the steps to the movie theater next to a person of female gender and, without taking the cigarette out of his mouth, asked, "So what, bitch, are we going or not?"

That is how his question was related to us – verbatim.

Pushing his friend aside, Vladik rushed to the gorilla, and the sidewalk, we should mention, is quite a ways off from the steps of the theater, so the gorilla had plenty of time to consider Vladik's approach. Vladik's intentions, however, were so unexpected, that the gorilla felt compelled to move his cigarette from the right corner of his chapped mouth to the left. Vladik slammed on the breaks right before the guy, and, breathing hard, demanded, "Apologize to the lady right this minute!"

The king of thugs – and the gorilla happened to be the notorious Grammar, may he rest in peace – made a step back and said to no one in particular, "I be killing him now."

The jab followed swiftly and caught Vladik on the bridge of his nose. Awash in blood, Vladik quickly got up and ran up to Grammar again.

"I repeat, you must apologize!" he demanded again, his voice breaking into a single extended sob.

"Naw," Grammar said, utterly confused. "I be killing him now for real."

He hit again and knocked Vladik down, but even that did not stop Kuznetsov. After he went down the fourth time, the presumably offended female party saw fit to interfere: she took Grammar by the arm, half-hugging his shoulder to contain his zeal, and said, "Let's go now, or else you might kill him for real."

"All right," Grammar said, and they left.

Vladik shouted after them – he still demanded an apology.

The person who told us this story swore that he remembered the face of a curious boy who happened to be hanging out on the scene, and many years later recognized him in the picture that accompanied a long article about the "Lyuberneggers" in *Ogonyok*: the protruding ears and the particular shape of the superciliary arch, he said, left no doubt about it.

But let us return to Vladik's first year at the University. Aside from his general physical stamina, his disdain for luxury, his persistence and motivation, Vladik was known for his humble Stargorodian roots.

"All my ancestors plowed land," he liked to say.

This insistence on rustic roots, which, admittedly, does not fit very well with the apocryphal narrative of the old man's split from the stockyard, has become such an integral part of Vladik's public persona that we feel it is perfectly legitimate to include his illuminating biography in our series of true life stories of the brilliant and ordinary people associated with Stargorod in one way or another.

As is frequently the case, Vladik was derailed by love. Cupid, that pesky, bare-assed troublemaker, took aim at Vladik right after the first exam session. Admittedly, he was not alone in his misery; moreover, consumed by his work on Cato the Elder, Vladik was the last of his classmates to become aware of the Varya K. phenomenon – by the time he finally noticed her, others had already had time to get over the charming yet unyielding art historian. Even the sailor Dyakovenko, blown from the North Sea Fleet decks into the marble halls by the stormy winds of the night-school quota enrollment, once, being significantly inebriated, complained to his friend Zhenya Rayev who came from distant Usol-Sibirsk, "I took her by the ass once, and you know how she hissed! That's a rotten shrew right there, but I'd still do her."

"True that, Sailor – she's out of our league, that one," Zhenya Rayev thoughtfully agreed.

After reaching this remarkable conclusion, the two friends set out for the dorms of the Soils Biology Department, where their visit produced a legendary series of events with broken windows and their pursuit of Aunt Klava the door-lady, performed naked and with a fire-extinguisher that had been previously discharged into the wall. The events, naturally, engendered quite a stir; in the aftermath, sailor Dyakovenko, since he was not involved in the unauthorized handling of fire-fighting equipment, got off with a reprimand, and Zhenya Rayev, to his own stunned glee, was expelled and sent back to his native Usol-Sibirsk, where we lost track of him forever.

Still, because we do not want to resort to citing, on rather questionable grounds, the even-more questionable fetish of liberal intellectuals, Dr. Freud, we will simply say: It was all Varenka K.'s fault.

She came from an old Moscow aristocratic family, whose name resonated just so with her given name – the simple Russian Varvara – which had become rare by the late 50s and was loaded, of course, with secret anti-Bolshevik sentiment, but which today has lost, unfortunately, its signifier. We, much to our own chagrin, do find ourselves employing, on occasion, the high-flying academese, not – as we're sure our reader will understand – due to any shortcoming of our magnificent native tongue, but rather compelled by our stubborn pursuit of the resulting musicality), the name, then, which in our own time... But you already know what's going on, without all this scholastic nonsense, don't you?

Varenka K. Her hair redder than a flame, trim, athletic, a brilliant gymnast, a bit of a ballerina – she was a creature that captivated the imagination and tempted the heart with coy green eyes, and, of course, she was fluent in French and played the piano. With a memory like a steel trap and her awesome natural talent, she beat Vladik 17 times in a row at Word Squares and thrice at Battleships one day when she ended up sitting next to him during a History of the Communist Party lecture.

Vladik was cut to the quick. Varenka was triumphant. Vladik followed her about like a puppy-dog. He carried her book-bag. Yes, exactly like a fifth-grader. He helped her into her coat. He pawed at the ground and haunted her large, professorial home until dark (and later). He was never allowed inside.

Was he truly suffering? At the time, several hypotheses circulated among his classmates; there were some who, because they envied him, said Vladik was merely seeking more cheap popularity, but we believe otherwise. Especially when one remembers the countless pages of Kuznetsov's love poems that were passed around the class and, of course, landed in Varenka's pretty hands. Did you notice that their initials were the same? This, for some reason, inspired in Vladik great confidence.

The number of poems rose in geometric progression. Sharp-tongued aesthetes found special delight in "Oh, you, whose hair is a fire's blaze" in which "blaze" rhymed with "craze," "maze," "braise," and "malaise," as well as "Like a general, valiant on the eve of battle," and the late-period "Oh, Roman courtesans..." (It is worth noting here that Vladik appears to have possessed the gift of foretelling: Varenka, after she married Vittorio Macini, a left-wing radical, now lives in Rome where, rumor has it, she teaches Russian grammar at the Jesuit collegium.) Sailor Dyakovenko was one of the sympathetic few, and found his poems pretty but worthless.

"She won't give you any, mate, trust me," he would say to Vladik, suggesting he instead come along to visit the soil biology girls.

Vladik refused every time, and instead went straight to his post outside his Muse's windows. He appeared not to notice when people made fun of him. He knew how to handle public opinion and worked at it patiently, until everyone, or almost everyone, got accustomed to seeing things his way. So it was that when another lost soul replaced him outside Varenka's windows – someone from mechanical mathematics, who was equipped with his father's Volga, and was also, to be fair, eventually discarded without ever having been allowed inside the house – most of the class mourned together with Vladik.

That's when Kuznetsov threw himself into his work, buried himself alive in the library with Cato the Elder's *De Agri Cultura* and produced the above-mentioned four hundred and fifteen brilliant pages.

* * *

The summer after Kuznetsov's first year passed in the shadow of The Newspaper Story.

Vladik's class was sent to an archaeological dig, where, according to witness testimony, Vladik had earned the honorable moniker "Bulldozer" for his incomparable ability to raze, stratum after stratum, ancient grave mounds. There was no job that he would refuse. He enjoyed climbing the piles of dirt and moving more dirt by shovelfuls, and it was there, in the trench one day that Vladik, lost in the rhythm of the work, brought his shovel down on his bare foot and sliced off a bit of skin. This happened in the middle of a workday, so there were plenty of witnesses. There was very little blood, but it must have been Vladik's own sudden, treacherous negligence that frightened, or rather, stunned him. At first, as was his custom,

Kuznetsov blushed red like a poppy, but in almost the same instant he began to turn pale, then completely white, and then he suddenly fainted. This disgusting weakness lasted mere seconds, but it was enough for Vladik to bear its shame forever. His resilience, his vigor, his stamina – all that failed him, and, utterly destroyed, he fled into the bushes and, it appears, even cried bitterly, because when he came out at the end of the day to board the truck back to the base-camp, Kuznetsov was described as having puffy eyes, bright purple cheeks, and a beaten-down expression.

From that moment, a new Vladik Kuznetsov begins.

From that day on, no one, not even sailor Dyakovenko who was a professional at the art of drinking, could ever outdrink Vladik Kuznetsov. By the end of the summer, Vladik's face acquired a distinct purple tinge, but that was it; every morning, Vladik rose before dawn, brushed his teeth, did a series of stretching exercises and went on his run. His hangover was purged by sweat, and afterwards Vladik swung his shovel just as methodically as before; only now he was really careful about his feet and wore his grandfather's cow-hide boots. Vladik's special affection for military style was not the same as the contemporary fashion fad indulged by his classmates: for them, uniforms were stylish only in a kitschy way, worn with a special carelessness that made the wearer resemble a carousing hussar. Vladik would not have any of it. When he put on his green shirt, it was also with a belt and a shoulder-belt; he was a whiz with foot-cloths (he thought socks a decadence), and, since the day of his shameful bloodletting, did not part with the heavy boots that his frugal grandfather had shod with cavalry-issue metal horseshoe taps.

Over a drink, Vladik liked to talk about the victories of the Russian military: aside from his dearly beloved Romans, he also admired Suvorov and reserved a special place in his heart for Marshal Zhukov, under whose command Vladik's own grandfather had the honor of serving. All this did not prevent Vladik from respecting Hitler as well; he even developed a peculiar way of greeting people by raising his arm from the shoulder, almost Nazi-like, with the invariable accompaniment of a resounding "Hi!" This behavior, naturally, only increased Vladik's scandalous popularity, but he remained democratic and drank with everyone. Since he was often the last man left standing, Vladik didn't mind cleaning up, until one day, sweeping the evidence of yet another party into a piece of paper he had found, Vladik made a mistake. We must mention that the head of the expedition was Professor Lokotov – a pedantic bore of a man, who had been wounded tragically in the Great War. On May 9, 1945, a snotty Hitler-Jugend kid shot Lokotov's tank with a Faustpatrone, killing his crew and leaving the future Professor one-armed. The injury made Lokotov anti-social, but it must have done wonders for his scholarly diligence, and by the mid-70s the old soldier had attained the rank of Professor, managed his own research group, and gained special fame in the academic community for his insistence on replacing, in his articles, the foreign borrowing "ceramics" with the simpler and more resonant phrase "broken pots."

So, Vladik, highly intoxicated but still securely vertical, was taking out the trash. Right at the street door (the students were housed in the village school) he lost his focus for a moment and almost fell on top of Professor Lokotov, who was entering. Drops of red goo from the leftovers of sardines in tomato sauce, a non-negotiable item on the student menu, fell onto the Professor's trousers. An empty bottle dropped from Vladik's grasp and hit Lokotov painfully on the foot. Vladik hastened to retreat, but was instantly trapped by the enraged archaeologist.

"What is this? What is it?" the former tank commander shoved Vladik's bundle of trash into his face. The paper into which Vladik had wrapped everything turned out to have been a school display; a picture of Lenin in the center had been pierced with a knife (Vladik recalled he sliced an onion there earlier) and the Leader of the Proletariat was smeared all over with the same red goo.

What happened next stunned everyone. Vladik – who may have been irked by the rough treatment, or insulted at being cornered like

Peter Aleshkovsky

that, or perhaps simply not in the right mood – suddenly shoved the
broken-pot luminary away and said, loud and clear:

"Fuck off, old man..."

The old soldier, we must admit, lost his bearings for an instant and
gave in. Vladik bolted through the opening, thundered out the door,
and fled to his cot accompanied by the angry clicking of his heel pads
on the brick floor.

As a result, there was a personal complaint about the behavior
of Komsomol member Kuznetsov. The History Department's
Komsomol Committee, however, was well acquainted with Professor
Lokotov; they had been dealing with the professor's personal
complaints for years – he never came back from an expedition without
a whole stack of them. It was, in fact, only the professor's reputation
with the Committee that saved Vladik from being expelled; he got
off with a reprimand.

Kuznetsov responded with words that are not fit to print,
expressing his disdain for such Komsomol nonsense.

The whole story appeared to have been the final blow to Vladik's
already shaky commitment to science. Marcus Porcius Cato the Elder,
who lived so many centuries ago, was cast into oblivion once again.
Instead, Vladik was consumed by the idea of creating his own political
party. He already had the greeting and the uniform; his ideology was
a mix of Cato's sense of entitlement, austerity and directness and
Suvorov's patriotism, with a dose of Nazi-smacking intolerance for
Jews and Armenians. The latter sentiment was something Vladik
developed following the advice of sailor Dyakovenko, who by then
had transferred to the History of the Communist Party Department.
Dyakovenko never made a secret of his intention to go back to the
North Fleet after graduation: with his blue buoy of a diploma he fully
expected to find a cushy political gig.

Vladik did not want a cushy gig. Vladik chose to fight. While he
respected his grandfather's lessons deeply, he was heard, in his inner
circle, bemoaning the fact that the old man had not quite seen the
things the way they were. Vladik was not satisfied by merely speaking

truth to power; as every true Russian, he cared about the oppressed masses and dreamed of liberation, while he continued to plan for his radically new party.

Vladik acquired a pair of bodyguards: Kolya Bolshoi and a guy named Footmanov from a once-noble family. No one knew where he found them; the three held court at the University's tap room and proselytized there without fear (and this was mid-70s, not today!), sometimes using their fists to make their arguments stick. Kolya Bolshoi's fists, we must observe, were as big as his last name.

What was keeping Vladik at the University at this point? It seemed there was one more thing he wanted – the military course, despised by everyone else. That's just the kind of man Vladik was – forever swimming against the flow, driven and stubborn.

Another story comes to mind.

A group of students led by Major Borodin, a well-known liberal, who had once aimed high but got burned (and was, people said, to remain a Major forever), an excellent military translator who had even been seen reading Salinger in the original on a subway train on his way to work – this group of students was ready to take in another class full of Major's stories about his adventures around the world. The students had developed a sure method for getting the Major to talk. Whenever they were supposed to be memorizing something incredibly boring about the American Minuteman or Polaris missiles, one of Major's favorites would raise his hand and ask, for example:

"Comrade Major, would you happen to know – can you see a submarine from a plane?"

Major Borodin would lean back on his chair and study his audience. When he was satisfied that indeed, everyone wanted to hear the answer, he would begin, "The Red Sea is home to a unique genus of giant sea-shells (here he would fire off an unpronounceable Latin name). If you are sailing, let's say, a small storm-boat, the shape of one of these sea shells looks very much like the contour of an enemy submarine at periscope depth, as seen from, let's say, a patrol helicopter."

On the day in question, things were proceeding as usual: the rapt audience was listening to the Major expounding on the distinguishing features of Ethiopian women (as compared to Somalis), when, at a rather important point, the lecture was interrupted by the measured thumping of someone marching in the hallway. The noise seemed to be approaching. The tactful Major Borodin allowed his face to acquire the look of a gourmand surreptitiously surveying the dinner table, to make sure that indeed, his roast snails have been served without the garlic-and-marjoram sauce. The thunder outside, meanwhile, climaxed in the command, "Halt!" followed by a distinct clack of heels snapped together. Then, Vladik's deep voice rumbled forth from behind the door:

"Permission to enter, Comrade Major!"

Major Borodin lifted himself from his chair just a bit, and, glancing at the door with growing alarm, replied almost according to the Manual, "Enter, granted."

A strong arm opened the door; Vladik entered – no, rather, Vladik filled the frame, closed the door behind himself neatly, then marched, heels clacking, the 15 feet from the door to the lecturer's desk and stood to attention.

"Permission to address, Comrade Major!"

"Yes, of course. Go ahead," Borodin said, making it clear he had no desire to continue this game.

"Comrade Major. Comrade Lieutenant Colonel Peredisty asked that I inform you that your spouse has called. She requested you call home subsequent to finishing the class. Permission to leave?"

"Thank you. You may go."

Only when the thunder of Vladik's boots faded completely at the far end of the hallway, did the Major dare ask, "Who was that?"

"Kuznetsov!" the class barked back as one.

"Well, well," the Major said, shaking his head, and continued his instruction.

✳ ✳ ✳

We could tell many, many more stories like that about Vladik, but that's the tragedy of our situation – we cannot, no matter how tempted we might be to do so, allow our narrative to slip into anecdotal levity; we are here to convey true information about a historical person, and we must pursue our goal with the seriousness it commands. Thus, we shall attempt to be brief. Vladik's biography, however, is rich in uncommon incidents and occurrences; we have a myriad to draw upon, and it would be impossible not to tell you about the training camp.

What wealth of amazing folklore has come out of that venerable summer institution, the military reserve training camp where students earn their officers' stripes and prove their mettle! Take just one song, the immortal *We are for Peace, but Our Guns Keep Reminding Us We're Soldiers* – this alone, a tune born somewhere in a deep trench to the accompaniment of the approaching IFV of the 'blue' team... Oh the songs, the old songs – they are all parts of the system.

But let us return to Vladik. Let us recall the story of Vladik being late to the training camp. He had both the right and the permission to be late! He and a group of his ancient-history colleagues was dispatched to strengthen the ties of Socialist Internationalism with theater students in Leipzig. The occasion was so important that the military department gave our guys permission to report to training three days late, but of course Vladik could not tolerate that. Instead, he snuck away from the Leipzig train and made his way back to the training camp, at its location in the middle of nowhere in the country. He wanted to be there on time. He was in such a hurry, he didn't even stop to visit his grandfather or to look for a barber; instead, he shaved his head himself, with a safe razor, balancing in front of the tiny mirror in the rickety toilet of the village train. He didn't have any water either. Try to repeat this Spartan feat! Vladik Kuznetsov's head, when he arrived to camp, looked like... Suffice it to say that when sailor Dyakovenko, in the midst of the barracks' howling mirth, took it upon himself to finish the job, the old sea wolf's hand shook as it came near Vladik's head and there was cold terror in the big man's eyes, terror mixed with disgust and deep pity. Vladik ground his teeth, but didn't make a sound; the sailor's hand shook, but did not make any new cuts – it was surprisingly gentle, that calloused hand.

But on, on with our story – we can feel you begin to doubt the veracity of our claims, dear reader, but there are witnesses, a whole battalion of them, more! For word of Vladik's determined pursuit of the mailman position spread far beyond his own battalion – everyone at camp knew it. Everyone knew Vladik rose first, before dawn, and ran to the camp's gate, so that he could pick up the rolled-up newspapers and run them back to the officers' quarters. He did this because – if you haven't guessed it already – the mailman's job came with a rank, and Vladik longed for the right to put a lance-corporal's stripe on his new shoulder-straps and become equal with the camp's veterans. It didn't matter to him that after the training everyone would receive their lieutenant stars; Vladik did as his grandfather taught him, and who could blame him? Who wouldn't admire his persistence and resilience, so uncommon among young people today? Stargorodians are a special tribe, you know?

And the story with the General? The General who came to inspect Vladik's camp; the General for whose arrival the whole division had been preparing for two days and two nights straight? Vladik spent both those days, the hottest mid-afternoon shifts standing watch at the entrance checkpoint – Vladik volunteered for this, he felt compelled to bear his share of the soldier's burden. He did it because he dreamed of being noticed. His dreams kept him at the checkpoint, until – alas! – his stomach played a dirty trick on him, and Vladik had to ask someone else to take his place so that he could dash off. He was gone a mere five minutes, no longer, but it was enough. Vladik had to watch from the bushes as the General's convoy pulled up, and as the General, surrounded with his retinue of officers, conversed with Arthur Melkonyan, the weasely Armenian who'd agreed to relieve Vladik from his post because he'd lost to sailor Dyakovenko the night before and had to take Dyakovenko's midday turn at the checkpoint.

Vladik watched from the bushes and, according to witness accounts, chewed his nails.

Someone reported Vladik's suffering to the higher-ups, and the Drill Sergeant singled Vladik out at the final parade, so on the train home Vladik was a bit overexcited.

And what about the time Vladik punished Academician Kombatov's boxer? That's a Greek tragedy right there! In his last year at the university, Vladik adopted a homeless mutt he'd found next to the One-Armed Man pub one day. The little dog was a comical creature, accustomed to lapping up beer from unfinished bottles left behind by kind patrons of the establishment; he could also stand on his back legs and do a few other tricks, and must have been tangentially related to poodles. Nonetheless, Vladik gave the dog a manly name, Ace. Those who tried to puppy-talk to Ace and address the little thing as Acey or Asik, were cut off at the spot by Kuznetsov's powerful throaty roar, "The dog's name is Ace. Is that clear?"

Following this, Kolya Bolshoi usually popped up from behind Vladik's back and everything ended peacefully, or not – depending on the circumstances.

So Ace became Vladik's faithful companion, following his owner everywhere in his mincing gait and waiting for him patiently on the lawn of the Humanities' Building until he returned from class. Man and dog were inseparable. They rode the train to Lyubertsy together; Vladik fashioned himself a special backpack for the express purpose of transporting Ace. Ace's shaggy face, popping out of the backpack, looked so endearing that everyone around fell under his spell, and no one, ever, had a single unflattering thing to say about the friendly little mutt.

And then a terrible thing happened.

One day, Vladik was walking next to Moscow State University's main building with Ace, as usual, trotting at his side. On a parallel course with them, but in the opposite direction, Academician Kombatov was walking his dog, a boxer named Prana. The Academician was credited with founding Soviet Indology, which he did by tracing the Slavic people's roots to ancient Hindustan. Kombatov found rich evidence in support of his theories; we refer those with a more-than-passing interest in this question to the full list of Academician Kombatov's publications available from the commemorative edition of Academician Kombatov: *80 Years of Soviet Indology*. Nothing at the scene foretold disaster. The men and their dogs aligned; suddenly and without any warning, Academician Kombatov's giant boxer rushed at poor Ace, and – imagine! – snapped the little dog's front paw in half. Vladik, as eyewitnesses told us, didn't lose a second. He dashed to the university's fence, ripped out a cast-iron rod (whether it was loose or badly attached, we don't know) and, wielding it like the Roman legionnaire he'd been brought up to emulate, struck the Academician's dog, piercing it through and causing it to expire on the spot, in the shocked Academician's arms. Then Kombatov had to run for his life, abandoning his pet's lifeless body on the scene – Vladik, like a heavily-armed hoplite swinging a bloody spear, pursued him to his door. Later, in a fit of righteous vengeance, the spear smashed an innocent telephone booth.

What else can we say? Vladik had enough of his wits about him to evade the police, and Ace was gone when Vladik came back for him, so the little mutt's ultimate fate remains unknown. We only know that Vladik took the loss of his companion very hard and for a while nurtured plans of setting the Academician's dacha on fire.

It was a rough year for Vladik. Right before his thesis defense, his old grandfather passed away in a veterans' hospital. Vladik was left without a soul in the world, alone in the two-room apartment in Lyubertsy. His grandfather's death affected him deeply; that summer, he built a memorial marker on the grave, topped with the Red Star, as is proper for veterans of all Soviet battles. There was no priest, of course, but still, for some reason, Vladik requested prayers to be said for 40 days straight at the church in Vagankovo Cemetery. Vladik defended his thesis and graduated, but only 'just' – people said, he drank heavily after his grandfather's death. He was assigned to the

Lyubertsy school,[22] and worked there for a few months, but was eventually fired on the grounds of "professional ineptitude," a charge painfully familiar to any free thinker at the time.

After that, Vladik's track grows cold. Someone who'd seen him told us that Vladik wanted to volunteer for the war in Afghanistan – he went to the recruitment office, suggesting his own plan of combat operations, but did not pass the medical exam. He somehow survived, year after year; he never worked as a historian. In the early days of perestroika, he was seen at Pushkin Square – alone, surrounded by a mob, arguing with the pressing human mass. People saw him, but were afraid to approach him.

The last person who can be reliably said to have spoken to Vladik Kuznetsov was Kolya Bolshoi, who is now Deputy Facilities Director at the Tretyakov Gallery. If one believes his account, which resulted from a visit to the Church of Assumption, in Vishnyaki (actually, Kolya usually goes to All Saints in Sokolovsk, but his mother-in-law lives in Vishnyaki), Vladik works there as a bell-ringer.

He has grown gaunt and pale; he wears a plain jacket and his apparently indestructible boots, does not shave, has let his hair grow long, and drinks only within reason (by Kolya's own definition). He is planning to go to the monastery city of Pechora, to learn ancient bell-ringing from its masters.

---

22. In the Soviet system, university graduates were often assigned to hard-to-fill jobs according to their specialty.

THE REAL LIFE

1

"Life, especially for those over 30, hurls forward increasingly fast, as if to match the speed of our day's new technologies, and one hardly finds a moment to simply approach a stranger and, looking him in the eye, say something non-trivial and pleasant. No, we have no moments like that, and even when we find them, we do something entirely different with them than we imagined. We talk about being charitable and merciful, and many join the recently resurrected societies of Friends of Animals and condemn with righteous rage the cruel dog-catchers. But would they act? Would they do anything, even if the action was humble and inconspicuous? Would I, myself, extend a helping hand to a homeless stranger, or at least to someone lost in this city – say, to that red-faced fellow sitting with his boxes on the park bench?.."

So, or approximately so, reasoned Rafa Stonov, a common office-worker, a road engineer. Rafa had always dreamed of erecting grand, leaping bridges and high-speed tunnels, but so far circumstances had prevented him from building any such thing, keeping him, for the time being, in the employ of the Asphalt and Tar Surfaces Department. To give him credit, he did develop a new method for laying concrete surfaces, and even defended a dissertation about it 12 years ago or so (his method is still being optimized for production at his research institute's testing facility). But Rafa had faith in progress. He also had faith in humankind. And if occasionally he did fall prey to Russian angst, likely somehow associated with the state of the roads it was his job to inspect, such episodes were no more or less frequent for him than is common. In his dark moments, Rafa would think of something very complex. This feeling cannot be decently explained except perhaps by means of a penetrating joke – but it is likely to be familiar to many of our compatriots: it's when life suddenly appears utterly unnatural and contrived, and one yearns for something hard to define, glimpsed once, perhaps, in childhood, through a crack in a fence.

That's why, as he was about to turn homeward during his Saturday walk, in a state of extreme inner anxiety, Rafa had to force himself to look closer at the random, red-faced fellow with his boxes, who had initially inspired in Rafa only aversion, diluted perhaps with small doses of curiosity and empathy.

The fellow, whose clothes and carefully concealed sense of dignity immediately marked him as a non-Muscovite, looked about anxiously, exhibiting all the signs typical of the concussion that results from a sudden encounter with Moscow reality. He would attempt to stand up and grab all his cargo at once, which he could not possibly accomplish, despite his impressive dimensions, broad shoulders, and, even more importantly, his incredibly capacious paws, which called to mind stereotypical pictures of native Siberian bear-hunters, descendants of the peasants who had saved a besieged Moscow in the frigid winter of 1941. When he failed, he would curse fiercely at his load, fall back onto the bench and address the passers-by with the entirely rhetorical question of "So how are we supposed to go on living?"

The passers-by, naturally, gave him a wide berth. All except Rafa, who plucked up his courage and took a seat on the fellow's bench. The fellow greeted him instantly, "I'm stuck, you see, with my girls here. I've got a return for tomorrow and nowhere to spend the night. Help us out, mate, or we'll perish just like the Swedes at Poltava."

Rafa smiled without saying much, and did not rush to offer customary Russian hospitality, although a small voice inside him already began to assure him that the fellow was not at all as dangerous as at first he appeared.

"Let me explain the disposition here," the red-faced man continued, slightly calmer. "I've come to the capital on chicken business. You'd be surprised, mate, but we chicken-breeders are a bit off, all to the last man. If I as much as catch a whisper that, say, somewhere in Tallinn someone's fixin' to sell some Cochin-chinas, I'm there in a blink. Bukhara, Vladivostok – the money's no object as they say. So, I got my return ticket well in advance, but now I'm stuck, after the deal went through lightning-quick. You go ahead, look, look into the box – I see you don't get it, not at all, it's written all over your face!"

He lifted a small flap cut into one of the boxes, like a window, and Rafa obligingly bent lower to see. A coquettish head popped up, attached to a creature that looked like a cross between a midget heron and a carrier pigeon. The head turned coyly, displaying itself, and hid back inside the box.

"Have you seen anything like this? Have you? In your eyes I can see you have not!" The fellow's face melted into a boyish smile that scattered the last shreds of Rafa's hesitation.

"So you'll put us up for the night, for real? The girls and I are quiet – no worries, guaranteed not to make a mess. I have a bottle with me, just in case, but I don't drink myself – I quit," the fellow patted his bulging briefcase as a manner of proof.

Then he rose from the bench, but instantly turned and slapped his hand on his forehead, "What a fool! I forgot – I'm Vovochka."

Rafa extended his hand and introduced himself informally, "Rafa."

He did not like his full name, Rafael. Being by education and upbringing a very modern person, he frequently begrudged his parents for giving him the distinction of such an old-fashioned name.

"Jew, are you?" Vovochka instantly asked, not especially politely but with great glee.

"No, why should…" Rafa began to say in his defense, but his new friend slapped him on the shoulder and explained with a giggle, "Why I asked? It's because your name's Jewish. I don't care – Greek,

Tatar or Jew – I've seen all kinds of people, mate. For me – as long as the man's alright! So, shall we?"

Flattered with the amazing congruence of their views and immediately reassured, Rafa bravely grabbed the boxes.

It was strange: he was absolutely certain that his wife and daughters would gladly welcome the unannounced guest – he had never had an adventure like this before.

2

Vovochka charmed Rafa's family instantly, and soon Rafa's twins were racing down the hallway to fetch the teapot, then the saucer, and then more water for the chickens, and everything in his two-room apartment oohed and delighted. And with good reason.

Have you ever heard of the black Bramah, feather-footed like a prize tumbler, barrel-chested and decorous, meek and serene like a village priest? Or of dwarf Cochins, those chick-sized, full-grown birds that had squeezed themselves into a clamoring clump under the armchair? Or of the fuzzy, high-stepping, crested and coquettish Paduas, which are more like a cross between a midget heron and a carrier pigeon? Or of the piebald, long-legged, muscle-rolled Orlov fighters – the pride and glory of any truly Russian chicken-man? Most people have no inkling whatsoever of their existence, and it was the same for Rafa until he beheld the creatures in his own home.

It's true, the air in the apartment was filled with something unimpeachably birdy, the parquet floors and rugs were covered with a fine dusting of wet sawdust, and tiny feathers flitted around in front of one's nose, but it was all worth it. It was a shame they couldn't open the window for more than fifteen minutes (strict instructions!) and they accidentally shattered the wife's favorite cup in their urgency to grind up an anti-stress powder of calcium and ascorbic acid, which the girls brought, running, from the pharmacy… and after all, they didn't get to marvel at the chickens for as long as they wanted: Vovochka, having performed his stress-reducing ministrations, all with winsome tenderness, settled his beauties into their boxes, tied them carefully shut and moved them to a dark corner.

And it was then, right after he ushered a chiseled pair of Orlov fighters into a box, that he suddenly grabbed the third Orlov hen and dashed to the window with such purpose as if he fully intended to jump, with the bird, from the seventeenth floor.

"Rafa, Rafa, send the girls out, I'm gonna' curse bad," he hollered, turning the uncharacteristically-meek avian princess in his hands and inspecting her claws, beak, head and crest. The girls burst out laughing, tactfully covering their mouths with their hands, and ran to the kitchen. Vovochka, gasping, explained his fit to Rafa:

"He conned me, that bitch-gutted Moskalev, conned me clean – slipped me a sick one. He must have switched them when I went out to flag a car. Now I can't breed them – two's not enough, you know, you have to cross them out. You viper, just you wait! And people told me, gave me fair warning – he's born into chickens!"

He stomped his feet and swore to find a way to send the whole Moskalev farm to chicken heaven with arsenic, and afterwards lay spent in the armchair trying to console himself somehow. Finally, the sense of pride and the dream-come-true feeling about the other birds won out. After all, the pair of the Orlovs he did get was excellent. And then, maybe, he'll soon have a chance to buy more; he knew for a fact that there were Orlovs in Riga, because just this morning at the Bird Market another expert told him so in exchange for news about the availability of some Dutch Kilzummers in Leningrad, as best Rafa could follow the story.

Vovochka pulled out his piebald hen and rooster, stroked their necks, admired their marbled wings and sighed ruefully:

"Did you see, they only have two colors – the third, the emerald green, the peacock green disappeared, except in tail feathers here and there, that's all they have left from their ancestors. But these few feathers give me the hope, no, not just hope – certainty! – that I will get it done, I'll bring back this vanished Russian breed. Rafa, Rafa, you keep smiling – don't laugh, mate, you don't know: last year at an auction in Italy a nest of stable Orlovs fetched two and a half million dollars! You ever heard of that? No? That's my point! I'm not talking about the Orlov trotters, about prize-winning horses – I'm talking about four hens and a rooster, and there's no wonder, just look at them, look at them, you philistine! A real bird – it's better than books that you traded for paperbacks, it's a symphony! A living being. The Orlovs are our national pride, they came from Count Orlov's own farms – yes, the same Count who created the trotters – and they were stronger and gamer than any Kokand or Bukharan. And now there aren't any left, even in Asia – I mean, the real, tricolored ones – and you say, he's crazy. Any man worth his salt is 'off' – and I have no time for the other kind."

He got up from the chair, flicked one girl and then the other on the nose, and together with Rafa went to move the dining table to the middle of the room. Next, the bulging briefcase made an appearance, and a half-liter bottle of "Russian" was extracted from it. The other, with a screw-on cap, was only briefly displayed.

"That one's for the conductors on the train, mate. People diplomacy," he said as if to explain that he wasn't hiding or holding anything back, but needed it for business.

Rafa nodded sympathetically, and Vovochka added:

"Don't worry – you'll have enough, I hardly drink any."

"Me either, really," Rafa confessed.

"Good deal, then," Vovochka nodded. "But surely you can get 150 down?" he roared and put his paws around Rafa to express his love, and smacked his lips enthusiastically in anticipation of a feast.

Galya fried a whole chicken for the occasion, opened a jar of pickled mushrooms, sliced some salted lard… and there they were, seated around the table, with Vovochka officiating, carving the chicken, pricking the sour-cream-baked crust, and serving the bird, in equal portions to everyone, with his bubbling chit-chat:

"Eat it up, eat up, you poor bastards, next time I'll bring you one of my Kholmogor geese, we'll bake it with apples!"

He poured the vodka into crystal shot glasses for Galya and Rafa and, after some hesitation, poured himself a whole glass.

"To our meeting and to take the edge off," he explained. "I just can't get that spider Moskalev out of my mind. He conned me good, didn't he? All right, my dears, ahead we forge!"

He raised his glass and drained it, in one great gulp.

"That's it!" Vovochka made a creaking noise somewhere inside and put the glass back on the table, upside down. "Gala, you forgive me for drinking like a truck-driver, usually I don't drink at all. It's all nerves."

Rafa and Galya clinked their crystal. God, Rafa thought, how lucky I was to pick him up! It was a fool that said no good deed goes unpunished, an honest-to-goodness idiot!

His thoughts jumped from one thing to the next; Vovochka's tales flowed like honey as he sat like some Emperor at a feast, refilled his hosts' glasses and told stories that made them laugh. We couldn't possibly not reproduce his tales here.

3

I've drunk my fill, in my time, to my heart's content you could say. It's now I'm with chickens and I don't allow myself much, you've seen them – they keep you busy. Up at half past four, do chores, and it's time to catch the bus, to the plant, and after my shift I'm back at their cages. I don't let Zoika anywhere near them – girls, women are no good.

I can talk forever, you know, my mother used to listen to me and listen, and then she'd spit, rub it into the ground with her foot, and go back inside, to hide from me. But I could get her even there, if I needed to, especially if I were tipsy. Or else I'd go to my hog – I called him Borka – fill his trough with beer, fix myself a drink about that big and sit there and watch him work his way through it. Made him a total wino, I did. But he was my true friend. My brother, younger one, would come up sometimes, "Vovka, pour me one." But I sent him packing – let him get it out of his wife, I was better off with

Borka, my brother, he, when he drank, wore me out. Blah-blah, blah-blah-blah – and I can do that myself, why the heck would I need another one! With Borka – it was great, we'd sit together and be quiet, I'd scratch his side now and then, or he'd oink a little at me. When we went after beer with him, they always let us through – "Let Vovochka and Co. through!" Guys laughed, but I didn't care and Borka oinked happily, he knew he'd get some too. And would you believe me – he drank from the mug and never spilled anything, not once! When 'twas time to cut him down, I left the house not to look, and never touched that pork.

Yeah, I remember some *khokhols* were around drinking beer with me,[23] and said, "Hey guys, check that out, he's growing his piglet something special, must be giving him beer to get more lard." How could you explain things to them – they feed their pigs horseshit to get them fat, people say. Borka, closer to the end, he did get pretty big, and just lay there and looked at me now and then. And, you know, I was never without some critters. Once, this local buddy gave me a little fox terrier. "Take him, Vovochka," he says, "I don't have much use of him, and really it's you I was thinking of when I got him." I called him Yeller – he was a big barker and a true watchdog, never let a stranger close. Mother would cuss at him, and he'd just glare back at her with his teeth all bared – and I'm just sleeping in the shed, with snow blowing in through the door, but what do I care? I've got extra pounds and a shearling coat to keep me warm, you could shoot a cannon at me, I wouldn't wake. Mother tried this and that, but Yeller wouldn't let her close – he knew his job. "You son of bitch," she says, "I'm the one who feeds you!" And he just goes, "Woof-woof!" and snaps at her finger. You couldn't chase him away with a yoke – he was one game dog. Afterwards, the guys said, the snake-eyes that were building a bridge in our town ate him. I didn't believe them until I lived with those folks for a while – but that was later, and first I had this idea of getting married. I was young and stupid then, had few brains left after wine.

23. *Khokhols* – a derogatory nickname for Ukrainians.

My mother-in-law and I, we would really go at it. The grandpa, after we'd drink together, was all right, but if I were on my own, even he would start looking at me askance. Because you know, I moved in with them in the city, into their big apartment. At first it was all fine and dandy, but then my better half started getting distracted. All right, I thought, I should give her something to keep her busy. So I got a pair of little black lambs from a local buddy that worked at the slaughterhouse – I thought we'd raise them, or, again, make her, the wife, a nice fur collar for her coat. When they bring sheep to the slaughter, you know, some give birth right there, so my buddy just picked them up and carried them out. I put them into a box, got on the bus home. And of course, they're going "blah-ah-ah," poor things, whimpering in that box. This one lady goes, "What's that you have in the box?" The wife, I say, brought a pair of unplanned twins into this world, so I'm goin' to the pond to drown 'em. She left me alone.

Great, I thought, sat back in my seat, almost dozed off, but everyone's around going "shoo-shoo-shoo" in whispers. So I got home, and everyone's already asleep. I went to bed too. Gramps got up in the middle of the night for a drink of water and thought delirium tremens had finally made him start seeing imps, roused my mother-in-law, and told her to call emergency services. She couldn't figure it out either, so they sat up all night in their room, without a wink of sleep. In the morning, sure thing – they made a ruckus. "The floor's covered in sheep crap, the carpet's ruined!" the three of them yelled at me in unison. So I said, to heck with you, got my lambs and went home to my mother. Never saw them again and didn't go to court for divorce – send me all the summonses you want, I burned them all. I had my own man in the police, Kolka the lieutenant, we went to school together. He kept at me: go somewhere, Vovochka, put yourself to use or else you'll drink yourself stupid, you've got a good head on you, forget your wench, just go. As to the good head, I know that myself – I was the best at math in school, put me to any machine – I'll puzzle it out, it's not a matter of rank at the factory, but of brains, and my pot, thank goodness, always boils.

Kolka the lieutenant tried to talk some sense into me. Once – wait, this is funny – he and I got into my garden, lay down under the currant bushes and had a good time. He's talking sense into me, but at the same time, because he's alright, he's keeping up: pick a berry, squish it with your tongue, then take a sip, and get another one. Mom had close to thirty bushes there – what else could a man want!

Suddenly I see these feet under the fence.

"Kolya," I whispered, "we've been tailed."

Sure enough, it's Filka Wolfov himself – he often liked to shave a free drink off of you. But this time… his feet don't follow each other straight, in one hand he's got the shaving brush, lathered up, in the other – the razor, and his head's like Frankenstein: left eye glued shut and the hair all greener than grass, and dried and spiky. Turns out his wife poured a can of paint over his head when he didn't make it all the way home and instead fell asleep in the shed. So he came 'round, you know, realized what happened and ran to me.

"Vovochka!" he bawls. "Shave it off! I can take, I can take it!"

First thing, we poured two glassfuls into him as an anesthetic, and then I set to scraping his scalp off–the paint had dried! I scraped as best I could, then washed him in kerosene several times, but the greenness got into his skin and he walked around for a while like that, painted. Since then he's become Crocodile, but before he had a manly name – Filya the Wolf. One day, not too long ago, I ran into him, and remembered the story, so of course I grinned ear to ear, and he hisses, "Shush, Vovochka! The guys just got over it!" So, I kept it zipped, absolutely.

Yeah, we had some good times, but I listened to Kolka the lieutenant, signed up for the surveyors' team and took off for Taymyr. Now that was life! I had two pals there – one was also Vovochka, we called him Paratrooper, and the other was Kolka Goldilocks – he was some sort of Veps, or a Karelian, probably Karelian, the Veps are meaner. Kolka was short, like this, barely up to my shoulder, but he was a game dude, and thick as a bull, muscles like granite. His hair was all smooth on top of his head – that's 'cause he never took his little stocking hat off, even in the labor camp – and below, down to his shoulders, he had these blonde curls like a girl. One old lady took him for a priest, called him Father… "I'm no Father," he says. "Fathers are all six feet under at Solovki." He was like that. So the three of us teamed up, and everyone respected us and feared us a bit, too. Kolka, I'm telling you, was chiseled out of granite, arms like excavator claws – he had his share of ax-swinging in logging camp and even when he got out, he never really left the woods. On a march, he could cover 50 kilometers like a prize stallion, no sweat. The Paratrooper was a different story, he was the brains, a smart man, only his head shook and his left eye blinked by itself – all from jumping. I don't know how many times he jumped exactly, with his parachute, but it was plenty. Those paratroopers are like us chicken-people – all nuts, maniacs. So the three of us made camp together in a ravine, and no one bothered us – they knew what they'd get back. Back in those days, I pushed 240 without a gram of fat, it's now that I spread out in winter and trim up in summer, when you gotta' run after the critters.

I lost Vovka stupidly. I flew home to Arzamas one month, and they stayed behind. Goldilocks didn't go on the next trek, he must've still had money, but Vovka did.

And the rivers there can flood like God forbid. So they came to this little stream and it's rushing full. The instructions always said to stretch a safety line first, but no one ever did that. Long story short, it took us a month to find him. Sent him back in a zinc coffin – you couldn't see much through its peephole, and there wasn't much in there to see. There he went and gave his precious life, without drink, clean as a whistle, we wouldn't drink for months when we were trekking.

After that Goldilocks and I went off – burned through a couple grand in a blink. One day we're sitting there, thinking what to do. Where we were, they sold wine in three-liter jars, and we only had one left – between the two of us, that was nothing. So we're sitting by this store and this Gypsy comes riding up on his horse. I point at him, meaning, look Kolka, how far the bastards have spread through the country.

"That," Kolka says, "is a gift from St. Nicholas. Exactly what we need."

He waves the Gypsy over and takes the bull by the horns: "How would you like it if I lifted your horse off the ground with one finger? Bet five jars."

Gypsy doesn't take long to convince – he's game, and folks gather round, curious, standing around, waiting for the show.

I'm staring right along with them – I figure Kolka's bluffing. But that was not his style. He climbed under the nag, whispered some spell to it from underneath, and kept stroking its belly until he found his spot – then when he did, he climbed out, stood by the horse's side and gave her a poke with his finger, and he had fingers like sixteen-penny nails, I tell you. The horsey, believe it or not, just sort of lifted off, not like rearing up or to kick, but just as it were standing, all four hooves off the ground at once, and all Goldilocks had to do was put his finger under her and lower her gently back.

The Gypsy zipped into the store without a word. Next thing you know he's got five jars and puts them down on the grass in front of Kolka.

"Show me the spot – I'll buy you ten more."

"Nah," Goldilocks says. "Give me a hundred rubles for a round count – I'll show you."

The Gypsy's game – he's already thinking how he'll strip his whole tribe naked. They must've been under that horse for half an hour, crawling on their knees and poking the poor thing all around the belly – but the Gypsy couldn't get it to work and with Kolka she just hung in the air, every time. So the horseman had to ride off empty-handed. He looked glum, that's for sure, but what can you do – he lost the bet fair and square.

Of course, folks all flocked to us, one thing led to another, and our five jars evaporated like they were never there. So we dragged ourselves to the local restaurant – and in this god-forsaken Ust-Tareya there was only one. It was always either our plantation crew there or the local officers – they had a construction garrison quartered there. So we sat quietly in the corner and kept to ourselves, but the soldiers were having a grand ol' time. Suddenly one of them whips out his gun and –bang! bang! – starts blasting into the air. It was later that we figured we didn't hear bullets whistling, so it was a signaling gun, and at the moment – howls, screams, women in hysterics, plates flying off the tables like rainbows – and we went to set things right. While we were busy stomping down that poor lieutenant and tying him up with tablecloths, the waitresses called the station and got us a ride. They packed us in all like rabbits, together with the tied-up sharpshooter, and then at the jailhouse they put him in one cell – and everyone else into the other. There were four of us, and we kept seeing more and more of them filing into our room. Well, I think to myself, they're gonna get you straightened out, Vovochka, put your affairs in order. I was all shaped up to take it like a man, when my Karelian, the shorty, pops up from under my elbow, comes up to their Captain, and says:

"Listen, mate, I wanna' show you something before we get started. Anyone got a five kopek piece?"

They found one for him – he bit it with his teeth, grabbed it with his fingers and – twist, twist! – twisted it into a corkscrew. Gave it back to the Captain as a souvenir and said, very clearly, "Mind you, guys, I like doing that to shoulder-blades, too." And reinstated himself in his corner quietly.

Naturally, they didn't believe him. Gave him another– he fashioned a bow-tie out of that too. And now what do you think? Our officers were all blooming like daisies in a flowerbed… They took us in, wined and dined us, and we parted as best friends – they turned out to be generous and well-mannered people.

4

"Yes..," Vovochka said, regarding Rafa and Galya who had long since pushed away from the table. "You eat, eat the jam, poor bastards, I'll keep to the tea – I miss the Indian stuff, we only get it before the November holidays. Yes, we drank to our hearts' content, those were the days. Later, my Karelian got bored and headed home, somewhere around Petrozavodsk. He asked me to come with him, but I didn't and went home to Arzamas instead. So we parted like that, and afterwards I never heard from him. He may be doing time again, or maybe got married, we both felt like settling down – you can only play that hard while you're young and loaded with easy Taymyr money. Since then I don't drink, only on holidays, and don't miss it in the least and highly recommend you do the same. Now, Zoika won't let me lie, I'm nuts about my chickens and don't need anyone else. When I get my Orlovs bred back –that's when we'll have one last party, and after that I can die happy!"

Tea made Vovochka flushed and somehow less solid; he spilled over the armchair and was quiet for a moment, but could not sit still for long.

"All right, girls, off to bed!" he shooed Rafa's twins. "Time, time, you've already stayed up way late." He grabbed one under each arm and dragged them off to their room.

After he put them to bed, Vovochka began to pack. He re-tied his boxes, sent Galya to wash dishes in the kitchen and explained to Rafa what to do with the sick hen, which he put into a separate box.

"Listen, do me a small favor, would you please? Just handle it without sentimentality. Take this poor thing back to Moskalev in Podolsk. I would stay myself, but first, I gotta be back at the plant the day after tomorrow and, second, I'm afraid I'd just strangle him like a chick if I lay eyes on him now. That's not right. Just give him the bird back and tell him he must've made a mistake in the dark. If he tries to give you 50 rubles back – don't take it, money's not the matter. Tell him it's his problem, I'll come back some other time. And don't worry – I won't touch him and certainly won't poison his birds, you should see how beautiful they are… too bad they got fixed up with such a shitty guy. I'll get the breed going, you can be sure of that, you'll marvel at them yet – Moskalev will come to me trying to buy, only I won't sell him any. Would you?"

And he looked at Rafa in such a way that he had to agree. What else was he going to do?

Then they went to bed and Vovochka disappeared into the bathroom – to wash up.

"He doesn't have any children of his own, but did you see how good he was with ours?" Galya said.

Rafa nodded and for some reason stroked his wife's hair.

"Go to sleep," whispered Galya, already half asleep. "Some people do find just the right thing to do with their lives."

They fell asleep with this thought.

5

In the morning, Vovochka rose before dawn, tiptoed into the kitchen and sat there quietly drinking tea until everyone else awoke. Galya rushed to make him breakfast, but he refused.

"Habit is second nature. I only have tea in the morning – by lunch time, or better still, by supper, that's when I can eat a horse. You go ahead and eat, don't mind me, I mean it, I'm fine."

And he didn't eat.

After breakfast Rafa went out to flag down a taxi and was planning to see Vovochka off at the train station, but Vovochka told him not to.

"You'd better, while it's Sunday, go to Podolsk, find that snake and give him the hen back. Will you, Rafa?"

And again he gave Rafa such a look that it was impossible to refuse.

"All right, guys, farewell, thanks for everything, and if you're ever in Arzamas make sure to stop by. Straight from the station – to my place, I wrote the address down for Galya on the fridge. That's it, let's go!"

And his taxi drove off, and the girls waved after him for a long time.

Then Rafa made his way to Podolsk.

He spent the entire trip anticipating how he would drop the cardboard box at the feet of the liar, and how he would turn down the money, and he got himself so worked up that he rang the doorbell with great determination and, as soon as someone opened the door, he stepped inside the apartment, holding the box in front of him like a bomb.

Moskalev, we must note, was a very shabby sort of a man, clearly pushy and unpleasantly unkempt. In his old sweatpants with baggy, threadbare knees, and a well-worn corduroy blazer dating back to the days when corduroy wasn't considered fashionable, with his cloudy, bulging eyes, he certainly fit the profile of an old con man, and the fact that he was visibly unnerved by Rafa's initial determination only proved that his conscience was not entirely spotless.

"Take back your hen, please. It's not very nice, you know, to take 50 rubles and pawn off half-dead goods. Vovochka asked me to tell you that when he comes next time…"

"What Vovochka?" the buggy-eyed Moskalev interrupted, grabbing the box and opening it. The hen, indeed, was barely alive: she rolled her eyes and feebly twitched one foot.

"What Vovochka?" Moskalev began, growing increasingly incensed. He shoved his fists onto his hips in a totally obnoxious way: "You mean Tolyanych from Stargorod, who came here yesterday?"

"What Tolyanych?" Rafa inquired, uncomprehending, but the old man cut him off:

"You must be from the same gang, then! I wonder why I haven't seen you at the Bird Market before…"

Moskalev made a threatening move towards Rafa and then – then things took a really ugly turn. Rafa could not and did not really want to get the story straight: apparently Vovochka – or Tolyanych – paid for Moskalev's Orlovs with three Kilzummers that promptly died during the night. Rafa couldn't quite grasp the difference in values, but someone owed someone a 25 and someone else gave someone a five-ruble break – it was all muddled in the horrendous noise and cursing that ensued.

To make the comedy complete, two enormous Moskalev-juniors emerged from a side door, pounced on Rafa and threw him out of the apartment in a rather dishonorable fashion. As if that were not enough, they festooned him with the three dead chickens, which were molting and certainly not as pretty as they had appeared only a day earlier.

On the train ride back, great sadness swept over Rafa. All he wanted was a good bath and not to think about anything. He was part of some terrible mistake, that much was clear.

At home, he told Galya everything, and when she bawled, Rafa, who could not stand anyone's tears, slapped the bathroom door shut behind him and locked himself in.

"Truly, girls and women are no good," he muttered angrily.

And that's when he spotted the familiar screw-cap bottle that was meant for "people's diplomacy." The bottle was shoved behind the laundry hamper. Next to it could be observed the plastic cup that normally held the toothbrushes. The bottle still had about a hundred and fifty grams on the bottom; Rafa, first replacing the glass back on its shelf, regarded the bottle for a while, shook his head, then suddenly swallowed its entire contents and stepped into a hot shower with a warm faith in humankind.

"No, it is true, it is: girls and women are no good," he muttered and smiled sweetly at some secret thought.

OX AND MOTHER LOVE

Since as early as the fifteenth century, it has been widely accepted in Stargorod that woman is a vessel of evil. It is interesting to note that the following story has come to us from two different, one could even say, independent, sources: one from our times and the other from times long past. The first time I heard the tale was in the steam room of Banya No. 2, on the Right Bank, from an ancient old-Believer. Later, the same anecdote was related to me by a researcher who, in the late Stagnation Era, had the miraculous opportunity to visit Mount Athos' Rossikon Monastery, where he found it, much to his embarrassment, among the fifteenth-century chronicles that had been transcribed, by the way, in Stargorod's own Sage-Nicholas Monastery.

Later comparisons revealed no significant discrepancies between the two narrators' stories; the "banya" version, admittedly, was spiced with more exuberant epithets and metaphors, not all of them fit to print, and there's surely a certain significance in this, but we, having resolved to relate the chronicler's version, will reproduce it here humbly, without deep philosophical digressions into the burlesque culture of the *skomorokh*, the longevity of this ancient novella, its relevance to the present-day and other similarly complex problems that shall remain untroubled by our probing minds.

Thus, once upon a time, there lived in the glorious city of Konstantinopolis a very pious priest. His chastity, modesty and humility made him famous far beyond his community. His wife was just as chaste and innocent, just as obedient and joyful. And so it came to pass that, just before Easter, at the very end of Lent, our priest was overtaken by the demon of lust, and so tightly did the devil clutch him, that, to put it somewhat metaphorically, the poor man grew a giant and unshakable horn. The sorry soul bowed and prayed, and donned an encolpion reliquary containing holy remains, but the demon would not let up, "turmenting muche." That's when the priest went after his wife, asking and begging her to give him that "which is his, but is prohibited."

The priest's wife, chaste "like duve," loving her husband deeply, answered him simply and straightforwardly, blushing "like poppie bloome":

"My dear spouse, you are, before our Lord Jesus Christ, my master and ruler of my life; I am your humble servant now and forever, but do not ask of me what is impossible – your torments will end soon. Bear your burden, my heart, for your suffering is nothing before our Savior's suffering on the cross. As soon as our Glorious King returns and the mystery of Resurrection is celebrated and complete, we shall be with each other, and I shall be yours, and you shall be mine. But this hour you must think of heavenly things and forget that which is worldly, for Satan is among us, desiring to undermine that which is holy, setting the pure of soul upon the road to perdition."

The priest left his wife and cried fiery tears, overjoyed as he was with his spouse's purity, yet despairing at his own weakness. He went to the manger and chewed on the thrashed straw, but the demon would not let him go. He turned the grinding wheels in the mill-house and milled loads of flour, but the horn of his lust still protruded. When he could tolerate it no longer, he went to the stable and made use of a jenny, and a nanny-goat, and then the jenny again, to the count of three, and only then did the cursed tempter leave him be.

Afterwards, the priest went back to the house, put on clean robes, and left for the church where he officiated the service, as was his duty. And the miracle came – Our Savior, who had been put to death by Pontius Pilate and died on the cross for our sins, rose and lived again, and the people's joy knew no end. And later, when it was time for everyone to depart after Mass, the father fell prostrate on the ambon and confessed his cruel sins to his congregation, and begged forgiveness for the jenny, and for the nanny-goat, and for the jenny again, to the count of three. And he was given the people's forgiveness, and his Christian brethren came and kissed him and praised Christ thrice.

And at that moment there came a fearsome sight: horrific copper-beaked birds of prey came from everywhere, flocking onto the church's roof. Their beaks and claws were sharper than a barber's blade, and in place of feathers they were bedecked of hard-cast arrows. The creatures flew in the skies, barking hideously, instilling fear in people's hearts, and not letting anyone go home.

Seeing this frightful sight, the priest's wife approached him, and helped him up from the ambon, kissed him thrice and led him to the door. Out they went into the yard, and the birds flew lower and lower, in circles smaller and smaller, until they dove all as one at the wife and tore her to little pieces. All that remained was her copper cross.

But this is an ancient myth, from bygone days. Our mission, however, is to chronicle recent history, and we believe the present-day version of the story gives us a no-less edifying plot than this doubtful tale, this Decameron-esque fare, this anti-clerical contrivance of some Firentsuolus who loses his mind after contracting the French disease. Stargorod is no place for vague eroticism – everything here is touchable and visible. Take, for instance, the story of Ox and Mother Love.

Exactly what brand of Christians the people in this story are – of that we cannot be sure: maybe they are Anabaptists, or Baptists, or maybe some sort of Adventists, but certainly not Khlysts. The folks who have lived for as long as anyone can remember on the Right Bank, behind the Rodina Hotel, have never done harm to anyone. In fact, no one has ever seen anything but aid and goodwill from them, and if they get together in one big house to read the Bible and sing their songs – who could complain about that? Come to think of it, they must be some sort of Old Believers, because Baptists don't sing like that – longingly, sweetly and melodically, so that the song pulls at your heartstrings, even though you don't understand a word of it – it's like the priest's chant at High Mass during Easter, when it's time to praise the Savior in Greek. But they don't have priests; that's a fact. Their old men all wear prayer beads wrapped around their wrists and those long cassocks, down to the ground, with upright collars. They bow so much when they pray that everyone has a little personal pillow – we think it's so they don't bludgeon their foreheads into mush, or maybe to keep their knees from callusing over.

What we don't know, we don't know, and there's plenty of that, because most of our information comes from our neighbors who, although good Christians all, can't always tell the difference between an akathist and an analogion, so we can't blame them for their less than perfect grasp of confessional differences.

When it's evening, the Right Bank community gathers in their prayer house. Lyubov Mikhailovna always arrives first, although she is almost always there anyway – cleaning, polishing, scrubbing. And when Serafim Danilovich comes (he's their holy man and Lyubov's husband), she bows to him, leaves the church and sits on a little bench outside, by the window. The congregation gathers. They often stop and visit with her, calling her kindly "Mother Love," because that's what her name means, and when done chatting, they bow to each other and part: folks go on to church and she stays on her bench. The bench sits on a wooden platform, and that's where she listens to the service, winter or summer. When it gets too hot, they open the windows, and she can hear everything, and even when it's all closed up, she still stays there, singing and bowing. All of the folks learn the Mass as kids, before their multiplication tables.

Tall cottonwoods and the fence around the prayer house hide her from strangers' eyes; in the winter, when it grows dark early, you can barely spot her from the top floor of the five-story apartment building next door: there she is, bowing, praying, always at her post.

Mother Love is small, but not hunched-over like many of the Right Bank women, and, in fact, not all that old. She must be about sixty, and one can still see the good Lord didn't deny her the gift of beauty when she was younger, and her eyes – enormous, deeper than the Lake – glow with a strange, utterly un-ascetic, exuberantly plucky fire. In a word, she is a spell of an old woman – once you've seen her, you don't forget her. However, we must give her husband his due, as well. Serafim Danilovich – he is tall and almost sickly thin, with a wispy little beard and a halting falsetto voice, but his eyes… His eyes compensate for the feebleness of his body – they are filled with glowing molten steel, with strength, and faith, and a truly prophetic certainty. Catch his eye in a crowd, and you won't feel blessed exactly, but you won't forget the man, either, because you'll glimpse the sort of strength that can turn rock into sand, the type of restless intellect that is always at work. But for his eyes and his fingers, which are always compelled by some internal impulse to work his well-worn antique amber prayer beads, like a weaver's shuttle through the shed, the man's whole figure would seem subdued and ethereal. He's got his spells, or so, at least, say the old retired ladies one to another – those women who are always shelling sunflower seed on benches before apartment buildings, keeping track of everyone else's business, 365 days a year, except, of course, during leap years.

Serafim Danilovich must be over 80, and he's always lived on the Right Bank, near Kopanka, close to their sect's cemetery, with its roofed wooden crosses and chapel of red coquina stone from beyond the Lake. He's always lived here, as did his parents, and his grandparents before that. He only left once – to go to war. Among our truly Orthodox folk, only Anastasia Petrovna Terentieva remembers him as a boy – they went to school together, before the war, that same war, of course.

"He was always so sickly," grandma Nastya remembers, "girls had no use for him, although he hadn't mangled himself yet, back then. But even then, it seems, he was an Ox."

Who knows what truth there is in her words, or where we might find it? What we know for sure is that when he came back from the war, they married him to Mother Love. She must've been very young, a girl, hardly fifteen then.

"She was one little daredevil. Eyes like dinner plates, not like now, but wily, crafty. Yet she went to the altar without a peep – her father ordered it so, and they have it strict, you know, not like we sinners," Grandma Nastya told us. "So, by and by, they lived together for about five years, didn't bear any children, but lived quietly, at peace, went to church, and during the day Serafim Danilovich worked as a barber in Banya No. 1 over the bridge. He was good too, the men respected him; sometimes they'd line up in the street to wait their turn – he shaved without cuts or pain, and didn't skimp on warm compresses. In a word, he was an expert."

And it would have gone on like that, but you know what times those were. After the war, in the nighttime, a man's life wasn't worth a kopek. And we had our share of those amnestied, or escaped ex-cons and bandits, hell knows where they came from. So, one time these two toughs stayed at Matryona Timofeyevna's place, this divorced lady we had. People rumored the two were on the run, but if anyone knew it for sure, they didn't tell. The men kept to themselves, Matryona brought them vodka and liver and innards from the sausage plant – that was where she worked. If she pleased one of them at night, we don't know which one it was, the old one or the young one. One was about 40 – he's the one we called "old" – and the other still wet behind the ears, but rotten already: foxy, beady, angry little eyes, mustache like a thread, stylish pants, and his whole body taut like a string – a viper about to bite. In the evenings, the old one would take a stool outside, sit on it and roll himself a cigarette; he'd sit there and smoke and watch the street, and his sidekick, like a pup, would be right there, just in case. Sometimes, the young one played cards with the boys, or pulled out his knife, just making threats, but the old one was always quiet, never messed with anyone's business, just watched silently and went inside by nightfall.

And that's when, as fate would have it, Serafim Danilovich got conscripted into hay mowing and was sent into the Lake Country, onto the islands there, leaving his Mother by herself. Except it's only now we call her Mother, because her husband is a righteous man in their faith, almost a saint, and back then she was just a girl, never mind she was married. And it seemed her husband didn't indulge her much, either. Or what have you – you know they live pretty strictly there.

So our Lyubasha was alone, no one to talk to, but she stayed away from the village youth, didn't go to their parties, turned off the light in the evenings to go to church, and afterward – straight to bed. And with first roosters – she was up, milking her cow, driving her out to pasture, doing chores, busy as a bee.

One day she was walking down our street, at nighttime after her service, and the hooligans came after her, teasing, pulling her braids, cat-calling, you know – she blushed like a poppy-bloom and made to run, but that's when the younger thug blocked her way. He pulled out his knife and grabbed her, in front of everyone. The poor thing couldn't even scream, or move – he held the blade to her chin. He pushed her to the little banya in the back, and there would've been trouble but the old one suddenly rose from his stool, motioned like so with his hand and snapped his fingers – the young one instantly forgot the girl, and dashed to his boss.

"Kneel!"

He fell to the ground like a cut sheaf. The old one reached behind him slowly, making a point, grabbed the stool and – wham! – smashed it against the young one's skull, splinters everywhere, the boy face down in the mud. When the boy came 'round and rubbed the blood out of his eyes, the old one pointed to the shards of the stool and said, "Have a new one here tomorrow." He was about to go in to Matryona, but stopped and looked a Lyubasha kindly – as she stood there, and the boys around her, neither alive nor dead, too scared to move.

"What's your name, pretty-eyes?"

She lit up as if with a spark.

"Lyubov."

"Fine, fine," the old man nodded. "Go on, sweetie, what are you afraid of? It'll be a lesson for this here goat." He shot one glance over her little figure and went home. And she dashed home, too – she couldn't have hoped for such a rescue.

After that day, people noticed that Lyubasha changed her path to walk past Matryona's house: she started fetching water at Kopanka, and she'd always gone the other way 'round, to Kosmodemyanskaya, before. What can you say? The old one must have won her over. Hooked her in, touched some string in the girl's heart. And of course, soon after there were rumors that he went to her at night. People gossiped, but no one dared to check – they also said the old man carried a gun on him.

All in all, they dallied like that for just over a week: Lyubasha bloomed like my lilac bush, even her gait changed – she used to skip around like a girl, and now she floated swan-like, and her eyes, the eyes – you wouldn't recognize her, she had these happy little impish sparks dancing in them... But all things end.

Serafim Danilovich returned, to his misfortune, at night – all the neighbors were asleep already. He went in – and there they were: caught red-handed. But what could he do against an ex-con? What all happened, I don't know, but the thug got him pinned down and shoved her into the pantry and told her to shush. And what then, what got into his head – but who would know those thugs, they're heartless after the camps, the girl only believed him out of her youth and foolishness – anyway, they had this old, banded trunk in the corner that held all her dowry: beads and necklaces, and money, too, for sure. He emptied it all into his sack, then dragged Serafim Danilovich, stripped of his pantaloons, to the trunk and clamped his manly stuff under the lid, the brute. Shut the trunk, locked it with the key, threw the key out the window, and placed Serafim's favorite German trophy razor on the lid. Just put it there and vanished – no one saw him or his pup after that. Robbed them, you know, locked him down, and ran.

They say the pain took Serafim Danilovich's power of speech – all he could do was moo a little; saying anything clearly or calling for help hurt like a white-hot iron brand, and Lyubasha was locked in the pantry, waiting, scared, not knowing what was going on and praying to every saint she could remember. He couldn't stand it for very long – he was shut tight and things started to swell. So the man grabbed his razor and – slash! – freed himself for the rest of his life. That's when he screamed. And she bawled, in the pantry, too, sensing woe. People ran in from everywhere; the old ones charmed his blood to stop and patched him up. When they freed Lyubasha from the pantry, you know, the first thing she cried out, before she knew what happened, was, "Don't beat my Nikolai (so that's what the thug's name was), it's all my fault, mine alone!" Of course, once she saw it and grasped what had happened, she went out like a light and for about a year afterwards no one heard her utter a word. Later, she started talking again, little by little.

Her father then visited Serafim Danilovich, asking him to throw her out, but Serafim didn't. He did not send her packing, but kept her on as a servant; he hardly talks to her in public, mostly gestures, and what happens at home, we don't know. And he punished her with a 50-year excommunication, which will last to 2001, which is soon, and which is also when they have prophesied the End of the World.

He probably won't make it – he's been ill a lot lately, but he doesn't let anyone into the house, she alone looks after him.

And that's their life.

After that, he never touched the razor again – the community gives them everything, and reveres him as a saint almost. People come to see him from other cities: he must forgive them their sins and such and, people say, he also casts out cancers with his hands.

Lyubasha, poor thing, has ever since dressed all in black, like a nun. Always on her knees, at the window, praying for forgiveness. Why wouldn't he let her go, with God? What use does he have for her?

This is all true, and so we can testify, having seen it with our own eyes out of grandma Nastya's window: beneath a November drizzle, in the cold, the woman kneeled – a tiny black silhouette, covered with a raincoat, at her post, bowing every so often, forehead to the ground.

What we don't know is what sense there can be in it, because if God is Love, then how do you explain this?

THE FOURTH DIMENSION

Critic Igumnov has been to America. To Washington, DC itself. And to New York City, too.

The New York subway scared him.

"It's a prison, a real prison," he told his listeners back in Moscow. "And blacks. You know, I'm not a racist, unlike the majority of our émigrés, but one does see some really scary black people. Poor, lazy. They have no desire to work – just stand on every corner and beg for quarters, but even a dollar won't buy you anything decent."

The listeners sighed devotedly. Igumnov sighed back.

"No, you wouldn't believe it: Manhattan is the city... it's the Yellow Devil! It's really embarrassing even to put it like that – makes me sound exactly like the newspapers, but there are many, so many problems there that we can't even imagine: everything's sold on credit, down to a microwave oven – your average American is in debt up to his ears."

"And what about sausage?"

For some reason, someone always asked this question, although they all knew, sons-of-bitches – and perfectly well – what the answer was.

"It's not about the sausage, believe me, man does not live on sausage alone," Igumnov sighed with even deeper concern. "It's impossible to explain this to you. You have to see and feel it. Sears stores, for example, don't open unless they have 30,000 different food items on the shelves. And what of it?"

"And what of it?" the listeners echoed, transfixed.

"I swear to you, guys, it's hard to communicate fully, but… it's stifling there – there's no soul. Everything wrapped in plastic, everything standardized. It's a nightmare."

The listeners nodded happily. Smiled their inward smiles. Proudly rubbed their hands together. Igumnov would end his story with a short conclusion:

"The one thing they don't have there, perhaps, is a kind of a fourth dimension."

And everyone would noisily drink vodka and praise the good man Igumnov. True, every so often there would be someone who'd say openly, with unconcealed sadness, "You're so full of shit, Igumnov," but no one listened much, and Igumnov would shake his head ruefully – what's to be done, you can't put your head on another man's shoulders. But he never entered arguments – he nipped them in the bud.

Things went on like this for about a month. Igumnov grew tired. Nothing was keeping him in Moscow: the story he'd promised the American magazine, "Europe or Asia? (A word of praise for Eurasians)," he'd written right away, with fresh impressions, and submitted it by fax. Drinking vodka and telling his American tales was growing old. His six-month stipend to Munich was still being processed. The televised debates from the Party Congress bored him to tears. The newly-minted Slavophiles were disgusting.

"Of course, today we're all about the roots, even me, with my universal perspective," he complained to his best friend. "But, you must understand, when they pulled me up, like a village bumpkin, in the late sixties… it was a different time – we were all together against the same thing, and now… No, the middle, the golden middle – the ancients had it right."

Igumnov deflected as many offers as he could, did not join any parties, kept to unorthodox magazines that occasionally printed his essays, and if the opportunity presented itself, garrulously criticized his employers among literary circles. Still, he was beginning to sense, could sense already, that he was irretrievably sliding to the left.

"You must understand, I can't very well go to April, April exhausted itself almost as soon as it was born," he moaned to the same friend.

All this "domestic" fuss grew unspeakably nettlesome. He wanted to rest, he wanted to go home, to the village, close to Stargorod, where, on the site of his mother's dilapidated hovel, he had finally built, four years ago, a sturdy, five-walled cabin. Lord, how many times did he dream of the Lake over there, in America!

The computer that he had bought with his earnings had yet to find a buyer, but the VHS player had already fetched 7,000. He found a good deal on new tires for his Zaporozhets, filled the trunk with a set of excellent fishing rods and tackle (a gift from an American colleague), kissed his wife and daughters, and set course for Stargorod.

Before he left, he called Piontkovsky and talked him into waiting a bit longer. Piontkovsky was about to receive, through the Literary Fund, a new car, a Model Nine, which prompted him to part with his almost-new Niva. Igumnov had offered to buy the Niva for a very good price – the money from the sale of the computer should be more than enough.

The wife packed, as always, substantially: a case of canned pork, four logs of bologna, little jars of instant coffee and Yugoslavian ham, and about 20 packs of 36-grade tea. The food was meant for the village where people expected Igumnov to bring gifts. There was no family left, and his classmates from school were also, nearly all of them, gone (after the army, following the usual formula, they all went anywhere but home). But not to bring gifts for the neighbors was, for Igumnov, unthinkable. People wouldn't understand if he came empty-handed; they wouldn't show it, of course, but they wouldn't understand.

The Zaporozhets struggled down the last ten miles of dirt road (it's a good thing we had a dry May) and Igumnov's native village welcomed him. They unloaded the food, and the case of vodka he bought on the outskirts of Moscow. They embraced.

It was early summer. The beginning of June. Leaves. The infinite Lake. Fish stew on a campfire. Smooth vodka. Talk. His soul relaxed, rested, awash in pure oxygen.

He didn't fear his American stories here. Quite the opposite – it was impossible not to tell them. His stories were sought after, waited for. People were proud of him. They did not hide their admiration when they inspected the waterproof Seiko on his left wrist, and, of course, they needled him, joked and peppered him with questions.

They listened just as raptly as his Moscow friends. Masking their curiosity with the Russian old-boy spirit, they attentively refilled his glass with his vodka. Shook their heads.

"And what about sausage?"

Oh! That eternally-expected question! Igumnov almost cried – people listened sympathetically.

"Well, what do you expect? – it's a strange land," commented tractor-driver Abrosimov on Igumnov's "fourth dimension," as it was self-evident, and for some reason, asked again, "So, you're saying, one can just walk up and buy a wind-up cock like it's no big deal?"

The whole company roared; the American theme was finished.

After about a week, after they finished all the provisions brought from Moscow, and Igumnov stoically switched to potatoes and fish soup, he began to experience an inextinguishable, tormenting longing. The locals, pretending to work, went on different errands in the mornings and came back only late, around dinnertime, followed by a search for more vodka or modest domestic chores. Increasingly, Igumnov found himself alone. Drinking Stargorod vodka didn't feel right and it bored him anyway. He was tired of pike soup. And, generally, fits of the familiar Moscow angst caught up with him, even in the country. Caught up and held him in their grip.

Against his instincts, he began to think. He wanted to convince himself that it wasn't, after all, about sausage. But what was it about? It was easy to talk about "the fourth dimension," but how could it be quantified? And was that necessary?

Take, for example, our national literature – what's the measure of quality there? Tradition? And what is this tradition? Western influence, through and through, especially after Peter the Great. And even before Peter… he kept thinking of Sophia Palaiologina and even saw her in a dream.[24] His obsession threatened to develop into a mania.

In the article he had sent to America, everything was nice and smooth, things were neatly explained by our geography, multiplied by our history. But this no longer satisfied him. Something mysterious had crawled into his subconscious. The voice of blood? Genes? Collective archetypal memory? The question tormented him; his American article seemed meaningless. On top of everything, the sky began to drizzle, lightly yet hopelessly. Igumnov hastened back to Moscow.

The neighbors brought him a bit of honey for his girls, and smoked some fish. Asked him to keep in touch. To come back sooner rather than later. And to make sure to bring sausage. The kind without fat. Two-ninety per kilo.

And Kolka Zhogin, a big fan of spoon bait, requested some cold-water spoon bait from Munich, along with Japanese fishing line.

Igumnov stepped on the gas.

He had almost made it to the paved road – about two miles from the asphalt – when his Zaporozhets sank into mud. Neither digging nor beech branches jammed under the wheels could extract the little car. After wearing himself out and getting dirty up to his ears, Igumnov relaxed. In about three hours, the co-op's Kirovets tractor would pass by on its milk delivery run. All he had to do was wait.

Igumnov unfolded his seat, lay back and took a nap. Right before he fell asleep, it occurred to him that the four-wheel-drive Niva would get through the mud no problem, and the thought made him happy.

---

24. Sophia Palaiologina: Grand Duchess of Moscow, was a niece of the last Byzantine emperor Constantine XI and second wife of Ivan III of Russia. She was also the grandmother of Ivan the Terrible.

He dreamt of a large supermarket shelf filled with little plastic lemons containing real lemon juice, for cooking.

He woke up to the drone of the Kirovets.

The big yellow tractor easily pulled the Zaporozhets onto the asphalt. The driver was a bit drunk, and unfamiliar – a wrinkle-faced little man from the neighboring village. Igumnov had no vodka to pay him with, so he promised to settle up next time.

"All right, America," the driver waved, "I see you don't know me, must be too proud now, or something. I'm Pashka Bokov, we were in the same class in school."

Igumnov gasped, mentally, and quickly started a sociable conversation. They talked for half an hour.

"All right America, Godspeed, I have to take this milk places," said the former classmate as he climbed back behind the wheel.

From there, over the growl of the Kirovets' engine, Igumnov heard a giggle and the excessively-upbeat, "And don't forget, when you come back, bring sausage for me, too!"

Igumnov returned to Moscow in dark and rotten spirits. He avoided his friends for a while, but it was not characteristic of him to hide out for long. Things returned to their well-oiled tracks and rolled along. Even with a kind of newly-emboldened abandon.

He still planned to go to Munich, although he changed the theme of his research to the poetics of Gogol's Mirgorod, which had been his focus before he took up Eurasianism. He bought Piontkovsky's Niva and sold his Zaporozhets for a good price. He surprised his friends with his new interest in videos. In his free time, he visited his neighbor, and together they watched detective and sci-fi movies.

On those occasions when his colleagues began talking about America, he cut them short with a single, inappropriate question, "Have you heard? They say a joint-venture factory in Saratov has obtained permission to manufacture wind-up polyurethane cocks."

The colleagues would exchange giddy glances, drop the painful topic and immediately start discussing women.

2010

A CHANGE OF CONSCIOUSNESS

Lent just ended. Sociologists from Moscow's Levada Center agency asserted that 79 percent of Russians had no intention of fasting or otherwise observing Lent. Two local hot-heads shot off fireworks during the church procession – I'll never forget how ashamed the boys looked when they were caught; they just wanted to make it better.

The Church continues to teach: prayer and repentance are the most important thing during Lent. The word "repentance" comes into Russian from the Greek "matanoia" meaning a change of consciousness and even the broadening of consciousness beyond the individual intelligence, sense. It implies a special spiritual procedure that can transport a believer's consciousness from one level of being to another. But then I also read in *The Stargorod Herald:* "Repentance is an identifying feature of our national character." I read that and didn't want to keep reading. It reminded me of a story.

In the late '80s I found some part-time work with a restoration team at the Old Believers' Pokrovsky Cathedral in the Rogozhsky neighborhood of Stargorod. The Old Believers were banned from building temples that looked like Orthodox churches, so when seen from the street, architect Kozakov's creation resembled a large box with a few domes on top. Inside, however, it was indistinguishable from, say, the Novgorod Sofia. A sweep of a ceiling. Stern icons in the ancient style. Monumental murals. Dusk, wax candles in massive silver candelabras. The smell of incense mixes with strangely Oriental, ancient harmonies, music that sounds mysterious and difficult to the modern ear, trained in Baroque polyphonies. At the entrance, an old lady vigilantly guarded this world against strangers.

Every morning for three weeks we climbed the scaffolding and washed the frescoed walls with a special concoction made with boiled soap, and for three weeks Maria Lukinichna, the door-woman, watched us with unconcealed disgust. Smoking on the temple grounds was strictly *verboten*, so when it was time for a break, we took our buckets of boiled-soap into the keeper's cottage, put them on the stove to heat, and went to the park next door. There, we smoked. When we came back, the gas under the buckets was almost invariably turned off. The old lady would come in to boil some tea and turn our stuff off just to spite us – we always left her a burner. When caught red-handed, she would not negotiate. She'd squeeze her lips into a disdainful line and stare at the floor. She observed her boycott as if it were a monastic vow. From the scaffolding, we could watch her: she spent her free time polishing the church's silver and scrubbing the floors, or else she prayed, bending again and again to the ground in countless bows. Once we heard her upbraiding a drunken reader:

"All you know is how to fill your gut! Watch my word – the Green Viper will get you!" she raged, and the poor little man could only mumble every so often, "I do repent, Mother..."

"I do repent, Father," Lukinichna would thunder back, bow, and pick up right where she left off, with fresh ire.

Then, a holy day of great significance was upon us. The Metropolitan himself was to come from Moscow. For two days before his scheduled arrival the old ladies scoured the church with zeal undreamt of by generals on the eve of a Marshal's inspection. On the day itself, the service went on forever – the Old Believers don't believe in hurrying their prayers. A few of our crew decided to wait the mass out on the scaffolding; myself and another guy, having finished what we had planned for the day, descended from the exulted heights, tip-toed around the faithful, and went outside. Not far from the church we found a *shashlyk* place where we had some kebabs with fries, washing it all down with the 777 port that at the time was served in "bombs" of 0.8 liters each. We ate and drank, then drank some more, bought more still to take with us, and then felt compelled, for reasons passing understanding, to go back to work.

Back in the church, we climbed the scaffolding to the top platform where I promptly slipped on a wet board and knocked down a bucket of dirty water. Its flight down to the bottom of the church remains branded into my memory to this day. It hit the floor and exploded, dousing the solemn gathering. But the Metropolitan did not shudder or make a noise out of order, and neither did the other priests – they only wiped their brows with the embroidered sleeves of their garments. The congregation did not stumble in its responses either, but carried on with the mass as if there had been no exploding bucket whatsoever. We took a nap up there on the scaffolds and retreated home when the coast cleared.

The next morning I came back to work; I was ashamed and scared. I prayed for the old door-lady to fall ill, to disappear, to vanish inexplicably from my life. Of course, that was not to be! A pair of burning eyes pinned me at the entrance to the church, alive and terrifying like the eyes of an Old Testament prophet in the icon above her. My legs folded of their own volition, I fell to my knees and blurted loudly, "Lukinichna, forgive this fool, I got drunk yesterday. I was the one who dropped the bucket."

Instantly, she dropped on the ground next to me – the way an axe falls on a log – and slammed her forehead against the floor. The sound of bone making contact with stone echoed through the church. Then she rose, and dropped her head again, and couldn't stop after that – she bowed and bowed, hitting her head against the very clean floor, sobbing, and saying, "You forgive me, brother! I thought you a godless pest, forgive me!"

I was shaking all over; I could feel no strength in my legs, no way to get up.

The old lady helped me up to a chair. She assessed my condition with one look, and said, "Go home, have a drink, take a nap."

I shook my head and went to climb the scaffolding.

No one ever turned off gas under our boiled soap again. Instead, Lukinichna now served us tea in the kitchen and chastised us gently for siding with Patriarch Nikon in the schism[1]. I don't drink port any more either, even the most expensive kind.

---

1. Patriarch Nikon's reforms of 1653, aimed to establish uniformity between the Greek and Russian church practices, caused a schism between the official church and the Old Believers movement.

THE HORIZONTAL AND THE VERTICAL

The other day, Styopa Morozov, director of Timber Concern No. 2, and I were summoned to tea at the home of the retired vice-mayor of Stargorod, Sergey Pavlovich Triflin. A short man, with intent, avian eyes that looked forever hungry, he had been the terror of the city in the early days of democracy. It was whispered in town that he very well might be a witch. Having outlasted two governors and three mayors, this 65-year-old man was finally fulfilled: he retired, and now spends his time doting on his prized German pointer Rida and taking an active part in the city's social life. Triflin is also a passionate photographer; his album *Wildflowers of Russia's Middle Zone* was published by a Moscow art-house. He is waiting for primroses now – spring is almost here. "I dream," he says, "of flowers in the snow."

We met three years ago, because of an old English rifle. I was the one who told him back then: it's a rare piece, a pre-Revolutionary W. W. Greener, with an elephant stamped on it and the safety button on the left side of the bed.

While we drank tea, the news on TV showed the former mayor of Vladivostok being arrested. Triflin commented on the story, then pulled a thick volume out of his bookcase and read to us an order by Peter the Great. In the year of our Lord 1719, on the 24th day of March, it was so ordered: "Smolensk vice-governor and associates to dispatch due statements of income and expenses. And if ye shalt not execute said errand the May of this year, then all ye, vice-governor as well as other subordinates, to be shackled at the ankles, chained by the neck and kept in the Chancellery until ye the above-mentioned duty fulfill."

"Now that's how they used to keep the vertical strong in the old days – and this here clown got flown by plane, and without a chain on his neck like a Gypsy bear. The progress is obvious!" Triflin smiled. "Charged with mismanagement of a million rubles – what kind of money is that! They'll find more, you can be sure, because you should remember the vertical, of course, but you must also keep a grip on the horizontal. We here, of course, figured this out back in the nineties."

And that's when Styopa asked how exactly one was different from the other. Triflin glanced at Styopa, quickly sized up his jeweled ring, as if snapping a picture of it, and began:

"It's simple. I had this lad under me, former military. One day, I pull up to work, and see this hot-pink Humvee parked right in front of city hall. No one around here ever had one of those. I barely made it to my office, and my phone's ringing. The mayor, Veslo Vasyl Petrovich, is on the line.

"Whose beauty is that out there?"

"I'm on it," I say, "post-haste!"

I asked around – turns out it's my own deputy's! I called him in.

"What happened?"

"Sergey Pavlovich," he says, "I admit I couldn't resist it – it's a gift."

"You," I said, "watch out – the mayor himself doesn't have wheels like that."

Next thing you know, our mayor is rolling around in style, in a pink Humvee. It didn't do much for him, though – he lives in Argentina now. And this lad of mine, the deputy, has gone far and climbed high in the capital, sends me cognac regularly, to thank me for having taught him about life. My other deputy, Khokhlov – he turns his nose up now, rules his own *kolkhoz* and drinks moonshine. So, as far as the horizontal went, we got that leveled out all right, and if Veslo couldn't take care of the vertical, I'm not one to judge him."

We sat for a while longer, drank tea with jam. Styopa, I noticed, was very nervous. Finally, we took our leave.

Outside the gate Styopa breathed a sigh of relief:

"I think we're all right now... That rifle he had you look at – he took it from me."

"You hold a grudge?"

"What's to grudge? Back then he signed over so much land, we logged for a year."

Styopa left in his beat-up jeep with the all-terrain wheels, exactly what he needs for driving around his logging plots. I stood for a minute at the fence, looking at Triflin's house, one of the first built in the village by the lake – people call the place "The Count's Ruins": A low-slung building in the shadow of cottonwood trees, with an inconspicuous second floor and a large basement (*banya*, garage, storage room), it stands in sharp contrast to the fashionable turreted castles surrounding it. Modestly extended horizontally, it is simple and comfortable inside. A tall antennae tower with a lightning rod pierces the sky; the national tricolor flag beats in the wind at its top.

And then I saw a magpie fly out an open second-floor window – a dart of black-and-white, and it was gone into the woods. Soon the bird returned and alit on the windowsill. In its paw, it held a brilliant object. I recognized Styopa's diamond ring. The bird seemed to admire its loot, then slowly turned what looked like a scrunched-up human face in my direction: it was Sergey Pavlovich looking at me. Reason failed me, for an instant, and when I could see clearly again, the magpie was gone.

All kinds of wondrous things happen in Stargorod. The actress Katya Kholodtsova, for instance, because of unrequited love drowned herself in one of Stargorod's channels and turned into a mermaid. Afterwards, many people saw her bathing there in the moonlight, and I am inclined to believe them. Now I also understood the fear Triflin inspired in local businessmen. No one seemed to know where he came from, but it only took him a year to take over the city.

I sighed, crossed myself, and went back to my local history museum, to work on the "G-whiz!" exhibit planned to mark "The Year of the Russian Language." The exhibit was why Triflin had called us in the first place: he decided to show his series *Thunderbolts of Our Native Land.* He charged me with preparing the catalogue and hanging the pictures; Styopa would be responsible for matting and framing.

53:76

The other day I came across a sensational clip on the internet: Koreans have bred carps with human faces. The picture showed a couple of fish with protruding snouts that, with a stretch, could be seen to resemble human features. Just another hybrid, nothing special. They should try coming here, to Stargorod, to catch the Catfish Man – but they ain't coming, are they? Our news is not big enough for the world-wide web.

Our national television couldn't care less for real marvels, they just fill the air with scary stories about thieves and cops. Somewhere in Stavropol region, a police captain fired his gun point-blank at an innocent family – the wife now rides around in a wheelchair and the husband got three years for "assault on an officer in the execution of his duty," but was amnestied right there in the courtroom. The policeman is now a colonel. There's no help for common folk. Every teenage boy in Stargorod knows this, and that is why they all worship our Sashka Pugachev, the people's avenger. They write on the District Police Station's wall, in spray paint: "Greetings from Pugachev! 53:76." Cadets paint it over the next morning, but the writing seems to bulge from the surface of the wall as if injected with the fashionable collagen that, if one believes the ads, "pushes out the wrinkles from the inside." The newspapers at first also wrote up a storm about Sashka, but even then they were afraid to tell the whole truth. Here's what happened.

Sashka, a born and raised Stargorodian who, after fighting in Afghanistan, lost all fear but not his soul, was doing well: he had two sawmills, eight small stores around the city, a construction supplies warehouse and the Lyubava tavern on the highway out of town,

serving tender chicken cutlets, stuffed fish from our river and girls in
the rooms upstairs. As well, there's the free gym, two schools' worth
of computers and a city soccer team – all paid for by the man himself.
Colonel Erikh Romanovich Mushtabel, the city's Chief of Police,
was a frequent guest at Sashka's table in Lyubava. He was also the one
who "protected" him and, once he got the taste for it, kept pushing
for a bigger share of the spoils. They got along fine, however, until
Sashka's love of fishing ruined him.

Mushtabel was also a devout fisherman, and they once made a bet
about who could catch a bigger catfish. Each went to his spot: one man
went upstream to Pimshin Dip, the other downstream – to the Ferry
Dip. Erikh hooked a 53-kilogram beast, but the one Sashka dragged
in weighed 76 kilos. Mushtabel took offense and declared war on
Pugachev. He found an excuse to close down Sashka's stores, took
away his sawmills, ordered a full inspection of Lyubava and publicly
threatened to burn the whorehouse down. So Pugachev decided to
go all in, told Mushtabel to meet him at night at the station, rolled in
with two AK-47s and let both rip from the hip, right in the doorway.
Three guys who just happened to be there went down, four more got
wounded, but the Chief was not in his office – he was waiting in an
ambush outside. The chase began.

They flew to the river. Pugachev had a chance to call out: "Don't
come to the water, I'll come for you as a catfish!" – and dove from
a tussock into the rapids. The police shone spotlights on the river,
opened fire, bullets rained on Pugachev. He swam, then went under.
No one ever saw him come up again. They never found the body,
although they searched hard.

Mushtabel didn't give much thought to the curse. He handled
the ensuing shit-storm and took over Lyubava, but it burned down
soon afterwards, and not a single girl got hurt, as though someone'd
warned them. Rumors of Pugachev's last words spread through
the city. Someone spray-painted "53:76 – That's how we do it!" on
Mushtabel's SUV, and the man just lost it. Plus, right at the same
time, fishermen started saying a monster of a catfish had turned up in

the river, no less than 200 kilos, tearing nets, letting their catch out, and there was no way to get him. The fishermen were also paying Mushtabel for "protection."

The colonel became obsessed with the idea of getting this fish – given that his authority in the city was rapidly approaching zero. Exactly what transpired when he went to the river at night, nobody knows, but people said Erikh Romanovich ran home covered in catfish slime, two fingers of his right hand bitten off at the root, his eyes filled with madness. He lost his speech, and could only moo – he pointed at the river and mooed, long and sad, like a terrified calf: "Oo-oooo-oogoooo!" At the hospital, they said he had a stroke, patched the old dog up, but, obviously, that was the end of his service. The colonel came down with hydrophobia: a mere glimpse of the river and he turned hysterical, like a baby. Once out of uniform, he turned into an old, sick man; kind people heap shame on him in the streets, reminding him about Pugachev. His wife didn't put up with it for long, packed up and moved the family to her Kalmykia – there's no water there to speak of. The fishing folks arranged for a church procession, prayed to the miracle-fish to get their fishing rights back. Some old man also advised them: if they caught a catfish, even a baby one, to always throw it back. So now you'll never find catfish cutlets anywhere on the menu in Stargorod – but we do have plenty of perch or zander.

It's been ten years, and boys still call out at discotheques "53!" and someone always shouts back "76!"

So don't you start with the Korean human-faced carp. But then, again, if you think about it – Oh, my God...

PICKLE AND LITTLE DRAGON

In the time before memory, in what would become the Stargorod district, there lived a people called the Komsi. They worked only so hard, drank themselves silly on *braga*,[2] and then soaked for weeks in *banyas* which in their tongue they called "saunas." When the hard-working Slavs arrived, they easily crushed the Komsi. The Komsi did not resist and, legend has it, retreated quietly beneath the earth.

Stargorodians who today live in the region are pure-blood Russians and visit *banyas* only on Saturdays. Having lost their jobs after the collapse of the *kolkhozes*, they drink cheap moonshine and swear that even if liquor turned to stone, they would gnaw on that rock – they have discovered no better medicine for their boredom.

It is said that moonshine kills 40,000 each year in our country. This horrific figure was pronounced by Putin himself, who proposed that the state take charge of alcohol production, so that it might be of the highest quality. Fortunately the Duma hit the brakes, and the plan was scrapped. We remember too well the two bottle limits of '87, and don't want to go back there.

Once the villagers polished off all the foreign alcohol known as Royal, they turned to a domestic product called Little Dragon, an oily, green, glowing beverage. I was assured that, if you stare long and hard into your glass, the liquid will congeal into a furious yellow snake that will spin on the surface of your drink like a resinous shard of pine wood in a spring puddle. The villagers drank Little Dragon without looking in the glass. Some lost their minds; others were carried straight to the churchyard. But the engine of history runs on

---

2. Fermented birch sap.

accidents: thanks to a miraculous confluence of events, the villagers have stopped consuming this poison.

Kolya Piklov, whose nickname was Pickle, downed a glass in the morning and then added two more at lunchtime, right there in the field, at which point he lost all interest in plowing, since he had a three-liter bottle of Little Dragon at home.

Pickle hopped behind the wheel of his Belarus tractor and rolled out onto the road. The next instant he was rammed by a new Audi A-8 that three goons were delivering to their commander, Anton Bes, the district's chief bootlegger.[3] Abandoning the tractor, Pickle fled as far as his legs could carry him, which was Bald Mountain, some ten kilometers from the village. There he sat down on a stump and began to think.

For ruining such an expensive foreign car, the Stargorodian thugs would definitely leash him up like a dog. Pickle became frightened and began to cry bitterly. Suddenly, he saw before him a snotty old woman in birch-bark shoes, who said, "Kiss me."

Since he had been a boy, Pickle had heard of a Komsi sorceress who, coming across a traveler, asked for a kiss. Those who did not show respect simply disappeared. So, without much ado, he gave her a peck on the cheek.

"You're a true Komsi, Pickle. What do you have to fear?" the hag laughed.

He told her of his woes. The sorceress gave him a vial of poison, and ordered him to drink it at home, then quietly lie down. Pickle thanked her and ran home. Meanwhile, the bandits drove the Audi in for repairs, then doubled back to beat the living daylights out of the tractor driver.

At home, Pickle poured the contents of the vial into his bottle of Little Dragon and gulped down a mouthful of the cocktail. His body suddenly began to bulge and broke out in pimples all over. Not quite

---

3. *Bes* is Russian for "Devil."

himself anymore, he stumbled out onto the porch, climbed into the bottom of his brining barrel and promptly turned into a large pickle.

The goons arrived and sat themselves down at his table. They sat for an hour... two... No sign of the master of the house. They got thirsty. Someone found Pickle's bottle. Someone else ran to the porch and brought back a ladleful of brine and a large pickle. They poured and drank, and the one who ran to the porch took a bite of the pickle. The poison worked instantly: two kicked the bucket and the third was transformed into a chimpanzee.

Pickle woke up on the table – either the brine had absorbed the poison or the effect of the drink had worn off. He had half an ear bitten off, but he was alive. Next to him were a whimpering chimpanzee and two stiffs.

The police pulled in. They did their tests and found cyanide in the Little Dragon. The case began to acquire the stench of prison, since everyone knew that the alcohol was supplied by Bes. The chief of police, Ivan Pankratovich Bolt, who had been protecting Bes' business, ruled thus: first, he would keep the Audi for himself; second, Bes would be forbidden from trading in Little Dragon.

Bes transitioned to Monolit, Mozaika and Maximka - "clear, colorless glass-cleaning liquids based on ethyl alcohol, without any mechanical additives." It's easy to order them: just search the internet for "Wholesale Liquor." They even offer home delivery.

The sorceress has not appeared to anyone since. Pickle brews *braga* and drinks nothing else, having completely stopped working. He proselytizes in the village that the Komsi will soon awake, as the time has come for their auras to be set free from their underground incarceration. When everyone laughs at him, Pickle goes home, climbs into his pickling barrel and soaks there for weeks, activating his *chakhras*.

The peasants now drink Maximka, which paralyzes the tongue for two days. But what is there to talk about, if everything is so clear? The chimpanzee lives in Bes' garage; at night he howls at the moon. Meanwhile, the chief of police has a new headache: the Duma has doubled traffic fines. What's good for a Muscovite is trouble for a Stargorodian. Each road police crew, which used to turn a hundred dollars a day over to the bosses, now has to deliver two hundred. The question is this: will people give them more money, and will it lead to public unrest?

THE HOLY MONKEY

A true miracle, as everyone knows, requires time to become accepted as such. The bandit Foma,[4] whom a spell by a Komsi-sorceress turned into a chimpanzee, lived in the garage of his former commander, Anton Bes. The latter dressed the chimpanzee in loafers, slacks, a padded jacket, a fur cap, and dark glasses with white rims, making him look like an unhinged clown. Bes had his fun and quickly forgot about the poor wretch.

Foma ran off to the city and hung about the cemetery church of St. Christopher. He begged for alms at the gates and bit by bit edged his way inside. An elder informed the abbot, Father Artemon, that Foma appeared to be a monkey. On one occasion, Artemon attempted to speak to him. Foma flung himself to his knees, seized his head in his hands, and froze in a repentant pose. The half-blind Father Artemon evaluated such zeal thus: "He's mute and a fool, but not without Christ; leave him be. St. Christopher also had the face of a beast; there's a reason he is portrayed with the head of a dog."

The *batushka*'s word is law, so Foma began to sweep the churchyard, and was even given a place to stay in the warm storeroom, where he slept in his clothes like a true holy fool. The old women began to say that Foma was a Hindu mute and that he was tormented by some exotic disease.

The church, naturally, had an icon of St. Christopher painted by an ancient hand, from a time when they portrayed the holy warrior with the head of a dog and a large sword. Only a few of these ancient images survive to this day, having evaded the order to paint over the

---

4.   The Russian equivalent of Thomas.

dogs' heads with human ones. Father Artemon prized the icon and, through all his 57 years of service, he humbly waited for it to perform a miracle.

A graveyard church is a profitable place, so they sent a second priest, Father Pavlin Pridvorov, to assist the abbot. Father Pavlin, having filled his head with street vendors' books, was consumed by the idea of canonizing Ivan the Terrible and preached that Holy Rus' could only be revived by a strong hand, which he had the temerity to assert in a letter to the Metropolitan. In reply, Father Pavlin was advised to display his intelligence less prominently.

Father Pavlin craved a cause. Someone related to him a local legend: in the graveyard church Ivan the Terrible had treated the orphan Ivashka to an apple. The boy ate the apple, lit up like an angel, and died. Father Pavlin felt it would be useful for the church to have a locally revered saint. So he issued an appeal and Young Guard activists excavated all over the church grounds, but they turned up no remains that could qualify as holy. Instead, for excavating without permission, they had to pay a fine to the Committee for the Protection of Culture. Father Artemon paid the fine and severely forbade Pridvorov from muddling the minds of parishioners with stories of false miracles. As a result, Father Pavlin bore a grudge against the abbot.

Meanwhile, Foma for some reason wandered back to his former boss and overheard a certain conversation: an order had arrived from Petersburg for the icon of St. Christopher. The boys who usually did the stealing didn't feel up to breaking into a church, so Bes boastfully declared that he himself would take care of it within twenty-four hours. At night, he slipped into the church. Barely had he pried the icon from the iconostasis when Foma sounded the alarm from the bell tower. The thief ran. Foma flew from the bell tower like an arrow, overtook Bes and ripped the icon from his hands. Bes struck him in the chest with a knife. Townspeople came running and surrounded the thief. The abbot joined them. Foma, not taking his eyes off the icon, died in the abbot's arms. And it was only at that moment that

Father Artemon realized that the savior of the church's treasure was in fact a chimpanzee.

The police were so fed up with Bes that they gave him the maximum sentence: twelve years of hard labor. Father Artemon prayed long and hard, and then wrote to his superiors about the Holy Monkey. Father Pavlin Pridvorov's denunciation followed shortly thereafter: it informed the authorities that the chimpanzee had attended liturgies, while, as everyone knows, the only animals allowed into churches are cats, because they alone do not eat their own feces.

As the bishop's bell ringer told it, the day before the bishop received the letters, the believers attending the Stargorod church, which was not even big enough to hold a service of extreme unction, beat the bishop's guards until they bled. Reading a letter about miracles of an all but heretical nature, and having grown weary of public unrest, the bishop quietly sent Father Artemon into retirement, then transferred Father Pavlin to the town of Soggy Tundra, to enlighten the pagans. News of the miracle flew through the city, and it was whispered that, before his death, Foma regained human form. The number of worshippers at the church increased. The hero-monkey was buried outside the walls of the church's graveyard, but pilgrims still beat a path to his grave. The profitable church was assigned to the monks of Boris and Gleb Monastery and Stargorod bandits gifted their Father Superior a new Jaguar, in order that he might pray for them. The people quickly christened the priest Jaguarius. Many take the name at face value…

No matter, it's a distinguished name, and it suits him well.

WINGS

Roza Musayevna Bakhtiyarova did not return to the capital after she was released from Stalin's camps. The ex-ballerina moved in with some distant relatives in the Tatar community and established a dance school under the auspices of the Bearings factory. She passed on quietly in 1995 and was buried in St. Christopher's Graveyard.

After Roza Musayevna's death, the dance troupe faded and eventually dissolved – without her genius, everything seemed pointless. Stargorod had become her fate; the school was the vocation of her ruined – as it seemed, once and for all – life. At one of her interrogations, right in front of her, the investigator had snapped in two the training wings gifted her (and passed through an English diplomat) by a half-crazed Nizhinsky.

She was strict and would sharply dismiss any of her girls' dazzling dreams of making it to the Bolshoi: "This is where you were born, and this is where you will be put to use."

Aigul Sarayev, the pride of our nation, the great flying ballerina, was her student. Her father, Rifat Sarayev, had wanted his daughter to master the art of gold embroidery, just like his wife, who had died young. Dance, he said, is not a profession; it is utter misfortune.

The girl worshipped her father, cried bitterly, but could not give up dancing. When, in her final year of high school, she fell in love with Vasya Peryshkin, her father, who had dreamed of wedding her to a Tatar, stopped talking to her altogether. Vasya was drafted into the army. He died in Grozny, during the first Chechen Campaign.

Spring arrived, and the birds sang their mating songs. Aigul fled the wake and wandered into the stall of old Kambiz, who since time immemorial had been trading all sorts of junk and antiques near the kremlin's entry tower. The Persian resembled a tower himself: ponderous and unscathed, he perched on a massive stool. His legs were like pillars; his wildly brilliant eyes like two searchlights.

The girl went inside; Kambiz blinked his eyes in greeting. Alongside the Pioneer bugles and the carved distaffs Aigul spotted a set of small wings mounted in a leather harness. Self-conscious in front of the old Persian, she tried them on before a mirror. The wings fit perfectly: they didn't restrict her movement, nor did they rub on her shoulder blades.

"Not afraid?" the old man asked.

"What's there to be afraid of anymore?" Aigul replied.

The stall owner took her small bill and brushed it on the shelves loaded with goods, as if sealing a deal with Fate.

The wings, fashioned to a one-eighth scale by some unknown craftsman in some unknown town, begat a new Aigul Sarayev. She staged the ballet *Eurydice*. Naked and wildly sensual, as flexible as a lash, she exploded the aura of tragedy, flying across the stage full of life – but landing as a sorrowful, discarded shadow from the Kingdom of the Dead. Aigul outlined her slanted eyes with make-up in a way that allowed her face to express something languid and bestial, just as the great Nizhinsky had done in *The Afternoon of a Faun*. Some imbecile lashed out at her innovative dance in an article in the *Stargorod Herald* titled "Sex on Stage," and she ran off to Petersburg, and then to Paris, and soon became famous the world over.

I watched *Night Flight*, which had made Aigul famous, with Roza Musayevna, on the government TV channel. The old ballerina was ill and I had stopped in to see her. Aigul flew across the stage in large, webbed wings crafted by a hereditary wing-maker in Verona, the last of his kind.

"The little bird flew away. No use for her here," the old teacher said of the performance.

A week later, Bakhtiyarova died. A month later, the shoemaker Rifat passed on. Aigul did not return to bury either of them, something the yellow press slobbered over for quite a while. Aigul doesn't give interviews, and basically talks to no one, always giving the impression that she lives on another planet, and thus she is often reproached for arrogance and haughtiness. The journalists have nicknamed Sarayev "the doleful diva" because she always performs tragic roles.

Not long ago I ran into Volokitin, the head of the Department of Culture, and chatted with him about the monument the city had promised to erect at the gravesite of Roza Musayevna.

"Now is not the time. National projects are the priority, and all money is going to teachers and doctors."

Out of sorts, I walked to the cemetery. A large Rolls Royce with darkened windows pulled out of the gate. Not the sort of car you see in Stargorod.

I brushed off last year's leaves from Bakhtiyarova's grave and suddenly I noticed, lying on the cement gravestone, a set of small, worn-out wings on a threadbare harness. I picked them up, and as I was looking at them, a girl of about fifteen popped up from behind me – I think I had seen her break-dancing in the park, near the monument to Kirov, where the kids hang out.

"May I?"

She snatched the wings from me and put them on. They fit her as if she was born for them. In the face of such impudence I lost my power of speech. The girl smiled lightly, leapt up, and soared into the air. Fragile, almost weightless, she flew above the gravestones and disappeared through the branches of the cemetery's linden trees.

CAT AND DREGS

Anyone who, having taken out an extended warranty on his new car, has ever found himself in need of replacing a warrantied part, has experienced moments of acute anxiety: what if instead of a new part, the garage sticks him with a used one? Fifteen years of free market later, one can safely say the insurance system has developed significantly. Here in Stargorod, everyone knows the story of Cat and Dregs.

Vassily Andreyevich Spitsyn saved up his fees from group portraits of kindergarten graduations and finally acquired his first "Volga".

He quickly painted it pink and equipped it with a pair of large brass wedding rings on the roof. Spitsyn Services, when it opened in 1991, was the first business of its kind in our city: Vassily Andreyevich worked as a hired driver and also offered his services as a wedding photographer, which maximized his earnings. He quickly became well known at the Wedding Palace as well as at the district wedding offices. Always a spendthrift, he paid the clerks there who referred couples to him with the chocolates and champagne that the newlyweds frequently shared with him.

He was always busy. The local gangsters, for instance, decided they liked hiring the only pink car in town to take them and their girlfriends to the Freedom Monument at night. They called it "trying the knot." The locals refer to the monument – a large, upturned bell resembling a giant shot glass, at the edge of town – as "one big drink". In 1014, the Novgorod army, after the battle at Soggy Tundra, expropriated our bells, but then the bells began to ring of their own volition, and the Novgorod folks promptly returned them, with their apologies. They had to drive them back to Stargorod upside down because the bells' indefatigable clamor had made them all deaf. As soon as they handed the bells over to the Stargorod bishop, however, the Novgorod crew miraculously regained their hearing and to celebrate their joy threw a feast for the locals where both sides drank themselves silly. So, as you can see, my compatriots have known since the olden days how to punish their enemies and how to forgive them.

Soon, the transmission on Spitsyn's pink Volga went out. Spitsyn went to the service shop Under the Bridge, which, according to his insurance contract, was obligated to fix his car for free. The prospect of doing so, however, held little appeal for mechanic Nikolai Perhavko. The freshly-minted entrepreneur was told, in no uncertain terms, that the transmission could be replaced, but first he had to get the car inspected all the way over in Gorky, which usually takes a month or two. In response, Spitsyn uttered four simple words: "See you in court." That was a knock-down.

"All right, we'll fix it up, come back tomorrow," the mechanic said, apparently in consent. Of course, no sooner had the client disappeared around the corner, than the furious Kolya jerked the car up on the lift. He did replace the transmission, but personally dropped cat feces ("dregs" as folks around here call them) into the new transmission oil. The gears shifted smoothly, Spitsyn drove out of the shop triumphant.

In a week, he came back.

"When it's cold, everything's fine, but once I've driven around for an hour or so, the stench in the car is unbelievable. What did you slip me? I give up – replace the transmission again, I'll pay cash this time."

He put a bottle of cognac on the hood as a peace offering.

The client's always right, as they say. Perhavko replaced the transmission with a used one; it creaked but worked. Since then, not a single person in Stargorod has called Spitsyn anything but "Dregs" behind his back.

Of course, the rules of the plot demand revenge. As luck would have it, Spitsyn heard that Perhavko was invited to an upcoming wedding as a friend of the groom; Spitsyn sent him a box with a present, making it look like it came from a friend of the bride, and enclosed a note asking Perhavko not to open the box until the big day. The box was delivered at lunchtime, after Perhavko had imbibed a respectable amount of vodka and was about to take his repose in the storage room. Intrigued, he untied the colored ribbon that held the box shut, and lifted the lid. A howling, catnip-mad female cat was instantly catapulted from inside the box and onto the mechanic's face. The cat's claws marked him for life, and the hero of this tale, as could only have been expected, was immediately christened with the name "Raggedy-Cat," whose first part was subsequently lost.

Spitsyn went on working hard. When a chance presented itself, he bought two more cars, and then a few more. He now sells imported cars. All his cars are insured and repaired in his own garage.

Once, during a break at the meeting of the "Friends of Stargorod" society I overheard Styopa, the director of Timber Concern No. 2 complain to Vassily Andreyevich about the 450 dollars Styopa had to pay at Spitsyn's garage for a routine oil and filter change on his new SUV.

"You bought yourself peace of mind," Spitsyn replied. "Everything's according to the law and your warranty contract. Or you could go to the Under the Bridge garage if you don't care about your car."

"But they say Cat now works for you," Styopa needled him.

"Cat, once he started to earn real money, forgot about his drink. We've reformed that fellow, and we'll change others too."

Styopa had nothing to say to that. They rang the bell, and we went back to the meeting room. Spitsyn railed at our businessmen for not contributing funds for the beautification of the main square and the monument to the architect Barsov, which was in need of repair. And you know, he shamed, squeezed, and banged the three million he wanted out of them – although not until he put his own million in the till.

It's been a long time since I heard anyone call Spitsyn "Dregs." People like to make fun of his love of cleanliness, some even call him eccentric, but they still respect him.

After the meeting, Spitsyn and I went downstairs together. All of a sudden, he grabbed my lapel and whispered, "Let's go get wasted – I've had it with them all, to be honest."

I was in no position to refuse Vassily Andreyevich, and really didn't want to. If I'm being honest.

HOW A SOLDIER SAVED HIMSELF FROM THE ARMY

Not so long ago, there was a debate on TV: should people of creative professions be required to serve in the army? Folks from the parliament took it up with the intelligentsia. They got quite worked up, I thought for sure there'd be a fist-fight, but they cooled off in the end and pronounced their verdict: the Army needs to professionalize, but until that happens, everyone just has to live with the draft. And one rather well-known politician publicly promised one well-known choreographer a deferment for all the guys in his troupe – struck a deal with his opponent, basically, as politicians are wont to do. Those guys got really lucky – like in a fairy tale. Although, we in Stargorod have seen our own share of fairytale luck.

Once upon a time, there was this soldier who decided to go AWOL. Before he got called up for service, he studied at an art college, but then he angered one of his professors: the boy didn't want to paint still-lifes; he only wished to do landscapes, *en plein air*. His mother earned little, and his little brother was ill with asthma and needed expensive drugs. His father watched a parking lot at night and read mystical books about reincarnation. He did not help the soldier's mother any, seeing as he'd taken such offense at her having divorced him. And they all lived in a tiny two-room apartment in a barrack-like apartment block. So it came to pass that our hero quit college and decided to serve his country. He went to the enlistment office and asked to be a Marine. Instead, they shaved his head and sent him off to the chemical weapons brigade, where they taught him to be quick and limber in a gas mask. And things would have just run their course, and he would have come home in just another six months, but as luck would have it, new winds came a-blowing through our good old army.

A whole bunch of new contracted privateers got sent to the soldier's brigade: every single one of them had done time, and was used to going about life not by the book but by their "notions." These privateers set to breaking in the rest of the enlistees, in order that they, too, would sign up as contractees. If everyone in the brigade did, Central Command promised them a ton of bacon. Some gave in; our soldier was the last hold-out. When the beasts promised to give him the blanket treatment after the evening roll-call, he called it quits and did what he'd been planning – dove out through a hole in the fence, and headed not to the village but out into the steppe.

So our soldier walked along the rail line and thought about putting a leg under a train – but when a train rolled along, he got cold feet, and didn't go through with it. He walked some more, and then kept walking, thinking his sad thoughts, until he came upon a great big palace where a general lived with his daughter. The general's daughter sat high up in a tower, watched "Animal Planet" thanks to a satellite dish, and thought sad thoughts. The general had a mind to get her married to the solicitor general's son, but the boy had bad breath. The general himself did not care all that much for the solicitor general, but knew he had to make the match for his daughter; it was the politically correct thing to do.

The general spotted the soldier at the gate; he thought they had sent him a *denshchik* (a day worker) – he's actually just asked for one. So he called out at the soldier, and ordered him to get the *banya* heated by 1600. The soldier went to work: chopped some firewood, got the fire going, and soaked the birch-bunches to bring them to life. Then the general's daughter showed up – brought the new *denshchik* bread slathered in lard to snack on. He ate tidily, then they worked over a handful of sunflower seeds, and took a great shine to one another. The girl went back into the house to do her nails, and the soldier sat down on the stoop of the *banya* to have a smoke.

And the general, it must be said, kept fancy black-cocked chickens from a distant land. So, one of these, the boldest hen, came up to the soldier, stood there and looked at him askance, but he was nice to her – didn't shoo her or throw a boot at her, and instead gave her some bread crumbs. The hen, for his kindness, gave him a magic grain. At 1600, the general's guests rolled in for their *banya*: it was the solicitor with his son. In they all went; the soldier slapped and whipped the birch-bunches on the solicitor's back – the solicitor only grunted, he liked it so much. He started asking the general to sell him his *banya* expert. The general wouldn't do it – he hadn't had his fill of him yet.

Once they got done steaming, they all sat down to vodka. Drank up a bucket, started on another. The solicitor started bragging about his son – what a beast he was, strong as an ox, breaks everyone's arms. That's when the General asked the soldier:

"Can you out-arm-wrestle the solicitor's pup?"

"Yes, sir," said the soldier, then tucked the magic grain the hen gave him behind his cheek, got big as a tiger, and ground the solicitor's son into the mud.

The solicitor took offense.

"You cheated, you rotten wolves!"

The general, without much ado, right-hooked him on the chin, then said, "You're the rotten wolf, and your kid's teeth stink!"

The solicitor left, hissing, "You'll be sorry you did this!"

"You wish!" hooted the general. "Our people always beat up on your people!" and made an indecent sign at the solicitor's back.

He was having such a grand time, he had the soldier sit down and drink some vodka with him. They drank one bucket; started on the next. The soldier held his own. The general liked this, hollered for his daughter. She was right there – she'd been peeking from behind a corner.

"This here common soldier saved you from the solicitor's pup," the general explained. "Wanna marry him?"

The girl agreed on the spot before her father changed his mind – she'd had it with sitting up in her tower. The general threw them a party, and got the soldier decommissioned. Afterwards, the newlyweds came to live in Stargorod, where the city allocated them a corner behind a curtain in a big communal apartment. The general's daughter stuck with it for a week, then ran away to Moscow, where she promptly landed a job with a modeling agency. She now advertises Blissful Ravioli and Tough-as-Nails Nail Polish. The soldier wasn't sad for long – the main thing was, he got out of the army. He went into carpentry, carves iconostases, makes good money, and doesn't dwell on the past. He told us his tale once – the guys all but fell over laughing: who now believes in fairy-tales?

Do you?

BOOTS AND BALLET SLIPPERS

There is a good reason why a boot is featured so prominently on Stargorod's crest. When the Muscovites, led by Vassily III, arrived to lay siege to Stargorod, the city's militia, all in leather boots, lined up atop the city walls. Prince Vladimir headed our forces.

"Heck," said the bast-shod Muscovites, "their last footman's got leather boots. We ain't getting far here."

And they beat their drums, and went back to where they'd come from. Prince Vladimir died soon afterwards, but a city tradition was born: every night, the citizens placed a pair of boots on his grave. Wearing these, the prince, invisible to the human eye, made his nightly rounds about the city, keeping guard and warding off various calamities. In 1917, the powers that be got skimpy and gave the prince a pair of worn-out, threadbare clogs. I don't need to remind you what happened after that.

Jean Borisovich Protege arrived in Stargorod during *perestroika*. He went to live in a humble communal apartment, where he soon struck up a friendship with his neighbor, a third-generation boot-maker named Nikifor. Prior to his relocation to Stargorod, Protege had run a small glove-making workshop in Tbilisi. In 1987, as a result of his conversations with Nikifor in the kitchen of that humble communal apartment, the cooperative The Sole was born. It produced boots, ankle-boots, and bootees for both genders. Protege was indefatigable: in the era of barter trading, he conceived and executed incredibly complicated chains of exchange, procuring for his enterprise raw leather, tanning supplies and imported dyes almost for nothing. Nikifor was his one-man Quality Control Department. He didn't squeeze a boot's toe with his fingers to see how the leather would crinkle, didn't drip water on a shoe to see if a stain would remain, didn't pull on fur lining to see if the pelt would separate – he merely rolled a bulging, blood-shot eye over all that was brought before him, then without fail tossed out any defective goods. By the end of the day, of course, he would get drunk as a cobbler, bragging that it was his way of maintaining the co-op's good reputation.

Nikifor told Jean about Prince Vladimir – Protege liked everything mystical. A young technologist named Sveta was charged with taking a pair of brand-new boots to the local hero's grave. Sveta, dreaming of promotion, diligently executed her duty. The boots always disappeared by morning; the prince must have liked them. The Sole's cheap products were selling like hot cakes. Jean Borisovich began to experiment with styles and colors. His new models found demand as far away as Moscow.

It was passion that became Protege's undoing. Sveta the technologist also showed great diligence in making eyes at him, and eventually got the aging entrepreneur to marry her. In the interest of her professional education, the young wife demanded to be taken on a tour of shoe-making capitals of the world. Protege took her to Europe. In their absence, there was no one left to take boots to Prince Vladimir's grave. The 1998 default all but bankrupted The Sole. Jean Borisovich grew feeble overnight, and soon died.

Now in charge, Sveta began by dispatching Nikifor into retirement. Then she erected a grand monument to her departed husband, at the ancient St. Christopher cemetery, next to Prince Vladimir's chapel. There, on a bench, in quiet, she contemplated the facts, considered the low purchasing power of her fellow citizens, and decided to take a risk. The factory began making cheap shoes out of synthetic leather, innocently pink ballet-slippers, brightly-colored, sexy sandals with strip-tease heels, and moccasins sewn of sturdy, clear plastic. Crystal-studded ankle-straps on acid-green alligator-print thongs; "retro" clogs of quilted black, periwinkle and purple leather on soles carved from local pine; scarlet lacquered soles and silver beading – she pulled out every trick she'd picked up abroad.

The Sole's products glimmered on store shelves like sparkling glass in a kaleidoscope. At the same time, a new female technologist was charged with taking a pair of boots made in the old facility to the prince's grave. The company turned around and began to turn a profit, which Sveta refused to share with city hall, entrusting her fate to her more exalted patron.

Nikifor founded Quality Control – a civic organization. They promoted native traditions, demonized the West, and accused The Sole of using low-quality materials and violating production standards. The lattermost, unfortunately, happened to be true. Sveta maintained a stony silence in the face of this criticism, until one day a furious Nikifor threw a pair of frivolous blue ballet-slippers onto her oak desk.

"Look – these were found on the prince's grave!"

The technologist was called in. She arrived, noiseless in her Nike sneakers, and confessed she only wanted to take the best product to the grave.

"And your boots – they're a throw-back, they suck!" she blurted, choking on tears. The next day, a high-profile city council commission descended upon the factory and discovered that The Sole was putting brand-name labels on their, basically, counterfeit shoes. The city hall wouldn't take Sveta's bribe. The factory was bankrupted.

The prince, her patron, took offense at this as incompatible with his medieval moral values, and that's a shame. The boots you can now buy in Stargorod look a great deal like the departed Jean Borisovich's products, except that their soles peel off in about a month. Young people prefer to save up and support foreign manufacturers. The girl was right: Protege's boots were a throw-back.

WINDS OF CHANGE

The Garden of Eden Estate, a federally protected historical landmark, lies about ten miles from Stargorod. One of our own, the famous architect Barsov, designed and built the place at the end of the eighteenth century for Tsar Pavel's General Ableukhov. The manor house, hunting lodges and magnificent park stood vacant and decaying for a long time. In the last couple of years, the property has tempted ten investors, each of whom, however, gave up soon after they started making renovations. Restoring a place like that is meticulous, expensive work that requires constant consultations with scholars, who tend to meddle and waver and fuss over every old pebble. All of this notwithstanding, one bright May day Garden of Eden was sold at auction for the eleventh time, this time with a 69-year lease.

Our new governor found new investors with very serious intentions. The way things were presented to them – packaged as the governor's Old Estate Project – was essentially no different from every previous venture, but the press trumpeted it as "the winds of change." There were two main contenders for the property: Vassily Paip, an oil magnate, a man who, in the highest echelons of power was simply referred to as The General. Few could appreciate the delicacy of the situation in which the governor found himself: his friendship with Paip was important in view of emerging profitable projects, but to slight The General meant to rock even harder the already-leaky boat of the governor's relationship with the current administration. The governor decided to sacrifice a pawn: the head of the Culture Department, Kim Volokitin, a civil servant of the old, Soviet school. Volokitin accepted his part and memorized his lines.

When the prospective investors were being taken on a tour of the park, Kim approached The General and mentioned to him, in passing, that the president visited "The Garden of Eden" once, on his way to the capital, spent a long time contemplating the melancholy cupids on the mansion's frieze, and then said, with an elegiac sigh: "Now here's a place to retire to – it's just perfect!" The General was not previously aware of this information, and swallowed the bait.

On the other hand, Paip's relations with the Kremlin were, at the time, highly neurotic. The General, while letting Paip outbid him, instantly conceived of a plan to present Paip's new purchase in the most unfavorable light to the Powers That Be. The oil magnate's company won the auction, and the fact was covered by the news the same evening. The General departed to feast at the governor's guest house, and stayed the night.

In the morning, strange howling was heard outside his door. The General stuck his head out into the hallway. Walking on his knees along the tufted carpet towards him was Kim Volokitin, naked to the waist, flailing himself unmercifully with a lash and whining monotonously: "Have mercy, it's my fault, the rats ate the wiring!"

A curt order to explain followed. With the lash held up for the distinguished guest in his outstretched arms, the head of Stargorodian culture recounted the misfortune: rats sniffed out the organic-rubber wiring under the hood of The General's Mercedes and gnawed it to shreds. The car now would not start, and for this he, the idiot who could take care of it, is asking to be whipped.

"I'll forgive you if you tell me who sent you to trick me," The General looked the trembling official straight in the eye – an experience few could bear. The General had a chance to make a few inquiries.

"General, sir, I thought of it myself, the fool, I thought it was for the better – ten investors already went bankrupt with the place, the foundations are built on quicksand."

"Fine work!" The General barked and went to get dressed.

History, as we all know, repeats itself. In 1767 Catherine the Great stopped in Stargorod in the guest palace on her way to the First Throne. Local yokels had an argument with the Tsarina's drivers, and beat them up. Someone instantly reported this to the monarch. An imperial order was issued: to whip every tenth man in the city. Then the city head with his entire cabinet prayed to the Mother Empress on their knees and gained the Most Benevolent's clemency for their wayward citizenry. Ever since then, on the feast day of Our Lady of Kazan (when the discomfiture originally transpired) they gave a thanksgiving service in the city hall. They did so every year, until the Soviets stopped it. This, however, did not save the Stargorodians from receiving, from the surrounding towns, the moniker "whipped"; still, it's no worse than the historical name given to the residents of Tver – "the goats," or the inhabitants of Torzhok – "crooks and snoops," or those from Kashin – "guzzlers."

I doubt Kim Volokitin was aware of his city's history. The General took his complaint to the governor, who was compelled, in the name of making amends, to let him have the above mentioned guest palace. It is now being converted into a boutique hotel with all the trappings of heavenly repose. This actually worked out well for the city: the school for mentally handicapped children that had been housed in the palace was moved from downtown to the edge of the city, but only time will tell how well the renovators will get along with the conservationists.

Kim Volokitin did not remain the head of the culture department for long: The General appreciated his acting talent and took him to Moscow. They say he is managing a super-secret garage there now, has been awarded his long-awaited colonel's rank, and could not be happier.

THE CURSED PLACE

The first thing a tourist has to deal with in Stargorod is our bridge. This is a cursed place for city fathers as much as it is for motorists, everyone knows that. The chronicler chose to record for posterity that, in 1011, *boyar* Kuksha, Stargorod's founder, drowned a Komsi priest here at the ford, and the pagan, in his last breath, cursed the *boyar* and all subsequent governments.

In 1696, Peter the Great, in a great hurry to Voronezh to supervise the building of his ships, arrived at the steep shores of our river, and, twisting his mustache in irritation, stood there waiting for a ferry. Right beside him there stood two old women – grocery peddlers.

"How much for the greens?" the tsar inquired.

"We let it go for half-penny, and the ferry costs a coin."

Two copper half-pennies at the time added up to a coin. The tsar, without wasting any more time, summoned the city head and ordered him to erect a bridge. Half a year later, returning from Voronezh back to the capital, the Tsar observed that the bridge hadn't even been started. He ordered the city head brought before him again.

"What, no money's been given you?"

"No, Your Majesty, they sent us the money, but we've no wits to puzzle out a thing like a bridge."

"Then here you go!" Peter exclaimed and slammed his fist on the poor man's bald skull so hard he almost died. And the city finished the bridge in no time.

In the Great War, the Germans bombed the bridge to smithereens. Under Zhukov's orders, the Red Army soldiers were trying to secure the crossing under heavy enemy fire. Right in the very thick of it, bullets and shrapnel pouring down, a jeep speeds up to the pontoons

– and the soldiers, the ones still alive, are all hiding in the trenches. Zhukov, with a cane, jumps out of the car. Bullets whiz past him – he pays them no mind: he was charmed, you see.

The marshal yells at the colonel, "God damn you, how much time were you given already?!" and smack! – whips his cane at the man's face; teeth fly!

"You!" Zhukov yelled at the first Captain he saw. "Make the crossing by nightfall, or I'll bury you alive!"

By nightfall, tanks were rolling across the pontoons, the enemy fled, the colonel was sent to Vorkuta, and the captain got a medal.

After the war, the job of rebuilding the bridge fell to the much-decorated Engineering Corps Lieutenant Colonel Shelest. Shelest was born a builder; he set to repairing the ruins with a team of soldiers who had fallen behind the front and stayed and a crew of German POWs. Eventually, the time came to send his soldiers home. Shelest's officers drafted a new crop of recruits from places no one had ever heard of. They finished the bridge, but then the draftees' term of service ended, and they, too, went home. Shelest, just for the heck of it, wrote to the appropriate authorities, asking for new soldiers. Instead, Cheka motorcyclists with machine guns rolled into town, but the war hero was gone. They never found him. Turns out, his unit had been disbanded right after the war – how did he manage to keep it working? Whatever he did, everyone – his officers and soldiers – served in the non-existent unit completely legitimately, and got due credit for it. People told many other stories about Shelest after this, but this one, at least, is true: he conned Stalin's regime all right, but he got the bridge built.

Since then, the bridge has gradually fallen into decay. Every new head of the city spared no asphalt on it, but somehow the potholes only grew bigger and deeper.

When Mikhail Yefremovich Nozdrevatykh – a Stargorodian born and raised, a retired air force general, and a chopper-pilot hero of the Afghan war – became the head of the city administration, he solemnly pledged to undertake a fundamental reconstruction of the bridge to bring it into tip-top shape. His old mother, people said, counseled him to have the bridge blessed with holy water and forget the crazy idea, but he did not listen.

Instead, Nozdrevatykh sent a request to the governor: a hundred million. The Governor right away countered: six hundred million, and not a penny less, or else it's not even worth the effort. That's where The General came in – an important man from Moscow, he had developed a big construction business in Stargorod. The General cut out the governor, got the contract himself, and procured three hundred million straight out of the federal budget. The ministry sent the money, but something happened to it somewhere along the way.

Exactly what transpired then between The General and Nozdrevatykh, we do not claim to know. However, there are others who witnessed their conversation, and here's what they report.

Mikhail Yefremovich is playing pool at the Old Tymes Club. Suddenly, The General, profoundly drunk, barges in and starts yelling, "You son of a bitch, what do you think you're doing? You stole the money, didn't you!"

"People," Nozdrevatykh replied, "shot Stinger missiles at me in Afghanistan and I wasn't scared. Get out of here. I'm not one to rob my own hometown."

In response, The General whispered something into the city head's ear – it had to have been a jinx – marched right out and climbed into his Mercedes, but didn't go very far. He slammed into the bridge's parapet – the car was totaled, and it was a miracle he himself didn't fall into the river below. And Nozdrevatykh was paralyzed on the spot – his legs folded under him and he couldn't feel them.

The money eventually turned up, albeit not all three hundred million – only a hundred. People said the governor found a way to skim off his cut after all. The General fudged and schemed, and paid Moscow back, but there was very little left for the bridge – just enough to roll on a new layer of asphalt using German technology. In the spring, the logging trucks came across and made the first dents in the road. Now, in the middle of the summer, traffic here crawls as usual – at a snail's pace, everyone worrying about their suspensions. Mikhail Yefremovich, for his honesty and forthrightness, gained great respect from the locals, but it hasn't given him his legs back. The bridge itself is holding up just fine – Shelestov with German POWs built it and that's, I tell you, something – not just some new German technology. I do wonder sometimes, though: would it have been better to sprinkle the bridge with holy water, and let it be?

DEMONS POSSESS US

Demons do possess us, that's a fact. Old Father Artemon often spoke of being possessed in his sermons, but also never neglected to warn his flock against false healers.

Not so long ago, in the Solombal district of Arkhangelsk region they found a body of an old woman who had died of multiple traumas – her ribcage was shattered. A certain Ms. Lagunova – a local self-proclaimed healer – apparently attempted to cast the demons out of the old lady's body "by means of jumping on her chest," as the police report put it. Such charlatans roam Russia in great numbers, no fewer than those of the demons that possess and torment us. Sometimes, however, the demons leave the soul of their poor victim when the fear of a greater force compels them.

Mikhail Yefremovich Nozdrevatykh – the head of the city administration, a retired general and combat helicopter pilot – suffered at the hands of an evil-eyed Moscow businessman known around here as The General. He, people say, whispered a jinx into Nozdrevatykh's ear, and the hero of the Afghan war was paralyzed from the waist down. This could not have transpired at a worse time: elections to the regional Duma were just around the corner, with our local philanthropist and millionaire Anton Porfiriyevich Nebendov running on the United Russia ticket. Anton Porfiriyevich badly needed a seat in the legislature: the region's new governor, in contrast to the previous one, who was now serving time for illegally logging a swath of land the size of one-seventh of France, proved to be intent on putting the free-wheeling local entrepreneurs (like Nebendov) under his thumb. For instance, he forced guys who poured a unique brand of iron to switch to producing the cheap vodka brand "For Unity." The metalworkers outwitted him though: they bottled the governor's vodka into elaborate cast-iron bottles which cost and weighed so much that people refused to buy them, thus bankrupting the governor's little home industry.

Now Anton Porfiriyevich, he came to Stargorod from Poltava some 25 years ago. A recent Polytechnic University grad, he was given a job at a small plant that manufactured trenching tools. Once it was allowed, Nebendo (that was his name then) privatized the plant, added the letter "v" to his Ukrainian last name to show he had no intention of going back to Poltava, and set to work. Now his "Stargorodian" makes construction cranes, lightweight motorboats, pumps and hydrants, spades, Halligan bars and cisterns for firefighters, needles, nails and meat-grinders. Imagine then having this iron-works empire being ordered to begin producing toilet paper! Nebendov did not say "no" to the governor per se, but immediately departed for the capital where the Commander-in-Chief of all firefighters made him a card-carrying member of United Russia.

The Stargorod's campaign headquarters' chief of staff – city head Nozdrevatykh – was supposed to ensure Nebendov's victory in the elections. If Nebendov made it to the legislature, the governor would leave him alone, but, on the eve of the elections the campaign found itself suddenly beheaded, or rather, be-legged: Nebendov's faithful lieutenants reported that Mikhail Yefremovich had fallen into a deep depression, locked himself up in his dacha, was seeing no one, and just sat with his old mother pouring holy water on his head and old Father Artemon in the corner mumbling prayers to cast the demons out of his paralyzed body.

"The Afghan hero's gone nuts, you say?" Nebendov shouted. "That's nothing! We'll fix him right up, my grandmother was the first witch at the Sorochynsky Fair – took off jinxes, evil eyes, and cast demons out too. Hitch up, boys!"

Fifteen minutes later, the official Mercedes delivered Nebendov to the city administration head's dacha. Inside, the paralyzed Nozdrevatykh sat in a leather armchair next to a big round table.

"Trust me, Anton," he said in a deflated voice, "it was easier for me in the war. I can't bear it – people elected me, but it's nothing but wolves and bloodsuckers out there."

"What are you talking about, Misha?! The war's just begun! Get up and crawl around the table, that's an order!" Nebendov thundered like an angel of the apocalypse, as he grabbed the armchair and pulled it out from under Nozdrevatykh. "Crawl three times around the table and you'll feel your legs, or else – great woe to you! I'm spending all the magic powers I got from my witch grandmother on you."

The sight of him was terrifying: he stood short, disheveled, with his tie askew and his eyes burning like hot embers, arms spread wide. Nozdrevatykh tried to crawl, but his legs would not obey him. One way or another, groaning and creaking, he circled the table three times.

"You didn't get it? Well, this'll be the end of me, but you won't live either!" and with these words, the Ukrainian exorcist whipped out a small firefighter's axe from behind his back and charged at his jinxed comrade. The battle-tested general howled like a Chinook at lift-off, jumped to his feet and leapt out the window.

Nebendov caught up with him only at the dacha's gate.

Two weeks later, the two were dining at the Olde Tymes, celebrating Nebendov's new seat in the regional legislature.

"You gave me quite a fright back then, Misha," Nebendov said.

"Shut up, I still get flashbacks of you with your axe," the city head admitted.

From the jukebox, a cracked voice began singing "Say You'll Haunt Me."

"Are you saying I haunt you?" Nebendov asked. "Nonsense. I'm the one who was haunted. And then today the governor congratulated me with victory – and not a word about toilet paper!"

And he slapped his comrade's exorcised knee – good and hard.

MEDICI

Our city's historic waterfront spent the Soviet years slowly dying. The buildings – an old hotel and nearby merchant villas – looked like the moth-beaten eighteenth century *kaftans* on rickety mannequins in the local museum. The once-proud street was unsightly, as though it had been recently bombed by the Germans and was good for nothing except maybe making movies about partisans.

With the arrival in Stargorod of Anton Porfiriyevich Nebendov, who steered the ne'er-do-well Stargorodian shovel factory to prosperity with an iron grip, the situation changed dramatically. Of course, the Poltava-born philanthropist could not be suspected of knowingly imitating the famous banker Cosimo Medici – instead, Nebendov acted instinctively. Cosimo, when he came to Florence in the middle of the fifteenth century, poured hundreds of thousands of florins into good works, and, by sponsoring ambitious church building all over the city, secured his position among the city fathers and enshrined his name for posterity. True, Cosimo's pious image was somewhat undermined by certain actions he took, but one can't repent unless one sins, can one?

Cosimo once said that he should designate himself the Lord's debtor in his accounting books, and if the Good Lord can wait for payment, he'd return the debt with interest. I think Anton Porfiriyevich would sign his name under those words had he had a chance. He bought up the crumbling buildings along the waterfront and restored them. A respectable restaurant materialized in the old hotel, together with hot running water, which had never before made an appearance there. United Russia's campaign office moved into the building adjacent to the hotel; the villas were given (charitably), one to the Stargorodian workers' union, another to the city itself, and even the architect who oversaw the renovations received a free studio in one of them. Then, Nebendov developed the vacant lots nearby, filling them with single-family houses in the "neo-Catherinian" style. He moved his family into one of these, but never entertained at home: the hotel and "the guest house" with a pool table, sauna, full bar and VIP suites accommodated all his social needs. The notoriously demanding Federal Preservation Committee gave the development its full and instant approval, and overnight the street became a textbook example of historically-sensitive construction – a turn which even Anton Porfiriyevich, with his truly Renaissance thirst for glory, could hardly have predicted.

Uplifted by his success, Nebendov put new roofs and a new coat of paint on the two churches on the other side of the river – both designed by the famous architect Barsov. People immediately began whispering that Nebendov had bought the bankrupt little factory on whose land the churches technically stood.

Naturally, the philanthropist's 50th birthday party became the social event of the year for the district and region. The lieutenant governor made a speech celebrating Anton Porfiriyevich's contribution to the revitalization of our community; his party comrades presented him with a statue of a bear carved of larch (he already had four), the game commissioner draped forty sable pelts atop the mountain of presents, and the local banker pinned the furs down with a gold nugget, which promptly made an appearance in the speech by the director of diocesan social services, who compared Nebendov himself to the precious metal. The city architect in his speech called Nebendov a new Russian Medici, which only added to the chagrin of the jealous audience.

The evening's most illustrious guest – Pal Sanych Koshel, chairman of the legislature, former lieutenant governor to the currently imprisoned former governor – took the celebrating Nebendov aside.

"A new Medici? Congratulations! So how come you got the churches painted but didn't pay for new crosses – you bought the factory and the land, didn't you?"

"Let the diocese take care of the crosses. The churches are right across from my windows, they spoiled the view – so I had them painted."

And, without answering the legislator's other question, Anton Porfiriyevich left the party and went outside.

"Cosimo Medici," he said to himself, savoring the sound of it and looked at the graceful old churches on the other side of the river.

He bought the factory a week ago, but the news of it hadn't spread through the region yet. He'd have to rebuild the factory, of course, to accommodate the new manufacturing line he'd already ordered from Spain, but it wasn't a big deal. Pal Sanych himself had long had his sights set on that factory, but he beat the chairman to it, and didn't even pay that much for the property. Come to think of it, why did he have the churches painted? Because he was the only one who could afford to do it? Or was it because he knew the gesture would appeal to the factory's owner, and he'd offer him a deal? Or because every newspaper in the region ran a story about it? Or was it because of that time when he was telling his granddaughter how people used to white-wash their old mud-walled houses in the villages around Poltava before Easter, and the girl glanced at the churches outside their window and asked him, "Why are those so dirty – will you paint them for Easter, too?" – and he didn't know what to say to her?

Nebendov took another deep breath of fresh air and went back inside his hotel to entertain his guests. Someone's drunken voice mumbled behind his back: "Had the churches painted, fucking millionaire! Couldn't do something for the children instead."

Anton Porfiriyevich recognized the voice as belonging to the director of the diocesan social services, to whom he recently donated a truckful of computers for the orphanage.

Anton Porfiriyevich knew decidedly nothing about Cosimo Medici, but determined to make a trip to Florence and learn about the man. He was curious, after all.

CANDY

About 15 years ago, in the last days of the old hippie "system," when its founding fathers – like Doughnut, Cockatoo, Noodle and Jimmie Mixer – were still around, and the various tolkienists, bikers, reconstructionists, gopniks and other sundry tribes were only beginning to emerge, a crew of very hairy people who called themselves "pipl" pitched its tents at the river a dozen miles from Stargorod. There was an excellent beach there, and a village with a grocery store nearby, but, most importantly, there was an expansive karst cave with labyrinths of corridors and passages that went on seemingly forever. The hippies meditated in a large black hall not far from the entrance, where they attempted to rid themselves of passions by letting the void into their souls.

Pipl also believed that it was here that the cave's guardian, She of Two Faces, found Dao. In pipl's memory She was a girl who went into the cave with her boyfriend, and fell into a crevice. The guy left her three candles, water and some bread, and then abandoned her, to his eternal shame. The rescue team found the food and the candles intact, but the girl disappeared. Now She sometimes appears to tourists in her old visage, and sometimes in the guise of an old hag. Those who meet the girl are advised to ask her to make one heart-felt wish come true. Her other shape is dangerous – those who see Her as a hag risk remaining underground forever.

In the year of this story, three people of interest joined the hippie slam: the legendary Noodle with his girl Olesya, and a photographer referred to as Botan, who held on to his brand-new Nikon camera even in his sleep. Pipl greeted their arrival with loud exclamations of "Wow!" Botan didn't get bent, didn't trip and didn't shoot the breeze

– he didn't have Noodle's storytelling gift, and when he wasn't staring at Olesya, with whom he'd been in love since high school, in mute adoration, he could be seen in nearby fields and meadows taking pictures of clouds and bugs. Any form of art was respected among the pipl, but Botan remained outside the "system" – they suffered him out of altruism.

Noodle had picked up Olesya on the street, right after prom: the girl was walking away from the party, crying – she'd just broken up with Botan, who was stupid enough to confess to her that he loved photography more than anything else in the world. An old-school hippie, Noodle chatted up the girl and later gave her "candy" as the hippies call their woven bracelets. There's something else they call "candy," too, though – and Noodle got Olesya addicted. For the pipl, an exchange of bracelets is a sacred ritual – they believe the gift tunes the receiver into the mind of the giver.

So, one night, the whole tribe decided to go to the underground room. There, they sat on their towels and began getting in touch with the void.

Naturally, the conversation turned to Dao, and then someone brought up She of Two Faces. Doughnut said that if you took the bracelet of someone who wanted to get off the needle and gave it to the cave's guardian, the person would instantly kick the habit, without any withdrawal pains. Olesya took off her bracelet right there and then and looked at Noodle. He shrugged indifferently. Before anyone could say anything, Botan snatched the bracelet from her hand, grabbed a single candle, a flashlight and his camera, and went underground.

He was gone for three days. On the fourth day, the pipl decided to call in the rescue squad, but right then, at dusk, he came to the campfire – the way a drama lead comes out from behind the curtain when the show is over and he's carried the day. Botan's underground wanderings left their mark: he was exhausted and worn, but utterly serene; he regarded the pipl with a calm, commanding gaze, his eyes pale like a pair of washed-out old jeans, and told them that he had seen She of Two Faces and given her Olesya's bracelet. Many, of course, did not believe him, but Olesya came up to the hero and took his hand. He looked straight through her, took his hand away, went to his tent and fell asleep.

The next morning, Botan went to Stargorod, printed his picture and brought it back to the pipl to prove his story. The picture showed a large cave with an arched ceiling. In the far corner, a softly outlined figure floated above the floor. Of those who knew the cave best, none had ever been to this room. And then suddenly – those who were there remember this clearly – the shape in the print began to vanish slowly and soon disappeared altogether, as though it had never been. The same day, Botan packed his things and left. Olesya also left, a few days later, and without Noodle. Pipl attributed her depressed mood to withdrawal, but that was just the thing: she didn't feel anything; she's got clean as easily as Doughnut had promised.

The hippie "system" soon collapsed – as did countless cultures of tribes and peoples who before seemed eternal. The story of Olesya's bracelet became part of local lore. These days, special guides take people to the cave for a fee, and at the entrance old ladies sell beaded, woven bracelets. In the room where the pipl used to seek Dao, drug addicts and tourists from all over the country leave the bracelets they've bought outside as an offering to She of Two Faces. Speleologists are looking for "Botan's room," but they haven't found it yet.

The photo editor of the *Stargorod Herald* likes to say, that if a photographer loves life more than he loves photography, he'll never get anywhere. Botan now shoots for *GEO* and *National Geographic*; he's traveled the world. Nothing is known about Olesya, but it is rumored among professionals that Botan still sleeps with his camera – and nothing else.

THE MERMAID

Katya Puck became Katya Kholodtsova after she married a man named Nikolai. He studied at the same drama school Katya entered after she ran away from Sakhalin. After her parents died, she was placed in an orphanage there, where she grew up reading books and dreaming of playing Ophelia.

By the time Katya joined Stargorod's theater company, she was alone. She starred in children's parties; her cropped hair and petite build doomed her to *travesti* roles. She spent the next five years playing principal boys, squirrels, and Thumbelina.

For five years, nothing changed in the one-room apartment the city had found for her: there were the same bookshelves with the same books, the same vanity, the same bed, and in the corner – a large wardrobe of Belorussian provenance. The model was called Sakhalin and Katya had bought the thing purely for its name. At nights, Katya thought about her Sakhalin childhood, when she still believed in miracles. On the island's beaches, after the storms, the sea leaves pieces of raw carnelian – a semi-precious gemstone; she remembered how, when she held the stones up to the sun, she could see through them.

One night she was so homesick, she decided to hide from her longing inside her wardrobe. Katya stepped into the thing – and suddenly found herself on a Sakhalin beach – on the shore of the Tartar Strait, at the foot of the Aniv lighthouse. She didn't feel in the least alarmed and walked toward the town – her favorite Aunt Lida Puck lived there. The aunt welcomed her with open arms, fed her a feast and put her to bed. In the morning, Aunt Lida gave Katya a gallon bucket of caviar, for the trip back.

The theater paid little; Katya climbed back into her room through the wardrobe and took the caviar to the market. In the fish rows, she saw Nodar – he was standing there, eating sunflower seeds. Katya fell in love at first sight. Nodar began selling her caviar for her.

He would wash down a bite of a caviar sandwich with sweet coffee and teach Katya about life, "One grain of caviar is nothing; a bucket of it is money. Money – that's freedom, and you keep talking about some miracle of art, phew, no one pays for that. I can't go through the wardrobe – I'm not allowed – but you can. There you go – that's your miracle right there. Now I'll eat the last piece of this sandwich and then I'll want a piece of you – isn't that a miracle, too?"

Nodar was wild, but passionate; Katya loved him.

In the meantime, the theater got a new director. He was young, and he staged *Hamlet*. Katya played Ophelia. Overnight, she became famous; she was even elected into the city's Cultural Council. Nodar stayed with Katya for a year, and then began disappearing for a week or two at a time. He told her he was busy expanding his business, but someone in the theater crowd started saying that he had gotten together with Lilya, the bartender from the Lyubava. At first, Katya didn't believe the rumor. She did, however, sit for long stretches of time at the beach. When she went through her wardrobe she'd hug herself in her sable fur-coat and linger, no longer hurrying to see her aunt. A very long time ago, back at the orphanage, she and her friend Alya used to read to each other their favorite story – Andersen's *The Little Mermaid* – at night. It made them feel warm inside, and wanting to cry.

In Stargorod, meanwhile, things changed again. The young director got an offer from the capital and left. His replacement put on a production of Ostrovsky's *The Storm*; it didn't have a part for Katya. Katya threw a fit in the dressing room, which prompted a jealous colleague to mock her: "Well, you're not gonna jump off a cliff over this, are you? Your caviar will feed you."

That evening, Nodar came home drunk, groped her and swore he loved her. Katya threw him out. Then she found an axe and chopped the wardrobe to pieces.

The next morning she got called to a meeting of the city's Cultural Council. The Mayor told them the Transportation Ministry decided to build a bypass, which meant a death sentence for Stargorod, which lived and died with the federal highway that went through it. A PR expert flown in from Moscow told them to come up with a local attraction immediately, something like the Mouse Museum they have in Mousino.

Not long after that, Stargorod celebrated its Founding Day. Katya played Thumbelina in the open-air production on the park's playground. In the crowd, she could see Nodar with the bartender; they were hugging each other, and did not look at her. After the show, Katya walked through the strolling public to the canal. She climbed one of the granite slabs that lined the embankment and leapt into the water.

Katya turned into a mermaid. We know this to be a fact because one famous photographer, when, for reasons unknown, he found himself in Stargorod, captured on film something that looked very much like an undine floating on the moonlit surface of the river. The uncanny picture was reprinted all over the world. Now, people reserve rooms in our hotels well in advance and at nights, packs of tourists stalk the embankments in the hopes of seeing the mermaid. Katya, however, is not very kind to them; in the past three years she's only showed herself twice.

A group of Japanese scientists offered to pay the city big money for the permission to study the phenomenon.

"How could we sell Katya – after she's saved our city?" the Mayor said, shaking his head. And then asked his deputy: "What's that Nodar character up to these days, anyway?"

"Selling nails in the market. Lilya broke up with him."

"Serves him right!"

The *Stargorod Herald* ran a story saying that the Moscow PR consultant got paid three million rubles for hyping the mermaid brand, but who believes a rag like that?

The decaying waterfront has been restored, covered with new granite and lined with wrought-iron streetlamps. People in Stargorod feel very proud about Katya; girls throw pieces of paper with their heart's desires written on them into the river. Some, they say, get what they wish for.

HAPPINESS

Until he turned 40, Genka hunted herring all over the northern seas, and with great success. Misfortune struck out of the blue: while he was at sea, his wife left him, and a nefarious scheme, of the kind that had come to be common in his industry, came to light on shore. The skipper lost his boat. On top of that, his mother became gravely ill. Genka found a job at the Angler tackle store in Murmansk. He perused the manufacturers' literature as meticulously as he used to study navigation charts, and became an irreplaceable expert in fishing and angling equipment. On weekends, he'd get away to one of the local bodies of water, and over the next ten years became so familiar with them that he was bored.

For his 50th birthday, Genka gave himself a present – a trip to The Three Rivers resort, on a lake about 10 miles from Stargorod. Genka managed to book himself early in the season, a fact which later caused him great pride. For the next five years, he vacationed only and exclusively at The Three Rivers; he came three times a year and among the regulars earned himself the nickname Murmansk Genka, which distinguished him from the crowd of the common show-offs who came to swim and entertain their women. The regulars – retired special forces, GRU officers, military contractors and manufacturers – were decidedly more important and richer than Genka, but his tackle was just as good. He always left his room before dawn and came back by nightfall, having missed both lunch and dinner, and even when no one else had a single bite that day, Genka always managed to bring back a respectable catch. He was made to fish just like a bird dog is made to hunt.

After dinner, the company usually gathered in the fireplace den, around the pool table. Genka would sit by himself, eyes wandering over the rooms' walls: he played poorly and didn't like losing. He drank little, and when he did, he would confess he could only think of coming back to The Three Rivers. It was Genka, by the way, who caught the record-setting 10.4-kilo pikeperch. He was well respected; men came to ask for his advice about equipment and ordered the newest and hottest items from him, which he sold to them at cost. There was only one thing that really irked him: the entire den was lined with photos of men with their trophies. His photo, however, was for reasons unknown missing, even though he broke Sashka Pugachev's record the very first year he came, when he reeled in a 79-kilo catfish. A year later, Kasym and his buddy Beard pulled out an 84-kilo beast from Babka's Dip and were instantly rewarded with three framed pictures right by the door.

Genka no longer had any friends in Murmansk; the vision of The Three Rivers sustained him – wind in his hair, the breaking waves at the lakeshore, the herons in the reeds, the quiet inlets and the deep, deep sloughs where the catfish sleep under the willows. Genka dreamt of catching a record-breaking 100-kilo fish; he knew where and how he would hunt for it, but he never told anyone of his dreams, afraid to jinx them. When he stood behind the counter in the Murmansk store, or took out his ill mother's bedpan, he would close his eyes and revel in the visions of his future glory.

Genka believed in his luck. Life, however, threw another banana peel under his feet. First, his mother died. Genka took care of the funeral, and felt out of sorts. He looked unwell – dark circles under the eyes, ghostly pale skin – and the store's owner sent him to see a doctor he knew at the district hospital. The doctor found leukemia.

"People live decades with this diagnosis," the doctor told Genka, and then ratted him out to the store's owner. The owner fired Genka on the spot, albeit with a 25,000-ruble bonus.

The fired Genka went home, and as he walked, for some reason, he no longer thought about his record-breaking catfish. With nothing particular in mind, he wandered into a mall, saw a cell-phone-card vending machine, paid, for no reason he could identify, for more airtime, pushed the button for "Beeline," and pulled out the receipt. He had no one and nowhere to call. Suddenly, among the familiar logos of service providers, he spotted a symbol he'd never seen before: a salmon leaping out of the water over a round sun. Under the logo, the unfussy serious-looking letters read: "Happiness." Genka fed a bill to the vending machine and pushed the button; the machine smoothly pulled in his money, growled, and returned a receipt which said: "Payment received, thank you!"

An hour later he got a call from the owner of The Three Rivers, Yegor. The resort had bought a large charter rig, and Yegor was calling to see if Genka would like to be her captain. Yegor wanted him there right away, but, purely for appearance's sake, Genka negotiated himself a week to get packed. This was a shameless lie: whenever Genka returned from The Three Rivers, he had his tackle and bag packed for the next trip three days later, as soon as the previous trip's laundry was dried and ironed. It was all there, ready, waiting for him in the closet. In the kitchen, Genka swallowed the pills his doctor had prescribed, and washed them down with *kefir*. He looked at the clock: he had plenty of time to catch his flight. On the way to the airport, Genka stopped at the mall, but the vending machine was no longer there.

"They took it away for maintenance, but you can pay at the customer service," the manager told him.

Genka smiled and shook his head. He kept smiling as he flew, and as he looked at the clouds and saw monster catfish slipping in and out of them. He's going to catch one just like that, for sure – he'll catch it in Babka's Dip and will personally nail the framed picture in the den, right above the fireplace!

THE HOURGLASS

Until he was old enough to start school, Seryoga Kuznetsov lived with his grandfather in the village, while his Mom, having lost her husband, was trying to fix her personal life in town. Seryoga and his grandfather together mowed grass for the rabbits and fed the chickens. The grandfather also had an hourglass: two bulbs of murky glass welded into a copper frame etched with a symbol that looked like a hut on crooked stilts. Grandfather brought the thing back from the Japanese war. The sand trickled from the top to the bottom so slowly that it seemed it didn't move at all. Playing with the hourglass was strictly prohibited.

In the evenings, after supper, grandfather would settle onto a little bench in front of his house, light a pipe and pronounce – as if it were a spell: "If you could turn back the clock, would things take the same course?" Leaving this question without an answer, he would send a thick ring of smoke up into the air, where it would melt and vanish. It was great fun living in the village; days there went on forever and did not end until sleep got the best of you.

Sergei graduated valedictorian of his class, to spite his mother – so she'd have one less fault to find with him. He also acted in the school theater, which he joined when he was in the ninth grade and was head over heels in love with Nastya K. When Nastya recited Katherine's monologue from *The Thunderstorm* – the one that begins with "Why is it people cannot fly?" – it took Sergei's breath away and it seemed to him that the very next instant a gust of wind would snatch his beloved from him and take her away forever. On their prom night, he took Nastya for a long walk along the riverfront and told her he loved her.

"You're going to Moscow next," she said, "and I want to live my life here, to make a difference in Stargorod. And, also, I don't love you."

He ran away to the village after that. His grandfather had died by then, the house stood vacant. Sergei did not sleep; he smoked and drank strong tea. The sand in the hourglass at the head of grandfather's bed seemed to trickle down faster now than it did back when he was a child, but Sergei didn't really notice it. He was thinking about Nastya. He promised himself that he would achieve anything he ever wanted, including winning her over.

Kuznetsov went to Moscow State University. After he graduated, he stopped in Stargorod to take care of his mother's funeral, and then flew on to France for an internship, and from there to Japan. He had no family left. He took grandfather's hourglass with him everywhere he went, but never showed it to anyone. How would he have explained that the sand now trickled down from the top bulb even faster, but the lower bulb always remained only half-full? He himself, for some reason, never felt any urge to solve this puzzle. But he did notice that as soon as he would turn the hourglass over, he started feeling apathetic, everything he was doing went wrong, and his heart lost its rhythm and beat unevenly, with starts and stops, as if struggling for oxygen.

To keep in working shape, Sergey worked out every morning, and then studied like crazy. In the nineties, time took off at a gallop, the country was desperately short of professionals with international experience, and Sergey did not miss his chance. At 24, he defended his doctoral dissertation in Economics and went to work for a very large and important company. Soon he became the youngest and most promising of the company's department heads. He was also one of the most desirable bachelors around, but he paid no attention to women.

He worked hard and did well, and one day he was offered the task of supervising the construction of the phosphate plant in Stargorod. The position came with the kind of authority in his native city that was comparable only to the governor's. Kuznetsov never forgot the promise he had made to himself. A trusted friend told him that Nastya, after school, graduated from the Pedagogical Institute, got married, had a son, got divorced and was now teaching math at their old school.

The first thing he did when he got to Stargorod was go and see her. Nastya was happy to see him, served him Lipton tea with strawberry jam, interrogated him about Japan and France and glanced, on the sly, at the one hundred roses he brought and she had put in an enameled bucket on a stool in the corner where she always set up her Christmas tree. Sergey suddenly realized that the woman sitting across the table from him did not in the least resemble the heroine of *The Thunderstorm* he had fallen in love with. The window was open; outside, the evening was muggy and hot. Nastya asked him for computers for the school. Then, she started ranting about the new Unified State Exam, and, once she really got into it, no longer listened to him when he told her about educational systems in France and Japan. After he'd been there an hour, Sergey took his leave. At the door, Nastya gave him a peck on the cheek.

The riverfront, where he had once confessed his love, was brightly illuminated. Sergey drove along slowly and looked at the oily surface of the river that reflected the streetlamps. A Japanese professor explained to him once that the hieroglyph on the hourglass's frame meant "time." Kuznetsov remembered his grandfather and what he used to say, arranged his fingers just so, and stuck his hand out the car window, at someone out there, in the night. At home, he automatically glanced at his hourglass: the sand poured down thick and fast, but there was never any more of it in the bottom bulb. Sergey opened his day planner, wrote down "Computers" on the 8:30 line, and turned off the light. He slept fitfully and twisted his sheet into a rope as he used to do some nights in the village, when he was little.

GOATS AND SHEEP

At the Institute of Asian and African Countries, Alisa defended the thesis "Kan-re-do: Bourgeois Ideology of the Civil Service in the Post-War Japan." Afterwards, while she was interning with Professor Yotiro Simada at the Tokyo University, she heard him formulate a civil servant's motto as follows: "A man must swim with the current in such a way that it does not drag him out to sea, where he may lose sight of land forever." Alisa framed her sensei's maxim in a cedar frame and put it above her desk. Another thing her professor taught her was breathing exercises. The sequence Alisa learned from him helped to focus one's inner force, "hara," on achieving one's goal, while remaining, outwardly, utterly unperturbed.

Alisa's father, a high-ranking Soviet official, as he pulled the strings to get his daughter a job, told her the tale of the lion who came to be sheriff in a new forest: "Just remember to send a goat or a sheep up to the bigger lions every so often, and you'll be fine."

That is how she did things. Bosses promoted Alisa for her agreeable disposition and sharp wits, and sprang to attention at the sight of her waspish waist, but Alisa remained faithful to one Olady Evlampovich, a successful artist she married after she returned from Japan. His position as secretary to the Soviet Artists' Union, however, proved to be not quite important enough in the new Russia. Alisa transferred to the Ministry of Culture and started helping her husband obtain commissions. She was always good at manipulating state funds, wasn't greedy, but never missed a good opportunity, knowing full well that a civil servant in traditional Russia is an immortal force, and no one and nothing would ever end the sheriffhood. Her daddy was right: the "goats and rams," transformed into the brick and mortar of her dacha on the Klyazma reservoir were mute just as one expects cattle to be.

In her work of implementing the government's priorities, Alisa often had to fight against conservatism and provincialism, but that was okay – she liked a good fight. For instance, take the recent government decision to cut federal funding for regional museums. It meant cultural institutions would have to learn how to make money on their own. The Pottery Museum in Stargorod fell victim to the cuts. The museum was undeniably provincial, with an inflated budget of a million dollars a year and its only claim to fame as an archaeological site was that Putin himself had visited and subsequently allocated funds to build an open-air dig. The director, loyal to Alisa, pocketed most of the money and gave her a kickback. And everything would have gone smoothly, if not for a small-time ram of a researcher who blew up the whole story in the local press. The director got cold feet, fired the researcher and shut down the dig.

Alisa flew out to Stargorod post-haste; she had to nip the scandal in the bud. They raked the director over coals of such heat that everyone knew right away: his days were numbered. The archaeologists and other museum employees, with the bitter provocateur in the rank of assistant professor at their helm, looked on with distrust. Alisa made sure to speak to them quietly, intimately, her eyes hidden under half-lowered eyelids, so that the overhead light did not allow them to read her expression (a trick she learned from her Japanese mentors); she called the director an embezzler, and asked the staff to give her a year to set things straight in the capital. They struck a deal: the museum would be disbanded, and then created anew. The archaeologists, in the meantime, were to organize themselves into an independent structure, a corporation that would later become the basis of the resurrected museum. A grant to continue exploration would ensure their independence of their old supervisor.

A glimmer of hope lit up in the eyes of the rebels – as if their scientific explorations could change anything. Big money was beginning to flow into Stargorod; a Moscow general (not without

Alisa's prompting) had begun a wholesale renovation of the city's historic center. As the Ministry's official, Alisa needed to implement archaeological and historical oversight over the renovation, but it didn't matter to her who would get to do it and file the reports.

As she departed, she said casually, "Come visit, I'm always happy to help."

That evening, at her dacha, Alisa sat in a rocking chair under an apple tree. The museum's director called. He apologized, made promises, flattered and fawned. The proud assistant professor did not call – did not send "a goat and a ram" up to the bigger lion – and missed his chance. In a year's time, the scandal would be forgotten; Alisa decided to forgive the loyal director.

A number of different animals lived at the dacha – it's fashionable now. Olady, seeing his wife in low spirits, brought to her Glasha, her favorite nanny-goat. Glasha took a piece of carrot from Alisa's hand and licked her fingers.

"Go milk her, I've had enough of this!"

The husband obediently led Glasha to the little barn in the back. Alisa had long been bored with Olady Evlampovich; getting any use out of him was like milking a billy-goat. Alisa closed her eyes, drew in the air and focused on her "hara"; she imagined herself swimming out into an endless ocean. The chair rocked gently, peacefully. With her narrow, exquisite foot, Alisa felt for the ground – just in case – and there it was, she hadn't lost it. She never will.

OUR PROGRESS

The military support base in Pankratovka – a village half sunk into the marshes north of Stargorod – was dismantled in the early 90s. Soon after the order was issued, the army stopped supplying coal for the base's boilers. The pipes of portable corn-stalk stoves emerged like bristles from the two-story lime-and-sand-brick housing units, which came to resemble a Pacific fleet flotilla awaiting its sad fate at Port Arthur.[5] The base veterans wrote to the Defense Ministry twice a year: they were entitled to new, comfortable apartments, but the Ministry had forgotten about them. Over the next 15 years, of the 82 officers' families that used to live on the base, only 43 were left in Pankratovka.

The very first year, the retirees planted orchards and vegetable gardens and would have become complete peasants were it not for Lieutenant Colonel Semyon Semyonovich Bulletov. Understanding that the men had to be kept busy, the former CO ripped the old banner "Our Progress Heads for the Woods!" from the gates of the base's garage and nailed up a new sign. It read "Automotive Club Varyag."

To start with, the men hauled a T-34 tank out of a nearby gulch and returned it to combat-ready condition. Then, in a marsh, someone found the shell of a light BT-7A tank. This machine was a rarity; you can count the surviving examples of this model on the fingers of one hand. The crew dug up original construction blueprints, restored the machine to its old glory and power, and added it to their fleet. Over the next decade and a half, the repair workshops of the former military

5. In 1904, the Russian fleet was destroyed by the Japanese at Port Arthur, in the Russo-Japanese War.

base gave new life to several ZIS 151 trucks (basically assembling them from snot and shoelaces), a three-ton army workhorse – the ZIS 5 (1934 vintage) with a 6x4 wheelbase, one each of a German and a Soviet AFV, and a legendary Nazi Tiger tank. The crown jewels of the collection were one of the first trucks of the 1940 Freightliner model, manufactured by James Leland and Co. at their Utah plant, before the corporation moved to Portland, and a GAZ-A which was said to be one of the cars that took part in the 1933 motor rally across the Karakum Desert, as described by Ilf and Petrov in *The Little Golden Calf*. Collectors would have offered insane sums for either of these two vehicles, but Varyag was not in the business of selling history. At the very dawn of the club's existence, Bulletov purchased, at scrap prices, a garageful of vintage Volgas, Pobedas, Moskviches, and ZIS and ZIM limousines; a special division – Varyag Corporation – restored and custom-tuned these for private clients.

In the new millennium, in light of the new trend for vintage vehicles, the business finally began to turn a profit. Twenty-two mechanics, four spare-parts experts, an accounting office and a crew of laborers – almost all of them retired military – worked under Semyon Semyonovich's management, and, what is most important, no one felt left out or short-changed.

The club began to attend vintage car and machinery shows; a TV crew made a show about them, and it was broadcast on national television. This brought it to the attention of the governor himself, a great lover of all things vintage. To line up the heroic machines in the Red Square, just before the elections to the federal Duma, where the Governor aspired to win a seat, struck him as a brilliant political move. On top of that, an influential person from one of the forces' ministries let it be known that, were the legendary GAZ-A to come into his possession, he could smooth out a few disagreements that had arisen between our Governor and the Kremlin.

The Governor sent a message to Bulletov.

Bulletov sternly demanded the long-promised apartments for his veterans.

At the end of April, a team of auditors descended upon the village and the prospect of serving time was revealed to Varyag's director.

On May 9,[6] a convoy of two tanks and three trucks delivered a strike-force of camouflage-clad Pankratov men to Stargorod's central square. The police let them through, thinking they were costumed actors from Moscow. Once on the square, the uniformed squad unfurled banners and signs: "We'll fight for the promised apartments!" The tanks aimed their guns at the Big House. The press snapped pictures. A special commission from the Ministry of Defense landed in Pankratovka a week later and signed a deal with the retirees that obliged the Ministry to move them all into warm apartments within two years. The event was covered in the national 9 o'clock news. The anchor spoke of the progressive trends in a government that finally dealt with its veterans. In the hubbub, Moscow quietly removed the Governor from his post. The machines were donated to the Stargorod museum. The important person never got the GAZ-A he wanted.

Bulletov won the battle and the war, but didn't move into a new apartment. Instead, he settled in a log house on the river, not far from the village, and took up beekeeping.

A *Stargorodian Herald* reporter once tried to interview him. The lieutenant colonel stunned him at the door by asking: "From the intellectual point of view, does technical progress move translationally?" And then he answered it himself: "Even if it does, I'm tired of it." Then he poured them both some mead, clinked his glass with the reporter's and drained it. The interview was not to be, the drunk correspondent was delivered home by a bread truck that happened by.

Bulletov was not so humble, however, as he made himself out to be. He didn't quite revert to getting around by horse and buggy; he drives a brand-new diesel UAZ and the corporation, which moved to Stargorod, pays him good dividends off its profits. When he works

---

6. Victory Day, celebrating the end of World War II.

on his beehives, he often sings an old army song about how every soldier has a right to rest at the river's edge.

KINDNESS

Turk's pained eyes haunted Marina all night long; she slept fitfully, kicked off her thin comforter and got cold – it was already autumn. She woke up bruised, barely made it to work on time, and worked on her client's make-up mechanically, although she regained her focus at the very end and finished by doing a good job. When Marina's client left, Artavaz – the owner of the Diarissimo beauty salon where Marina had been working for the past two weeks – started lecturing her.

"Don't prettify the client, attack their style. If she comes in blonde – dye her into a brunette, quit being nice to them, you can't let them set the terms!"

The day before, he told Marina he couldn't have her cutting the clients' hair and banished her, as punishment, to the make-up row. Marina hadn't said anything then, and didn't contradict her Armenian star of a boss now. She walked the city streets in the clean, cold air. She walked and thought that it was time to get a down comforter. Seven years ago, she took in a sick Doberman from the street, nursed him to health and named him Turk. Her husband told her to put the dog down, he was afraid of him, or maybe he was jealous. Marina refused, and the husband divorced her. And now Turk had died.

Women who came to be ravaged by Artavaz would stand up from the chairs, turning their suddenly foreign heads and straightening their shoulders as if they were about to leap off a cliff. They were at pains to hide their panic; the mirrors on the salon walls both beckoned to them and frightened them. Artavaz was *macho*, many liked him. Marina's clients, on the other hand, shied from dramatic makeovers. She loved finding the subtle touches that could bring out the image her client had chosen herself. Likely she needed to look for a different place to work. But Diarissimo was right in the center of the city, which was very convenient for clients, and this was the rub.

On Posad square, an old woman with a tote caught Marina's eye. She had thin hair in a pitiful perm, a coat that was just as pitiful, and threadbare cloth slippers. The woman peered pleadingly into the faces of the passersby, asked them something, repeatedly got a curt reply, but stubbornly persisted. Marina came up to her.

"Sweetie, could you tell me where Garibaldi street is? I seem to be lost..," the woman asked.

Marina had never heard of such a street. The old woman couldn't tell her with any degree of coherence how she had found her way to the square. Marina took her to the police.

When he heard their story, the sergeant on duty barked, "No such street in this town! Wait over there, we'll write up the paperwork for the asylum."

The grandma squeezed her lips into a thin line, which made her look like a sick pigeon.

"Take me home with you, I'd pay you for your trouble," she asked, all of a sudden.

The request left Marina stunned; the old lady stood before her, blinking in her confusion. So Marina took her home, gave her a bath and a warm meal, and put her to bed. Before falling asleep, she told her, for no particular reason, about her quarrels with Artavaz and about Turk's death. The old woman listened and nodded with a wise expression. In the morning, she made herself at home, made *blinchiki* with meat and a pot of soup, but didn't seem to want to go outside, afraid of getting lost again.

The next day, she disappeared. She left Marina a mound of cutlets in a deep dish on the stove, turned off the gas, and put the key under the doormat, just as Marina had asked. Nothing was missing; the old lady must have gone out to the store and wandered off again.

Three days later, the woman pulled up to Marina's apartment building in a large American car, accompanied by a driver/bodyguard.

The old lady had her hair died a soft reddish-brown, an excellent choice for a naturally dark-haired woman, and no longer looked wilted and unwanted.

"I promised to pay you back," she said from the door, and put an envelope on Marina's kitchen table. "My experiment on the square – I did it because I read on the internet that sociologists say people, basically, are growing kinder by the day. 69 percent of responders say we ought to help the homeless get medical care and jobs, while just 23 percent believe vagrancy should be banned and all the homeless rounded up and sent to special camps, like they did in the old days."

She smiled.

"I'd spent three hours on that square before I met you. Don't fuss over the money; my son was a businessman, he died a month ago, had no kids. I couldn't possibly spend all his money, it'll still be there when I'm gone. There's a former bakery for sale on Malaya Posadskaya – buy it, refit it, and cut hair however you think is best, I'll be your first client. Get a puppy and cheer up."

She put down the cup of tea that Marina had poured for her and, very satisfied with the impression she'd made, left.

Soon after that, Marina bought the place the woman suggested, hired a few people, and is now flourishing. The puppy has grown up into an elegant Doberman who protects his mistress on walks, and if you happen to be one of the people who think this breed is dangerous, Marina would love a chance to dissuade you, explaining that it's all about kindness and proper training.

It is foolish to contradict her: as soon as Arto the Doberman raises his almond-shaped eyes at you, your hand, of its own volition, reaches out to pet him, something the smart dog benevolently permits from all normal people who are kind to his goddess. And as far as the sociologists' findings go, well, they are highly educated people – I'm sure they know what they're talking about.

KAMBIZ

On the nights when passersby glimpsed the red flickers of flame bouncing off the walls of a small room in the small brick house that huddles against the gate tower of the Stargorod kremlin, they knew – Kambiz was doing his witching. The old Persian believed in the Good that persists in its grueling war with Evil. I doubt you could find, in central Russia, even a dozen experts who could correctly pronounce the ancient words *khumata, khukhta, khvarshta* – the holy triad of Zoroastrianism, "good thoughts, good words, good deeds," that constitute the foundation of any true Zoroastrian's life. The Persian, with his unruly mob of white hair and bulging eyes, seemed to people to be a kind of a magus, and it was widely believed that he could foretell the future and cure incurable diseases.

Nina Timofeyevna Shlionskaya, a math teacher from the First *gymnasium*, never in her wildest dreams could have imagined that she would have to turn to the wizard for help, but, defeated by family troubles and having lost her faith in doctors, she decided to take her chances – her last chance, as her neighbor Klavdia Ivanovna insisted – with the Persian. The man had cured Klavdia Ivanovna's husband of alcoholism in a single session.

Kambiz sat before the fireplace in which soggy logs were slowly beginning to burn. Unable to hold back her tears, Shlionskaya told him about her daughter Katya. Abandoned by the scoundrel who had seduced her, the girl was suffering from a mental affliction, had turned inward and withdrawn from the world. Doctors – and they'd been to all kinds of doctors – could do nothing to help her. And then this cult – the New Life Fraternity, as it called itself – showed up. The girl went to their meetings. Soon she wanted her parents to join as well – but the new life, into which Katya dove head-first, frightened them more than her earlier withdrawal: Katya now seemed to live in a scary fairytale from which there was no return. Recently, she announced that she would gift her parents' apartment to the fraternity, sign over ownership to her Teacher, and move "into the cells" with her sisters. They were all brothers and sisters, chanting spells and beginning their prayers with a peace pipe passed around a circle, after which they would be given visions of the new life they all aspired to. If Katya sold the apartment, she would doom her aging parents to homelessness, but she did not think about that.

"You'll come live with me, it'll be better for you that way," she said. She has become a zombie.

"What's to come of us? What?" Nina Timofeyevna asked Kambiz.

Kambiz threw a pinch of white powder on the logs. Smoke billowed and rose, the logs caught fire instantly. The Persian took a magical crystal off a shelf and looked at the fire through it.

"Where do they meet?"

"The building that used to be the movie theater."

"Go home now, everything will be fine tomorrow."

For some reason, Nina Timofeyevna believed him, and left – the Persian emanated true magical power. Kambiz, after she left, spoke to someone on the phone.

The next morning Kambiz attended the fraternity's meeting. The teacher – a well-nourished man with a shaved head who was wrapped in an orange bed sheet – greeted the newcomer with a happy smile and offered him the peace pipe. The rite had already begun – about a hundred adepts sat in a circle on small ottomans, and their pin-head-sized pupils told Kambiz they were already seeing visions.

"Do you know the future?" Kambiz asked the teacher in his thundering voice.

"Of course I do, brother, and so will you if you join."

"You do not know the future. You are a liar. You will be taken to the police now, and then you'll stand trial, and get eight years in a high security prison for distributing drugs, and then will come the camp, concrete floors, tuberculosis and death."

Kambiz waved his arm. Two SWAT teams poured in through the doors. The teacher was promptly handcuffed and led away. In the back room they found a stockpile of hard drugs. Lieutenant Colonel Ivanov, who was in charge of the operation and who tracked down the entire supply chain (the teacher cracked right away and gave the police all his dealers) got a medal and was promoted. Katya returned home, went through detox, and never mentions selling her parents' apartment anymore. Does she still dream of a new life? History is silent on that count. The common citizens of our city saw the raid as just more proof of the Persian's prophetic gifts.

After the raid, Kambiz returned home to sit in front of his fireplace and stare at the sacred flames. He thought about the great wisdom of Ahura Mazda. He had used an ancient remedy – a weak opiate solution – to cure Lieutenant Colonel Ivanov's wife of hysteria and insomnia, and restored peace back to that family. And yet, used for ill, the same drugs almost ruined a hundred other families. Kambiz pulled his piece of rock-crystal from the shelf, played with it for a bit, then put it back. People needed theater, otherwise, it was too hard for them to believe a simple truth: Good fights Evil all the time, and a virtuous man who follows the path of Truth, must also work hard not to stray, for Evil often comes dressed in Good's clothes.

The Persian fed a dry log to his fire; his lips habitually uttered the three ancient incantations. Someone knocked hesitantly on his door.

"Come in, the door's unlocked!" Kambiz said in a thunderous voice and made his eyes bulge to give his face a ferocious expression.

REPTILE

They called him Lizard at first. Red-haired and green-eyed, the gleam in his pupils ferocious, he was quick and hungry, and learned the law early: fear no one and strike first, or else they'll eat you alive. After his first night on the street, one old "wolf" pounced on him:

"Share what you've got."

"I've nothing."

"Then give me your 'nothing'."

Lizard nodded to his pillow, "There, go take it."

The "wolf" shook down the stash.

"There's nothing here, you punk!"

"So I told you – you can have your share of that."

Later, when he came to be Reptile, he tested the newbies himself. Recruited a band of the fearless. Ruled over them more with his look and his word than his fist, having learned well that man has yet to invent a weapon sharper than a look and more accurate than a word; stole his words from the old-timers, did homework. Most didn't. For the time being, hid his eyes – saved his look. He seemed in no hurry, but only seemed – in fact, he fought tooth and claw to be on top, and fought his way in. Changed his flag – became Captain, the one at the wheel, looked after Stargorod. Set his course under Gorbachev; the Gypsies then joked: "As long as the Gorbach's in Kremlin, our horses will eat with gold teeth!" But he didn't fuss over dough, and wasn't one to show off, did not wear bling like a suit to work. Built himself a house across from the Governor's and lived a quiet life, waved from the driveway and dropped by for *shashlyk*. Judged his people by the code, punished by the law, and over the next 20 years filled his house with stuff, but not with a family – bowed to the code on that count, he did, knew how it goes: a family drags you down – and it weren't fools that cut you your shirt, so don't go turning it inside out. Pinned a flag to his lapel, got a party card, and sat in the assembly, but put the business of power into expert hands – sent in Spade and Badger, who did accounting long before girls on TV sang about the job. Himself stayed in the back, didn't go far, put his pieces on the board and got bored. Life's a string – you give it some slack, it'll twist into a noose on your own neck.

Did rounds of the city every day. He'd go to the gas station – they'd pour him a shot of 95, he'd down it straight, and see better. If things didn't look sharper, it meant boys were mixing the good stuff with 76, he'd send the whole crew to the logging farm, "to the mosquitoes," they'd straighten up in a blink – he wasn't Yakuza or something, never chopped fingers. Then he'd visit his laundries, walk between spinning drums, watch his money dry, with the tips of his fingers he could sense second-rate work, punished the slackers, rewarded a beautiful job. Stuffed his pockets with bills, but didn't take dirty ones – didn't like the way they'd stick and wad up. Drove to his restaurant, held court, heard complaints, helped some folks, broke fights, rarely showed his teeth. Really, he only came to life if there was a raid, but raids were few and far between – his pawns in the proper corridors ran like clockwork. On City Day he stood on the Archdeacon's right, and held his candle straight. The crowd whispered about him behind his back, in fear and awe.

He went abroad once – didn't like it. Started running away to the woods, to a hut that looked like the one in which he'd been born. He went to hunt, the story was. Deep in the woods, alone, he'd drop his clothes, do a flip and his body would turn – scaly and covered with reddish-gray fur. He'd spend the night roaming under the trees, startling pigs, would sometimes wrangle a moose and drink the blood from its throat – to keep fit. His bodyguards knew nothing – he told himself; he could no longer see the way people looked at him when he came back. They looked with fear, they fawned: at night in the woods, the gleam in his eyes burned bright and dyed his pupils red, and the eyes would give him away, but he wasn't one to look in the mirrors when he came back.

And still, in the woods he also got bored. No beast was his match – in speed, in wits, in pure strength – none of the many he'd seen in his life, all ferocious and merciless. Those who crossed him cooled their heels in the graveyard, and those who were smarter left him alone, and he did not bother them. And so it went, as the story goes.

Then – he must've lost his grip and slipped. Was walking in the forest, came to a clearing, sniffed – something seemed wrong. Looked up, scanned the tree line. All was quiet – too quiet indeed. You can't hear a bullet lying inside the gun. You don't smell a trigger yield.

He flew back a few steps, fell and died.

Three men in camouflage dropped from tree stands. Approached carefully, guns cocked.

"Look... his ears are down."

Spade, who was in charge of the hunt, prodded the now harmless bulk of him, and pulled out his cell phone.

"Done, Comrade General. Positive – dead as a doornail."

And fished for his flask in his backpack.

"Good job, boys, you're all going to the Maldives. Bury him here," he offered a drink to his whippers-in. "Whiskey, 12 years old."

"And this 'un here – all he drank was gas... Gave me an ulcer. Now this! That's good shit."

"What if we saved his head and stuffed it?"

"Are you nuts? They'd pack us in for poaching – these things all died out, he's the last big one that was left! Damn reptile."

"Don't be so harsh, Vasya, let's drink to the repose of his soul, poor sinner. His time's over, it's our time now," the man drank, exhaled, and laughed with relief – a horsey, giggling laugh.

A neigh called back from the river – a young stallion tried out his voice, happy to be alive. The men spit into their hands, pulled the shovels they'd brought with them from the bushes and started digging a reptile-sized grave.

KARAOKE

Hardy, orange-tinted apples hung on the branches. Father Artemon kept watch over the tree all through September, happy with how the Antonov apples were ripening. On the first Sunday in November – the bishop's name day – Father Artemon rose before dawn and gathered a large basketful. So as not to spoil the beauty of the fruit, he did not wipe off the cool, damp droplets of evening rain. He walked through the city to the bishop's residence and was let into the waiting room by a servant. He sat down on a chair outside the high office. The bishop had yet to arrive, and the church high priest and secretary of the eparchy were waiting for him in his office. The door was ajar and Father Artemon heard the servant's voice: "…has come to intercede for Pavlin."

"Three years he's been interceding. That monkey-lover just won't let it go," the secretary sneered.

Four years earlier, the bishop sent the old priest into retirement: with his poor eyesight, Father Artemon had, in his church, administered communion to a chimpanzee, taking him to be a holy fool. Father Artemon, to be fair, had a different view of things: Foma the monkey had saved the church icon from a ferocious thief, laying down his life in the process, and Father Artemon faithfully believed that the monkey was an enchanted human being, and not a mute beast, but he had obeyed the bishop's order. Now he stood through church services alongside the choir, thinking of how he might atone his sin: because of him, another priest – Father Pavlin Pridvorov, the one who had informed on Father Artemon – had also been banished from the city, to serve in Soggy Tundra. Pavlin, owing to his youthful mind, had entertained wild ideas and thirsted for a career. This was always repugnant to Father Artemon, but he had only to recall the poverty and utter hopelessness of his rural childhood, and he would begin to feel sorry for Pavlin's six children,[7] banished to the land of mosquitoes for their father's mistake. Father Artemon had the dream of restoring the disgraced priest to the lush city post before he died. He believed that the bishop would listen to his entreaties and at first did not attach any significance to the secretary's evil tongue.

The voice of the high priest floated out the office door: "…He wrote a letter to the chief conservationist: 'All the princes and persons of eminence in this world have given to the church, so why can't the artist show his generosity and, out of his honorarium, give Father Pavlin a karaoke machine, in addition to the refrigerator and television he had already contributed, for which he would be inscribed in the church rosters as a warden and be eternally commemorated throughout the parish.' That's something, eh?"

"He's indulging his fancy… We all know what he wants that karaoke for," the secretary replied. "He is weaving intrigues. When we go out to sanctify that church, you keep Pavlin away from the Minister, while I keep him from the bishop. We keep our eyes peeled, and we'll get through cleanly. I'll get the message to the artist to not gift that karaoke."

Father Artemon left the bucket with its greeting card in the corridor and quietly retreated. At home, he took his savings from beneath an icon and bought the best karaoke machine he could find in the department store, then boarded a bus for Soggy Tundra.

The Minister who is now all-powerful was born 57 years ago in Soggy Tundra. And now, as has become the custom at the pinnacles of power, he decided to restore the single little church in his tiny hometown. The restoration team had been working for two years, and the opening of the church was planned for Christmas, in the presence of the church leadership, politicians and the press. Everyone knew that after the holiday feast both the Minister and the bishop loved to

---

7. Priests in the Orthodox Church can be married before taking their vows and thus have children.

sing Russian folk songs using a karaoke machine. Thus the lachrymose appeal to the brigadier of the restorers, which had somehow been intercepted by the eparchy. Father Pavlin's calculations were precise: after the lavish feast and libations, the bishop's and minister's souls would thaw, songs would soften them to tears, and it would be the perfect moment to throw oneself at their feet and beg for forgiveness and a transfer – it hardly seemed likely that the bishop could refuse him in front of the worldly boss.

Father Artemon rode on the bus and fervently thanked Providence for sending him to the right place at the right time. His apples and cards had been ignored for three years. No, he had fallen behind the times, so far behind, and it was right that they sent him into retirement. He, with his unsophisticated nature, would never have come up with a plan such as this, but these envious fools, they're quick on the uptake and just get in the way.

Father Pavlin welcomed him warmly. Rural life had been good to him. His children were healthy and did not look like a gang of ragamuffins; their childhood was nothing like his before the war. But the main thing was that Father Pavlin had become warmer and more easy-going; the first thing he did was embrace the old priest and ask his forgiveness. Gratefully accepting the karaoke machine and learning of the intrigues being woven at the eparchy, he broke down sobbing and called Father Artemon "sweet Father."

They parted warmly the next day. The priest's wife packed a basket of pies and fresh boiled eggs for Father Artemon. The old priest rode the bus and looked out the window at the November sky. No tracks are left in the heavens, he thought, for some reason; even the birds have flown away. The clouds hung low and thick, covering the endless, happy azure beyond like armor. Father Artemon closed his eyes and died quietly and joyfully, as he had lived.

THE MAGIC LETTER

When Misha was little, his Mom always told him: "Don't you go aiming high, Misha – you're soft, anyone can squeeze you however they want, and eat you on a bun." Misha didn't listen to his mother's words.

At the institute he did skits with the KVN team,[8] and caught the eye of Sergey Pavlovich Triflin himself; Triflin brought him into the Stargorod mayoral administration and kept him close. So it came to pass that Misha put on his stone boots. Their agreement was that, when he wore out seven pairs, they'd give him an iron staff. If he then wore down 12 iron staffs and did not err – they'd make him a sheriff. Every night Misha delivered a postman's bag of cash to Triflin's safe. He learned his trade on the fly – threatened here, flattered there, but one way or the other delivered what was Caesar's better than all the other young guns. Soon, they moved him up a floor.

Misha developed the taste for double-breasted blazers with crested buttons and ties with a sparkle, but always half-a-shade dimmer than his master's. He wore his boots out in two years, put on a pair of Salamander suede zip-ups and kicked it up a notch: you should've seen him then, with his iron staff doing toe-loops on the asphalt – only sparks flew! He got an office, too, with a double paneled door and brass handles all carved in curlicues like an iconostasis. Around his seventh staff, Misha got to ride around in the bank's collectors' van with two porters to help him, and found

---

8. KVN - Клуб Весёлых и Находчивых – a popular game show that has been on Russian/Soviet TV since the late 1950s, in which teams of contestants compete to answer questions with humor, do extemporaneous improvisations, and present prepared skits.

a trick for his staff, too: every day the knife grinder at the market worked off a quarter-inch on his wheel for him. The levies were enough to keep Misha in bread-and-butter, but he wasn't greedy, and his master didn't mind.

One morning, Triflin gave Misha in his usual pile of paperwork a "Good Luck letter" – you've probably seen them: "The original is being kept in Amsterdam, copy this letter five times and send it to good people, Count Blondenquist did the same and won a million, Khrushchev forgot – and was deposed the next morning."

Misha lost the letter in the daily hustle, and three days later – boom! – a scandal: he was supposed to get it to the Governor himself, who wanted to stitch the letter into the lining of his suit coat that he would wear to his appointment with the President. They flew a copy in from the museum in Amsterdam, barely made it. Triflin didn't care that Misha had only one more iron staff to wear off – banished him to manage the rotten Boozersk *kolkhoz*. All the money Misha had saved had to be doled out – the governor's crew threatened to put him in jail and the Mayor left him to bail himself out.

Misha understood he was punished for violating democratic centralism's primary principle: he nearly put a higher authority in a bind, and let down his boss. The Magic Letter doesn't forgive – born in 1264, it's still doing its work around the world!

At the *kolkhoz*, Misha made do: loosed a lumber gang into the forest – they mowed it down in a blink – sold all the old machinery for scrap, but there was no way he could raise the kind of cash he had gotten used to in Stargorod.

Misha started to drink.

Fortunately, he still had enough brains to make the move, once he ate his way through the *kolkhoz*, for the position of the local administration's Election Commission head – a quiet harbor, but there was no money in it. Misha's lean years dragged on; the administration forgot about him, so he sat in his middle of nowhere and wracked his brain over how he could remind Them of his existence. Once he read in the paper a quote from Metropolitan Bishop Cyril, who stated that "he would very much like to see the moral condition of our society restore itself, so that, perhaps, one day we could yet see an Orthodox monarchy." Misha armed himself with this quote and told a bunch of visiting reporters that it's time to anoint our President to the throne. And that's when he got fired.

"Why me? All I did was repeat what the Metropolitan said!"

"The Metropolitan can say it, but you can't. It's still too early, plus look how wisely he put it: "perhaps, one day, we could yet." And you just dropped it into their laps like a done deal – what were you thinking? Gone feral in your woods is what you did."

Misha drank hard then, spent everything he had. Next morning he dug into his wallet for something with which to buy a cure for his hangover, and found the old wrinkled "Good Luck letter." All these years he'd been carrying his misfortune right under his heart! It was then he remembered his mother's words. What made him mess with the higher-ups, really? They almost ate him alive.

He went to his cousin in Udomlya and bought from him 50 female rabbits to breed, built a bunch of cages and fenced off his yard, so the rabbits could come out and graze. Raising one rabbit costs 28 lbs of feed, 14 lbs of hay, and 3 rubles' worth of electricity. Total over four months: 80 rubles. For that you get: fresh meat, almost 6 lbs, equals 400 rubles, liver 50 rubles, fat 50 rubles, pelt 25 rubles, total 525 rubles. You clear 445 rubles from one animal, and an average female rabbit has 40 pups in a single year.

There was only one thing he tried to keep secret – and still it got out somehow: before he got into rabbits, he copied the magic letter five times and sent it to people he knew, and the very first copy went up to the Governor certified mail. Make of it what you will. Misha now is doing just fine, bought a Gazelle van, hired two hobos to look after the rabbits, and drives around without a care in the world, delivering meat to restaurants.

No, it wasn't his mother's advice that saved him – ask anyone in Boozersk, they'll tell you. They're still mad that Misha, the bastard, kept the Good Luck letter to himself, didn't share it with his own kind when he should have. So now the guys are all waiting, hoping the letter will make it back to Boozersk somehow. People say it's got a five-year-cycle and then comes back around. Here's hoping it's sooner rather than later – this life will grind anyone down.

STONE SOUP

Folks have been working fields around Stargorod for centuries, but every year, new boulders come up from under the ground. The pagan Komsi tribe that used to live on these lands believed that a fire-breathing dragon lived in the depths of the earth and the boulders and rocks were the petrified tears he shed mourning the people's hard lot. The Soviet government, when it arrived, explained everything: our region lies at the foot of a large plateau and for that reason is rich in highly valuable construction materials – they started quarries everywhere and caravans of trucks loaded with high-quality gravel began crawling daily to the Stargorod's railway station. They even began building a narrow-gauge line to the quarry in Kozhin, the local army unit engineered bridges for it and raised a levy, but then *perestroika* happened, and the unit was disbanded. The rail line soon disappeared in thickets of wild raspberry and mushrooms; carps found their way into the quarry's flooded pits.

For a long time, no one had any use for the abandoned piles of gravel and cobblestone, until a man named Rashid arrived in our lands – the fourteenth son of an Azerbaijani farmer, he had wandered to Stargorod in search of a better life. Rashid turned stone into money: he hired cheap trucks and had hobos load them up in exchange for booze, then sent his cargo to Moscow and sold it there on the Rublyov market. Rashid paid Musa the Chechen "for protection," and his trucks made their way to Moscow without any trouble. One day, Musa introduced Rashid to a hot-shot Muscovite. "So, you're in the gravel business?" the Muscovite asked Rashid.

"A little."

"The *kolkhoz* has been divided into individual lots – get me the whole package for Kozhino, and I'm especially interested in the lots that border the old quarry. A hundred and forty hectares altogether, ten owners – get me the lot, I'm paying triple."

"Five times, and I'm getting the signatures," Rashid said sternly and glanced at Musa. Musa nodded silently.

The Muscovite shook his hand – they had a deal. In the *kolkhoz* administration, a bottle of cognac and a box of chocolates produced the records Rashid needed. He copied down the owners' names and drove to Kozhino. He was not a stranger there: every fall he came to buy sheep he supplied to Stargorod's Muslim diaspora. After two neighbors got ten thousand in cash each, the rest lined up to see Rashid by themselves; Rashid told them he wanted to build a pig farm in Kozhino. He had eight deeds in a blink. Simple math showed that at the price of 1800 rubles per hectare, each 14-hectare lot made him 152,000 rubles in profit. But to get the ninth lot, Rashid had to face the old witch Alevtina Pimenova. And she wouldn't budge.

"My father wrung this lot out of the *kolkhoz*. It used to be my great-grandfather's way before the revolution. Father said we could make soup from these stones for the next hundred years."

They sat there for four hours, bickering; Rashid went hoarse, Pimenova, without him noticing, got him to agree to pay 40,000 more than he'd started with. Her lot was right next to the quarry, Rashid could not let it slip.

Cursing the hag under his breath, Rashid paid up, grabbed the deed, and went to find the last address on his list. Kolya Piklov, also known as Pickle, was waiting for him.

"You're after the stone, aren't you?" he inquired of the entrepreneur.

"I'm building a pig farm."

"Don't play with me, pal. There's a dragon guards our rocks – you gotta give him something, or else there'll be trouble. We the

Komsi know how to do it. And as far as selling the land – I'll sell, why not, what do I want with it."

Pickle went to the pantry and returned with a strange-looking rock with a hole in it.

"Here, put this rock under Pimenova's deed; she's my cousin once removed, I'll do spells for our blood. And you, here, have some beer in the meantime – we, the Komsi, don't do deals otherwise." Being a well brought up Azerbaijani, Rashid did not dare violate the ancestral law and took a sip of the beer. The world spun around him, and he fainted. When he woke up, it was night, and he was sitting in his car parked somewhere in the middle of a forest. He counted the deeds – there were eight. The ninth one, Pimenova's, was gone.

Musa, when he heard Rashid's story, said simply:

"You got conned. You don't have the whole lot – the Muscovite won't give you the money."

Then he offered Rashid a hundred thousand rubles for the eight deeds that he did have. Rashid was afraid of Musa and did not refuse. The quarry, of course, in due time opened anyway. The Muscovite's corporation bought out the last two lots, for a totally different price. Alevtina had long been living with Pickle, and now they used their money to buy a small cottage at the edge of Stargorod. With gas and hot water.

Pickle still drinks his homemade beer, same as always. Alevtina grumbles, but she knows – he's a Komsi, and Komsi can't go without. The other folks in Kozhino drank through their cash in a week, had themselves a grand ol' time, spent another week hung-over, and went back to living their lives as they had before. They never bore a grudge against Pimenova and Pickle; quite the opposite – the Kozhino folks take great pride in them, and whenever they make their way to town, come to visit and stay until either Alevtina or Pickle throws them out.

Rashid, soon after, ran into Pickle in the market, offered him his hand, and gave him a slap on the shoulder, "You're a wily son-of-a-bitch, but whatever, I'm not angry."

Pickle shook the hand of the Azerbaijani farmer's fourteenth son and said, "The dragon, Rashid, is crying under the ground there, mourns us every day, wails and sobs, and we live like we're not brothers – that's our problem."

BEAUTY AND THE BEAST

Katya was a beauty. For five years, she fought with her husband, Sashka, a drunk and a good-for-nothing. In return, Sashka regularly beat her. Finally, Katya took their little daughter Sveta and left him. The commonly accepted maxim, "If he beats you – he must love you," did not sit well with her.

Stargorod's hospital, where Katya worked as a nurse, took pity on her and found her a one-room flat in an old barrack still heated with firewood. The neighborhood women only shook their heads: Sashka was known far and wide for being ferociously vindictive. Katya's neighbor, Aunt Klava, pitying her, called the young woman "my *kamikaze*." Several times Sashka tried to break through Katya's door at night and broke her windows. Katya would call the police, they would put him in the slammer for 15 days, but every time he came out he'd go after her again – the official divorce seemed to have done nothing but rile him up more.

Katya's life turned into a nightmare. She would gladly sign up for a job in the North, but she had neither the energy nor the money to pull up roots and move to a new place with a small child: under the auspices of a new national program, the hospital's clinic and emergency room doctors got a 10,000 ruble raise, and the nurses saw a grand total of 700 added to their monthly 3,000. Katya worked two full-time shifts and could barely make ends meet.

One night Katya was walking home after her shift; it was late, already dark. She had to walk past St. Christopher's cemetery, about which people liked to tell many scary stories – many featured werewolves who gnawed on buried skeletons at night, robbed passersby and demanded pay-offs from passing cars. Katya walked faster along the cemetery's fence; she could hear someone breathing heavily behind her, catching up with her.

"Wait, bitch, I gotta talk to you!"

Katya recognized Sashka's voice. Facing him in this deserted place, at night, alone did not bode well at all – Sashka had long been threatening to stab her. Katya gripped the handle of her purse harder and prepared to defend herself. Her ex pounced at her like a rabid animal, drunk and vicious, knocked the useless purse out of her hand, and twisted her arm behind her back; she saw the gleam of a blade. Realizing she was done for, Katya screamed.

Suddenly, the nearest bushes shook and a thing, a creature, something so dreadful it could only be called a Beast climbed out. Without idle talk, it struck Sashka on the jaw, knocked him off his feet and went to work on him, saying: "I see you bother this beauty one more time, I'll bury you right here." Sashka whimpered in horror and pain and swore to forget Katya forever.

The Beast turned out not as scary as it was in the cartoon Katya watched with little Sveta. It had a pleasant voice and spoke kind words to Katya, comforting her as she wept with relief from the terror she'd survived, and it stroked her hair in a way that sent electric sparks flying all over her body and instantly robbed her of any sense. The Beast saw Katya home, went through her door and told her not to turn on the light. "Shh, keep quiet, lest we wake up the kid."

The Beast seemed to have paralyzed Katya's will; she felt no fear whatsoever towards him. Everything happened in a blink, almost like in the cartoon. No – it was better, much better, so much better. No movie could ever hope to match what happened between them.

At dawn, Katya woke and stoked the wood-burning stove – she had to start potatoes boiling in the cast-iron vat for the piglet she kept in the yard. The Beast was sleeping, arms spread wide on the bed, and his linen-blond curly hair gleamed on the pillow. Last night, before they climbed into bed, he told her specifically not to touch the skin he shed on the floor. Katya considered the prohibition, thought about all the trouble that usually ensued in fairy-tales when such orders were disobeyed, and decided not to listen. Be what may! She bundled the whole pile together, threw it into the stove, and added a few logs for a good measure. The flames shot up high, red flashes leaped around the room. Katya made sure the skin couldn't be saved, then went back to the room, climbed under the blanket and pressed close to her Beast. He mumbled something in his sleep, and put one arm around her shoulder.

And that's when the bullets began to explode inside the stove.

Lieutenant Ivanets jumped up as if someone had scalded him; a terrified Sveta howled from behind the curtain. Katya prepared to receive her well-deserved death.

Ivanets dashed to the stove, grabbed a pale of water and splashed it onto the fire. Then he grabbed a poker and spread out what was left of his uniform. Seeing that he wouldn't be able to save any of it, he looked reproachfully at Katya. She, chin held proudly high, explained, "I was afraid that you would turn into a Beast again and leave us."

At those words, Kolya Ivanets looked at her with awe and, suddenly finding the courage, said, "Now not in a million years!" and stuck his tongue out at Svetka who poked her head out from behind the curtain.

For leaving his post without permission and for negligence in handling his personal weapon Lieutenant Ivanets was discharged from the State Traffic Police.

"I've done my turn as a werewolf in uniform – that was plenty," he declared, returning to Katya's apartment with a bottle of champagne and a bouquet. "Tomorrow, I'll submit an application to the fire brigade, the guys promised to find a spot for me." "You do know how to handle a fire," Katya said as she came up to the Beast and kissed him.

Everyone knows since times immemorial that the Beauty got seriously lucky with the Beast – but why is it that those who make it their business to write such stories never bothered to wonder: and what about the Beast?

BRIBE

Ivan Nikanorovich Lyapunov took great pride in his ancestor Lyapun, the source of his last name. In 1546, scrivener Lyapun, sent to Bakhchisarai as the head of the tsar's embassy, refused to pay "the staff duty" to Khan Sakhib-Girey's *murzas*. The *murzas* – Crimean nobles – had the custom of meeting Moscow's emissaries before the Khan's palace and throwing their walking staffs under the Russians' feet; they demanded a significant sum as the price for free passage. This wasn't merely about having to bribe them: the payee, by virtue of having to buy himself entrance to the palace, acknowledged the supremacy of the Khan and his own lowly position as a payer of tribute – something upon which the Crimean Khans, who traced their lineage to Genghis Khan himself, were keen to insist. The poor Lyapun was stripped naked and paraded around the market with his nostrils and ears sewn shut to shame him before Bakhchisarai's citizenry, but he did not give in and returned to Moscow never having gained an audience with the Khan or having signed a new treaty. Upon his return, Lyapun was promoted to clerk and sent to Stargorod, where he was destined to beget the famous Lyapunovs.

In the early days of democratization, Ivan Nikanorovich spent two years working as Stargorod's mayor's deputy, but he didn't fit into the system, for he despised bribing as a phenomenon. So he returned to his old position at Stargorod University, where he taught Russian history and was a department chair.

He was just about to deliver his lecture about the relations between the Rus and the Golden Horde one day when an unexpected question made him revise his narrative: a student asked where bribes came from. Ivan Nikanorovich began with the Byzantine Empire, in which the administration was broken up into districts called dioceses (from the Latin *dioecesis*). Each diocese had its own judge and its own bishop. The judge was responsible for adjudicating civil disputes, and the bishop for keeping the spiritual peace, correcting violations of moral and religious norms. Neither official was ever paid a decent regular salary, as, for instance, judges in the West would later receive from the government, so they had to rely on whatever the parties to the suit could donate to the court for having justice done – and that's how the bribe was born. No one saw it necessary to set a standard for the donations, so corruption quickly became the norm in the state's apparatus. Over time, the state weakened and fell – easy prey to bloodthirsty Turks. In the West, where governments inherited Roman law, bribing was seen as a great shame and was punished severely. However, it was Byzantine customs that were imported to Rus along with Eastern Christianity; a prince, for instance, who was expected to act as a judge, received lands "to feed from" – basically, a token maintenance – and how much he charged privately for solving a citizen's dispute was never discussed. The nobles and the common people traditionally looked the other way.

"Do you mean to say that bribing is in our blood and we can do nothing to root it out?" the student asked.

"I believe it is wrong to give bribes, and that we should fight this," Lyapunov answered and ended the discussion.

After class, Kostya Stupin came by Ivan Nikanorovich's office – Kostya was his graduate student and a fourth-generation fisherman from the Lake Country.

"Ivan Nikanorovich, dad sent you some fish," Kostya said shyly offering the professor a box of smoked zanders.

"Are you offering me a bribe?"

"We caught these together, I smoked them myself, I just wanted to share – try them, it's from the heart!"

To refuse would have meant to offend the boy. Lyapunov shook his head and took the box.

Later that day he went to visit his mother – she lived in a village, a dozen miles outside of town. His mother loved fish, so the zanders came at a perfect time. He drove through the gathering dusk, having forgotten to fasten his seat belt or to turn on the lights, and thought that he really should not have accepted the fish. At St. Christopher's Cemetery, something – an apparition with a sergeant's shoulder-straps jumped out of the bushes and waved the traffic police stick at him; Lyapunov pulled over. The apparition was skinny as a child: it had an almost-bald skull with a bit of thin hair on it, and its big-knuckled fingers ended in razor-sharp nails.

"Driving without lights, without the seat belt, and when you made that turn you traveled into the facing lane! Oh, is that fish you got there?" the skeletal apparition wheezed happily, poking its head into the window and looking over Lyapunov's shoulder into the back seat.

"I won't give you any money," Lyapunov said sternly.

All of a sudden, the skeleton broke apart into three small boys in tattered clothes.

"Mister, we're hungry, help us, ple-e-ase!" they sang out in unison. Their gaunt little faces would make a rock cry.

"To heck with you – here!" Lyapunov threw a couple of fishes out the window. The boys snatched them and vanished into the bushes.

In the village, he complained to his mother about the traffic police – they're way out of line!

"You're always judging people, Vanya," his mother said. "And you should know better. To hear you say it, everyone's just getting fat, and there are all kinds of people out there. Take Katya Pimenova – she lives on the other end of the village – her husband's in the traffic police, and he's skin and bones, a breeze could tip him over, but he works hard and does all the chores at home, and they have three kids, and he doesn't drink but they're poor all the same. Power's gone to your head, Vanya – why did you ever want to mess with it?"

Ivan Nikanorovich did not argue with his mother, but threw back a shot of vodka, bit a pickle and went outside. It was frosty; the sky was pierced with stars. For some reason, he suddenly imagined his ancestor – how he walked across the Bakhchisarai market, naked, with his ears and nostrils sewn shut, the crowds cursing him with words he couldn't understand. The vodka spread warm throughout Ivan Nikanorovich's body. He brushed off a quick tear, turned, and went inside, to sleep.

INSTITUTE OF DREAMS

A small diesel engine pulled a local train along the narrow-gauge line between Soggy Tundra and Stargorod. It was December 24, and Nikita Yurievich Kostochkin was on his way home from a business trip. It had been three years since his wife Alyona died, leaving him alone with his daughter Masha, now a student at the university. Masha's boyfriend was an asshole, but Kostochkin did not believe he had the right to talk to his daughter about this, and, on top of that, he was afraid of being abandoned by her in their three-room apartment. At the moment, however, on his way home, he wanted nothing less than to walk in on the boyfriend staring idiotically into the TV in his kitchen.

There was a time when Nikita Yurievich worked at a museum, where he collected folklore by traveling around the region. In the 90s, the position at the museum was cut, so he found work at a new place called The Institute of Dreams. Its 10 employees published dream interpretation guides, read coffee-grounds, recorded Gypsy predictions about the future of the country, and had a director who in all seriousness declared that their mission was to teach people to see and appreciate their dreams on a whole new level – to become what he called "cognizant dreamers." Nikita Yurievich did not bother to look for a deeper meaning in the director's bullshit, and instead continued to collect the same old folklore he'd always cared about – along with the new legends that were being born right before his eyes.

Kostochkin always traveled second-class – he could count on meeting fascinating characters there. This day was no exception: a drifter who boarded the train in Emmaus informed him that the station had been named after one Emma Us, an old-timey landlady who was built like a grenadier and loved nothing more than shooting hares.

"She'd shoot 240 of them in a day!" the drifter boasted, as proud as if he'd counted the bodies himself.

The drifter had never heard of the vision of the Risen Christ that had appeared in Emmaus to some travelers, only snorted dismissively when Nikita Yurievich mentioned it, then turned to the old lady on the seat next to him and proceeded to enlighten her about the ongoing battle between the forces of White and Black magic. The forces of Light were currently being represented by Kaloyev, the guy who stabbed a Swissair traffic controller, and who had just been let out of Swiss jail.

"Because he fought a German!" the hobo proudly declared.

"You mean a Swiss," Kostochkin corrected.

"How's that different?" the hobo snapped back. "Those Krauts opened a gravel pit in Kozhino, next thing you know they'll take the whole country down, stone by stone. One of our guys has had a dream about it."

"It's German Christmas today," the old lady piped in. "Whatever dream you get will come true. Only the dreams tonight don't bode well – that's because the Laodokian Angel leaves his post to revere St. Nicholas; we are orphaned for the night. My neighbor dreamt on this night in 1991 about Gorbachev, and the spot on his head shrank in her dream into a dot. And the very next morning he said goodbye to everyone on TV, and they lowered the Soviet flag over the Kremlin!"

Nikita Yurievich sat there silently, listening, committing things to memory. He's already collected a bookful of such stories heard on the road. Traditional dreams – the kind in which a fish means pregnancy, a dog is a friend, and losing one's teeth betokens death – have come to seem common and boring to him; they were a legacy of another time, and gravitated to notions popularized in Martyn Zadeka's fortune-telling book that enjoyed great popularity among the Russians in the middle of the nineteenth century. The new folklore, in its living, passionate, confusing, sometimes raving spontaneity, reflected the condition of the common mind and was, to Nikita Yurievich, far more interesting.

His fellow travelers, having bonded over their long and substantive conversation, got off the train together at some small station. The diesel engine strained, the car rocked hard on the rails, and the storm tossed handfuls of snow against the window. Kostochkin fell asleep. He dreamed of a child, a girl of magnificent beauty – they were picking mushrooms in the forest together and laughing happily about something. The girl looked both like his daughter Masha and his late wife Alyona.

When Kostochkin woke up, the train was already pulling up to Stargorod's platform. He took the back way home from the railway station, cutting through the dark yards, and yet he couldn't shake off his dream. If you see a maiden, that means a marvel, a miracle is near, Zadeka maintained – a naive interpretation based on the similarity between the words "maiden" and "marvel." Kostochkin expected no miracles.

Masha, fortunately, was home alone. On the occasion of Christmas, albeit Catholic, she had roasted a duck with sour Antonov apples, and bought a bottle of champagne. Nikita Yurievich told her about his dream and, jokingly, suggested they drink to a miracle. That's when his daughter broke down and told him she was pregnant, but added sternly that she would never even consider marrying the child's father, and called him an asshole.

"That's great – there'll be three of us!" Nikita Yurievich hugged his daughter and spent a long time holding her and stroking her hair.

That night he dreamed he saw the Angel of Laodokia, carved into a schooner's bow. The ship flew up to visit St. Nicholas. He, Kostochkin, stood at the helm, and a fishing net long as the Milky Way hung down from the stern. Snow fell all around them, flakes coming to rest atop Martyn Zadeka's book, forgotten on the ground below. Suddenly, the volume changed its shape and turned into the map of his country, except that instead of its name the letters written across its curving expanse spelled "The Institute of Dreams."

Tiny trains sped through the snowstorm in all directions, their passengers slept, and their dreams, colorful like candy wrappers, flew up and fluttered towards the stars, but were caught instead in the mesh of the ship's fishing net. Nikita Yurievich realized that he was inside a "cognizant" dream. In his sleep, he hid his face in his hands, to make sure he wouldn't wake up, the way he used to do a long time ago, when he was a little boy.

A CARAMEL ROOSTER FOR CHRISTMAS

It was Christmas Eve, and Nikolai M was beset by unpleasant thoughts.

In the morning, he found in his mailbox a card from his daughter, who'd run away to live in Germany, only to find out that his daughter and her husband were celebrating Christmas in Morocco this year, instead of visiting him in Stargorod. Then his publisher, who'd been feeding him one excuse after another, finally admitted that, unless a sponsor suddenly materialized out of thin air, they wouldn't be able to publish Nikolai M's fundamental study of Stargorod's history for another year. And really, who cares that St. Christopher's Monastery, founded by St. Ephrem back in the 11th century, is today, after Ukraine's independence, the oldest monastery in our country? The day before, he visited both the church and the city council, and neither gave him any money to publish the book.

It is the pinnacle of insanity to believe that we have solid footing. In fact, our history attempts to convince us of the opposite from the very beginning. We thought we were moving forward by walking on hard ground beneath our feet, and all of a sudden we learn that there's nothing even remotely resembling ground there, and, what's more – there's nothing that could be called movement. The democratic transformations – an object of M's heartfelt faith – fizzled out; the city did not want his work, his daughter did not want him, and the people in the street met his beret and eyeglasses with cold, unfriendly looks. He dreaded even imagining their eyes in times of trouble. In 1611, the crowds hung pharmacist Von Rhode right here, on the midtown wall – they thought he was a Swedish spy. Indeed, the word "neighbor" means nothing in big cities. Perhaps it is still relevant in villages, where everyone knows everyone else, and everybody can still love and hate each other in a true neighborly fashion?

Thus obsessing, M came out onto Bolshaya Square. In the middle, the city had put up its Christmas tree; somewhere nearby children were screaming happily. A Gypsy woman pounced on M, stuck a rooster candy-on-a-stick into his fingers, snatched a hundred rubles from his wallet, and, running away, promised that he would meet his happiness today.

M sat on a bench, unwrapped the rooster from its cellophane wrapper and put it into his mouth. The taste of burnt sugar reminded him how he and his friend Vaska used to slide down ice hills here, in the park by the Stargorod kremlin. Back in the day, the caretakers of the city park made those ice hills especially for the kids. It was also here that the boys snuck to smoke Dymok cigarettes, then hid the rest of the pack in a secret cache, and went home, happy and drenched, sucking on rooster stick-candies just like this to mask their tobacco breath. Or chewing on almonds – which were disgusting and filled your mouth with a sort of perfumey after-taste, but cost less than two roosters.

Eight years ago, Vaska was in a bad accident that killed his wife and daughter, and left him crippled. He drank himself almost to death after that. M suddenly decided to visit him.

Vaska still lived in the same Stalin-era apartment building where M himself was born 45 years ago, in the same communal flat with two other families. He was very happy to see Nikolai, showed him to his room, pulled some canned fish out of the fridge, put out black bread and poured them vodka. Very quickly, however, the joy of their reunion was gone without a trace – Vaska got drunk and broke down crying: two days before he had buried his beloved shepherd dog Rada, the only other soul that loved him. Drunk, restless, in panic, he kept saying he would kill himself. M tried to comfort his school friend, thought of kind, soothing things to say to him, and, in the process of talking him off the ledge, somehow discovered that he had lifted himself out of his earlier despair. They finished the vodka, hugged, and sat there for a while, reminiscing about their childhood. Then Vaska lay down on his threadbare couch and zonked out. Nikolai found a blanket, tucked his friend in, and went home.

He walked and thought that the surest way of conquering one's own madness was to visit someone who was even madder. So your dog died – get another one; so they didn't publish your book – write another one. He works for history, after all, and on the historical scale, a year or two don't mean a hill of beans. When he was climbing the stairs to his apartment, he heard his neighbor Nastya call his name: shyly, she invited him to celebrate Christmas together. He accepted, hurried home, took a shower, put on a suit and a white shirt, and got a bottle of Champagne out of the fridge.

And then he talked, and she listened. It turned out that Nastya used to attend his lectures at the university. She was born in a village. It was hard for her to get out of there, and she did not miss it in the least. Now she was happily working at the museum; she lived alone. Nikolai, without quite realizing it, retold his entire book to her – and Nastya wasn't bored! There was only one thing he couldn't understand: how was it that he had never noticed her before?

Everything that is supposed to happen after dinners like that happened. In the morning, M. woke up early, snuck out of bed, dressed and rushed to the square. He was possessed by the need to buy Nastya a rooster on a stick. But the Gypsy woman was not there – instead, there was snow, fluffy and new, and it erased the gloomy city of the day before. Passersby, all to a man, smiled at the bespectacled man in his beret.

M. bought a rose bouquet instead of candy – and that's exactly what he said to Nastya when he gave it to her, that and many other words. Piling his plate with eggs and breakfast sausage, Nastya asked, "So does this mean that the word 'neighbor' is not completely meaningless in big cities?"

The only thing left for M to do was to admit his own stupidity, which he did, promptly and happily.

THE PENCIL STUB

The pencil stub served me faithfully and reliably for an entire year, just like the man who had given it to me – Parfyon Dmitriyevich Malygin.

I met Parfyon Dmitriyevich in the tap-room at the old market, where I went in the hopes of overhearing a good story. Writing a story a week, I'm here to tell you, is pure madness, but a happy madness nonetheless. I lived it for a year – I forgot everything else, I listened to the human choir around me and stole from it everything that was worth stealing.

Some of it, when written down, inevitably lost its sheen, but I survived, owing much to Parfyon Dmitriyevich, who was always there to critique, edit, and supply a new twist borrowed from one of the ancient newspapers he read in his retirement. Parfyon Dmitriyevich, the son of a geography teacher and the grandson of a village priest persecuted by the Soviets, spent his life as a purveyor of stationery. First on foot, with a suitcase, then in a broken-down GAZ four-wheeler, and by the end of his long career – driving a Gazelle mini-van, he had crisscrossed the entire Stargorod region a million times. He sold simple sets of colored pencils, purple and blue ink, cheap fountain pens, presser feet for sewing machines, graph paper, slide rules, and, closer to the end of his service, markers in colors wildly divergent from the natural hues of the rainbow.

Countless Grandfather Frosts, Snowmaidens, bunny-rabbits and sad crocodiles, posters and certificates of birth came into this world thanks to his labors. Love letters and denunciations, sympathy notes and recipes for *blinchiki* with mushrooms would not have been preserved and would not have reached their addressees if it hadn't been for Parfyon Dmitriyevich. And the great volumes of milk and potatoes, pickles and barley that were accounted for in parallel columns on the pages torn from school notebooks, the baseline of a life now long gone? The world does not exist thanks to the atomic bomb, Parfyon Dmitriyevich used to teach me over a shot of vodka, but by the singular grace of stationery that enables people to describe the world around them, to convey its breath to a loved one, a neighbor, or the humblest log hut in Soggy Tundra, where a woman everyone knows only as Ivanovna, once the mistress of a Detective Krotov whom she alone remembers, is living out her days.

In the tap-room at the old market, Parfyon Malygin shared a *cheburek* and a fifth with me and gave me the gift of soulful conversation and a simple magical pencil stub.

"You're going to tell me they don't make them like this anymore, aren't you?" I prodded.

"Of course they don't!" he said and stamped the table conclusively with his glass. "You'll see what I mean, when it's time."

He went on to talk about the Truth of Life, which has much in common with the truth of fairy tales, and about the newspaper fairy tales that have nothing whatsoever to do with life. He spoke simply; we were instantly fast friends. I went to visit him many times over my year of writing a story a week, and read him the stories that seemed to spool from under the hard, sharp tip of his magical pencil almost against my will. Parfyon listened, sometimes grunting in protest, sometimes nodding in agreement, but most often he would interrupt and start on a story of his own, which led to another, and then the third, and that's how we spent our evenings. He was ill for the entire year and sat there behind his enormous writing desk, huddled in an ancient wool blanket, his bare feet stuck inside soft *valenki*.

"Take speech, words," he would begin meaningfully and fix me with his soft eyes bleached to the color of blotting paper. "Words are magic," he would declare, hold a solemn pause, and then burst out in giggles like a proper girl who's just heard a dirty joke.

He was fading, slowly and quietly – he knew this, but did not complain. Every day, he would shrivel another quarter of an inch – a fact recorded by pencil lines on the bathroom doorframe.

Two days ago, when I first had the idea for a Christmas story, the last in the series, I went to get his advice. The pencil he'd given me had turned into a meager stump by then, and secretly I was praying that perhaps he'd find me another one somewhere in his stocks – the prospect of life without the assistance of magic frightened me.

Parfyon Dmitriyevich looked at me with his characteristic smile:

"Will the story have miracles in it?"

"Of course."

"Well, good then – and Merry Christmas!"

His eyes gleamed, the blanket emitted a strange rustle, and his head suddenly disappeared from behind the desk. I called his name; he didn't answer. I went around the desk: the *valenki* were there on the floor, and the blanket pooled around them, empty. When I lifted the blanket, I found a brand new pencil – the new shape into which my dear friend changed himself. I left the apartment on tiptoe, slinking along the walls like a thief. At home, I read the letters impressed on the pencil: "Travels."

"Enough of your stories, try another genre, don't bore your reader, you can't just spin tales out of thin air all your life," Malygin used to tell me.

Having crisscrossed the Stargorod terrain a million times, Parfyon was trying to push me out the door and into the wide world beyond.

I, too, felt like trying something new, and so I listened to my friend's wish. I packed quickly, threw a bunch of socks and shirts into my backpack, and topped it with a spare pair of pants. I put my new pencil carefully into a sturdy pencil case. I opened the door. It was snowing; the weather was beautiful. I started my car, let the engine warm up, and drove out of the yard.

Ahead of me spread a vast land, no better or worse than the Stargorod country, a land where life glowed quietly, awaiting the great magical holiday. Someone would be selling stationery out there too. I'll buy myself a school notebook and write in it, and if my fingers get cold, I'll hold them in the breath of the world and warm them.

About the Author

Peter Aleshkovsky was born in 1957 and graduated some two decades later from Moscow State University. He worked for several years as an archaeologist in Central Asia and as a historical preservationist in the Russian North before turning full-time to literature in the mid-1990s. He has authored a dozen books and first attained literary success with *Stargorod*, followed by the works *Seagulls; Skunk: A Life* (translated into English by Glas); *Vladimir Chigrintsev, The Institute of Dreams* and *The Other Side of the Moon*. Aleshkovsky has thrice been short-listed for the Russian Booker Prize, most recently in 2006, for *Fish: A History of One Migration*, which was published in 2010 by Russian Life Books.

About the Translator

Translator Nina Shevchuk-Murray was born and raised in the western Ukrainian city of Lviv. She holds degrees in English linguistics and Creative Writing. She translates both poetry and prose from the Russian and Ukrainian languages. Her translations and original poetry have been published in a number of literary magazines. With Ladette Randolph, she co-edited the anthology of Nebraska non-fiction *The Big Empty* (U of NE Press, 2007). Her translation of Peter Aleshkovsky's novel, *Fish: A History of One Migration*, was long-listed for the Rossica Translation Prize. In 2012, her translation of Oksana Zabuzhko's *Museum of Abandoned Secrets* (AmazonCrossing) was released.

34610721R00200

Made in the USA
Lexington, KY
12 August 2014